Incident

in

Baltimore

A Novel
By

Arley Owens, Jr.

SHORTY MAE PRODUCTIONS

Cover Art: CL Owens
Editor: Pitman Sanders

First Printing May 2013
Printed in the U.S.A.

Soft Cover Edition
ISBN: 978-0-9848195-6-0

SHORTY MAE PRODUCTIONS
P.O. BOX 81102
MIDLAND, TEXAS 79708

I GET AROUND
Composed by Brian Wilson and Mike Love

DOWN UNDER
Composed by Colin Hay, Ron Strykert,
Marion Sinclair

INCENSE AND PEPPERMINTS
Composed by John S Carter and Tim Gilbert

WIPE OUT
Composed by Bob Berryhill, Pat Connolly,
Jim Fuller, Ron Wilson

HIT THE ROAD JACK
Composed by Percy Mayfield

LOVE IS ALL AROUND
Composed by Reg Presley

To

Todd Glasgow
Rest in Peace, Bro

28 Years Ago

She sat down to pee and idly gazed at the body of a beautiful horse, ruined by a yucky bearded man with a hairy chest about to shoot an arrow. His hips merged with the horse's shoulders just below an ugly tallywacker that stuck straight out like a huge summer sausage. The painting, done by her talented mother, always came off the bathroom wall when they had company, except when her two aunts came over.

So did all the others.

They'd first appeared the day after her father's funeral. All but the one in her parent's bedroom hung on a wall. It sat on an easel beside a portrait of her mother with no clothes on. A professional artist had painted both of those.

"Why are you messing up horses on purpose?" she'd asked.

Her mom had laughed and said, "They're not horses, darling, they're depictions of an extraordinary being called a centaur."

"Why do you hide them when we have company?"

"I'll explain when you're a little older. You wouldn't understand the reason if I were to tell you now."

"Is that why I'm forbidden to mention them to anybody?"

"Mm hmm."

She was a year older now but still hadn't been told why.

Finished with her business, she tore some toilet paper from the roll, daubed her twat, and dropped it in the bowl. While turning to flush she spotted red stains seeping from the paper floating on the water. She breathlessly folded up a long stream of toilet paper, lined the bottom of her panties with it, pulled them up, fastened her jeans, and stormed for the living room.

"Mommy, it happened, it happened, it happened!"

Her mom looked up from a bootie she was knitting, and frowned. "What have I told you about running in the house, Veronica?"

"Sorry, but I'm *so* excited!" She pointed to her midsection. "I went to the bathroom to pee and I'm bleeding down there just like you said I would when you explained why my boobs started growing!"

The strangest smile appeared on her mother's beautiful face. She put the bootie aside and rose from the couch. "Oh, my little towhead, you're no longer a child but a young woman—your menstrual cycle has begun. Now I can share a wonderful secret with you. It came to me in a dream I had two months before we lost your father."

A wave of sadness rolled over her, washing away curiosity about the secret. Veronica had been so proud that her dad was a fireman, but now she wished he'd had a boring safe job because he'd died while trying to rescue a baby from a blazing apartment. Her mother had gotten a lot of money because of it and was having a new house built out in the country. "I don't wanna move, Mama. I want to stay in this house where Daddy lived."

"Don't be glum about that, Veronica. He'd want you to live in a better house, and you'll like it so much more than this one, I promise. And guess what? I'm having a very special room constructed where you and I and your aunts will have such grand times together."

Hearing about a special room titillated her. "Can I invite some of my friends?"

"No. It's sort of like a secret clubhouse and only four people can know about it. We're going to have so much fun."

Veronica pouted and crossed her arms over the plum-size knots that had recently developed on her chest—growths she'd been assured would get much larger, perhaps even as big as her mom's. "Well it won't be any fun for me if my friends can't see it. I want to stay here."

Her mother tousled her hair and grinned. "Oh you're going to love the new house and the special room."

"What's so special about it?"

"Well, hon, it's going to be sort of like a magic room."

"Really?" she said excitedly, curiosity beginning to override the dread of moving. "What's the wonderful secret you were going to share?"

"I'll tell you in a day or two, after you stop bleeding. For now I need to show you how to use a tampon."

She suddenly felt scared. "Will it hurt?"

"No, dear." A sigh slipped through her mother's pretty lips. "Let's just hope you don't develop premenstrual syndrome like my two sisters. It runs in the family, I'm afraid. I always hated being the youngest child until I started having my period and learned it had skipped me. Your grandma suffered from it horribly."

That *really* worried her. "I'm not sure I wanna turn into a woman."

"So you'd rather remain a tomboy for life?"

She nodded and her mom let out a hearty laugh. "Well I'm afraid there's not a thing you can do about it. Every child has to grow up, dear. But there are pleasures in being a grown woman that are far more thrilling than anything childhood has to offer."

ONE

The Present

Taylor Cain's dining table could seat twenty but he'd be breaking bread alone tonight. Not that it mattered much. Even when circumstances were different, loneliness still prevailed—it had for the last nine years. He sat at the end of the gleaming rectangle of cherry wood, scrutinizing a beef roast being nervously carved by his maid Suzanne, whom he'd chastised for not setting the table properly. Steam and clear juices with a hint of pink oozed from the savory tenderloin with each incision. She positioned a thick slice on his plate, surrounded it with vegetables and a pile of gravy-laden whipped potatoes, then quickly unfolded a napkin.

He raised his chin, Suzanne gently tucked it inside his collar, and scurried off to the kitchen, passing his butler Jim. Regretting the tongue lashing he'd given her, he stroked his beard and gazed at the fireplace, little noting Jim place a dessert tray beside the main entrée. The cheery glow of flames languidly devouring a batch of fresh logs seemed to mock him. White flakes drifted past an arched window in his peripheral vision, introducing a steady snowfall.

Perfunctorily turning his attention to the sterling silver flatware gracing both sides of his plate, he selected a fork and knife. Thoughts of happier days taunted him—his brother's infectious laugh, his sister-in-law's great sense of humor, his niece's inability to correctly pronounce his name when she was a toddler. Unca Tawor, she'd called him.

Suzanne returned with the bowl she'd forgotten. While shoveling banana pudding into the bone china dinnerware, she timidly asked if he'd like more wine. Responding to his single nod, she filled his glass and stood at attention beside Jim.

Taylor separated a narrow tip from the rest of the beef, brought the dripping bite to his mouth, and grimaced when he began to chew. "This roast is tough!"

Suzanne's face paled. "So sorry, Sir."

"You didn't cook it. Tell Alfred to get in here."

"Right away, Sir."

She came back with the cook in a matter of seconds.

The anxious expression on Alfred's facade matched that of Suzanne's. "Sorry, Sir."

"Sorry . . .?" he glared at the Englishman who'd been part of his household staff for the last twelve years. "Do I pay you to be sorry?"

"No, Sir."

"I pay you to cook for me, and I don't expect to chew leather when I'm served beef, now do I?"

"No, Sir."

Taylor stabbed the cutlet and thrust it towards him. "Now tell me, did I order tough?"

"No, Sir. I prepared it the same as always. It must have been an inferior cut."

"An inferior cut or inferiorly prepared by a bungling buffoon?"

The cook lowered his chin.

He flicked his wrist and sent the meat sailing before purposefully dropping the fork. It hit the bare spot of the china with a sharp clang. "Now what do you propose I eat for dinner since you screwed up the roast, hmm?"

Alfred raised his head but didn't make eye contact. "There's pheasant left over from last night's dinner. I could warm it up for you, or perhaps you'd prefer Jim to relieve me as you usually do when my cuisine displeases you, and have him fix you something."

Taylor wanted to shout that he wasn't paying him to serve leftovers, but took a deep breath and blew out a sigh of irritation instead. "You think you can do that without screwing up?"

"Yes, Sir."

"Then get to it, and take that leather with you." He pointed at the roast platter.

Alfred hoisted it immediately and hurried to the kitchen. Jim retrieved the cutlet from the newly varnished hardwood floor and followed him.

Taylor turned his weary eyes to the drifting snow.

¶

Nanatobi stood at her bedroom window on the third floor, watching snowfall grow increasingly heavier past the black metal bars lurking beyond the frosty pane. They'd been placed there to prevent her from trying to escape even though there wasn't a ledge and jumping from that height would be suicidal. The door was locked and would remain so until her uncle finished dinner, after which the maid would bring hers to be imbibed in the confines of her room. She was being punished for breaking her curfew. Her penance consisted of a week in her room with dinner served late and limited phone privileges. When the meal arrived her conventional telephone would be taken away and not returned until tomorrow's breakfast. She wouldn't get her cell phone, computer, or television back until her sentence had been served.

She'd been living under her uncle's domineering thumb for almost a decade now but time was finally on her side. Only one more semester to go and she'd graduate from the University of Maryland. In eighty-four days she'd turn twenty-one and receive her inheritance which would enable her to bid good riddance to her miserly caretaker. For now, she had to play by his rules because as much as she detested him, she disliked work even more. If not for the stipulation in her father's will that she had to attain the status of a college senior by her twenty-first birthday or the inheritance would be deferred until she turned twenty-five, she wouldn't have bothered with college. That had originally only pertained to a trust fund he'd set up for her, but after her parents' death a judge placed their entire estate under the proviso as well. It was Friday, the sixth of January, and she wouldn't turn twenty-one until March thirty-first. Come April Fool's Day she'd finally be free of her fool of an uncle once and for all.

Her reflection stared back from the misty glass, stopping just above her petite waist. Flaming red hair hung past her shoulders in thick luxurious waves, framing large green eyes, a small nose, and full lips on a pale freckled face.

"You are dangerously pretty, my dear," she whispered to the icy glass. The words had been spoken to her long ago by her mother whom she'd lost, along with her father, at eleven. She too had been a redhead with a pale complexion, but hers had been spotless. So had Nanatobi's father's—a black haired man like his older brother, her uncle, whose hair and beard had turned salt-and-pepper through the years. No one else on either side of the family had been cursed with mottled skin, only her.

Moving her shoulders back and forth, she placed a hand on each hip, puckered, and lowered her eyes to the two dimensional image of her ample breasts, bulging against a frilly blouse. Men always took note when she walked into a room. She loved the sensation of being the object of lust but fretted they didn't properly appreciate the features above her neck. Every paramour had praised her beauty but she feared their impassioned phrases were more inspired by a spectacular figure rather than her heavily freckled countenance.

The sound of a key turning in the latch made her look towards the door.

"Here's your dinner, Ma'am." Suzanne placed a covered tray

on a small table near her canopy bed.

"What is it?" she asked as the thick-waisted English woman unplugged her red landline phone.

"Roast beef, but it's a little tough, I'm afraid. At least your uncle said it was. I cut your portion into several thin slices just in case."

Nanatobi laughed. "I bet somebody's missing a piece of their ass."

"Yes, Ma'am."

"Alfred or Jim?"

"It was Alfred."

"So this time the butler didn't do it." She sat down on a dainty chair and scooted up to the table.

Holding the phone in one hand, Suzanne removed a silver dome from the tray with the other. Mashed potatoes with brown gravy, peas and carrots, French bread, and banana pudding accompanied the roast beef. Nanatobi picked up a slice of meat with her fingers and bit into it. "Mmm, delicious and tender. Taylor's full of it as always."

¶

A blip suddenly appeared on the radar. Charley Hudson put a hand over the mouthpiece of his headset and shouted, "Unidentified aircraft at thirty-eight thousand feet!"

It had popped on the screen from out of nowhere. The other air traffic controllers saw it too. One of the flights Charley monitored was circling at the same altitude as the mysterious orb. He tried to sound calm but nearly yelled, "American eighty-five increase altitude five hundred feet."

"Roger, Baltimore."

The blip vanished. Charley once again covered his mouthpiece. "My black middle-aged ass is too wore out for this shit. Keep everybody away from thirty-eight thousand, that damn thing's liable to pop up again."

And it did, this time appearing on the screen at thirty-four thousand feet. Charley heard the controller to his right bellow, "United sixty-four, descend five hundred feet!"

They weren't supposed to show emotion when talking to the pilots, especially not fear, but he knew the poor guy couldn't help it any more than he'd been able to. The object inexplicably disappeared once more only to show up again at twenty-nine thousand feet.

Charley had been looking forward to an upcoming vacation from Baltimore Washington International Airport which he desperately needed, being precariously close to burnout. The inexplicable blip rattled him to the core, shredding his already frayed nerves, making him all the more anxious to get away from this place.

¶

Arnon Green had been praying when a flash of light shot across the interior of his closed eyelids like an angry comet, leaving a dreadful intuition in its wake. Rising from his knees, he went to the lone window punctuating the stone walls and observed the snow falling from an icy night sky. He ignored the dim image staring back at him. Though only forty-eight, his wiry hair and beard were hoary which made him look like an old Uncle Tom. Born at seven minutes past seven on the seventh day of the seventh month, he was the seventh son of a seventh son of a seventh son—an interesting fact in which he put no stock.

But many of his family members did.

The room served as his sanctuary. He'd built it years ago, back in his twenties. Located on his small Maryland farm, the round rock-and-cement edifice stood twelve feet high. He resorted here when the need arose to commune with the Lord through prayer and fasting, for it contained no distractions. Heated by a wood burning stove, illuminated by a single kerosene lantern, the building had no electricity. A cot, metal folding chair, and an old TV tray—upon which sat his Bible, notebook, and a can stuffed with pencils—were the only furnishings. The tiny bathroom housed a toilet and a wall-mounted mineral-stained porcelain lavatory without hot water.

He pulled a pair of gold wire-frame glasses from his wide nose and ran a handkerchief across his forehead before using it to clean them. Returning the checkered cloth to a back pocket of his overalls with one hand, he used the other to reacquire the lenses.

The flash he'd seen in his spirit was unquestionably an omen, and it filled him with dread. His visions always came to pass, though sometimes much differently than what he anticipated upon receiving them. He could only hope his interpretation of this one was diametrically opposed to his hunch, otherwise bad and evil times were surely nigh at hand.

Obeying a sudden nudge in his spirit Arnon stepped outside without bothering to put on his coat. The freezing breeze cut him to the bone as he dropped to his knees and raised his hands towards the snowy heavens. "Almighty God, in the name of the Lord Jesus Christ I beg for deliverance for those to be affected by whatever this thing is I fear you have warned me has arrived . . . ."

TWO

Brad Barron had lived in Baltimore all his twenty-nine years. A stylist kept his blonde hair immaculately trimmed and a manicurist tended to his nails twice weekly. An exclusive salon insured he maintained a good tan, and regular dental visits kept his perfectly straight teeth gleaming white. Being the personnel director at Mirror Tech, a company that created and developed computer software, afforded such amenities. Barely standing five-six, he compensated for what he felt to be his only other flaw by wearing lifts inside footwear with generous heels. The Italian boots he'd chosen to shod his feet for the occasion enhanced his stature several inches.

"It *would* have to snow tonight," he sighed aloud, looking towards the patio through sliding glass doors. Thrusting his left arm out so the wrist of his white shirt protruded beyond the sleeve of a beige Armani sports coat, he adjusted a diamond cufflink and strolled to a wet bar that had cost him a small fortune. Satisfied with the hors d'oeuvres, liquor, set ups, and ice bucket, he crossed the living room to double check the CD player. All the slots were filled. He turned it on, fine tuned the equalization, and adjusted the volume.

Someone rang the bell. On his way to answer the door he tightened the knot of an inordinately expensive red and navy-blue silk tie purchased for the party.

"Lou! Entree, my man."

Lou Cotton, his best friend since high school, who towered over him when both were barefoot, walked in removing a worn denim jacket which he slung over his shoulder. "I must be early."

Grinning, Brad looked down his nose at his buddy's plaid western shirt—faded from too many visits to the washing machine—threadbare jeans, and scuffed cowboy boots. "I see you dressed for the occasion as usual."

"Hey, I am dressed up. These are my Sunday-go-to-meeting jeans."

"Right . . . well I hope you won't feel too out of place."

Lou tossed the blue jean snap-up on the back of the couch, lumbered to the bar, and started making himself a drink. "Your snooty friends aren't going to bother me."

Brad knew that all too well without hearing it. Lou never felt ill at ease no matter what he wore. Everybody liked him, especially women. He kept his brown hair at shoulder length and always sported a few days growth on his ruggedly handsome face. Plopping down on the sofa in front of his shabby coat, Lou nonchalantly crossed his heels on the coffee table and took a swig of rum and coke. A man's man, he always exuded confidence without a trace of arrogance. Brad wished such self assurance came as naturally to him. He'd been extremely jealous of the Okie in the early stages of their friendship but it had long since dissipated.

They'd met the summer Lou moved to Baltimore from Oklahoma a couple of months before they started tenth grade. By that Christmas they'd become best friends. After graduation he'd gone to college but Lou, arguing he was a natural born mechanic, had talked his parents into letting him start his own business with the money they'd saved for his higher education. His father had liked the idea and went along, despite his mother protesting it was too much of a gamble. But the gamble paid off. It turned out Lou also had a talent for business as well. He now owned three prosperous auto repair shops and employed a dozen mechanics in each. Though he still loved getting his hands greasy working on car engines, something Brad would never be able to relate to, he didn't spend much time at any of his shops anymore, preferring to "just hang around town like a bum" as Lou put it.

Again the doorbell rang. He smoothed his lapels and went

to answer it.

Lou snickered. "I swear, Bradley Boston Barron, you're about as anal as they come."

"Up yours, Lou."

He opened the door for two of his coworkers, Nelly Branch and Sally Gretch. Nelly was a tall extroverted blonde, heavyset and plain, but blissfully untroubled by it. Sally had brown hair and wore glasses. She would have been an inch taller than him if not for his lifts and heels. Both were his age and single, but he had no romantic interest in either.

"Welcome, ladies, glad you could make it." He gave each a light hug.

Wearing a large grin, Nelly looked past him. "Hello, Lou!"

Lou grinned back. "Howdy."

"I don't believe you've met Sally. He hasn't has he, Brad? Lou, this is Sally Gretch."

"Nice to meet you, Sally." The prosperous business man, dressed like a poor ranch hand, tipped his glass at her in a salutatory gesture.

"Hi," she replied with a shy tone.

"Let me take your coats."

They obliged and Brad promptly hung them in a closet by the front door. "Refreshments are on the bar, help yourselves."

They headed towards it as more guests arrived—Coy and Lucy Sax, an older couple who'd celebrated their twentieth anniversary last week. He'd met Coy through Lucy who worked at Mirror Tech. He hadn't finished welcoming them when Ursula Winston, Ava Blanc, and Hilda Weiss walked in without bothering to ring the bell. All three answered to him from nine to five every week day.

Ursula was a tall dishwater blonde that stood out in any crowd. Her gorgeous face and impeccable body rivaled that of any Playboy Playmate or Penthouse Pet, and in his opinion she had a perfect nose. The two dainty nostrils beneath her delicately sculpted bridge sometimes flared slightly when she talked. When she giggled it wrinkled a tad, forcing the nostrils to spread, and the action aroused him. He'd told her once of his admiration of it and asked if she'd had it done.

"Heavens no, but thank you for the compliment," she'd replied. "I've heard of leg men but you're the first nose man I've ever ran into."

"I'm not a nose man," he'd assured, "but if I were, I'd rate yours a perfect ten."

Though quite attractive, Ava Blanc's mood dictated the degree he found her likeable. When she showed up for work all radiant and vivacious he couldn't get enough of her, but when her disposition fell to the other end of the spectrum he tried his best to avoid the blue-eyed brunette. Hilda Weiss stood about five-five, an inch taller than Ava. She was rather bland in both appearance and personality, but worked hard and never complained. All three of them knew Lou, and each vied for his attention at get-togethers like this. Lou ate it up and loved razzing him about it afterwards. By the time he'd gotten their coats put away Ursula was settled on the sofa beside his best friend cooing, "Be a dear, Lou, and make me a dry martini . . . ."

¶

He'd finally done the deed and it looked good, all that shiny skin. Ronnie Garr pulled a Ravens cap over his bald scalp and smiled at the bathroom mirror. He turned to check his new look from the side with the hat on. That also pleased him. Mats of brown hair he'd just cut and shaved off his head covered the sink. He grabbed what locks he could and tossed them into a waste basket. While washing the rest down the drain, he took off the hat to get one more look at his gleaming dome. It felt so liberating. Rubbing a hand over it, he exulted in its smoothness until seeing some residual follicles were sticking to the sides of the lavatory. Once he got that taken care of he turned off the faucet, slipped the cap back on, grabbed his coat, and walked out of his tiny rundown apartment.

Whizzing down the boulevard in his black Thunderbird with the radio blaring, he kept alternating between cap and scalp, rubbing the latter every time he bared his head. He drove towards her house even though he had little hope of seeing Renee Van Cedar. She lived with her parents a few miles outside the city in a ritzy development called Wine's Gate. The emerald-eyed beauty with curly auburn hair didn't know it yet but she was destined to become his wife. They weren't dating, in fact they'd never even spoken to each other, but he knew destiny had brought them together the first time he saw her. Whatever course she'd taken last semester had been in the proximity of his anatomy class at the University of Maryland and he'd spotted her in the hall several times. He'd learned her name when a guy tried to hit on her, and wouldn't have known she still lived at home if he hadn't overheard her telling a classmate. She was listed in the phonebook so it had been a cinch getting the address.

Every time he'd managed to work up the nerve to speak to her something had thwarted him. On his initial try a girl had ran up to her and gushed, "Renee, guess who just asked me out! Danny Hill!" Ronnie didn't know Danny Hill, but he was obviously a big hit with Renee as well because she'd exclaimed, "No way! Oh I hate you!" Then the two girls had broken into giggly madness and started jabbering endlessly about the dude, so he'd slumped silently away. After three more botched attempts, including one where he'd followed Renee to her car, he'd never been able to spot her alone. The semester ended in mid December and twenty-three days had passed since he'd last set eyes on the woman of his dreams.

The odds were against him seeing her at college again so now he'd have to initiate contact outside of school. He didn't think calling would do anything but put her off since she didn't know him, so he somehow had to get her face to face. Though the effort would most likely once again prove futile, he hoped to catch her leaving her parents' house so he could follow her, and when she arrived at whatever destination, pretend to accidentally run into her. Providing the setting was a public place of course. In the same conversation he'd eavesdropped on and learned she still lived with her parents, Renee had also said she usually flew the coop right after dinner on Fridays, date or no. Luckily, she'd also mentioned what time her mother punctually served the evening meal.

After graduating high school he'd drifted through countless odd jobs, worried about nothing, partying like there was no tomorrow, before waking up to the fact his life had no direction and he'd been wasting it. With no particular goals, he'd taken some night classes at a no-name college while working a full time job. Choosing English and history since every degree plan required ex amount of both, he figured by the time he got those two academics out of the way a career path would present itself. In the end it had proved too unrewarding for the amount of work involved and he hadn't been able to see any light at the end of the tunnel.

While watching TV one day a marine recruitment commercial inspired him to become one of the few and proud. During his four year hitch he'd learned two important things: discipline, and the fact that whatever career path he chose, it needed to be mentally oriented because the vigor of youth wouldn't remain with him forever. A fellow jarhead with aspirations of becoming a doctor had instilled the latter in him. The dude was always reading science books and medical journals. Ronnie occasionally skimmed through some of them and had developed an interest in biology by the time he'd gotten honorably discharged.

He'd recently turned twenty-eight and had one semester left before earning his bachelor of science degree. After that he'd get his masters, then his doctorate, and become a college professor. He planned to change Renee's last name to Garr as soon as possible afterwards. There wouldn't be any family members at the wedding from his side. He didn't have any siblings and his parents were dead. A free spirited hippy type, his father had died in a motorcycle accident before his mother learned she was pregnant. She'd died of breast cancer six years ago. Both had been estranged from their families so he'd never met any grandparents, uncles, aunts, or cousins.

For the second time in as many Fridays he drove by Renee's house. Her white Camaro convertible was parked in the drive of a stylish residence with a two-car garage and a balcony-covered porch. Every window facing the street blazed with yellow light. The snow covered roof and feathery crystals drifting in front of the panes gave off the effect of a Christmas card springing to life. A few blocks away the street ended in a cul-de-sac, so he braked and swerved around. Before he got back to Renee's house she pulled out of the drive and headed towards Baltimore.

"Whoa, I finally caught a break!" He grabbed the Ravens cap from the passenger seat and slapped it atop his freshly scalped head. Adrenalin coursed through his veins at the possibility of meeting her at long last. She didn't know he existed so there'd be no reason for Renee to think the T-Bird tailing her at a distance wasn't coincidentally heading for the city. But then she made a turn that took her, and therefore him, the opposite direction from town.

"Renee, where are you going . . .?"

¶

The doorbell rang. Jim Dogensworth promptly set his tea down and went to answer it. His employer glanced up from perusing *The Wall Street Journal* as he passed the parlor on the way to the front door.

"Hi, Jim, is Nan in?"

He smiled politely at the lovely Renee Van Cedar, Nanatobi's best friend. "Yes, but I'm afraid she's indisposed."

She pursed her lips and looked at him rather dubiously, a goodly amount of doubt in her pretty eyes, whose color was remarkably similar to Nanatobi's. "Indisposed, huh?"

"Yes, I'm afraid so." He didn't want to say that a twenty-year-old had been grounded and wasn't allowed visitors. It seemed uncouth.

"Hmm . . ." she continued perusing him. "You can't let me in, can you."

"I'm afraid not."

"Well tell her I dropped by to see her. Can you at least do that?"

Relieved she hadn't inquired further he replied, "Happy to."

"Okay then, see ya."

¶

Renee had stopped at the entrance of a long drive leading to a massive stone manor—rolled down her window, punched a code pad perched on a marble pedestal, two wrought iron gates had opened, and she'd driven through. He'd viewed the action from his rearview mirror after driving on. Coasting down the road at little more than an idle, Ronnie had the sinking feeling she'd be spending the evening there. Heaving a bitter sigh, he finally turned around, retraced the route at forty miles an hour and quickly slowed down when he saw her getting into the Camaro as he passed the gates. A few minutes later she sped around him. Scarcely believing his good fortune, he accelerated—giddily thinking that maybe shaving one's head brought good luck.

Gliding past snow-glazed fences and crystallized trees, Ronnie's heart danced as he navigated his Thunderbird through the frosty mist. Windshield wipers faithfully keeping old man winter from blocking his view, the warm red brilliance of Renee's taillights lured him towards Baltimore.

¶

"Get that will you, Lou?" said Brad, referring to the ringing telephone, barely audible because of the music. He was at the bar mixing himself another drink. A dash of vermouth in a pool of gin, an olive on a toothpick, and *Viola!* a perfect martini. He surveyed the room, taking a sip from his glass. Nelly was dancing with Coy Sax to the tune of The Beach Boys' *I Get Around* while his wife laughed at him from the sofa. Ava and Hilda cavorted with each other. Sally Gretch sat cross-legged on the floor in front of his entertainment center looking at CD's. Lou had paired up with Ursula for the song but left her dancing alone in order to answer the phone.

Everyone he'd invited had come except Jesse Van Cedar and his wife Veronica. The vice president of Mirror Tech and his boss, Jesse seldom fraternized with coworkers outside the workplace but he never failed to invite him. He actually came once and appeared to enjoy himself, really hitting it off with Lou, but his wife had seemed aloof and bored throughout the evening, so a repeat appearance seemed unlikely.

"You and my daughter share the same musical taste— golden oldies," Jesse had said.

"In that case tell her she has an open invitation any time I throw a bash," he'd replied.

"I've seen the way you look at her when she comes to the office. No way I'm letting her near a hound like you."

"She's way out of my conference," Brad had confessed with a laugh. "She wouldn't give me the time of day. Now you'd have to worry about Lou. But me? Not a problem."

Jesse had chuckled along with Lou, and the matter ended with his boss's assurance he'd relay the offer to his daughter. Renee Van Cedar—though beautiful, thoughtful, and bright—was a tall girl, which automatically put her *out of his conference.*

Lou hung up the phone and joined him at the bar.

"Who was that?"

"Someone needing directions to the party. She said her name was Renee Van Cedar."

THREE

He'd been careful to tail Renee from a safe distance, at times having to do so from behind as many as three vehicles. Now only a van stood between them. It shot ahead when she turned right at a sign that read *VISITOR'S PARKING*. It belonged to an apartment complex in the Northern District. Dejectedly feeling he'd struck out again, Ronnie started to drive on but a sudden idea made him swerve in behind her. Though a risky maneuver, it might be his golden opportunity if he could intercept her before she got to the apartment she was heading for. He parked in the first available space and hurriedly got out of his car. Keeping his eyes glued to the Camaro, he watched her select a spot sixty or seventy feet away and waited until she started walking towards a sidewalk dividing the small front lawns of a line of townhouses.

Trotting until he got near her, he slowed to a walk and put his plan into action. "Renee, is that you?"

She turned her pretty head towards him as he advanced. Her dark-green eyes were wary. "Do I know you?"

Heart pounding in his chest, he drew in a breath. "I used to see you in the hall last semester at Maryland, before and after my anatomy class. My name's Ronnie Garr."

"How did you know mine?"

"Um, I overheard you telling someone."

That seemed to worry her. Brow wrinkling, she studied him for a long moment, then a smile of recognition appeared. "Oh yeah, I recall seeing you too. You look different with a hat on."

"Ah, so you knew I was alive after all." He'd managed to sound nonchalant, but knowing she'd actually taken note of him made his insides tremor with joy. It also gave him a much needed boost of confidence. "Are you doing anything special tonight?"

Two gorgeous orbs of exquisite jade narrowed on a

beautiful face that immediately turned guarded over his question. "Why?"

He braced himself for probable rejection due to her expression and response. Nothing had ever affected him like the fireworks that exploded in his soul when she'd crossed his field of vision while he'd been casually ambling down the hall his first day of anatomy class. Consequently he had no past experience to draw from. Instinct warned him not to speak his mind or he'd scare her away, so he tried to come off like he was merely lonely and bored. "Um, I was just out and about because I got tired of sitting home alone, and would sure enjoy some company."

She didn't say anything, merely gave him a menacingly sexy glare. He nervously slipped the cap off his head and scratched at his scalp.

Her jaw dropped. "You shaved off your pretty hair!"

"Huh?" The compliment floored him.

"I loved your hair. Why'd you shave it off?" She ran a wooly glove over his scalp, looking concerned as if feeling a wound.

Even more taken aback, he gulped with excitement. "I'm surprised you noticed I had hair."

"Oh I noticed . . ." she lowered her hand. "I also noticed you trying to talk to me a few times, and I thought maybe it was because you wanted to ask me out."

"It was—I tried!" he ejaculated excitedly.

"Why?"

"Why?" His throat went dry as he took in her intoxicating beauty. "Because I like you."

An eternity passed before she answered, and when she did, it was only to repeat the single word question.

"I just do, that's all."

She tossed him an impish grin. "How do you know you like me? You don't even know me."

He plopped the Ravens hat back on his head. "I know I like

you, okay?"

"How do I know I like you?"

Grasping the bill with his right hand, he bobbed the cap up and down, searching for a clever remark. "Because I've got pretty hair?"

That invoked a big smile. "But you shaved it off just like Sampson and Curly the stooge."

"As I recall Delilah shaved Sampson's head. Got no idea who did Curly's, but didn't he wear a buzz cut?"

The vapor of a short laugh streamed through her gorgeous lips, then she frowned. "You live here?"

"Uh, no."

"Here to see somebody then?"

"Yeah."

"Who?"

"You."

"Me? I don't live here. I'm going to a party."

"Maybe they'd let me crash it."

A confident smirk rose on her face. "I'm sure it wouldn't be a problem since the man who's throwing the party works for my dad."

He glanced down at his jeans. "Hope it's not black tie."

"Who cares? How tall are you?"

"Six three. Why do you ask?"

"Just curious that's all. Let's see, that makes you six inches taller than me."

"So you're five nine."

"Yeah. Your being tall means I can wear heels when we go out."

His heart leapt with elation and he couldn't hold back a giddy grin. "So you're saying you'll go out with me?"

"If you promise to grow your hair back."

"You got it!"

She hooked an arm around his. "Okay, Curly Sampson, let's

go to the party . . . ."

¶

Brad opened the door and there stood Renee Van Cedar with a tall powerfully-built skinhead holding a Ravens cap in his hand. She removed her gloves while stepping inside. "Hi, Brad, this is Ronnie Garr. Ronnie, meet Brad Barron."

He shook Ronnie's hand and tried not to wince from his vice-like grip. "Nice to meet you. Love your hair."

The skinhead chuckled which relieved him. He'd hoped the small joke wouldn't be taken as an insult. Ronnie Garr was clearly not the type of man one would want to offend. Rubbing his hand to regain circulation, he introduced them to everyone. "You'll find libations on the bar, help yourselves. Uh, you are over twenty-one aren't you, Renee?"

She smiled and leaned her head on Ronnie's shoulder. "I am twenty-one. Have been since November."

"Good. Wouldn't want to be guilty of serving liquor to a minor . . . ."

¶

Ronnie surveyed the room from the bar with Renee at his side. He thought Brad seemed nice enough, though a bit pretentious. The dude certainly wasn't a cheapskate by any means—he had three different high-dollar brands of gin, whiskey, vodka, tequila, and rum sitting atop a fancy bar, along with an eclectic array of mixes, juices, and finger foods. Except for Ursula Winston, who kept sneaking peeks at him as she danced with a longhaired redneck, he couldn't recall the names of Brad's other guests. He wanted a beer but the stash in the fridge was imported. Afraid to take a chance, he'd settled for Crown and water. Renee sipped on a tequila sunrise he'd mixed for her. The song ended and a slow tune started playing on the stereo. She smiled at him. "Dance with me, Curly Sampson."

Taking her right hand with his left, he eased his other onto her lower back and they started moving to the music. The touch of her soft palm was electrifying. He pulled her closer until their upper bodies lightly made contact. She gave his hand a squeeze of acceptance which thrilled him. Then, to his delight, she released it and pressed into him, throwing her arms around his neck. He clasped his hands together at the base of her spine as she rested her head on his shoulder, spurring a profusion of emotions. Renee smelt sweetly musky and he knew he'd always associate all the abstract feelings swirling inside him with that scent. Intoxicated by a euphoria known only to one falling desperately in love, he exulted in the magic moment, keenly aware he'd savor the precious memory of it until the day he died.

"I love your perfume," he whispered in her ear, relishing the feel of her large breasts pressing against him.

"It's Blue de Chanel. I hate your cologne."

"It's Old Spice," he snickered, "and it's aftershave, not cologne."

The song ended. With his arm around her waist, he walked Renee back to the bar where the redneck was mixing a drink for Ursula Winston.

Ronnie handed Renee the remainder of her sunrise, took a sip from his glass, and returned it to the counter. Meanwhile the redneck wandered towards Brad, talking to an older man in front of a set of sliding glass doors.

The sultry blonde turned towards him. "So what do you do?"

"Going to college on my G.I. Bill." He noticed Renee's face brighten when he said G.I.

"What's your major?"

"Biology."

"Going to be a doctor or scientist, huh? How interesting."

"No, a teacher."

"Oh . . ." Ursula raised her right hand above his head. "May I?"

"Uh, sure."

She kneaded his scalp with her long fingers. The action embarrassed him and he could tell it irritated Renee. Ursula stopped and glanced her way. "You don't mind do you?"

"Not at all." A fake smile had quickly replaced the scowl she'd worn. Renee set her drink on the bar and assaulted his head with both hands, vigorously rubbing it. "There's nothing like the feel of a human bowling ball."

Ursula laughed and refocused on him. "What branch of the service were you in?"

"The marines." He grabbed Renee's hands and forced them to her sides.

"Eeew, the marines. I dated a marine once." She looked past him. "Whoops gotta go. Lou wants to dance."

He watched her join the long-haired redneck whose name finally registered in his memory, then cut his eyes to Renee. "You wanna get out of here?"

She frowned. "We just got here. Where are you wanting to go?"

"Any place you like."

"You in a dorm or what?"

"Apartment."

"Cool."

"Yeah well, it's a hole but it's home."

Brad approached. "You kids having fun?"

"Oh we're just having a ball," Renee chided with a dry tone conveying boredom.

The peppy dude grabbed at his chest and grinned. "Hurt

me to my heart!"

"Just teasing, we are having fun. Aren't we, Ronnie."

"If you say so . . ." he picked up his drink and took a long pull.

"Your dad said we have the same taste in music. What would you like?"

"How about some Justin Timberlake?"

Brad raised his brows. "I think Jesse must have been mistaken. He told me you liked golden oldies like me."

"Oh I do! Got any Men At Work?"

"Sure, all of them. What's your pleasure?"

"Hmm . . ." she cupped her right elbow and tapped her chin with a long index finger. Renee's hands were naturally pretty but her pointed clear-shellacked nails made them all the more alluring. "What am I in the mood for by those guys? How about *Down Under.*"

Their host walked briskly to the stereo, rifled through a mass of CD's, and inserted one after the song finished playing. Soon the sound of a flute lead-in filled the air.

Bouncing her knees lightly to the rhythm of the tune, Renee surveyed the room. He imbibed a nip of aqua-diluted whiskey and idly watched the metrical gyrations of Ursula and Lou, who suddenly disappeared when the apartment turned dark and silent.

¶

The damn thing had fallen all the way to fifteen-thousand where it vanished, only to reappear on the radar a few minutes later at eleven-thousand feet. Then the emergency generators kicked on due to a blackout, and Charley's exhausted eyes beheld the blip no more.

¶

Nanatobi had been flipping through the current issue of *Cosmopolitan* when the lights went out. Expecting the power to return any second, she remained stretched out on her bed and impatiently waited. The darkness persisted, so she got up and stepped cautiously across the floor, hands reaching out, awaiting contact with a chest of drawers, atop which lay her purse. With that mission accomplished, she snapped it open and rummaged through her keys, wallet, hairbrush, makeup compact, mini-pack of tissues, lipstick, and a mascara tube before finally locating a penlight which she switched on immediately.

A dim beam cut through the blackness. "Need to replace the batteries," she muttered aloud. Opening the drawer of her nightstand, she grabbed a box of wooden matches kept on hand to light an array of scented candles adorning her vanity. Three stood in silver holders on either side of a large round antique mirror. She ignited each one. By virtue of a half dozen flames she could see her reflection, the flickering lights causing little shadows to dance across the freckled face in the looking glass. A sweet blend of cinnamon, vanilla, blueberry, raspberry, cherry, and jasmine emanated from them.

Carrying two at a time, she placed the flaming sticks of wax on the nightstand and ambled to the far corner of her bed to check the time. She aimed the penlight at a large clock centered on the face of a clown—a treasured heirloom her mother had given her as a child. Hanging on the wall near the hallway leading to her dressing room, closets, and bathroom, it looked ghostly in the semi-twilight. The battery-powered hands pointed out the time as nine forty-eight. At least ten minutes had passed since the electricity went off she figured. Making her way back to the nightstand, she switched off the flashlight and stashed it beside the matches. Then she crawled back atop her red velvet bedspread and tried to resume reading. Thick darkness looming beyond the illuminated area spooked her, so she returned half the candles to the vanity. The maneuver did nothing to dispel the gloom on the other side of the room but she kept her focus on the magazine and tried not to think about it. She could make out the words but had to strain her eyes.

Hearing a key turn in the lock, she sat up. Suzanne soon walked in, bearing a bright flashlight. "Are you okay, Ma'am?"

"Yeah, but you'd better leave the door unlocked. I don't relish the idea of being locked in with no lights."

"I understand, Ma'am, but your uncle—"

"Piss on my uncle, leave the damn door unlocked! Please?"

Suzanne had moved to America when her husband accepted a promotion in one of the overseas subsidiaries of T-Cain Corporation that required relocation. She'd replaced Auntie Bessie, the name Nanatobi had grown up calling the previous maid even though they weren't related. Bessie had been wanting to return to her native England so Taylor, who'd never had a live-in servant that wasn't British, asked Suzanne to consider joining his household staff when her husband unexpectedly died of a stroke. He paid her well, as he did all his employees, and it was the only thing Nanatobi presently admired about the man. Of course if he didn't, none of them would have been willing to put up with his petty perfectionism which sometimes led to tantrums. And a tantrum was just what Suzanne feared she'd incur if she left the door unlocked, judging by the pale look on her face.

"Sorry, Ma'am. I'd like to, but I just don't think it wise to do so. Can I bring you anything before I retire?"

"Yeah, a hack saw."

"Oh, Ma'am." Covering her mouth to muffle a giggle, Suzanne stepped into the hall and promptly closed the door.

Then locked it.

Nanatobi threw the magazine across the room. "Dammit to hell!"

She lay on her bed and fumed with anger—longing to give Taylor a taste of his own medicine, let him know what it felt like to be treated like a fucking slave. Of course the bastard was too prim and proper to disobey rules so he'd never have to worry about such consequences if she were his guardian, no matter how strict or ridiculous the guidelines. Thinking of him obsequiously minding her caused a snigger to tickle its way out of her nose. A pleasant memory from the past tried to surface but she quickly dismissed it, retrieved the publication, and almost went blind straining to read in such weak illumination.

The power finally returned and the sudden brightness beaming from the lamps on either side of the bed forced her eyes closed for a moment. The digital display of her radio alarm kept blinking twelve a.m. She crawled to the edge of the bed to check the clown clock, then rolled towards the nightstand and set the time. Like the light bulbs, it had been rendered dormant for almost an hour. Lacking only a few paragraphs from finishing a celeb exposé, she decided to complete it before blowing out the candles.

¶

"Hey the lights are back!" shouted Brad as the stereo started playing again. "Anyone in the mood for one hit wonders? I defy any of you to name one I don't have."

"How about Strawberry Alarm Clock?" Ronnie challenged. "Back in the sixties they did a song my mom loved called *Incense and Peppermints*. She had the forty-five and I got a spanking for using it as a Frisbee."

It delighted him that Ronnie had loosened up as they'd all drank and chitchatted during the blackout. "*Incense and*

Peppermints it is . . . ."

¶

   She'd barely finished the exposé when a tingling sensation tickled her skin and a surge of vertigo seized her. Dazed and utterly thunderstruck, Nanatobi found herself hovering above a small group of people, some of whom were dancing. Though able to see, hear, and smell, she seemed to be floating beneath the ceiling without a corporeal body. Her best friend was talking to a virile young man with a shaved head, but she didn't recognize anyone else. Music blared—a song she'd heard a few times on the golden oldies station called *Incense and Peppermints.*

FOUR

When the nightmare shift finally ended he went straight to a bar near BWI. His bartender buddy grinned as he took a stool.

"The usual, Charley?"

"Yeah, Johnny Black—neat—and keep them coming until my hands stop shaking . . . ."

¶

Renee danced with Lou while he cut the rug with Ursula to a fast instrumental tune called *Wipe Out,* so there wasn't any body contact, a fact Ronnie felt grateful for. Not that he wouldn't have liked rubbing up against the sexy blonde, but he didn't want Lou groping Renee. During the blackout they'd all gotten to know each other a little, drinking and talking by candlelight, and he'd managed to enjoy the party even though he hadn't gotten Renee alone like he'd hoped.

When the song ended Brad shouted, "Last Call, folks. What's your pleasure?"

¶

He walked Renee to her car a little after midnight. "Is there any way I can talk you into staying out a little later instead of going home?"

"I'm afraid not, Ronnie."

"Do I at least get a goodnight kiss?"

Her eyes bore holes through him, the twinkling green highlighted by snowflakes languidly falling in front of them. "Not on the first date, sorry."

The negative reply embarrassed him, he really hadn't expected her to resist. But then he hadn't anticipated she'd call it a night either. Not knowing what to say, he looked down at the snow covered parking lot, feeling like a fool.

"I'm in the book. Give me a call, okay?"

He raised his head and forced a smile. "Sure."

Apparently sensing how awkward he felt, she patted his shoulder. "I had fun, Curly Sampson, but now it's time to say goodnight . . . ."

¶

The peculiar incident had been strangely intriguing but frightening—so outlandish it couldn't have really happened, yet so vivid he couldn't state with any amount of certainty it hadn't. Brad didn't know what to make of it. It had taken all his resolve to conceal his disquiet for the sake of his guests. Now all of them were gone except Lou, and anxiety had dwindled into confusion infused with curiosity. He filled two cups with coffee, doused his with a generous amount of creamer, lightly sweetened it, and carried them to the living room.

Lou reached up from the couch and relieved him of the unaltered cup.

"Well you seemed to enjoy yourself this evening," Brad said on his way to the bar.

"Yeah, I had a pretty good time, but I'm pretty wore out." Lou gulped a swallow of sobering caffeine and cut one of his shit-eating grins. "Those chicks that work with you just won't leave me alone."

"You poor thing. I can't believe how long that blackout lasted."

"But it made the party, man. That skinhead Ronnie Garr finally chilled and I think it was only because of the blackout. That dude wanted to leave as soon as he got here. I think all he had on his mind was getting into Van Cedar's panties."

He shot him a sarcastic smile and raised his cup. "Like you

didn't."

"Sure, who wouldn't? But I had my eye on Ursula."

"So who didn't?" He took a sip, set the cup on the bar, and folded his arms across his chest. "I know you'll think I'm crazy, Lou, but the weirdest thing happened during the party."

"Oh yeah? What?"

"A little while after the lights came back on I could have sworn I was someplace else."

"Someplace else? What do you mean?"

He studied the frowning Okie for a moment, wondering how he'd react if the tables were turned and Lou relayed the odd occurrence to him. "I was in a swish bedroom with a red canopy bed and a funny looking clown clock. There were three candles burning on an antique vanity and three by the bed like they were being used for illumination even though the lights were on."

Lou chuckled. "I didn't know you were an acid head, Brad."

"Told you you'd think I was crazy. I was looking at everything from above, like a fly on the ceiling."

Finally realizing he wasn't joking, Lou leaned forward, whiskered face etched with puzzlement. "An out of body experience? Thought those were only supposed to happen during sleep."

"I wouldn't know about that, but I'm not exaggerating. I'd gone to the bathroom to adjust the lift in my left boot and sat down on the edge of the bathtub to pull it off. The next thing I knew I was floating in that bedroom and then I was laying sideways in the tub like I'd fallen backwards. But I have no memory whatsoever of falling into it."

Lou squinted at him with a worried scowl. "You'd better get a checkup, man. You must have passed out and dreamed all that shit."

"No, I'm sure I was never unconscious."

¶

Naked beneath the covers, Nanatobi lay on her side writing in her diary, a ritual she practiced at the close of each day. The hands on the clown's face portrayed the time as two minutes past one a.m.

I heard the song Incense and Peppermints and saw the following: Renee with a bald man, a tall blonde woman, a handsome redneck in need of a shave, four other women and an older man. They were partying hearty. What does it all mean? Haven't a clue. Did I fall asleep and dream it or did it really happen? Will find out when I talk to Renee tomorrow.

She locked the book, slid it beneath the mattress, and switched off the lamps.

¶

Suzanne brought breakfast and the telephone at eight-thirty. As soon as she locked the door behind her, Nanatobi called Renee's cell, ignoring the scrambled eggs, bacon, toast, jam, coffee, and orange juice.

"*H-Hullo?*"

"Renee?"

"*Huh?*"

"Renee, wake up. It's Nanatobi."

"*Huh?*"

"Listen, the strangest thing happened last night. Where were you?"

"*W-Where was I?*"

"Yeah, where were you? Did you go to a party?"

"*Party? Uh . . . yeah.*"

"Listen, sweetie, this is very important—it was the strangest thing. Were you by any chance with a bald man?"

"Bald man? No."

"Are you sure you weren't with a bald man?"

"Huh? Yeah . . . sure."

"Okay then, go back to sleep. Give me a call when you wake up."

Frowning with disappointment, she hung up the phone. Renee had shot down the thrilling notion that she'd really left her body last night. She took a bite of scrambled eggs and almost gagged.

They'd gotten cold.

¶

Ronnie could feel a few sprigs already invading the smoothness of his bald head and wanted to shave it again. Of course he wouldn't for Renee's sake. Ironically, after finally summoning the guts to see if the hairless look fit him, he thought the style enhanced his appearance, only to discover his dream woman deplored it. Before last night the closest he'd come was the buzz-cut he'd received in boot camp. *After I win her over I'll shave it again.* An inward smile turned to a frown as he thought, *If I win her over.*

Sitting at a rickety wooden table in his kitchen, he breakfasted on scrambled egg whites, dry wheat toast, and black coffee. It was Saturday which meant he had to be at work at nine-thirty. He held down two jobs. During the week he tried to squeeze in twenty hours at a grocery store, the most he could manage and still go to school full time. That job paid minimum wage. From nine-thirty to four-thirty every Saturday, he did routine maintenance on trucks at Palloy Transportation, a trucking company owned by a great guy named Ben Palloy, who paid him twelve dollars an hour. Ben really liked him and wanted him to get his degree. Every once in awhile, for no reason, he'd lay a fifty on him.

He fixated on Renee while driving to work—the magic he'd felt while holding her as they danced, the agony that had riveted him when she'd refused a goodnight kiss.

¶

Still wearing her bath robe, Renee leaned against the refrigerator sipping orange juice, hearing but not listening to her parents conversing in the dining room over Saturday brunch. As they rambled, she planned her next few moves. When she finished her juice she'd go upstairs, get dressed, and call Nan. Thinking of her stirred a vague recollection. Had she called earlier? It seemed like she had and asked about a bald man. *Why was she asking about a bald man? Did she really call?* Carrying the juice with her, she went upstairs and phoned her. Nan didn't answer her cell so she tried her bedroom phone.

"Hello?"

"Nan?"

"Ah, so you finally woke up."

She yawned. "Yeah, finally. Listen, did you call me this morning?"

"Sure did."

"Thought so. And did you say something about a bald man?"

"Sure did."

"Why?"

"Doesn't matter since you weren't with one."

"But I was."

"You were? You told me you weren't."

"I was practically talking in my sleep, silly, there's no telling what I said."

"Is the bald guy tall and good looking in a tough guy sense?"

"Yeah . . ." she yawned again. "How did you know?"

"Listen, don't say anything, just let me talk, okay?"

She giggled, wondering what had Nan so wound up. "Okay."

"There was a song playing, Incense and Peppermints. *Did you hear a song with the line incense and peppermints while you were with the bald guy?"*

"Yeah, but how did you know?"

"Never mind that now. Just answer my questions, I'll explain in a minute. Was there a tall blonde woman with a handsome redneck with long hair in need of a shave?"

A chill raced up her spine. "Yeah, how did you know?"

"Were there five other women and an older man, liquor and snacks on a fancy bar?"

"There was! How do you know all that?"

"Amazing! Amazing! Ab-so-lute-ly fucking amazing!"

"But how did you know?" she demanded.

"I know, because I was there."

"What? You weren't there—you were home. At least Jim said you were. I only went to the party because Jim wouldn't let me in. Said you were *indisposed.*" She voiced the last in her best attempt at a stuffy British accent which brought a laugh from Nan.

"Try imprisoned."

"So Taylor's at it again, huh?"

"Yeah, the ass wipe. Sorry you drove all the way out here for nothing. I should have called and told you I got grounded yesterday. One of housekeepers came downstairs for a late night snack and caught me sneaking in after curfew night before last. The little snitch told Taylor and he grounded me for a fucking week."

"So what gives? You weren't there so how did you know about all those people and that song playing?"

Nan drew in an audible breath. *"I was there, Renee, only*

my body wasn't."

"Come again?" she laughed.

"I'm being serious, sweetie. We had a blackout last night that lasted for the longest damn time, and not long after the lights finally came back on I—"

"There was a blackout where I was too, at the party."

"Well, I was lying on my bed when all of a sudden I went all tingly, and was suddenly hovering below a ceiling and it really freaked me out. The next thing I knew I saw you and that bald man. I saw the others and heard the song playing. Next thing I knew I was back in my bed. Weird, huh?"

"My god, Nan! How is that possible?"

"Don't know, but it happened—you just confirmed it did and I'll prove it to you." Nan perfectly described the living room and everyone at the party except Brad.

"You're sure that's all the people you saw?"

"Positive."

"Well you're missing one."

"I am?"

"Yeah, the man who lives there."

"He must have been one of the three dudes I saw, maybe the older guy."

"No, he's young."

A few seconds went by before Nan spoke again. *"Hmm . . . well he must not have been in the room at the time."*

"But he was. He's the one that played the song."

"You believe me, don't you?"

"Well yeah. I'm just curious why you didn't see Brad, that's all."

"I don't know. What's the bald guy's name?"

A smile sprang to her face. "Ronnie. He's the guy I told you about that was always ogling me in the hall last semester."

"The dude with the pretty hair?"

"Mm hmm."

"And he shaved it off?"
"Yep."
"Did you tell him to?"
She winced. "Hell no!"
"Then why did he do it?"
"I have no idea."
"So he's Ronnie, right?"
"Right. Ronnie Garr."
"And the redneck?"
"That's Lou."
"The older dude?"
"Can't remember his name."
"Hmm. Well that's all the men I saw. It's like photocopied in my skull. I can still see it all so clearly."
"This is totally wild, Nan!"
"I'm telling ya."

¶

A severe itch developed under Ronnie's nose. Resisting the urge to relieve it with his fingers like he'd failed to do on numerous occasions when his hands were covered with used motor oil, he used his left bicep to rub the irritation away.

Ben Palloy, who'd just gotten out of the truck after jotting down the mileage, laughed at him. "Finally learned didn't you, son."

He laughed back. "Don't know what it is about getting my hands oily that makes my nose itch."

"Shows you got a nose for the business. I see you shaved your head since you were here last Saturday. What possessed you to do that?"

"I've been wanting to for a long time. My hair grows really fast and I have to let it get long and shaggy in between haircuts because they're too expensive for me to keep it neatly trimmed. It doesn't cost me a cent to shave it but I was worried the bald look might not fit me. Finally got the cojones to do it last night and was real pleased with the results, but now I've got to let it grow back."

"Why so?"

"My girlfriend doesn't like it."

Ben responded with a tight-lip grin and perused a checklist fastened to the clipboard he held with a brawny right hand. Despite being sixty the only thing soft on the barrel-chested man with Popeye-like forearms was a slight beer belly. Though a naturally strong man himself, Ronnie felt a certain kinship with him that went beyond brute strength. They were both leathernecks. Ben fought in Viet Nam and had been awarded a bronze star along with a purple heart. The burly guy's wife had told him about the medals but refused to say how her brave hubby earned the purple heart. Ben wouldn't talk about it either. He speculated it must have been some sort of groin injury due to their silence and the fact they'd married young and didn't have any kids.

"How long have you been seeing each other?"

"Since last night."

Ben chuckled. "One of these long term relationships, huh?"

"Has been for me . . ." he wiped his hands dry with a shop rag. "I knew she was the one the moment I saw her."

"And you finally won her over last night did you."

A twinge of doubt plagued him over Renee refusing the kiss. "Hope so."

Ronnie replaced the filter and screwed the plug back in the oil pan. As he began to fill the engine with clean oil, Ben walked over and stuffed a hundred dollar bill into the pocket of his work shirt, a sentimental smile clinging to his broad face.

"What's that for?"

"Take her out for a nice dinner on me and the missus."

"Oh man—" he raised a grateful hand. "Thanks a million, Ben!"

The jarhead slapped his palm. "Simper Fi."

Echoing the sacred marine sentiment, he thought wistfully, *Now if she'll only accept the invitation . . . .*

¶

Ronnie called Renee the moment he got home from work. Not only had Ben surprised him with the cash gift, he'd let him off two hours early without docking the time from his pay.

"Hello?" said a woman he assumed was her mother.

"May I speak to Renee please?"

"Just a moment. Renee, you're wanted on the phone . . . ."

"Hello?"

"Renee?"

"Well hello, Curly Sampson."

Her recognizing his voice put a grin on his face, but her ambivalent tone made him uneasy. "Are you busy tonight?"

"That depends on you I guess."

The statement thrilled him. "Well, I'd like to take you to dinner if you don't have any other plans."

"Sounds great. What time?"

"You call it . . . ."

He pulled into her driveway at four-thirty, the time he'd normally be leaving Palloy Transportation. A gorgeous white-haired woman, built like Renee but several inches shorter, answered the door. Her haunting eyes were such a dark shade of brown they looked black at first sight. If not for the smile lines beginning to deepen on the sides of her full sensuous lips she could easily pass for a woman his age.

"You must be Ronnie. I'm Veronica, Renee's mother."

"Nice to meet you."

"The pleasure's all mine." She led him into a large living room with an elevated ceiling. Looking up towards a second story banister edging an open hallway she hollered, "Renee, your date's here!" Then she turned to him. "Make yourself comfortable, she'll be down momentarily."

An inordinately long sectional sofa, two armchairs, and a recliner were situated in a semicircle for convenient viewing of a gigantic plasma television perched above a multi-speaker sound system. Choosing the armchair closest to him, he sat down.

"If you'll excuse me, I've got a cake that's ready to come out of the oven."

Less than a minute after she left the room, he heard a door open upstairs. He raised his eyes to see Renee step through it, looking sensational in a short black skirt with nylons and pumps the same color. Her large breasts were straining at a long-sleeved white blouse with collar, buttons, and cuffs of ebony. Smiling down at him, she balanced a purse on the banister long enough to don her coat, strolled to the landing, and gracefully descended the stairs.

"Mom, we're leaving now," she said as they passed a pair of swinging doors.

"What time can I expect you home?"

"Probably around midnight or a little past."

"Well don't make it too far past."

He followed Renee outside but hurried ahead of her when they neared his car.

She giggled as he opened the passenger door for her. "How gallant of you, Curly Sampson. Are you always so chivalrous?"

"Always," he said with a grin. "Now get in the damn car!"

Snickering at his pop off, she seated herself and he closed the door.

Having never eaten at a pricey joint in Baltimore, Ronnie had asked his boss which one he would choose to impress the woman of his dreams. Following Ben's advice, he took her to the jarhead's favorite Italian restaurant. They'd beaten the dinner crowd so got seated right away.

Until their food arrived the conversation centered on his stint in the marines, which she'd brought up and wanted to hear all about. He'd seen little action during his tour of duty in the middle east and Renee seemed disappointed he didn't have any glorious war stories to tell. Thankfully she hadn't asked who he'd really gone to see at that apartment complex last night. When their relationship rested on solid ground instead of floating in the topsy-turvy ether of initial courtship, he'd tell her. Until then, he hoped it wouldn't cross her mind.

For the last few minutes they'd been dining in silence. He'd been deliberating on how to bring the mood to a more intimate level and finally settled on a tactic. "I really enjoyed dancing with you."

Focusing on her food, she twirled noodles around a fork, raised the implement, and cast her beautiful emerald eyes upon him while sensuously chewing a bite of Chicken Alfredo. She swallowed and reached for her wine. "You're quite a dancer yourself, Curly Sampson."

"I hate I didn't get a goodnight kiss."

She took a sip and lowered the glass. "Maybe you'll have better luck tonight."

His heart seemed to skip a beat.

"I wish you hadn't shaved your head."

"If I'd known you liked my hair I never would have, believe me."

The corners of her mouth turned up with a sealed smile that tantalized him. He loved her delicate lips and had fantasized about kissing them since first seeing the auburn stunner. Unlike her eyes—always ablaze with fiery confidence, revealing she was acutely aware of her astounding beauty— they appeared vulnerable, tender, endearingly wary as if constantly requiring a passionate smooch to be reassured of their worthiness. An inward sigh rose within him as they parted to receive another small portion of creamy pasta.

Barely tasting his own, due to adrenaline, he nonetheless consumed everything the waiter had sat before him, finding it hard not to merely sit and ogle her for nourishment.

After the early dinner he took her to his apartment.

Renee glanced around his tiny abode, able to see everything except the bathroom and bedroom, accessed by a short hall. Only a strip of metal running along a junction of dingy gray carpet and worn yellow vinyl separated the living room from the kitchen. She took off her jacket and handed it to him. "You weren't kidding, this *is* a hole."

"Any port in a storm, as they say." He draped her coat around the back of an old office chair situated at his small desk, and spun it around. "Here, it's the best seat in the house."

She sat down and crossed her long shapely legs. The stylish attire she wore radically clashed with the shabby furnishings of his apartment, making him wish he hadn't invited her to dinner. Instead of spending eighty-five percent of Ben's unexpected gift at that expensive restaurant, he could have taken her clubbing instead of being forced to bring her here. "I'm fresh out of beer so all I can offer is pop or coffee, I'm afraid."

"A soda will be fine."

"It's generic cola. I stay pretty well stocked because I get it for half price at Riley's Grocery where I work part time. Are you sure you wouldn't prefer coffee?"

"No, I'll have the soda."

He fetched two from the kitchen, handed her one, and took a load off on a dilapidated recliner, the only other place to sit in the living room. The mood he'd tried to establish at the restaurant had pretty much dissipated. Feeling a little awkward and unsure of himself, he searched for something to say besides how beautiful she was and how much he adored her.

"The freakiest thing happened to my best friend last night," she said, relieving him of his burden.

"Oh?" He tried to appear interested but couldn't care less. All he wanted was to make love to her.

"She lives in the country but the blackout reached her area too. Shortly after it ended she apparently left her body. I know, sounds really strange. Anyway, she was floating along Brad Barron's ceiling and saw us at the party."

He let out a laugh and grinned at her like she was crazy. "And you believe her?"

"Oh yeah, there's no doubt it really happened. Remember asking for that song *Incense and Peppermints*?"

Eyes drawn to her pretty lips he so badly wanted to feel pressed to his, he nodded.

"Well it was playing while she was there. She told me all about the layout of Brad's living room and perfectly described everyone except Brad, who she didn't see for some reason. There's no way she could have known all that."

The expression of wonderment on her face blew his mind, and he couldn't keep from laughing again. Renee didn't appear to have a gullible bone in her body much less the capacity to swallow a load of bullshit like this. "Look, she's probably been to that apartment before and saw everybody leaving last night. You must have mentioned the song before she told you about it. She made the whole thing up, and I can't believe you fell for it."

Renee firmly shook her head. "She brought it up first. She doesn't know Brad and she was locked up in her room all night. She has a warden for a guardian. He's her uncle and he grounded her. She could escape from jail easier than she could break out of her room. I went to her house last night before I went to Brad's, and the butler wouldn't let me in. I suspected she was grounded, and then when I talked to her on the phone today she confirmed it. Believe me, her body never left that house."

That must have been the mansion she stopped at. He took a moment to digest her argument. "Okay, she says she left her body and wound up at the party. Did she float there, fly there, how did she get there?"

"She doesn't know. That song was playing and she saw all of us except Brad, and then the next thing she knew she was back in her body. She wasn't sure it really happened until I confirmed that I was with a quote-unquote bald man."

"Bald man?"

She grinned. "You, Curly Sampson."

"Oh. Well I don't believe in astral projection any more than I do psychics or fortune tellers. You're just remembering wrong that's all. She must have dreamed about a party and subconsciously read everybody at Brad's into it when you told her about them."

Her thick auburn curls swayed with another decisive head shake. "Nope. As a matter of fact after I confirmed I was with a bald man she told me not to say anything and let her talk. So how could it have been a dream, Ronnie? The exact same people, the exact same song? Give me a break."

"Stranger coincidences have happened."

"That's a load of shit," she spat defiantly. "There's just no other way she could have described everything in such detail without being there."

He chuckled again because from her perspective she was right. Not wanting to piss her off he resisted the urge to point out the obvious—one of the people who'd gone to the party must have told her friend about it and the friend decided to have a little fun with her. "Well I can see there's no changing your mind, but I still think she lied to you."

"Mm mm. I know Nan better than anybody on the planet

and she's not a liar."

"Nan?"

"Yeah, Nanatobi Cain. Her uncle's Taylor Cain—*the* Taylor Cain."

"Wow." There wasn't a soul on the eastern seaboard that didn't know that name. He figured Renee moved in elite social circles but had no idea she rubbed elbows with members of the highest echelon. A weight of negativity tugged at his gut that he might not have a prayer of winning her over. Reminding himself that she'd gone out with him in spite of his lowly financial status did little to dispel the notion. Dating a poor guy was one thing, marrying one a horse of a radically different color. He wouldn't always be impoverished but riches didn't lie at the end of a professor's rainbow, at least not his.

Her purse started ringing. She opened it and pulled out a cell phone. "Hello? . . . Hi, Nan . . . You're kidding? . . . Oh my god, how is that possible? . . . Well we have a skeptic, the bald man Ronnie . . . Yeah, I told him all about last night and he doesn't believe me. I'd like for you to tell him what you just told me."

Wearing an I-told-you-so grin, she thrust the phone at him.

Totally mystified, he took it from her. "Hello?"

"Hello, Ronnie, I'm Nanatobi Cain, Renee's best friend." The excited voice had a sexy edge to it.

"Yeah?"

"I just got back from your place where I was hovering over you and Renee. You're wearing a white shirt and blue slacks. The two of you are each holding a can of soda pop, at least you were a moment ago, and . . ." she went on to describe Renee's attire and his apartment.

"Okay, I don't know what you and Renee are up to but I don't believe you were just at my apartment."

"I have to go now, the maid's here for the phone. Tell

Renee I said bye." Her tone had shifted from exhilaration to irritation but still sounded provocative.

He handed Renee's cell back. "She told me to tell you bye."

"I wonder why she got off so suddenly?"

"She said the maid was there for the phone."

A bitter hiss, vaguely resembling a sigh, departed her beguiling mouth. "Of course, Taylor's stupid telephone rule. When Nan's grounded she can't have her phone from dinner till breakfast. How come you told her you don't believe her. How can you not?"

"You guys are pulling some sort of joke."

"How could we be, Ronnie? I've never been to this apartment before and you'd have heard me if I'd told her anything about it or you. There's no explanation other than she was really here."

¶

Brad lifted his face from a plate of squished sushi. He'd been sitting at the table eating dinner, yet somehow found himself in the room with the canopy bed again. Fear mounted as he tried to reason out what happened. He must have passed out and hallucinated the bedroom scene during his unconscious state just as he had the night of the party. Luckily the side of his face had hit the soft wrapped fish or he'd have smashed his nose. Lou was right, he needed to see a doctor. As he pondered what might cause such strange phenomena a horrid thought came to him.

I hope I don't have a brain tumor!

¶

"Well why doesn't she just move out?" Ronnie asked,

referring to Nanatobi allowing her uncle to hold her prisoner.

"She will at the end of March when she turns twenty-one and gets her inheritance, but until then she's totally dependent on Taylor."

"Why doesn't she get a job so she can move out?"

Renee snorted a short laugh and eyeballed him like he'd just asked the most ridiculous question imaginable. "Nanatobi Cain and work are mutually exclusive terms. Besides, she'd need to make about ten thousand dollars a week to maintain the lifestyle to which she's been accustomed since Taylor became her guardian. He might let her keep the Porsche he bought her but he'd definitely cut off her allowance and take back all her credit cards if she moved out. She's just a college student like us so no one would pay her that kind of money even if she was willing to go to work. Anyway, back to her out of body experiences. I wonder why she pops up where we are when she has them?"

¶

It really is happening! Nanatobi hastily scribbled, growing hotter by the second. *It was so exciting, floating along the ceiling and seeing them, knowing they had no idea I was there. Got a real good look at Ronnie and must have him.*

She stashed the diary, quickly undressed, and stretched out on the bed. Fondling her breasts with one hand while mauling her pussy with the other, she fantasized Ronnie was dicking the shit out of her. After being satisfied by her imaginary lover, she got up and hurriedly put her clothes back on. Suzanne would be returning for the dinner tray any minute.

¶

"So what's your story, Ronnie Garr?"

"My story?"

"Yeah," said Renee, narrowing her eyes with a cute squint. "Where are you from, why biology, why the University of Maryland, etcetera, etcetera?"

Her curiosity titillated him. He hoped she really wanted to know and wasn't just making small talk. "I was born in Denver and lived in a lot of different Colorado towns while growing up. Near the end of my marine hitch I got assigned to Camp David which brought me to Maryland. I don't have any family, and no real ties with anybody in Colorado, so I had no reason to go back there."

"Why do you want to teach biology?"

"I got intrigued by it when I was in the corps. I don't want to be a physician, and though I sometimes toy around with the idea of becoming a research scientist, right now my plan is to teach instead."

She grimaced. "You couldn't pay me enough to teach high school."

"No, not high school. I'm shooting for my doctorate so I can teach at the most renowned university that'll have me. How about yourself? What's your goal?"

"Oh I'm doing just enough to get a liberal arts degree to placate my dad." She stretched her long arms, causing her breasts to strain so hard against the snug-fitting blouse he marveled buttons weren't popping off. "I don't have any career goals. I plan on entrapping some good looking millionaire in the near future and retiring."

The fortune hunter remark sounded like a joke and he hoped that's all it was. "Sounds like a definite career goal to me."

An ironic smile trailed a light giggle. "I guess it does, now that you mention it."

Studying her beautiful face, he felt a dull pain worm its

way through his insides at the thought of not sharing her life. Instinct advised against it, but he geared up to make his move anyway because his feelings for her were too strong to allow this opportunity to pass. "What if I were to predict your future for you. How'd that be?"

"Predict away, Nostradamus," she permitted with a playful grin.

He summoned his courage and cleared his throat. "I'm betting you won't be marrying a millionaire but are going to wind up hitched to an ex-marine who will ultimately make his living as a biology professor. That's my prediction for your future."

The stunned glower that came over her made his gonads shrivel. "Fat chance, Curly Sampson."

His intuition had been right, he'd moved too fast, but it was too late to turn back, so like a compulsive gambler he went for broke—placing all his chips on one square as the roulette wheel began spinning. A little voice inside his head assured him the steel ball wouldn't land on his number but he had to let her know how he felt. "I didn't believe in love at first sight until I saw you in the hall last semester and knew it had happened to me. Whatever it takes to win you over, I'll do it. There's no one else in this world for me, Renee. No one."

The apprehension flaring in her jade eyes as she firmly set her jaw and tightened her lips assured him he'd seriously crossed the line. She gazed at him with that same wary expression for what seemed like forever before finally giving a verbal response. "Keep it light, Ronnie. I like you and am willing to have fun with you—*real* fun—but I won't marry you. Put that crazy notion out of your mind and don't ever mention such nonsense again."

There wasn't a shred of doubt she meant it.

Torrents of unbelievable agony crippled him inside. She'd ripped him apart—heart and soul—and had done so as thoughtlessly as if merely dismantling a tinker toy man. He felt infinitesimally small, as if he was nothing but a stupid, inept, undeniable fool for even thinking he could win her love.

The hurt must have shown on his face because a look of pity formed on hers. "I'm sorry. I never would have agreed to date you if I'd known you were that serious about me. I think you'd better take me home."

Tears streamed down his face as she gathered her coat and purse.

He wanted to die.

¶

"Renee, your date's here!" she turned to him. "Make yourself comfortable, she'll be down momentarily."

Radically confused—wanting to ask Veronica Van Cedar if she remembered saying those exact words to him before, but unable to because she'd think he was a loon—Ronnie sat down.

"If you'll excuse me, I've got a cake that's ready to come out of the oven." She strolled to the other side of the room and disappeared through a set of swinging doors.

A regular door opened upstairs and Renee appeared.

His mind reeled. At first he'd attributed everything to an unbelievably strong and very lengthy sense of déjà vu but that wasn't the case at all. She came down the stairs wearing the same clothes she'd worn earlier, confirming all of this really *had* happened before—only a few hours ago.

The whole evening repeated itself. Everything played out exactly as it had before with the exception of Renee asking him if something was wrong when she caught him deep in thought about this weird reenactment of a slice of time. He answered with a question. "Does anything strike you as odd since we left your house?"

"No," she replied—tone indifferent, expression untroubled. Renee obviously didn't have a clue.

"Are you sure?"

"Well yes I'm sure," she laughingly affirmed. "I would know wouldn't I? What are you getting at?"

"Um . . . nothing."

"So what's your story, Ronnie Garr?"

Remembering the disastrous turn of events that soon followed her question when she'd asked it earlier, he wasn't about to let that play out again. He didn't know what the hell was going on but he'd miraculously been given a second chance. After reciting a synopsis of his life for the second time, he veered back to a subject he'd avoided before. "What happened to Nanatobi is truly remarkable."

Her brows rose with surprise. "So you believe her now?"

"Well yeah, I sure do."

"Your last word on the matter was for me to change the subject. So what changed your mind?"

"Logic. The only thing that makes sense is she's telling the truth. Impossible though it seems." On the previous go-round he'd wanted time to think on it before committing himself to the notion Renee's best friend really had paid a ghostly visit to his apartment.

"Isn't it weird?"

"Yeah, totally baffling." Recalling her saying she was willing to have *real* fun with him when he'd brought her here the first time, he made his approach. Words of love hadn't won her over, maybe the physical act would. "There's no point in discussing it though. We'll most likely never know why it happened. Instead of talking about your friend's freaky experience, I vote we go get some liquor and come back here and get naked."

Renee bolted to her feet. "If you think you're going to get

into my pants with that lame line you're full of shit! I'm nobody's cheap whore. I think you'd better take me home."

Incomprehension cramped his brain. He'd somehow been given a second shot at Renee but managed to blow that one too . . . .

He kept playing the two scenarios over in his mind while driving back from Wine's Gate. The same events had happened twice which meant he'd either gone back in time after first taking Renee home or had been given a vision of the future that had seemed so real he might as well have lived through it. He didn't know which was the case, but kept hoping for a third chance at it.

Unfortunately no such opportunity came.

¶

Ronnie spent the day sulking—wishing he hadn't burned his bridges with Renee last night, racking his brains trying to figure out how he'd lived the same segment of time twice. Those thoughts and emotions whirled around the bizarre fact that Renee hadn't been aware the exact same things were reoccurring. Her mom and the people at the restaurant hadn't appeared cognizant of it either. Neither had Nanatobi Cain when she'd repeated the exact same phone call. That could only mean none of it really happened the first time, which left but one conclusion—he'd envisioned a portion of the future he thought he'd actually lived through.

FIVE

After an agonizing twenty minutes of isolation spent in a room the nurse had taken him to from the waiting room where he'd already suffered a half hour of worse case scenarios torturing his mind, a gulp of fear lodged in Brad's throat when the neurologist finally stepped through the door. He'd made an appointment the Monday following the Saturday he'd woken up with his jaw pressed against a pillow of raw fish and seaweed. Ten days later the tests had been run and four days had passed since. Now he'd learn the results.

"Your two blackouts weren't caused by a tumor," said the physician, scanning the contents of an open folder. "The x-rays were negative and the cat-scan confirms it. Your blood pressure's normal, the blood tests show you to be fit as a fiddle, so there's nothing physiologically wrong with you. Since you say they weren't caused by drugs or alcohol, and you had no other symptoms indicating an extreme allergic reaction, and you're certain emotional stress wasn't the culprit, they must be psychosomatic in nature . . . ."

Brad drove home elated. Whatever had twice rendered his body unconscious while inducing his brain to produce a micro-movie of him floating beneath a bedroom ceiling wasn't a side effect of some terminal disease, and that called for a celebration. He phoned Lou, then everyone at the office, and told them he was throwing a bash at his place this coming Saturday night.

¶

Having served her sentence, Nanatobi could now come and go as she pleased, so long as she gave her uncle a detailed itinerary of her whereabouts: who she'd be with, where, and how long. She found Ronnie Garr listed in the phone book, wrote down his address, and lied to Taylor about going to Renee's.

¶

On his way to work, Ronnie reached for the knob but someone knocked before he could turn it. He opened the door to find a woman smiling at him. An aura of wealth and privilege hung about her. She looked like the quintessential debutante—used to getting her way and having things done for her due to her station in life and astounding beauty, flawed only by a complexion splotched with freckles. Her coat, gloves, pants, shoes, and purse were red like her hair. The young lady standing before him could be none other than Renee's astral-traveling friend, he assumed.

"Hello, Ronnie, I'm Nanatobi Cain. We spoke on the phone a while back when Renee was here."

He couldn't help grinning over correctly ascertaining her identity beforehand. "Well hello, Nanatobi, nice to meet you in person. I'm afraid you've caught me at a bad time. I was just on my way to work."

"You work at night?"

"Yeah, at a grocery store. I'm a starving college student and have to put food on the table some way. If you'll excuse me, I don't want to be late."

A cute pout captured her speckled face. "Can't you call in sick? I really need to talk to you about what happened the other day."

Scheduled to work from eight till the store closed at eleven, the stunt would cost him three hours pay. "I can't afford to lose the money."

"Tell you what . . ." she fished a shiny red billfold from her purse. "I'll give you fifty dollars if you'll call in and say you'll be a little late, and I promise I won't stay long. You can go on to work afterwards and make even more money."

She held out a fifty dollar bill.

Eyeballing the tempting greenback, Ronnie knew he should refuse her offer because it entailed lying to his boss. The world was full of irresponsible people and he'd made a commitment to himself long ago not to be one of them. But he wouldn't make that much working his shift, so he accepted the cash and motioned her inside.

Nanatobi took off her gloves and dropped them on the recliner beside her purse as he dialed the store. When a tight scarlet blouse bulging at the bust, and the hip section of snug-fitting pants were no longer hidden by a knee-length coat, he couldn't believe his eyes—the woman had a body to die for. Instead of lying, he told his boss he had an opportunity to make a quick fifty bucks if he'd permit him to come in at nine, which the good sport did.

He spun his office chair around. "Have a seat. Do you want something to drink? All I can offer you is generic cola, coffee, or water."

"No thanks, I'm all set."

As she made herself comfortable, he fetched a kitchen chair, not wanting to disturb her stuff piled on the recliner.

"I'm sorry. You can toss my things anywhere. I didn't mean to deprive you of your chair."

"Not a problem." He lowered himself onto the wobbly wooden seat.

"Okay, I'll get right to it. I've been thinking about what happened to me, and I think it has something to do with you."

"Why's that?"

"Because the two times I left my body I've gone to where you were—that party and here. I think there's some sort of metaphysical connection interlocking the two of us."

She seemed excited about the possibility. He wondered why. "I was with Renee both times, so maybe your connection is between you and her rather than you and I."

"I don't think so. I've known Renee since first grade and it never happened until the other night. If the link was her it seems to me it would have happened long ago. At least that's my theory. Please tell me about yourself, maybe there's a clue there."

Nanatobi's boobs were eye-magnets and he had a hard time keeping his off them. But her green irises painfully made him think of Renee, making it difficult to focus on her face. Giving his fingernails a phony inspection he said, "I'm still not convinced you had an out of body experience, and I don't see how talking about myself is going to help. But I think I may know what happened to you, because something similar happened to me."

"You had an out of body experience?" she asked excitedly.

"No . . ." he lowered his hands and looked at her. "How many times do you remember talking to me on the phone?"

A confused grin appeared. "Why only once of course. Why would you ask such a peculiar thing?"

He palmed his knees and sighed. "That's what I thought you'd say. I lived through a segment of time twice that day. Only the people who experienced it with me didn't realize it was happening a second time, including you since we had the same conversation two times and you only recall one. So I've concluded that I somehow had a vision of future incidents that seemed so real I thought I was living them out before they actually happened."

Her dappled façade shifted into a beacon of childlike eagerness. "That's fucking amazing, tell me what happened."

Surprised she so readily believed him, he recounted his date with Renee, even the part of trying to change the outcome.

"And Renee had no idea all this happened twice?"

"No. Neither did her mom or any of the people I interacted

with that night. And that's what I think happened to you. I think you had a vision of something while it was happening, but you weren't really there even though you thought you were."

"Nuh-uh, I'm certain I was right up there—" she pointed towards the ceiling "—and you were sitting right where my coat is, and Renee was sitting in this very chair I'm sitting in."

He shook his head. "You don't understand what I mean. In your case you saw something that actually happened but you weren't there when it did, you just thought you were. That's how your visions worked. In my case, I actually lived it out after envisioning it."

She was thoughtful for a moment. "Well either way it still involves you, doesn't it?"

"I don't think so. I've been thinking a lot about what happened to you because of what happened to me. The night of that party there was a blackout. Remember?"

"Yes."

"And you say nothing like that ever happened to you before then, right?"

"Right."

"Well I heard on the news that no one's been able to figure out what caused it. I followed Renee that night and she stopped by your place before going to Brad Barron's apartment, which means I also drove by your house. When Renee stopped I continued down the road a ways. My guess is that some type of a freak undetectable energy field developed somewhere between your house and the place I turned around, and started moving towards Baltimore. I drove through it but Renee left before it reached your place, affecting you like it did me. Though Renee didn't get contaminated she was in the vicinity. I think whatever happened to you and I centers around her because she's your best friend and I'm crazy about her. My vision involved her, and you always go to where she is. I think when that energy field, or whatever you want to call it, got to the heart of the city it had gained so much strength that it caused the blackout and either exploded or dissipated or just kept moving on. If I hadn't followed her that night and you hadn't been exactly where you were when that thing passed through, I don't think anything paranormal would have ever happened to either of us."

"Wow, what a cool theory!" Her freckled countenance blazed with excitement. "So you think whatever caused the blackout caused me to leave my body."

Her childlike enthusiasm struck him so humorous he had a hard time restricting laughter to a mere grin. "Only I don't think you really left your body, I think you had a vision. Why I didn't have my vision until the next day I couldn't say, but that's what I think brought it on because nothing like that has ever happened to me before."

"Why were you following Renee? Why didn't you both just ride in the same car?"

At first he started to lie, but what difference did it make now? Nanatobi would very likely tell her, but it couldn't do any more damage than he'd already done. "Renee didn't know I was following her. Still doesn't as a matter of fact."

"Oh . . ." she gave him a shame-on-you grin. "But the two of you were together at the party. How did you wind up together?"

"I had driven by her house and when I turned around she was pulling out of the drive, so I just followed her—to your house and on to the party. We hooked up in the parking lot where I acted like it was a coincidence we bumped into each other."

"So you didn't know any of the people at the party? Besides Renee, I mean."

"No."

"Well Brad Barron's having another party and this time I'm going with Renee."

His stomach soured at hearing that. "And this time I won't be."

Going right past his statement she said, "He's the one person I didn't see that night, and I can't imagine why I didn't. Renee's certain he was in the room the same time I was there."

"When you envisioned you were there," he corrected.

"Whatever. We're going to the party so I can have a look at him and see if it rings any bells."

He rubbed his sprouting scalp, feeling sick about Renee going to that party without him.

¶

Nanatobi surveyed the room. Renee was dancing with Lou, the redneck she'd seen on her first astral trip. The tall blonde woman seemed upset about it. It felt strange being there in person, standing on the floor. Except for Ronnie, everyone she'd observed from the ceiling was there, only this time she could see Brad. Handsome but a bit geeky, she wondered how short he'd be without the high-heeled boots he wore. He gave off a slightly effeminate air but wasn't gay. The look on his face when Renee introduced them to each other belied that, and she'd caught him ogling her several times afterwards.

Lou had asked her to dance right after Brad introduced him, but she'd declined, not wanting to show everyone up. She'd only been three years old when her mother started teaching her ballet after discovering she had a gift for gracefully whirling to melody. Her professional lessons began at age four and continued until Taylor had given her the right to make her own choice on the matter at thirteen. After achieving the title of prima ballerina of her class, the lack of a higher rank to strive for had weakened her interest, so she'd quit. Besides not knowing how to tone down her superior abilities, she didn't particularly enjoy dancing to modern music. Though she could twirl masterfully to any musical genre, she preferred classics such as Tchaikovsky's *Swan Lake* and Pugni's *La Esmeralda*. As she stood at the bar sipping a wine cooler, it occurred to her Brad hadn't danced a single time either.

¶

Charley had his television turned up as loud as he could stand it but the damn music still overrode the sound. He didn't want to be a troublemaker but enough was enough so he tossed the remote, bailed from his recliner, and went next door to reason with his noisy neighbor.

Brad answered the doorbell and smiled with surprise. "Charley! Come on in and join the party, my man."

"Thanks, maybe some other time. I'm on vacation and right now I just want to chill in front of the boob tube. Would you please turn it down a little so I can hear my show?"

"Oh—sorry, Charley, of course."

"Thanks, I appreciate it . . . ."

He'd been away from the control room for a couple of days and his nerves were beginning to settle. His ex wife had called earlier and set them on edge like she always did, but now he had his hot buttered popcorn, pickle juice, and could actually hear the TV.

For awhile.

By the time he'd emptied his bowl and glass, the stereo next door was once more blaring through the walls. Knowing the volume would eventually creep back up if he complained again, he decided to fight fire with fire. He'd spend the rest of the evening with Ray Charles and cold beer—let the blues and brews take his cares away. Already hearing *Hit The Road Jack* in his head, he opened the refrigerator, reached inside the box, and groaned when his fingers encountered only two bottles.

¶

Ronnie had been driving around North Baltimore stewing over Renee, fearing she'd hook up with Lou Cotton at Brad Barron's party. He thought about splurging for a bottle of booze and getting drunk but that wouldn't accomplish anything but a hangover. Besides, he couldn't spare the cash after allowing himself the luxury of wasting gas on this cold lonely Saturday night. He adjusted his Ravens cap, now covering hair long enough to lay down instead of sticking straight up. Even though Renee didn't want him, he'd let it keep growing because somehow, someway he had to win her over—he couldn't give up on her. Passing Brad Barron's apartment complex for the fourth time, he resisted the urge to pull into the visitor's parking lot again. He'd already confirmed Renee's Camaro was parked within. A couple of miles later his engine stalled.

He coasted to the shoulder of the road and popped the hood. A nearby streetlight made it unnecessary to bother with the flashlight in his glove box. The battery cables were properly tight so he checked the high tension leads. They all fit snugly on the plugs and distributor. Using his pocket knife to pop the catches, he removed the distributor cap and inspected the insides. The terminals and rotor were clean, so carbon buildup wasn't the problem. He put the cap back on and fetched a toolbox from the trunk.

Before long he'd narrowed the problem down to either the fuel pump or fuel filter, which he'd determined by loosening the outlet line. It should have spewed some gas but didn't, which meant fuel either wasn't being delivered to the filter or couldn't get past it. His back began to protest being bent over in the same position too long. He backed away from the engine and countered the sensation with a quick arch of his spine.

"This is not good," he mumbled while scanning the area. Nothing nearby could be of any help. He couldn't afford a tow truck but didn't dare leave the car overnight, it would be stripped by morning. He'd never wanted a cell phone, and couldn't keep up with the monthly payments even if he did. Wishing he had one now, he closed the hood, stowed his tool box, locked the doors, and started down the road, opposite the direction he'd driven.

A Cadillac whizzed past after he'd hiked about half a mile. It slowed to a stop and reversed back to him. The driver's window powered down to reveal a big black man behind the wheel. "You belong to that T-Bird back there?"

"Yeah," Ronnie answered with a hopeful tone. The dude looked like the type of guy who'd be willing to help out a stranded motorist.

"What seems to be the problem?"

"It's either the fuel pump or fuel filter, I don't know which."

"Oh what a shame. Want me to call a tow truck for you?"

"Can't afford one. I was trying to find a payphone and call my boss to come help me."

"What's the number?" He produced a cell while saying it.

Ronnie told him and watched the index finger of a huge black hand punch the tiny buttons before being given the device.

"Hello?"

"Ben, it's Ronnie."

"What's up?"

He conveyed his dilemma and handed the phone back. "Thanks a million. My boss is going to tow it for me."

"Good. Well hop in and I'll give you a ride back to your car."

The dude scooted a twelve pack of beer to his side as he got in, and thrust a hand towards him. "Charley Hudson."

"Ronnie Garr," he said while shaking it.

His new acquaintance shifted into drive, made a u-turn, and cruised towards his car. "So what do you do, Ronnie?"

"I'm majoring in biology at Maryland and work part time at Palloy Transportation and a grocery store. How about yourself?"

A weary sigh emerged. "I'm an air traffic controller and proud to say I'm presently on vacation."

"Good for you."

"Yeah, I'm really enjoying it except for tonight."

"Why's that?"

"There's a party going on in one of the apartments next to mine and the music's so loud I can't hear my TV. I asked my neighbor to turn it down and he did, but somebody jacked it back up."

"A partying neighbor is an irritating neighbor," said Ronnie sympathetically.

"Nah, ol' Brad's a good neighbor. It's just those damn parties he throws every once in awhile. Usually I'm at work when he has one because most times he opts for a Friday to have a shindig. But even if he hadn't decided on a Saturday bash this time I'd have still been home since my vacation started two days ago and I've got no plans but to lay around my place like a lazy hound dog."

Surely it couldn't be Renee's Brad. "So he ran you out of your apartment, huh?"

The big guy laughed and patted the twelve pack. "No, I was low on beer and am on my way back home. I live right down the road from here."

So did the Brad he knew. "Your neighbor's last name wouldn't happen to be Barron would it?"

Charley cut his eyes to him. "Well it sure is."

"Real tan, blonde hair, perfect teeth?"

"That's him."

An ache rose from the pit of his gut like a painful air bubble. He blew out a breath to relieve it as if expelling a burp, but it didn't do any good. "It just so happens my girlfriend's at that party."

"Well if your girlfriend's there, why aren't you?" quizzed Charley, face scrunched with a frown.

"She dumped me."

"Oh what a shame . . . ."

¶

Twenty minutes after he waved goodbye to the friendly black man, Ben arrived in one of his winch trucks and they hauled his car to the shop. While Ronnie unhooked the cable Ben told him to borrow one of the company pickups. Then he laid a fifty on him. "I'll take care of your car, whatever it needs is on me. You go have some fun."

He let out a sad laugh. "I really appreciate your generosity, Ben, but it's eleven o'clock."

"What, you gonna turn into a pumpkin at midnight? The night is young . . . ."

Ronnie stopped at a convenience store near the shop, picked up a case of beer, and drove to Brad Barron's apartment complex. He parked a few spaces down from the white Camaro, stashed the beer in the pickup bed to keep it cold, and waited.

¶

Nanatobi sat cross legged on the floor in front of Brad Barron's coffee table, facing the couch, upon which sat Renee and Lou Cotton, a couple of feet apart. Everyone else had gone home. Brad served coffee and remained on his feet. "I hope you had a good time, Nanatobi, even though you never danced."

She didn't want to waste any time getting to the point. "Actually I had an ulterior motive in coming with Renee tonight, Brad. The last time she was here something odd happened, and I'd like to talk to you about it . . . ."

¶

Nanatobi's astounding tale thoroughly rattled him. Lou, on the other hand, seemed more intrigued than apprehensive. Brad took a minute to compose himself before responding to her. "So you saw everyone but me?"

"Yes, and that's why I wanted to talk to you. Renee said you were in the room when that song was playing, but I didn't see you. I thought for certain she had to be mistaken, but since you remember being present too, I'm at a loss."

"This is unreal," said Lou. "Tell them what happened to you that night, man."

"What happened?" Nanatobi quickly demanded, more than asked. She seemed thrilled about her astral trip rather than concerned like him.

"Something very similar to what happened to you."

"Wow, tell me all about it." Anticipation zoomed from her pretty eyes like two green laser beams.

"Well, I seemed to be floating beneath a ceiling the same way you described, only I didn't see any people and don't have a clue where I was."

"What *did* you see?"

He took a nerve-settling sip of coffee, puzzled as to why she too wasn't worried about the strange experience which had evidently really happened. "I was hovering over a red canopy bed and saw candles burning on an antique vanity in a very upscale bedroom. There was a large analog clock on the face of a clown hanging on one wall and—"

"My god, your describing Nan's bedroom!" gasped Renee.

The declaration turned him instantly feverish. He felt dizzy, disoriented, and quite frightened. "R-Really?"

"Most definitely," affirmed Nanatobi, whose face had lit up like downtown Las Vegas upon hearing his report. "I was using the candles for light during the blackout and left them burning a good while after it finally ended. Now we're getting somewhere."

Lou placed his cup on the coffee table and swooped his hair back with both hands before resuming his slouching position on the couch. "Dude, I just remembered something. You weren't in the living room the whole time *Incense and Peppermints* was playing. You left before it ended. You'd challenged everyone to name a one hit wonder that you didn't have and Ursula hollered as you stepped into the hall that she was going to nail you when you got back."

He remembered thinking Ursula had indeed won the challenge before she'd confessed to making up the group and their only hit song. Fresh off the out of body experience, he'd been too unnerved to laugh at her joke. Feeling much like that now, he thought back to Ronnie Garr requesting the song, and inched his memory slowly forward from there. A few seconds later he popped his forehead with the heels of his palms. "You're right, Lou. That song *was* still playing when I went to the bathroom to uh . . . well anyway that's where the bedroom scenario happened."

"That explains why I didn't see you while I was here!" Nanatobi gleefully shouted. "Ronnie told me he thinks what happened has something to do with the blackout."

Renee glared at her. "When did Ronnie tell you that?"

"I went to his apartment to talk to him the other day. I

meant to tell you but it slipped my mind."

"Why did you go see Ronnie?" she demanded suspiciously.

Nanatobi threw her an incensed smirk. "To talk to him about the out of body experiences. Only he thinks I was having a vision like him."

"A vision like him? He never told me anything about having any visions."

Brad's already tangled nerves lurched into high tension. Renee was growing angrier by the second and he feared a catfight might be ensuing.

"Where is Ronnie anyway?" quipped Lou with a disarming smile, clearly trying to lighten the mood. "Why didn't he come to the party?"

Still hurling hand grenades at Nanatobi with her eyes Renee muttered, "I didn't invite him."

"Why not?"

The two girls kept staring at one another, each gorgeous visage burning with ferocity. Renee didn't answer, but at length Nanatobi clenched her teeth and said, "Because she dumped him, that's why. And since you dumped him, you've got a lot of nerve giving me the third degree over going to see him."

Renee indignantly dropped her jaw. "Is that what he told you, that I dumped him?"

"More or less."

"Well I didn't!"

"Well he sure thinks you did."

"Are you certain it was your bedroom I saw?" Brad gingerly intruded.

Nanatobi cut her eyes to him. "The clown clock confirms it."

"Beyond doubt," said Renee.

Lou started scratching his whiskered chin. "This is the weirdest thing I've ever heard. What do you think is going on with this shit, Brad?"

"I don't know, but it happened again the next day. I was floating around that same room and woke up to find I'd collapsed at my table. It scared me so badly I went to a neurologist, afraid a brain tumor was causing me to pass out and hallucinate that bedroom scene. But thankfully I don't have one. Now I'm dealing with fear of the unknown since those apparently really were astral projections."

"Do you remember what time it happened again?" said Nanatobi. Curiosity had replaced the anger on her face when he'd mentioned leaving his body a second time. Renee appeared inquisitive as well, but still looked slightly ticked off.

"Not the exact minute but it was somewhere between six and seven because that's when I eat dinner. I came to with my face lying in a pile of sushi."

Lou laughed, as did Renee, but Nanatobi frowned with thought while eyeballing her. "Remember me calling you right after I saw you and Ronnie at his place?"

She nodded.

"That was around dinnertime. I'll bet when I left my body, Brad left his just like what happened the first time we went astral. I think Ronnie's right. Whatever caused the blackout is responsible for the experiences Brad and I had, and the vision or whatever Ronnie had."

Renee groaned. "What vision are you talking about? Remember he didn't tell me about it."

"He didn't tell you about it because you dumped him."

"I did not dump him!"

"Well whatever you want to call it . . ." Nanatobi rolled her eyes. "He said he lived the same sequence of events twice. He picked you up for your date, took you to dinner, then to his apartment, and you made him take you home. Some time later that entire evening reoccurred exactly the way it had before, but only *he* knew it was all happening a second time."

"That's impossible," spouted Lou.

She sneered at him. "Oh, and what happened to Brad and I isn't?"

The Okie thought on that a moment and grinned. "I see your point."

"Anyway, Renee, Ronnie finally concluded it couldn't have really happened twice or you and everyone else he was in contact with would have realized it too. So he surmised he must have envisioned it but everything seemed so real he thought he'd lived it the first time, when in fact it was only a vision of what was going to happen."

A cynical laugh sprang out of Lou. "I'll bet he made all that up just to freak you out."

Nanatobi shrugged. "You're entitled to your opinion, but I believe him. He thinks what happened to me was a vision also, and it seemed so real I thought I was there. But now I know he's mistaken about that since it happened to Brad too."

Brad felt that had some merit to it. "Not necessarily. Maybe I really didn't go to your bedroom but only dreamed I did."

"Well I know what happened to me wasn't a vision or any dream."

"It didn't seem like that to me either," he asserted, "but were you aware of reentering your body or did you just seem to wake up?"

Nanatobi donned a faraway look. "You know, it *was* like waking up."

"So you see what I mean? We could have envisioned everything in dreams that were so vivid we thought we were hovering over the scene but never actually left our bodies."

"Hold on there, partner," said Lou. "According to both your accounts neither of you had gone to sleep before you wound up in an astral state, so how could you have dreamed it?"

SIX

Renee left Brad Barron's apartment complex at twelve-forty. Relieved to see her leaving with Nanatobi and not Lou Cotton, Ronnie followed without fear of Renee getting wise to it since he wasn't in his T-Bird. Once it became clear they were heading for Nanatobi's house he turned around, grateful to be able to sleep tonight. Thoughts of her hooking up with the redneck had tormented him since Nanatobi told him about tonight's party. Now he could relax.

Ben had insisted he enjoy himself, and wouldn't hear of him paying for gas while using the company pickup, so he cruised the city streets for awhile before calling it a night.

A shocking yet wonderful surprise awaited him when he arrived at his slummy apartment complex—Renee getting out of her car. He parked where she couldn't see him and tailed her on foot to his place. Toting the case of beer, he arrived just as she began knocking on the door.

"Nobody's home."

She whirled around with a gasp. "Ronnie?"

"So what brings you here?"

Smiling prettily, she put a hand on his shoulder. "I'm sorry I got upset with you."

It hadn't occurred to him until that moment that he didn't know which scenario she'd actually experienced on their strange repeated date. If his assessment was correct it had to be the second one. "Um, the old memory needs refreshing. Exactly why *did* you get upset with me?"

"Let's go inside first, it's freezing out here."

He opened the door and followed her into the living room. "Can I offer you a beer?"

"No thanks, I've had enough alcohol tonight. Brad Barron threw another party and Nan and I went to it. I'll take a soft drink if you have one."

Removing a beer from the box, he stashed the rest of the case in the fridge, and grabbed a cola. Renee seated herself in the recliner and he handed it to her. "Okay, remind me why you got upset."

"For talking to me like a cheap whore just like I told you."

So she *had* experienced the second scenario. "Well let me apologize for that. I'm really sorry."

"Apology accepted, all's forgiven."

His insides twisted as he recalled the cruel directness in her voice when she'd said she would never marry him. He loved her too much to be just another guy, but he couldn't give up on her either. There had to be a way to win her heart, he'd just have to find it. Cracking his beer open, he studied it while figuring the best approach to take, and took a swig upon reaching a decision. "Great. Now we can start over."

Her expression seemed to indicate she wasn't particularly interested in discussing their new beginning. "Nan met Brad Barron tonight, and boy did he have a tale to tell. It seems he also had an out of body experience, and get this—he was floating around in Nan's bedroom. It happened to him twice just like it did to Nan, and he apparently leaves his body at the same time she leaves hers."

"How weird." That amazed him, but not to the degree Renee's detour hurt. He gulped another mouthful of suds.

"And Nan had something interesting to relay as well. She said you had a vision. Why didn't you tell me about it?"

Renee showing more interest in his vision than their relationship felt like a hot knife twisting in his gullet, but he forced the emotion to a back burner. "Because I didn't realize that's what had happened until after you dumped me."

"What's with that? That's how Nan put it too. I didn't dump you, Ronnie."

"What would you call it then?"

"I was angry and I asked you to take me home. That doesn't

mean I dumped you."

He pulled off his cap and tossed it on the desk.

"Oh it's growing back fast!"

"Yeah . . ." he ran a hand over his head and took another pull from his can.

"Okay, so tell me your vision."

Renee's eagerness offended him but he shook it off. "The same string of events went down twice. The second time I realized early on it was happening again. I was sure the first one had really taken place until I realized that neither you, your mom, nor the people at the restaurant we interacted with knew it was reoccurring. So I can only assume it was some sort of precognition that was so graphic I thought I'd gone back in time and relived it. I suspected only the second date actually happened, but didn't know for sure until you confirmed it.

"When your mom said the exact same things the second time, it dawned on me everything was repeating itself. I knew what you'd be wearing when you walked down the stairs, and I knew what you and your mom were going to say to each other as we were leaving."

Her sexy auburn brows moved towards each other, but the frown conveyed acceptance. "So everything happened the second time exactly as it did the first time?"

"Well, not exactly."

"What do you mean?"

"Since I knew the evening was going to end with you demanding that I take you home, I had the opportunity to change what I said that prompted you to do that, hoping for a different outcome. Unfortunately, even though I changed combat tactics it still ended in disaster."

"Combat tactics," she giggled. "I'm curious. What did you change?"

"No, first tell me what you remember me saying just before

you wanted to go home."

"You wanted to get some liquor and come back here so we could quote-unquote get naked. What did you say the first time?"

He cleared his throat and drank beer.

"Come on, tell me. What did you say the first time?"

Reminding himself to remain calm no matter how she responded, he grinned as if finding the matter humorous. "That I wanted to marry you."

"You're kidding," she laughed out.

"Scout's honor."

"And I got mad at you for that?"

"You sure did."

For the first time she seemed to doubt him—her blazing green eyes were boring a skeptical hole through him. "Why can't I remember that if it really happened?"

"Because it didn't happen to you, only to me. The second time around was when everything really transpired. You'd said we could have *real* fun together but you'd never marry me, and that's what prompted my crass suggestion the second go round."

The statement apparently extricated any disbelief. Her gaze turned warmly receptive. "Nan said you think all this has something to do with the blackout."

"Yeah. I believe whatever caused it is responsible for what happened to Nanatobi and me. Hearing Brad went astral the same time she did and landed in her room while she went to his apartment gives my theory a boost."

"Why do you think it's connected to the blackout?"

"Because that oddball power failure is the only thing out of the ordinary that happened that night. It's just a guess, I could be wrong. I'm certainly not going to be dogmatic about it."

She yawned and glanced at her watch. "Oh my gosh, it's almost two o'clock."

"Well you can't demand that I take you home this time because you drove yourself."

"So who said anything about going home, Curly Sampson?"

That confused him. When he'd driven her home as she'd demanded on both dates, it appeared to be over for good. Now she wanted to spend the night. Why? "Um, I don't get it."

"Don't get what?"

"Why you're willing tonight but weren't before."

"I didn't realize how much I liked you until Nan told me she came to see you. It just inflamed me with jealousy."

A geyser of hope sprang up within him. "You were jealous?"

"Yeah. But not enough to marry you, so don't get the wrong idea. And why would you want to marry me anyway?"

"Not sure I do anymore," he lied as the geyser dropped to his bowels, turning them bitter. Her countenance fell and she appeared totally vulnerable. Maybe it was vengeance, perhaps stubborn pride, or merely stupid male ego forcing him to pass up the opportunity—which he'd probably hate himself for doing in the morning—but he couldn't sleep with her on these terms. "I think you'd better get along home now."

¶

Nanatobi gasped—arched her back and moaned—then totally relaxed, slowly sliding her hand from between her wet inner thighs. Breathing evenly now, she lay in the darkness of her room thinking of Ronnie. Then suddenly she was in his apartment peering down at him and Renee, who sat in his recliner looking shocked and hurt as he took a drink from a can of beer.

"Why do you want me to go home?" she heard Renee say.

"I don't have any interest in starting a relationship that has no future."

"I didn't say there wasn't a future for us. I just said I wouldn't marry you."

"Whatever . . ." Ronnie got up and squashed his beer can. "Look, I'm tired and I want to get some sleep. Come on, I'll walk you to your car."

¶

Brad hovered above the red canopy, under which Nanatobi Cain presumably lay sleeping. The lights were off yet he could clearly see the clown clock, the antique vanity, a chest of drawers with girly knickknacks splayed across the top, a dainty table with a single chair, a hope chest, a bricolage sculpture, a settee covered in scarlet velour, a huge Elvis poster next to a plasma TV, a mannequin wearing a ballet tutu, and a burgundy-stained desk, atop which sat a computer. Awaking to find himself in his bed, he pounded his pillow, turned over on his side, and feeling too drowsy to worry about the experience, went back to sleep.

¶

Ronnie returned to his apartment after walking a stunned Renee to her car. He took off his shirt and was about to slip out of his pants when the phone rang.

"Hello?"

"Ronnie? It's Nanatobi."

"It's a little late to be calling isn't it?" His voice reflected the irritation he felt.

"I know, but I knew you were awake."

"How did you know that?"

"Because I just saw you and Renee."

"Oh really?"

"Really. You were drinking a beer and Renee was wanting to know why you wanted her to go home."

She'd been there all right. "How long were you here?"

"Not long. Can you believe it happened again? It was no vision, Ronnie, I'm certain I was there."

Though shocked to learn her astral projections were the real deal and not extrasensory perceptions like the one he'd experienced, exhaustion forced a yawn from his throat as if he was bored. "Look, give me a call tomorrow and we'll talk some more about it. Right now I need to hit the hay."

"How about I just come by after lunch?"

"Fine. See you then."

SEVEN

As Nanatobi made herself comfortable in his office chair, Ronnie eased into the recliner. Knowing he had no chance of marrying Renee, he didn't refrain from feasting his eyes on the redhead's incredible bust.

It rose with an excited breath. "I called Brad Barron to see if he left his body again and he did. He was in my bedroom while I was here, just like I theorized."

He slowly shook his head. "This is too much. So when you leave your body he leaves his, only he always goes to your bedroom while you've been to two locations—his place and my apartment. Very peculiar. And you went to where Renee and I were every time."

A sexy grin sprang up. "But I still don't think Renee has anything to do with it. I think I just go where you are."

She obviously wanted that to be the case, and it stirred his hormones, but he didn't agree, not seeing any logic in it. "I don't know why you say that since she's always there too."

"Listen, this is embarrassing but I think I have another clue." Her demeanor shifted from girlish eagerness to a glow of womanly passion. "Before I came here last night I was thinking about you."

Nanatobi's face was hauntingly beautiful and very unique, in that it took time to notice the true magnificence of her features due to the myriad brown splotches that first caught the eye. He hadn't realized until she'd donned that sultry look just how gorgeous it really was. "Okay, you were thinking about me, that doesn't prove anything."

"No, you don't understand. I was *really* thinking about you. You know, in the erotic sense."

The statement, along with her expression, aroused him further. "Okay."

"And the next thing I knew I was here."

"Well I hate to shoot a hole in your theory but you couldn't have been thinking about me the first time it happened because you didn't even know I existed."

Her freckles spread with a knowing smile. "I wasn't thinking about you the second time either but I knew about you because Renee had mentioned you. I didn't know your name, only that you were the hunk with the pretty hair she'd seen several times at the university. When I called her that next day and told her I'd seen her with a bald man, she told me it was you."

Though flattered to hear Renee had called him a hunk, the excitement Nanatobi had induced when saying she'd been *really* thinking about him completely overrode the emotion. He couldn't help wondering what this gorgeous redhead was like in bed, something that never would have crossed his mind if the woman of his dreams hadn't been so adamant she'd never be his alone.

"So anyway, I think just as Brad Barron for whatever reason is drawn to my bedroom when he leaves his body, I get drawn to wherever you are."

A hot expression came over her that ignited a lust-surge he'd never experienced before. Incapable of resisting an overwhelming urge to do so—like an automaton being controlled by someone else—he stood up, unzipped his pants, wrestled his rapidly inflating penis through the fly, and radically freaked over his inability to stop the crazy action, heard himself say, "Well right now I think you're drawn to this."

Nanatobi's eyes went wide, but not with fear. She dropped to her knees in front of him. Despite his dumbfounded state he couldn't help moaning with pleasure while watching the top of her red hair bob rapidly back and forth at his crotch.

"Ronnie, are you listening to me?"

Pulse pounding his temples, he gaped at her blankly,

utterly flabbergasted. It had seemed so real . . . but he was still sitting in the recliner, she'd never left his office chair. "I-I'm sorry, guess I got lost in thought there. What were you saying?"

She resumed speaking but he couldn't listen properly from reeling with shock over the wild hallucination. *What the hell just happened, am I going insane?*

"Are you okay, Ronnie? You suddenly don't look well."

"Um . . . yeah, go on."

¶

Brad stepped outside for a breath of fresh air. The temperature had reached sixty, a welcome change. It hadn't risen above forty in weeks. An enticing aroma caused him to peek through a knothole in a cedar picket of his patio fence. Charley Hudson had a steak sizzling over charcoal, enjoying an early Sunday afternoon beer as he tended it.

"Barbecue sure smells good, Charley!"

Charley glanced his direction and grinned. "Is that you playing peeping tom, Brad?"

"Yeah."

"Well there's more if you want one. Be glad to grill one for you if you haven't had lunch yet."

His mouth watered at the thought. "Are you sure you don't mind me barging in?"

"Not at all. Come on over and grab yourself a beer."

Forty minutes later they were sitting at Charley's dining table.

"Had a funny thing happen last night," said his host. "While I was making a beer run I picked up a guy whose car broke down, and he knows you."

"Really? What's is name?"

"Ronnie Garr."

"Oh. I met Ronnie when one of my guests brought him to my party the night we had that blackout."

Charley winced. "Man, don't even mention that night."

"Why? I know the music didn't bother you because you were at work. At least you were for most of it."

"Indeed I was—" he drug a serrated blade across a portion of seared club steak, cutting off a juicy wedge which he brought to his mouth and began to chew. "That had to be the weirdest damn shift I ever worked."

Brad did likewise, finding the meat exquisitely savory and quite tender. "Why's that?"

"There was this blip on the radar, jumping all over the place, appearing then disappearing. Then the blackout happened and the emergency generators kicked on just as it vanished for good. We never did figure out what it was, but I just knew there was going to be a midair collision before it was all over with."

"But there wasn't was there? I don't recall hearing anything on the news."

"No. But it's a damn miracle there wasn't. Whatever that thing was, I hope to God it never comes back."

He took a swig of the domestic beer his chef had graciously offered. "Probably a small plane, I would think."

Charley raised a forkful of baked potato dripping with butter to his lips and held it there. "Not a chance. It covered thousands of feet in no time flat. It bopped around on the screen for a good while and then just vanished when that blackout occurred that nobody's been able to account for. The two events are related, I guarantee you. And I wouldn't be surprised if that damn blip isn't what caused all the lights in Baltimore to go out." He finally relieved the fork of its burden.

A chill ran through Brad as he recalled Nanatobi saying Ronnie Garr thought her astral projections were a direct result of whatever caused the blackout. "Um, let me ask you something. Do you think it's possible for someone to have an out of body experience?"

Nodding as he chewed, Charley swallowed and reached for his beer. "I've got a cousin that had one when we were kids. We were sleeping in the same bed and he had this luminous clock on the nightstand. He said some time after we went to sleep he was hovering above his body and saw me snoozing next to the clock. Then he suddenly woke up and thought he'd dreamed the whole thing until he looked at the clock. The time was the same as he'd noticed while floating in the air. That next morning he asked me if I'd ever had one of those *out of body dreams.*" A chuckle accentuated the term. "That's what he called it. Why do you ask?"

"Because I had one the night of the blackout."

"Oh?" Charley wiped his mouth and set the napkin on the table.

"You don't believe me do you." He started carving another bite of steak.

"Well now why wouldn't I? You've never lied to me before so why would you start now? Tell me about it."

Brad relinquished the fork and knife and locked his fingers together. "I was in this woman's room, floating in the air just like your cousin. I looked around for a few seconds and then wound up back in my body at my apartment. It's happened twice since, and I went to that same bedroom both times."

A concerned frown verified he wasn't being patronized. "Whose bedroom is it, or don't you know?"

"I didn't at first but that's what's so weird, Charley. The bedroom belongs to a young woman named Nanatobi Cain, and her best friend came to my party that night—the girl who brought Ronnie Garr as a matter of fact. And she brought Nanatobi to the party last night so she could meet me because the night of the blackout she had an out of body experience and was hovering beneath the ceiling in my apartment. She saw everybody there except me. Then after I went to bed last night I'll be damned if I didn't pop into her bedroom again. I'm beginning to wonder if all this doesn't have something to do with the blackout, especially now that you've told me about that blip."

Visibly taken aback, Charley started rubbing his jaw, hand slightly trembling. "All I know is I've never seen anything like that in my twenty-two years in front of a radar screen."

He'd obviously been traumatized by the mysterious object. Brad couldn't recall ever seeing his hands quiver before. "What do you think that thing was, Charley?"

"Man . . . I don't have a clue. Nobody does."

¶

Nanatobi got up and started stretching. "I'm getting hungry."

They'd been talking for hours and it was almost six o'clock. Ronnie had to make himself look away for fear he'd have another hallucination because of a compelling desire to say, "And I know what you're hungry for." He barely managed not to voice it.

She purred an erotic sigh and gazed down at him. The gleam of a different type of craving danced in her eyes. "Why don't you pull your dick out and let me suck on it? Maybe a mouthful of jism will tide me over."

Besieged with astonishment, he just sat there, not knowing what to do. Had she said it or was he only imagining things again? She stared at him expectantly, indicating the enticing invitation had really been offered, but he wanted proof. "Um, did you just say something?"

"Well *yeah.*"

Loins swelling with feral lust, he rose to his feet and started to unzip his pants, not believing he was actually doing it, while at the same time eagerly awaiting her pretty mouth.

It fell open. "What the fuck are you're doing?!"

Oh no—it happened again! He immediately dropped his hands. "What did you say awhile ago?"

"I said I was hungry," she giggled.

Completely stupefied and drastically embarrassed, he tried to explain himself. "Listen, I'm sorry. I thought you said something else after that."

"What did you think I said?"

Face burning with shame he muttered, "I thought you asked me to . . . ."

"To what?"

"To . . . take it out . . . you know my—" he pointed towards his crotch.

A shrill laugh shot out of her throat. "Why would you think that? All I said was I was hungry."

He collapsed into the recliner. "I must be losing my mind."

She sat back down as well and leaned over, elbows on knees. "Let me get this straight. You thought I asked you to take it out?"

"Yeah."

"And what was supposed to happen after that?"

"I thought you said you wanted to . . . ."

"Suck it? Is that what you thought I said?"

Knowing she'd really spoken the provocative words this time, the lustful glow on her face as they left her sexy lips almost made him cream his jeans. Relieved he hadn't trashed his underwear, he blew out a sigh and nodded.

Nanatobi smiled and shook her head, with amazement rather than disbelief. "This is getting weirder, Ronnie."

"I know and I'm sorry. I humbly apologize. Like I said, I must be losing my mind."

The smile intensified. "No, Ronnie, you're not losing your mind. You were reading mine."

"Huh?"

"Yeah. Right after saying I was hungry I fantasized about telling you that what I was really hungry for was you, and that maybe if you filled my mouth with jism it would tide me over."

He gasped. "Are you sure you didn't say that out loud?"

"Positive. Tell me what you thought I said, word for word."

Feeling totally discombobulated, he rubbed his eyes, halfway thinking all this might be nothing but a vivid dream.

"Tell me, Ronnie, don't be shy. Tell me what you thought you heard me say."

"After you said you were hungry I could have sworn I heard you say 'Why don't you pull your dick out and let me suck on it? Maybe a mouthful of jism will tide me over.' Excuse my French but that's what I thought I heard."

She turned flush, but wantonness in her excited expression left no doubt it wasn't embarrassment coloring her cheeks. "That's exactly what I fantasized."

"Wow."

"This is so wild, Ronnie. You can read my mind."

He started massaging his forehead with his fingertips. "There was another incident earlier I thought happened, and it freaked the shit out of me when I realized it didn't."

"What?" she exclaimed, eagerly awaiting the information.

"I thought you were actually doing what you said you fantasized."

"You thought I was going down on you?"

"Yeah."

"When was this?"

"Earlier when you were first talking about being drawn to wherever I was when you leave your body."

Nanatobi grabbed her hair with both hands, making

temporary dog ears of flaming red. "Oh man, Ronnie, this is too fucking weird! Right after I said I believed I was drawn to wherever you were, I fantasized that you stood up and pulled out your joystick, shook it at me, and said 'Well right now I think you're being drawn to this.' Then I hit my knees and started giving you a blowjob."

A rush of adrenaline evaporated all the moisture in his throat. "That's what I thought really happened."

"This is so amazing!"

"Yeah . . ." he had to shift in the chair to accommodate an oncoming erection.

Taking note, she eyeballed the bulge in his pants and pointed at it. "Want me to take care of that for you?"

He raised his brows. "Did you just ask me to do it, or are you fantasizing again?"

Features radiant with passion, the sumptuous redhead licked her lips while rising to her feet, and started towards him. "No, this time it's happening for real . . . ."

EIGHT

Crimson fingertips deftly working the buttons of a red blouse, exposing the upper mounds of large breasts imprisoned in a scarlet brassiere, she gracefully lowered herself to her knees—looking up at him the whole time, ravenous desire burning in her lust-ridden eyes. Cotton-mouthed, he yanked his zipper down as she took off the blouse and reached back to unfasten her bra. But before she completed the transaction and he could free his stiff cock, her forehead hit his hands and she rolled to the floor unconscious. Panicked, Ronnie grabbed her shoulders and started shaking them, pleading for Nanatobi to wake up.

¶

Charley bailed from his recliner and hurried to the couch, stepping on the wet carpet soaked with beer spewing from the bottle his neighbor had dropped on the floor when he'd keeled over. "Brad! Can you hear me? Come on, man, open your eyes!"

¶

Jim closed the front door and started for the dining room to assist Suzanne in preparations for dinner.

"Who was that at the door?" Taylor asked as he passed the parlor.

"Renee Van Cedar, Sir, asking to see Nanatobi."

"Nanatobi's supposed to be spending the day with her!"

¶

A shrill gasp erupted from Nanatobi as her eyes flew open. She grabbed her blouse and hastily got to her feet. "Oh shit, I'm in for it! My uncle's going to ground me again."

Ronnie's heart was nearly beating its way out of his chest. "You scared me to death. Are you okay?"

In mere seconds she had her magnificent cleavage covered and quickly gathered her things. "Oh, Ronnie, I guess it is Renee I'm drawn to. She was at my front door. I was floating above her and saw her talking to our butler. I told my uncle I was spending the day with her. I've got to call her and try to come up with something to explain this away or Taylor's going to kill me!"

As the sexy redhead bounded out the door, he zipped his pants and heaved a tormented breath of bitter frustration.

¶

"Sorry about dropping my beer."

Charley got up from the floor where he'd been soaking up the spill with a wad of paper towels. "Don't worry about that damn beer, Brad. You just passed out cold. You must be coming down with something serious. You'd better see a doctor."

He shook his head and sighed. Though quite confused about the matter, he was no longer afraid. "No, Charley, it was another out of body experience. I was in Nanatobi's bedroom again . . . ."

¶

Nanatobi and Renee walked into the dining room all smiles. His employer scowled at them. Jim stood stiffly at attention a few feet away from Suzanne, who did likewise.

Taylor slid a half finished plate of lasagna to the side of the table as a signal for it to be taken away, angry focus now affixed solely on his disobedient niece.

"What have you got to say for yourself, young lady?"

She winced with surprise. "Whatever do you mean?"

"You didn't spend the day with Renee like you told me you were going to. Where were you? I know you weren't with her."

"Why of course I was. What a thing to say."

Renee nodded. "She really was, Mister Cain."

"Then why were you here asking for her earlier?"

"I wasn't. This is the only time I've been here today."

"Jim said you were." Taylor shifted his menacing gaze towards him, then back to Renee, who donned a disarming smile.

"I'll bet it was Betty. She looks a lot like me."

"Betty?"

"Yeah, Betty Solomon. People confuse us as sisters all the time."

Taylor's glower intensified. "Jim?"

He slowly looked Renee over and turned to Taylor. "I stand corrected, Sir. The young lady was dressed nothing like Miss Van Cedar but the resemblance *is* very remarkable."

Taylor narrowed his eyes at Nanatobi. "Why is it I've never met this Betty before?"

She put her hands on her hips. "Taylor, I have lots of friends you've never met."

"I'm aware of that, but they don't come to call on you here, only Renee does."

"Well there's a first time for everything isn't there."

"Don't get smart with me, young lady. How did she know the gate code?"

Nanatobi lowered her hands. "Sorry, didn't mean to be insolent. I gave it to her at the university Friday. She's as trustworthy as Renee, she won't tell anyone."

He studied both girls for several moments. "Jim, if this Betty comes to call again I want to meet her."

"Very well, Sir. Sorry for the mishap."

"It's not your fault you thought it was Renee."

"Thank you, Sir."

Nanatobi took a cherry tart from the dessert tray. "I just popped in to get some clothes. I'm spending the night with Renee if that's all right."

Taylor folded his hands and granted her request with a nod. "What time will you be coming home tomorrow?"

"I'll be home by dinnertime . . . ."

"Thanks for everything, Jim," said Renee with a grateful smile as she and Nanatobi walked out the door.

He couldn't prevent a sly grin from forming. "You're very welcome, *Betty.*"

¶

Two hours after Nanatobi had fled from his apartment, she'd returned with Renee. They were gathered round his decrepit kitchen table. He and Renee were drinking beer. Nanatobi, who'd opted for a soda, explained how she'd escaped her uncle's wrath.

No longer frustrated over not receiving oral satisfaction, Renee's presence actually made him feel relieved Nanatobi's astral flight had prevented her from completing the act. He didn't understand why exactly, since his love for the auburn heartache would remain unrequited. "Well I'm glad you didn't get grounded."

"Thanks to Renee and Jim, I'm free as a bird."

Renee grinned. "So what are you going to do when Taylor finds out there's no such person as Betty Solomon?"

"Oh yes there is," Nanatobi quipped with a laugh. "We'll

just do your hair up different, put some heavy makeup and gaudy clothes on you, you'll lower your voice, and you'll become her."

A giggle dispelled a doubtful frown as Renee considered it a moment. "You know? That might actually work."

"Hopefully we'll never have to resort to it. Oh by the way, Ronnie, I called Brad earlier to see if he went astral again when I did but he didn't answer. I left your number on his machine and asked him to call me here if he couldn't reach my cell which has been acting up. Hope you don't mind."

"Not a problem," he assured.

She glanced at Renee. "You're not going to believe this but Ronnie can read my mind. Whatever caused him to be able to relive the same thing twice apparently equipped him with the ability to read my mind as well. This whole phenom has like really interconnected us big time."

Jealousy poured over Renee as tangibly as if Nanatobi had dumped a bucket of water over her head. She shot him a hurt look that reeked with the agony of betrayal—her pouting lips appeared more vulnerable than ever. "Is that true, Ronnie?"

Not wanting to add fuel to the fire Nanatobi had kindled, he proceeded cautiously. "Well I didn't exactly read her mind. I thought something happened but found out it really hadn't, she'd only been thinking about it. It was really weird."

"And it interconnected you with her?"

"Um . . . yeah, sort of, I guess."

Suddenly brandishing a large knife, Renee lunged to her feet and got behind Nanatobi in a flash—grabbed a handful of red hair, yanked her head back, and sliced her freckled throat.

"Noooooooo!" he screamed while leaping from his chair, only to find Nanatobi unscathed and Renee gaping at him, slack-jawed and dumbstruck.

Shockwaves reverberated through his brain. It had seemed so real.

Renee leaned forward, face etched with a squint. "Are you okay?"

"Um, yeah . . ." he slowly sat back down. "I am now."

"Why did you do that?"

Before he could answer Renee, Nanatobi gave him a sheepish smile and said, "If you just read my mind again, I'm afraid it will have to wait for a more apropos time."

Still stunned, but accepting he'd only imagined the morbid scene, he shook his head. "No, I wasn't reading your mind. I think I must have just read Renee's."

Renee swept back a curly lock from her forehead. "So what was I thinking?"

"That you'd like to cut Nanatobi's throat."

She gasped but Nanatobi laughed as if he was just popping off. Features paled with awe, she stared at him for a long moment before turning to Nanatobi. "He wasn't joking . . . that's exactly what was going through my mind."

All humor vacated the redhead. "Why would you want to do that?"

"Because I'm jealous of you and Ronnie."

"Oh yeah . . .?" Nanatobi's freckles spread with a wicked grin. "Well if you knew what almost went down before I was snatched from my body you'd really be jealous."

Auburn brows arching, emerald orbs ablaze, Renee exhaled a ragged breath and said, "What almost went down?"

"It was more like what was up if you know what I mean. First Ronnie thought it really happened but it didn't. I was only fantasizing about it and he saw my fantasy literally come to life. Then after I discovered he'd read my mind, we were about to do it for real."

Renee zeroed in on him, angry suspicion looming like green daggers in her eyes. "What's she talking about, Ronnie?"

He looked towards the fridge.

"Ronnie?" she demanded.

Still taking in the worn apparatus that rattled every time the compressor kicked on he said, "You started this, Nanatobi, and you can finish it."

"Gladly," she giggled. "I almost deep throated his johnson."

Sensing Renee glaring at him, he kept appraising the refrigerator as if it were a Rembrandt rather than an appliance on its last legs.

"You wouldn't sleep with me but you were going to let Nan give you a blowjob?"

He finally turned to face her. "I wouldn't sleep with you because you dumped me."

"For Pete's sake, how many times do I have to say it? I did not dump you!"

Nanatobi let out a piercing laugh. "Renee tried to get you in bed and you turned her down? Oh that's priceless!"

"Shut up, Nan!" Renee ejaculated venomously.

"Shut up yourself! I'll damn well talk if I want to."

"Fine. Just don't expect me to listen." She took an angry slurp of beer and glowered at him. "I thought you liked me. You even said you wanted to marry me. What happened?"

"I've already told you," he answered with a shrug. "I'm not interested in a relationship with no future."

"And there's a future with you sticking your dick in Nan's mouth? Give me a break! You sure have a double standard don't you, Ronnie Garr."

"There could be a future for me and Ronnie, you don't know."

Renee rolled her eyes with scorn. "I'm not listening to you, Nan."

The phone rang and he got up to answer it, grateful for the interruption. Brad Barron asked for Nanatobi. Ronnie pointed the receiver towards her. "It's him."

He went back to the table and listened to Nanatobi relate her latest astral trip to Brad. Renee kept heatedly staring at him without saying anything.

Nanatobi hung up the phone. "Brad wants us to come over to discuss everything. An air traffic controller told him he saw something on radar the night of the blackout that couldn't have been a normal aircraft . . . ."

¶

". . . and then it just vanished," Brad concluded after explaining Charley's mysterious radar blip. He had prefaced it with the out of body experience that occurred while he'd been next door.

"That seriously adds credibility to my theory," said Ronnie Garr, sitting on the couch between the two girls. Renee appeared angry with Ronnie while Nanatobi seemed to be competing for his attention. He'd been standing since their arrival but would love to sit by that gorgeous redhead. Alas, she hadn't shown any interest in him. Her beauty loomed in the highest regions of the sex scale like Renee's, and to see them sitting on either side of the tall virile ex-marine made him extremely envious.

"Well that's all I've got . . ." he brought his hands together with a clap and grinned at the lucky guy book-ended by two sensuous Tens. "I see you're letting your hair grow out."

Ronnie started rubbing the back of his muscular neck. "Yeah, but I might shave it off again, I don't know."

Renee turned up her nose. "Go ahead, see if I care."

"I like you bald," said Nanatobi with an energized smile. Then she looked his way. "There's a new development, Brad. Wonder Boy here has discovered he can read minds."

"Oh really?" With all that had happened of late he didn't find the notion hard to swallow. "I wonder if the three of us might have acquired other strange powers yet to make their presence known. Okay, I'm thinking of a number. What number am I thinking of?"

Ronnie lowered his arm. "That's not how it works, and I can't do it at will. When it happens, it's like whatever's being thought actually springs to life."

Nanatobi cast a knowing grin at the ex-skinhead. "Yeah, it's really strange."

"Oh it's *strange* all right," said Renee bitterly, glaring at Nanatobi.

¶

Renee and Nanatobi had been verbally sparring for several minutes. Though neither appeared angry anymore, they kept at it. The grudge match had somehow turned into a lark and they seemed to be enjoying putting on a show for Brad and him. Then suddenly they were naked—writhing on the carpet, kissing and fondling each other, begging Brad to fuck them as he stood there throttling his mammoth pecker. Ronnie didn't have to wait for a return to reality to know none of it was real. Brad's height had increased at least ten inches and a stud horse would have been envious of his dick. When he snapped to with the girls on the couch and Brad standing at the bar, he cleared his throat and rose to his feet. "Um, I know you weren't intending for me to know it but I can tell you what's on your mind, or at least was a moment ago if you're interested."

An edgy smile surfaced. "You can?"

"Yeah, but I think I'd better whisper it to you."

Brad turned red as a beet upon being informed.

¶

Renee fought her way to the middle of the seat when the three of them got into his borrowed pickup. "So what was Brad thinking?"

"You don't wanna know." Ronnie backed out of the parking space and drove away from Brad Barron's apartment complex.

Nanatobi leaned forward to face him. "Come on, Ronnie, fess up. What was he thinking? I know it had to be erotic or the two of you wouldn't have been so secretive. He's bi isn't he? Was he fantasizing about you?"

"Why would you say bi?" giggled Renee. "If he was fantasizing about Ronnie, he's gay."

"Because I've caught him looking me over too many times for him to only prefer men. Come on, Ronnie, tell us."

He didn't want to embarrass Brad, but if he was in the man's shoes he'd rather have the truth out in the open rather than have anyone question his sexual orientation. "Okay I'll tell you, but only because I don't want you to think he's not hetero. He was daydreaming about the two of you getting it on with each other while he watched."

"Gross!" shouted Renee.

Nanatobi laughed. "I don't know, I try to keep an open mind."

Renee scooted closer to him which made Nanatobi chuckle again.

"I wonder why it only happens to me when someone's having a sexual fantasy?"

"You call me cutting Nan's throat a sexual fantasy? What kind of pervert are you?"

"Duh, there's certainly nothing sexual about that." He heaved a sigh. "I wish this shit would stop. I feel violated, like I'm no longer in control of my own mind. If only I knew *why* it's happening, maybe I could do something to prevent it."

"It must have something to do with anger as well as sex," said Nanatobi. "Renee was furious with me when she had those bad thoughts."

"She's right, Ronnie. Nan has a valid point."

Nanatobi slapped the dashboard. "I've got it! It's not just sex or anger. I bet you can pick up on anyone around you who's feeling really passionate about something. Passion—that's what prompts you to live other people's thoughts."

Renee agreed and put a hand on his knee. "Would you mind swinging by my house?"

"You want me to take you home?"

"No, silly, I drove my car to your apartment. But I want to change clothes."

"What's wrong with what you're wearing?" The sweater and jeans she had on looked very comfortable.

"My sweater's making me itch."

They discussed Nanatobi's theory all the way to Wine's Gate. He pulled into Renee's drive and killed the engine. "I'll just wait here."

"No, come in, I want you to meet my dad . . . ."

After introducing him to her father, Renee and Nanatobi went upstairs, leaving him sitting in an armchair next to Jesse Van Cedar, a tall man with dark-green eyes. Renee had obviously inherited those two traits from him, and owed her voluptuous figure to Veronica. The genes responsible for her father's dark brown hair and her mom's white tresses had apparently reached an auburn compromise when Renee was conceived. Stretched out on a recliner, he'd muted the TV so they could talk. Veronica was lounging on the sectional couch. Both were drinking daiquiris. She'd offered to fix him one but he'd thankfully declined.

Jesse took a sip of his and asked what he did for a living.

Ronnie explained that he went to college full time, worked most weeknights at Riley's Grocery, usually from eight until the store closed at eleven, and maintained the trucks at Palloy's Transportation every Saturday.

"Where is Riley's Grocery?" asked Veronica.

He told her and immediately diverted his eyes. Maybe it was her natural expression when being informed about something, but it sure looked like a bedroom stare to him. Unaware of it, her husband un-muted the TV and resumed watching his movie. Ronnie focused on the television screen as well, but couldn't help noticing her continual ogling from his peripheral vision. A knot formed in his stomach when she got up and started towards him.

"Come into the kitchen with me, Ronnie, there's something I want to show you."

He glanced at Jesse, expecting to see an angry scowl on the man's face because of the seductiveness in his wife's voice. Incredibly, he seemed oblivious to the statement. Ronnie gulped as Veronica pulled him from the chair by the hand. She led him across the living room and through the swinging doors but didn't stop in the kitchen. They wound up in a hobby room.

"Wait here, I'll be right back."

Wanting to run, he stood there instead, hoping he'd misread her intentions. It wasn't long before that hope vanished.

Veronica stepped into the room completely naked, locked the door, and began fondling her extraordinary breasts as she hiked her right leg onto a chair. "Get down on your knees and lick me, Ronnie."

Suddenly back in the armchair, he couldn't believe how real it had all seemed. She hadn't uttered a word about the kitchen and neither of them had left their seats. He kept his eyes glued to the gargantuan television, ignoring her continuing hungry glare. Straining to resist a hormonal firestorm ignited by her fantasy, he conjured the grossest thoughts he could in order to prevent a hard on. He wanted to get the hell out of there as soon as possible.

Renee, who'd swapped the sweater for a blouse, finally descended the stairs and promised her father she'd be home by one at the latest. When he stopped behind Nanatobi near the front door, waiting for Renee to open it, something soft yet firm pressed against his back. The woman had unquestionably shoved her breasts against him on purpose. He turned around to see Veronica looking up at him, brazen lust burning in her dark eyes.

"Come see us again, Ronnie."

¶

"What's wrong?" Renee asked him from the other side of Nanatobi, who'd won the battle of sitting next to him this time. They were almost at his apartment.

"Nothing, why?"

"You've seemed distant ever since we left my house."

"Yeah, you have," agreed Nanatobi.

"Did Dad say something to upset you?"

"No, nothing like that. He's a real nice guy."

"Then what's the matter?"

"Nothing's the matter." He wasn't about to tell Renee that her mother had not only fantasized about him but had came on to him in real life as well. To make matters worse, he couldn't shake the image tattooed in his brain of Veronica's gorgeous naked body or the erotic memory of feeling her big tits pressed against his back.

Badly needing to pee, Ronnie headed for the bathroom first thing when they got to his apartment. Questions pounded at his skull. Why was he living out people's fantasies? Did Renee know her mother was a slut? Was Veronica really a slut or just a cock-tease? What had the woman hoped to accomplish by that stunt at the front door? Didn't she fear he might tell her daughter? Did Jesse know what kind of woman shared his bed? If not for her fantasy he could excuse Veronica's boob-press as a move to test his character, see if he appeared offended or aroused—tell Renee to stay away from him if the latter showed on his face, which it probably had.

Head swimming with confusion, feeling ashamed of the arousal stewing inside him from Veronica's actions, he returned to the living room. Nanatobi sat in the office chair and Renee had chosen the recliner, so he brought a chair in from the kitchen.

"I'm dying to know if Renee's dad has the hots for me like I've always suspected," said Nanatobi, freckles stretched with a naughty smile.

Renee sighed. "You know he does."

"Well I want to know if he was fantasizing about me. Was he, Ronnie?"

Feeling insulted for Renee's sake, instead of answering the licentious insensitive redhead, he got up and fetched a beer.

Nanatobi continued pestering him about Jesse Van Cedar. Seeing she wouldn't let up, he decided to mess with her mind. "Yeah, he fantasized about you."

"Yes! Tell me everything!" She started rubbing her hands together. Renee turned away and covered her ears.

"He had you in handcuffs hanging from the ceiling naked, and was beating you with a whip. You kept telling him, *Harder! Hit me harder!*"

"Oh I love it! How marvelously perverse."

"You're sick, Nan." Renee closed her eyes and rubbed her temples as if to relieve a headache. "God, and so is my dad. Gross!"

Ronnie had the perfect cover to camouflage the mood he'd been in, but it would be totally unfair to the man he'd just met to let this go any further. "I was just teasing Nanatobi. You're father didn't fantasize about anything."

"Oh you little shit!" Nanatobi swatted the air.

"Sorry, couldn't resist. You were so persistent I just made one up."

"Well something happened at my house," said Renee, skeptically eyeballing him. She kept it up for a few seconds, then suddenly her features twisted into a mortified gape. "Oh god it was my mother wasn't it—you read her mind! What happened?"

"Nothing happened."

"I can tell you're lying, Ronnie."

"No I'm not."

"Yes you are!"

"All right!" he snapped. "She did fantasize, but trust me—you *do not* want to hear the sordid details."

Renee looked nauseous. "I'll take your word for it. Let's not discuss this any further."

"Bullshit, I want to hear all about it!" screeched Nanatobi.

He started to tell her to drop the matter but the words froze in his throat. Butt naked, stretched out on his back, he craned his neck to behold Renee and Nanatobi, also nude, lying on their stomachs facing each other at his groin, taking turns going down on him and occasionally kissing each other. They were on a bed so large the girls' feet didn't reach the edges and his toes lacked at least forty inches from touching Veronica Van Cedar, standing at the foot wearing only a wanton grin. She crawled up the bed, straddled his face, and demanded he eat her. She'd no sooner barked the command when he found himself standing off to the side, watching the three women deal with another man who'd apparently taken his place. The guy's face was hidden from view because Veronica's undulating hips covered it. A second later he snapped to.

Mind-bogglingly astounded by what had just gone down, he glanced at Nanatobi, certain she'd produced the erotic vision. There were no tale-tell signs on her face but it couldn't have stemmed from Renee because her mother was in it.

"Why are you looking at me like that?" the frisky redhead asked.

"Uh . . . were you thinking about sex a moment ago?"

She grinned. "Nope, but I'd love to hear all about it."

A deep blush pounced on Renee's face when he turned to her. The fantasy had undoubtedly been hers, but why would such an off the wall sexual arrangement appeal to her? Another thing that blew his mind was the coincidence of Veronica demanding oral satisfaction in her fantasy and Renee picturing her doing the same.

Responding to his confused inquiring gaze she said, "I was thinking about what I feared might have been going through my mother's mind while you were at my house."

Jaw sagging, he gaped at her as if she was a ghost that had just materialized. Why would Renee think her mother even capable of such perverse thoughts, much less worry she'd entertained them? He collected himself and cleared his throat. "Well um . . . that's uh . . . that's quite a fantasy."

"Well tell me!" squealed Nanatobi.

"Ronnie, don't you dare!"

Her panic radically contrasted with the excitement she'd exhibited while working his tool with Nanatobi. "Don't worry, I won't. But I have to ask, why did you think she fantasized that?"

Renee's eyes flew wide. "Don't tell me she did!"

"No. But what makes you think she could have? That's really out there."

"I can't stand it, you two are driving me mad! Please tell me what Renee thought her mother was thinking."

"Leave it alone, Nan, I don't want to hear it . . . ."

As the two of them argued, he continued to ponder why Renee feared her mother would have that particular fantasy.

What type of woman entertained the notion of an orgy with her daughter in it? He thought about Renee's reaction when he'd told them about Brad's wishful musing. She'd called it gross, yet when thinking of what her mother might have fantasized, she'd certainly appeared to enjoy locking lips with Nanatobi. By the time the argument ceased and the freckled redhead finally gave up trying to force him to tell all, he'd concluded Renee was lying. She hadn't thought her mother fantasized it. She'd come up with it on her own and feared he'd tell Nanatobi.

She got up and put on her coat. Nanatobi did likewise.

"I take it you guys are leaving?"

"Yeah, I need to get home."

"I have to go too. I'm spending the night with Renee."

That didn't jive with what she'd told her father. She had thirty minutes to spare before having to leave in order to get home by one. He figured she wanted to bail before he dug any deeper. Since she'd fantasized about her mother, he couldn't help wondering if the man who'd replaced him might have been Jesse Van Cedar.

What the hell have I stumbled into? he thought morbidly. Pain ripped at his heart and disgust churned his entrails over learning a sick perversity lurked inside Renee's beautiful head. It made him despise the creepy ability to witness other people's passionate thoughts. He'd give a king's ransom to erase the depraved fantasy from his memory. Despite the shock engulfing him over being forced to witness her dark side, it didn't diminish his love for Renee at all, only made him feel miserable and hopeless.

After she and Nanatobi left, he immediately went to bed. While trying to find sleep Veronica's fantasy suddenly parted his mental curtains and played out in intricate detail as if he were sitting in a theater viewing it on a silver screen. In the beginning he tried to make it go away but soon stopped resisting. Veronica's wishful escapade strangely comforted him because the farther lust raised his dick, the less he thought of Renee.

Before long he started pumping it, envisioning himself fulfilling Veronica's request in the hobby room, only doing so with reciprocation from her as they lay on the floor in a tight sixty-nine. Then Renee entered the scene and his fingers lost their grip before he reached climax.

As his hard deflated, agony grew, making him wish he'd gone back to Colorado after his discharge. If he'd attended college there he never would have seen that auburn-haired goddess walking down the hall at Maryland, and he'd have dodged the heartache of knowing he could never have the thing he wanted most and always would: Renee Van Cedar as his lawfully wedded and eternally faithful wife.

NINE

Ronnie's shift ended an hour before the store closed. He made for his Thunderbird in the parking lot of Riley's Grocery, removing a dingy smock in the process. Before reaching the vehicle, repaired earlier in the day by one of Ben's mechanics, he saw Veronica Van Cedar get out of a silver BMW and stroll into the store, shapely hips accentuating her swaggered gait.

It couldn't be coincidence. There were far too many supermarkets closer to Wine's Gate for her to patronize Riley's, a modest size facility with only three cash registers in a fairly rough neighborhood. She'd obviously come here expecting to find him. In light of what happened last night, he knew she hadn't sought him out merely to chitchat.

If Renee hadn't been adamant that she'd never marry him, he would have kept his lust for her mother in check. When he hadn't allowed her to stay overnight, far from cursing himself the next morning, an awakening had occurred as to what had intuitively prompted his refusal. He couldn't allow himself to sleep with her, knowing she'd never be his alone. The thought of Renee being with another man already caused him enough pain without the compounded torment he'd experience if they ever made love. Though already completely obsessed with her, at least he didn't know what he was missing in that area, and he dared not ever find out. It would cause him to love her even more. Her mother evoked no such emotions in him, and when she'd pressed her large breasts against his back, the turn on had been electrifying.

She's a married woman, Ronnie, his conscience repeatedly warned as he tossed the smock onto the passenger seat, closed the door, and went back inside the store. Yeah, Veronica Van Cedar was married all right, but she'd hit on him, not the other way around. The stirring in his gonads overrode all sense of guilt. Spotting her in the coffee aisle, he strolled down the one next to it and almost bumped into her when he came around the corner.

"Ronnie?"

Though the surprised look on her face was genuine due to being startled, he had no doubt she'd fully expected to find him somewhere in Riley's. "Hello, Mrs. Van Cedar."

Her ebony eyes hungrily looked him up and down. "Please, call me Veronica."

He smiled. "Okay, Veronica."

Glancing nervously around, she reached for a can of Maxwell House. "Just stopped in to pick up some coffee. Fancy meeting you here."

"Yeah, I work here." *Which you damn well knew.* "Just got off as a matter of fact."

"Oh did you now?" A blush rose up her face, signaling a hormonal surge. "And where were you heading from here?"

"Home."

She put the coffee back. "Silly me. Just remembered I bought coffee yesterday."

"Well it was nice seeing you. Guess I'll shove off now." If she didn't say something to stop him, he'd have to play out his bluff to force her hand, and head home.

"How's your back?" she said after he'd taken a few steps.

Arousal kicking into high gear, he halted and turned around. Her bearing exuded lasciviousness, further raising his blood pressure. "Great. Got a real nice massage just before I left your house last night."

"Glad you liked it. Where can we go?"

"My place is a hole but we can go there if you'd like."

She laughed. "A hole, huh? In that case why don't you follow me . . .?"

Ronnie tailed her to a swank motel and within ten minutes after parking their cars they were standing in front of a room. She slipped the key card through a slot and the door unlatched. He walked in behind her and turned to pull it closed. When he again faced the room she threw her arms around his neck, pulled him down to her upturned face, and plunged her tongue into his mouth. It had been a long time since he'd slept with a woman. Desire flared through him like a lighted match tossed into a pool of gasoline. He grabbed her breasts and she shoved her right hand against his crotch, cupping it for a second or two before rubbing it madly, fingers furiously groping.

"Oh—" she tore her sexy lips from his and glared at him, black eyes smoldering with lust. "You make me so hot I swear if you don't fuck me right now I'll spontaneously combust and my death will be on your hands."

They swiftly undressed and fell onto the bed, entangled in each other's groping arms. Before long she clawed at his back, surging into a stormy orgasm that forced him to explode inside her clutching tunnel.

Guilt over what he'd just done flaring, he eased out of her and rolled over on his back.

Veronica exhaled a blissful sigh and reached for his shrinking wet penis. "Oh I needed that so badly." She gave it a light squeeze and rested her fingers on it. "When you walked in with Renee and Nanatobi last night something just came over me. I've been growing hornier for you ever since."

Hearing Renee's name brought him even more painfully down to earth. "You got my motor running when you shoved your tits in my back. I don't fool around with married women but you broke my will. Now that I've let off steam, I feel guilty as hell."

"Don't. No one will ever know except you and I."

"Doesn't matter, I'll always know."

"But you enjoyed making love to me, didn't you?"

Having obtained relief, his genitals couldn't begin to compete with his filth-stained conscience. *What the hell was I thinking?*

"Answer me, Ronnie. Did you enjoy fucking me or not?"

"You're a very beautiful woman," he managed at length, "of course I did."

"As much as Renee?"

"I can't believe you just asked me that."

She started kneading his balls. "I want to know."

"I can't compare you to Renee because we've never made love."

Her fingers froze. "The two of you haven't had sex yet?" She said it like a date without sex was something unheard of. What kind of woman had he so foolishly given up his peace of mind for?

"We've never so much as kissed." He slid his hands behind his head.

Veronica turned over on her side, causing one long tit to press against him while the other rested on his chest. "Why not?"

"Just one of those things." He lowered his left hand to the breast lying atop his own and began fondling it, hoping arousal would ease the guilt.

It did to a small degree.

"Mmm . . ." she closed her eyes. "That feels good."

Seeing how carnal and conscienceless her mother was, he realized Renee hadn't lied after all. She really *had* feared her mother might have been thinking of the orgy. That meant there'd been a real one. He'd been wondering if the mystery man in Renee's fantasy was her father. An idea presented itself as to how he might find out. He tweaked Veronica's nipple and said, "Do you do this with all of Renee's boyfriends?"

Her eyes flew open. "Of course not."

"Then to what do I owe this honor? I just turn you on or what?"

"Yeah, you turn me on, that's all."

"You know what turns me on?"

"What?" she whispered provocatively through a lazy smile.

"The thought of you and Renee at the same time."

Her sexy features twisted into an angry scowl, laced with apprehension. "Why did you say that?"

"Because it's true," he replied nonchalantly, taking full note of the worry her livid expression failed to conceal. "Know what would make it even sweeter? Having Nanatobi join in. I could just see you sitting on my face while they took turns giving me a knob job. What a rush that would be."

Now blatantly alarmed, she rolled off the bed and stood over him, hands cinching her narrow waist. "What all has Renee told you?"

"Enough for me to know some lucky guy has already had the pleasure of sharing the three of you." Ronnie hoped she'd say who that man was.

Her beautiful breasts heaved with a sigh of resignation. "Then you know we're witches . . . ."

TEN

His newly acquired ability had inadvertently exposed the fact that Renee and Nanatobi practiced witchcraft. Since Veronica said the coven must be kept secret at all costs, he never would have found out without experiencing Renee's fantasy. Alone in his bed, staring into darkness, Ronnie's thoughts centered on what Veronica had told him at the motel a few hours ago. Her best friend had talked her into joining the coven. A few years later Renee had been inducted upon reaching puberty. At fourteen years of age Nanatobi had joined. Twelve witches and one warlock currently comprised the group of pagans but a member had died and they needed another female to bring the number of women to thirteen. She wouldn't tell him any more than that.

The man who'd replaced him in Renee's fantasized orgy couldn't have been Jesse Van Cedar after all. The warlock who headed the cult had to have been the recipient of the sexual favors simultaneously administered by Renee, Nanatobi, and Veronica. He'd deduced that after learning Jesse didn't know anything about the coven and the secret activities of his wife and daughter. The three women had to have been with the warlock at the same time or Veronica wouldn't have drawn the conclusion that Renee had told him they were witches.

Not wanting to get Renee in trouble with her mother, he'd confessed she hadn't told him anything. Veronica had gotten super pissed at him for tricking her. Whether she believed the claim that his fabricated fantasy had been purely coincidental he didn't know. He hadn't said anything to Veronica about Nanatobi's out of body experiences or his own paranormal activities. She'd made him promise not to tell anyone about the coven, and after calming down had insisted he make love to her again. Ironically, not once did she ask him to perform cunnilingus.

¶

Ronnie shut off the alarm and rolled out of bed. A stab of grief shattered the notion that maybe last night had only been a bad dream. Apparently his subconscious had convinced him as such during slumber because the sordid reality seemed harder to face than before he'd finally dozed off.

Renee's secret life tortured him during his morning exercises, haunted him all through breakfast, and pulverized his mind with renewed strength when she called after he washed the dishes.

He soon discovered Nanatobi was on the line as well.

"Nan and I just had a heart to heart with Mom."

"Yeah?" His voice betrayed how nervous he felt. Veronica had apparently told them everything.

"So now you know."

"Yeah . . . now I know."

"So how was Mom?" Renee said it with no more emotion than if asking who'd won a ballgame.

"What do you mean?"

"Don't be naive, Ronnie. How was she in bed?"

"She was great, wasn't she," Nanatobi knowingly declared.

"Um . . . yeah." He didn't know what else to say.

"Mom wants to know when you want to do it."

"Do what?"

"You're being naive again, Ronnie."

He gulped. What he'd told Veronica had only been a bluff, merely a ruse to ascertain the identity of the man the three of them had been with. Learning she wanted it to happen for real left him speechless.

A sigh hissed in his ear and Renee said, *"Oh never mind, we'll decide when. Now, Ronnie, you mustn't tell a living soul about the coven."*

"Uh, no, I won't tell anyone."

"Good. Talk to you later, bye."

He'd never had much interest in religion but knew the Bible condemned witchcraft. *Thou shalt not suffer a witch to live*, he remembered reading once when holed up in a fleabag motel with a broken TV, flipping through a Gideon's Bible for something to do. Why did the woman he loved have to be one? Worse yet, why did she have to be involved in the type of pagan worship that incorporated group sex and even incest?

Renee's lack of concern over him sleeping with her mother profoundly disturbed him. So did her desire to have a love-fest with him that included her mom and best friend. But he didn't have to worry about her trying to convert him. According to Veronica, only one male could be a part of their coven and that slot had already been taken.

The idea of an orgy with the three of them actually frightened more than enticed him, and he didn't want to sleep with Renee anyway. Even though she'd turned out to be a witch and a presumed slut, he couldn't help his feelings for her. He dared not let them deepen, it would drive him insane. He'd never had sex with two women at the same time, much less three, and an orgy with a mother and daughter struck him as disgustingly immoral.

Of course sleeping with another man's wife wasn't right either, and he'd already done that. The more he thought about his tryst with Veronica, the worse his conscience bothered him. To win Renee's hand and make her his bride had been all he wanted, yet he'd wound up screwing her mother instead. Then everything got really fucked up in his psyche upon learning Renee not only knew about it, but wanted a rating on her mother's performance just as her mom had inquired about how she'd stacked up against Renee. Now both were expecting to bed him simultaneously.

He believed in right and wrong, marriage, and a basic

morality binding to all, so he had to admit he'd sinned against the common decency he adhered to. That awareness sickened him. *A stiff prick has no conscience*, the old saying went. While that might be true enough, the big head wasn't supposed to let the little head do the thinking like he'd so idiotically done.

¶

Nanatobi groaned with pleasure as Veronica's tongue slithered all over her hot slit while she pummeled Renee's with her own. They were in a circle on Renee's bed, mouths pressed to pussies—Veronica's on hers, hers on Renee's, Renee's on Veronica's.

ELEVEN

Brad's office door opened and in walked Jesse Van Cedar carrying a folder which he dropped on his desk. "This is the dossier of a close friend's son. I want you to process it for me. If everything checks out set up an interview for tomorrow at one o'clock."

"Sure thing . . ." he reached for the file. "Did Renee tell you she came to my party Saturday night? She even brought one of her friends."

"Yeah, she mentioned it." A slow grin inched its way across Jesse's pronouncedly handsome face. "What did you think of Nanatobi?"

"Oh she's a heartbreaker, Boss."

"That's putting it mildly. So is she in your conference?"

"Sir?"

"You told me Renee was out of your conference, and I just wondered if Nanatobi was as well."

Brad laughed. "I'm not sure. How tall do you think she is?"

"Oh, I'd say about five-five."

"Well if she's shorter than five-six, she's definitely in my conference." Sadly, Jesse being a tall man and therefore not self conscious about the matter, probably wasn't as good a judge of height as he. Nanatobi had worn heels to the party and his enhanced altitude hadn't seemed any taller than hers, so he figured she was more like five-seven. When she came over with Renee and Ronnie, he'd been so dumbfounded by their discussion it hadn't occurred to him to compare their stature at the time.

"Are you aware of who she is?" Jesse posed the question like Nanatobi was some sort of celebrity.

"Um, no, I guess not. Who is she?"

"Taylor Cain's niece. She's lived with him since her parents died when she was eleven."

He swallowed a lump of incredulity. Nanatobi's height no longer mattered—she wouldn't give him the time of day even if he stood six-six. Only an extremely wealthy man with an exalted social status dared attempt to court a live-in relative of the renowned Taylor Cain. To learn his astral body always freely entered the billionaire's estate and went straight to his niece's boudoir flabbergasted him. His physical carcass wouldn't be permitted past the gates.

Jesse turned to leave but paused at the door. "That girl's not your run of the mill type. She's a little different."

When it closed behind him Brad muttered, "If you only knew how different . . . ."

¶

It had been a long time since he'd been out in this neck of the woods. The scenery comforted him. All the cows, sheep, horses, trees, and fences were planted on terra firma and needed no guidance from below to keep them from colliding with their own kind. As Charley drove to his cousin's farm, he thought about the *out of body dream* and chuckled again at the terminology. He was on his way to see him because of what had been happening to Brad. They spoke on the phone every once in a blue moon but hadn't seen each other in years. The ol' boy had always been a smart cuss even when they were kids, and he'd grown up to become a wise old owl. Because he had all those sevens connected to him, some members of the family almost deified him.

Sentimental anticipation warmed his insides when he turned onto the old familiar drive and parked his car. It grew as he climbed the porch steps, making him realize how much he missed his cousin. The front door swung open before he reached it.

"Well by golly I thought I heard a car drive up! Shut my mouth if it ain't the uppity negro from Baltimore."

"How you doing, Arnon, you old fool?" They grabbed each other in a joyful hug.

Arnon pulled him inside by the arm. "So what brings you out to the sticks? Man, what's it been, ten years since we laid eyeballs on each other?"

"Oh I don't think it's been that long has it?"

"Sure does seem like it to me. Of course it's got to where years are seeming to fly by like months. Let me see . . ." he brought a finger to his thick lips, tapping it against them as he thought it through. "It was Christmas time last time I saw you, I'm sure of that. And it was at Aunt Betty Louise's house, I'm sure of that too."

Charley nodded. "That's sounds about right."

"Well come on and let's get you comfortable. Have a seat and I'll fetch us up some tea."

He sat down on the couch and hollered, "Do you still play like a monk in your tower like you used to?"

Arnon laughed from the kitchen. "Don't know why everybody calls it a tower, but yeah I still play like a monk in it every once in awhile."

Like everyone else that really knew Arnon Green, he had the greatest respect for his spirituality. And the thing Charley admired most about his cousin was the fact that even though he took his beliefs very seriously, he could always laugh at all the jokes about his eccentricities surrounding it. Arnon had *The Sight*, and most everybody close to him knew it, though the younger generation of the family seemed incapable of comprehending it for some odd reason.

When he returned from the kitchen Charley rose to accept a teacup perched on a saucer, then sat back down while Arnon chose an old stuffed rocking chair to rest on.

"Why didn't you call ahead? I'd have gone to the store and

got us something fancy for supper. As it is I'm afraid you'll just have to settle for last night's leftovers, chicken and dumplings."

"Mm-mm-mmm!" he exclaimed at the notion. "Been a coon's age since I've had any. Glad I didn't call ahead. Where's Mary Jo?"

"Off to her sister Martha's for a spell."

"Oh . . .?" he took a sip of Arnon's savory tea.

"Yeah, she's feeling mighty poorly since her man died a few weeks ago."

"Oh what a shame."

"Yeah. Had a heart attack in his sleep."

"Well now that's the way to go."

"Yes it is, ain't it?"

"She took the kids with her I guess."

Arnon cackled and slapped his thigh. "My two daughters have done grown up and left the nest. Bessie became a nurse and moved to Annapolis. Beatrice is living with her and studying to be a veterinarian. Seems like I remember telling you all about it on the phone here while back."

He shook his head while laughing at himself. "Well hell, Arnon, you darn sure did, didn't you. It's been so long since I was here, I guess I was expecting everything to be like it was. Bessie and Bea running in and out the door, Mary Jo yelling at them to stay in or stay out."

A wistful smile sprang up. "My, that seems like a million years ago, Charley."

"Yeah, it sure does."

"So any chance of you and Loretta getting back together?"

"Nah, it's over. Besides, I'm really enjoying my freedom."

"And your job? How's it going?"

"Not good. I think I'm going to have to look for another line of work. My ol' nerves just aren't what they used to be."

Arnon slurped some tea and billowed a sigh. "Well you

knew going in you'd have to sometime because of the pressure."

"True enough. An air traffic controller shouldn't work at it more than ten years if you ask me."

"Well I sure wouldn't be no good at it. And you've been at it how many years?"

"Twelve too many." He set his tea on the coffee table and folded his arms across his chest. "You remember when we were kids and you had that *out of body dream* as you called it?"

Arnon nodded. "I was floating above my body and saw you cuttin' Zees. Why you asking about that, Charley?"

"My neighbor's been having the same thing happen to him, and it started one particular night when I had a bad time at work." He inhaled a deep breath and let it out slowly. "There was a blip on the radar acting real crazy, then the whole city of Baltimore blacked out. And it's been happening to this girl he knows. Every time she leaves her body, he leaves his and winds up floating around her bedroom."

Brow furrowing, lips drooping, Arnon looked extremely concerned. "When was it you saw that blip?"

"A few weeks ago."

"The exact date I mean."

"January sixth."

"Did the sixth fall on the first Friday in January?"

"Yeah, it sure did."

"Oh my . . . oh my, my, my."

Arnon's morbid reaction made him shudder. "What are you my-myin' about, cuz?"

"I had a vision while I was praying that night. It was just a flash of light, came and went real sudden. I felt deep down in my spirit that it was a dire omen. While I don't know that it's a bad thing that's happening to the girl and your neighbor, I'm real troubled that it started that same night."

¶

"And the coefficient will be commensurate with the weight of the atomic mass . . . ."

Physics class lasted an hour every Monday, Wednesday, and Friday. The professor spoke with a dull monotone and had deep set eyes beneath an abnormally low hairline, giving his upper face a gorilla-like appearance. Ronnie always looked slightly to either side of him during a lecture to keep from being distracted by the comical mix of his voice and odd physique.

He tried to focus but found it increasingly difficult to stay alert. Though he'd managed to record important points of the lecture thus far, his fatigue-scribbled notes were barely legible. Compounding the problem, his thoughts kept wandering back to Renee. Ever since she'd called the morning after his fling with her mother seven days ago, he'd felt disconsolate and had a hard time sleeping at night. When she phoned after that, he'd lied about coming down with something and promised to call when he felt better. Nanatobi had been given the same fabrication. He didn't want to talk to either of them until he could sort everything out, and having group sex with them and Veronica—which was all they seemed to want to talk about—would only complicate things further.

After physics he had two more Monday classes to attend before going to work at Riley's, and he'd have to manage with only three hours sleep. His pen ran out of ink and he cursed under his breath. Struggling to keep the professor's drone from lulling him to dreamland, he pulled a pencil from his notebook.

¶

Wearing new scarlet heels and a red tailor-made pant suit with a top designed to show cleavage, she stepped through the glass doors of Mirror Tech. A receptionist sitting inside a circle of gleaming brass smiled as she waltzed up and asked how to find Brad Barron. Upon receiving the information she took an elevator to the second floor and entered his office unannounced.

"Nanatobi, what a fantastic surprise! What are you doing here?" Brad's expression betrayed he had a testosterone tempest swirling inside—his eyes see-sawed between her face and boobs as he made his way towards her.

She gave the aroused exec a light hug, recognizing a trace of juniper in his pleasant cologne. "I was in the neighborhood, so thought I'd pop in and say hi."

¶

Nanatobi knocked on the office door but didn't wait for anyone to answer. She stepped inside to find the tall blonde sitting at a computer, wearing glasses. "Hi there, remember me?"

Smiling, Ursula Winston removed the spectacles while rising from her desk. "Yes, I remember you. How are you?"

"Doing great, thank you." She'd visited Brad first solely to give the appearance that saying hello to Ursula had been a mere afterthought. Renee and Veronica both knew the voluptuous blonde worked with him but there was no reason for Brad to assume she did. Bringing up the people she'd met at the party had been pure manipulation. She'd asked about Lou, noting a touch of jealousy when he'd answered those questions. Then, pretending their names had escaped her, she'd inquired about *that older couple* and quizzed him about *that girl with black hair.* Careful to show no more interest than she had while making the other queries, she'd asked the name of *that tall blonde woman.*

"Ursula Winston," Brad had answered.

"So what does she do for a living?"

"She works here as a matter of fact. She's my assistant."

"Oh, well in that case I guess I should tell her hello too. Wouldn't want her to think me rude."

She'd planned to hang around until lunchtime but her visit with Brad hadn't lasted as long as anticipated due to him being quite busy. Assuming Ursula's break came at noon, she had to figure out a way to loiter for another twenty minutes without arousing her suspicion. They couldn't talk here, she'd most likely overreact at first, and it would be disastrous if anyone were to hear why. Since they barely knew each other, the provocative target might sense an ulterior motive if she asked her to lunch now. The invitation had to appear spontaneous, merely a polite gesture resulting from the coincidence of happening to be there when Ursula was ready to eat her midday meal.

"So what brings you to Mirror Tech?"

Nanatobi locked eyes with her and smiled. "I was in the neighborhood and decided to drop by and say hello to Brad. We got to talking about the people at his party and he told me you worked here too, so thought I'd pop in and say hi."

"Well it's good to see you again." Ursula reseated herself, put her glasses back on, and picked up the phone while scanning the computer monitor. "Excuse me for a sec, need to make a call."

". . . I see, so he *has* been employed there for the last eight years? . . . You would rehire him? . . . Very good. Thank you for your time."

Ursula hung up and removed the corrective lenses she apparently only used for reading. "So wanna do lunch?"

¶

Ronnie yanked a lever to squeeze excess suds from the mop and began swabbing a section of seamless gray tiles between two rubber cones with *WARNING WET FLOOR* inscribed on them. A pair of black high heels strolled up to one and stopped. He raised his head to find Veronica Van Cedar standing in them. She smiled but didn't utter a word.

"Hello, Ronnie."

Turning towards the voice, he spotted Renee standing by a rack of potato chips at the other end of the aisle. She looked more beautiful than ever. Seeing her again turned his stomach cold at the thought she'd never be his.

"Hi there, Ronnie."

He swung around to find Nanatobi now standing beside Veronica, who walked up to him and caressed his cheek. "The time has come . . . ."

Despite the fact he still didn't want the foursome to happen, he felt compelled to follow Veronica to a heavily wooded area in the country where she finally pulled into the drive of an isolated single-storey house that had to be at least a hundred feet wide if not more. The lights of her BMW went dark and he saw four women get out of the car. Three of them went into the lengthy structure but Renee approached him as he got out of his Thunderbird.

"I'm proud of you, Ronnie. I was afraid you might chicken out." She looked towards the house and back at him. "This is the place where we hold our meetings. My grandmother had it built when Mom was twelve. She inherited it when Grandma passed away. Come on, let's go inside."

Ronnie grabbed her arm. "I didn't come here for a witch's convocation. If that's what you have in mind I'm leaving."

Of course he knew why they were there, Veronica had

picked the time for the orgy. But the presence of the fourth woman troubled him. Even though he'd been told no male could join the coven, that didn't mean they weren't planning on practicing their particular brand of voodoo on him, and he wanted no part of that. He'd been leery about coming to begin with, and now wished he hadn't.

Patting his clutching hand she said, "I promise, we brought you here for your body, not your spirit. There'll be no witchcraft of any kind."

Her statement sounded sincere, though insulting. He released her. "Who's the other woman?"

"You'll see . . . ."

Renee escorted him into a normal looking living room which surprised him. He'd expected some sort of occult atmosphere—black walls illuminated by candlelight, a pentagram on the floor, a large portrait of a goat's head, something along those lines. Instead only a couch, loveseat, several chairs, some small tables, and an entertainment center greeted him. A narrow opening along one wall led to a hallway while a wider cavity on another revealed a kitchen. There were several pictures of Renee, Veronica, and some women he didn't know arranged on the mantel of a fireplace. He figured they had to be Veronica's relatives since Nanatobi wasn't in any of them.

The other three women weren't there. He feared they'd gone in back to change into whatever witch's attire this sect wore. An image of them walking in chanting, wearing black robes and pointy hats, worried its way into his mind. Renee told him to make himself comfortable and opened a closet door from which she took out an odd-looking armless chair with a narrow seat indented for buttocks. Ronnie sat down on a normal one beside a small table.

Placing the chair near the hall opening, she went to the kitchen and soon returned with a tall glass in each hand, one of which she gave him. "I think you'll like it. Drink up."

She took a sip and he followed suit. It was some sort of fruit based concoction with a trace of liquor. Sourly-sweet on the way down, it left a very pleasant aftertaste. Renee turned up her glass again. Her beauty cut him to the core as he watched those devastating green eyes glisten with delight while her delicate lips imbibed the blue fluid. It killed him to know his dream of them becoming man and wife had been forever shattered. The woman he'd fallen for was a witch and an incestuous pervert, a fact no outsider would ever suspect for Renee looked as wholesome as she did sexy—the type of girl that had a lock on becoming Miss America if she ever entered the pageant.

Downing another swallow, he followed it closely with a couple more as a sense of euphoria began to overcome his melancholia over Renee. Yet the sensation didn't prevent his nerves from staying on edge.

"I'll be right back." She sat her glass on the table near him and disappeared down the hall. A moment later Nanatobi entered the room wearing a floor-length translucent gown with sleeves that belled at the wrists. In Renee's fantasy hers and Nanatobi's backsides had been in view but he hadn't seen the fronts of their bodies. Brad had imagined each had the same prototypical centerfold torsos since the guy had never seen them nude before. Ronnie's throat went dry as he stared at Nanatobi's protruding pink nipples and red pubic hair, conspicuously looming beneath the sheer silk like they were almost phosphorescent. She strolled to the kitchen and returned a moment later with a drink like those Renee had made. Despite his nervousness, he felt himself growing erect.

Nanatobi cast him a devilish smile. "This is a special mixture. It's a very powerful aphrodisiac." She seated herself in the chair closest to him, took a long pull from her glass, and crossed her legs. "We have a little surprise for you—a blonde treat."

As if being cued the mysterious fourth woman walked in, wearing an identical garment. It radically shocked him to see the surprise was Ursula Winston. A Greek Goddess would have been jealous over her body if not for a red heart tattooed just above the V-shaped splotch of curly hair at her crotch, revealing her to be a true blonde. He didn't make her for the tattoo type, she seemed far too classy for such foolishness. Tattoos on a beautiful woman struck him as disfiguring as a fake moustache on a pretty girl. Nonetheless hers didn't prevent his cock from zooming towards its zenith.

She seemed nervous but appeared to enjoy his blatant stare. "Hello, Ronnie. Remember me?"

"What are you doing here?"

"I guess I'm here for the same reason you are." Ursula had lost the self assured air she'd possessed the night he met her. She looked apprehensive yet excited, like a girl about to ride a roller coaster for the first time.

"Sit here." Nanatobi stood up and offered her chair. Ursula took it as the redhead went to the kitchen and returned with a drink. She handed it to Ursula before curling up on the floor at his feet with her own glass in hand. Meanwhile Renee and Veronica walked in wearing their see-through apparel. Renee's astounding build mesmerized him as he watched her maneuver the armless chair to the center of the room. Her large breasts bobbed with each movement, forcing him to adjust his pants to accommodate a rock-solid hard on.

"Plant your sweet butt in front of me, Ronnie," commanded Renee, standing behind the curious chair.

He tried to do as she said but Nanatobi grabbed his legs. "First we need to get you naked." She took off his shoes and soon had his pants pulled down to his ankles, forcing him to step out of them by tugging the waist against his heels. Then she unbuttoned his shirt and took it off.

"Remove his briefs, Ursula," said Veronica.

The tall blonde complied, now looking highly aroused.

Veronica went in the kitchen as Nanatobi guided Ursula near the chair. The fruity potion had completely neutralized any inhibitions he normally would have had, being naked in front of four women. With his steely penis jutting towards the ceiling at a steep angle, he walked towards Renee.

Her perfume seduced his nostrils. He sniffed deeply—filling his lungs with the enthralling fragrance—and sat down. She stood behind him massaging his shoulders for a few moments, then leaned over, assaulted his neck with hungry wet kisses, and gingerly traced her tongue up to his ear. After giving it a gentle nibble, she started rubbing her silk-covered breasts against his upper back in slow rhythmic motions as her talented hands explored his chest.

Returning from the kitchen with her drink, Veronica stopped several feet in front of him and took a long pull. She crossed her left arm beneath her breasts and cradled her right elbow, holding the intoxicating mixture close to her face. Her swollen nipples looked like two extruding pebbles beneath the silky transparency. Flaming with lust, her dark eyes fastened themselves to his groin as she moistened her full lips with an eager tongue. At length she said, "You girls get to work."

Ursula seemed confused but Nanatobi obviously knew exactly what to do. She took off her gown, reached for the hem of the newbie's, and pulled it up the blonde's body. Still looking bewildered, Ursula raised her arms to assist the disrobing. The two women were staggering in their naked splendor.

He stared with wild wonder as Nanatobi wrapped her hands around Ursula's left breast, lowered her face to the nipple, and excitedly sucked it into her mouth. Astonished and repulsed, the tall blonde pushed her away. "I'm not into that shit!"

Laughing, Nanatobi shoved her right hand beneath the

heart tattoo and kept pace with Ursula's rapid back-stepping until a wall prevented any further retreat. Then, standing tiptoe like a ballerina, she planted her lips on the protesting blonde's. Ursula's eyes flew wide with rude surprise but Nanatobi kept their mouths welded together while continuing to rapidly finger her. Ursula's shock-parted lids fluttered helplessly and snapped closed. Resistance clearly defeated, she moaned while passionately returning Nanatobi's kiss, snaked a hand between two freckled thighs, and a deep raspy groan resonated from the redhead.

Veronica separated the smooching, groping women—guided them towards the chair, nudged them down on the floor in front of him—and came out of her gown.

Ursula immediately took him into her mouth and reluctantly acquiesced when Nanatobi pulled his shaft towards hers. Lustful moans surged from her freckled throat as she gobbled his throbbing hardness with furious urgency. He almost came but Veronica pulled her off, and the few seconds that passed before the black-eyed witch took her turn enabled him to hold back. Before long all three women alternated between licking his scrotum, mouthing his tool, and kissing one another while Renee continued massaging his chest with her hands, and his upper back with her luscious breasts.

Nanatobi once again almost made him lose control but Renee shouted "I'm ready!" and the bodacious redhead backed off an instant before he would have spewed into her incredibly gifted mouth. Veronica and Nanatobi each grabbed an arm to help Ursula off the floor. As they guided her back a few feet, Renee stepped in front of him and stripped, tossing the robe thoughtlessly aside.

Agony shot through him like a high-voltage electric current, torturing him as he beheld the feminine grandeur of the woman he loved—the girl who held his very soul in the palm of her pretty hand. The dense triangle of auburn curls between Renee's long sculpted legs, the taut reddish-pink nipples terminating the loveliest breasts he'd ever seen, mercilessly taunted him—silently reminding that her dazzling womanhood and unbelievable tits, swaying as she positioned her excruciatingly voluptuous body over his rod, would never belong to him alone. Though his dick throbbed, and his balls tingled, and his mouth salivated, and his pulse raced with anticipation—his heart was breaking.

Kissing him hungrily, thrusting her tongue against his, Renee eased her hot, tight wetness onto his pulsing rigidity. The thrill was maddening. She moved her hips slowly at first, as if testing the sensation of having him inside her, but soon she increased the pace, assaulting his iron manhood with furious intensity. Gasping and groaning as she undulated— her movements so frantic that her teeth clacked against his several times—she forced their mouths to remain cemented together, as if the ecstasy of their sexual union depended upon the unification of their ravenous lips as much as their thrashing genitals.

He'd closed his eyes when the long wet kiss began but opened them upon hearing an ecstatic shriek issue from one of the other women. Ursula stood with her legs spread wide while Nanatobi and Veronica, kneeling before her, lashed at her slit with their tongues.

Renee finally broke free of the kiss and threw her head back. "Oh fuck, Ronnie . . . oh it's so fucking beautiful . . . oh f-fuuuuuuuck . . .!"

He grabbed her glorious butt and expelled his semen inside her thrusting canal, the powerful climax unlike any he'd ever known. Renee slumped forward and slid her face past his. Raising his hands to her back, he held her, relishing the hot exhalations blowing across his shoulder as she caught her breath.

Ursula cried out again—one set of clawing fingers grasping a handful of red hair, the other clutching white. She emitted one last exhilarated wail, then immediately tried to push them away shouting, "Okay! . . . Okay! . . . Okay!"

Pulling away from Ursula—lips slimy with the blonde's love-juice—Nanatobi shoved Veronica onto her back and mounted her. She pressed her crotch against Veronica's face, buried her own between the white-blonde's legs, and they humped each other with animal frenzy until both squealed with satisfaction.

Nanatobi got up and flung herself onto the love seat. Head tilted back against the cushiony upper rim, she stared at the ceiling—her lengthy, pointy, freckled breasts rising and falling in rhythm to her panting chest. "Oh, that was wickedly wonderful."

Renee gave him a kiss and slithered to the floor. Resting her head on his upper thigh, she lovingly stroked his shin. "You were fantastic, Curly Sampson."

Her compliment made him want to cry. A dark ache overtook him as he sat collapsed in the chair, every muscle in his body totally relaxed except for his throbbing rod which inexplicably remained rigid as a flagpole. How many other men would hear those words? If only he could be the only one, he'd be soaring above the heavens with joy unspeakable. Instead, he faced a lifetime of bitter loneliness because no one could take her place.

No one.

She'd stolen his heart and there wasn't a chance in hell he'd ever get it back. Now the thing he had tried to avoid made it even worse, just as he'd known it would. His love for Renee had grown unbearably stronger, even though it was merely an act of meaningless sex to her. He wished he'd never laid eyes on the beautiful bitch.

"Oh my, that was something else," sighed Ursula, slouched

in a chair, big boobs jiggling as she fanned her face with both hands. "When do I get to do it with Ronnie?"

"After me," said Nanatobi.

"I'm next," Veronica insisted.

"Nuh-uh!" Nanatobi straightened in the love seat and glared at her. "You've fucked him already. It's my turn next."

Veronica laughed. "Point well taken. I have boinked him already, twice as a matter of fact."

Seemingly oblivious to the other women, Renee looked up at him with a tender smile as she slowly moved her hand up his leg and caressed his balls while rising to her knees. Then she ran her tongue all over his blood-gorged shaft, took it between her pretty lips, and her heavy auburn curls began rapidly bobbing up and down.

The feeling blew his mind, temporarily overriding his heartache. He'd never known such intense surges of erotic pleasure. Whether it felt so good because Renee's precious mouth administered it, or was simply the best blowjob he'd ever had, he couldn't hold back. "Pull off, Renee, or I'm gonna let loose in your mouth!"

That only made her suck harder and faster, escalating him to heights of ecstasy that forced him to cry out with pleasure. When his sperm gushed into the back of her throat, her gurgling moans assured she'd wanted him to do it.

She raised her head from his lap and craned her neck to look longingly into his eyes. "Now I have your seed within my womb *and* my stomach." Her emerald eyes held him spellbound before she closed them and again rested her face on his thigh. Stroking his shin once more she whispered, "I love you."

He snapped to between two rubber cones at Riley's Grocery, holding the mop, standing exactly where he'd been when the three women had surprised him. The dizzying sensation that he'd once again experienced an impossible event almost overwhelmed him. It hadn't really happened.

His throat went bone dry when Veronica appeared and from the opposite end of the aisle he heard Renee say, "Hello, Ronnie."

When they'd shown up the first time he'd been unable to keep from following them for some crazy reason. But now he knew precisely what to do. When Veronica started towards him he motioned for her to stop. "I take it you guys are here because you've decided it's time for the party."

"That's right, Ronnie," she said with a sultry smile. "You're not going to disappoint us with a case of cold feet are you?"

"Oh no, I'm ready."

"How soon can you get out of here?"

"Right after I finish mopping this aisle."

"Good. We'll be waiting for you in the parking lot in my car. Just follow us . . . ."

When Veronica's BMW pulled out of the parking lot and made a right at the highway, he turned left and headed for a doughnut shop where he planned to hang out until midnight in case Renee directed her mom to his apartment to try again. He wasn't going anywhere near that house in the country, knowing his dream hadn't been in vain after all. His heart pounded in his chest, but with rapturous joy rather than anxiousness over all that had happened. Renee loved him— she'd said so—and that's all he needed to know. Somehow, someway, he'd get her away from that coven and help his beloved get her head straight. Eventually they were going to live happily ever after.

He'd mysteriously been granted the ability to relive the same scenario twice in a row again, and this time there'd be a happy, wholesome conclusion. Though it had all been firmly implanted in his memory, it wouldn't be in Renee's. She'd only remember the second outcome. In her reality, as well as the other three women's, none of it had or would happen.

Whatever the four of them wound up doing tonight, he wouldn't be a part of it. The only fly in the ointment was the fact that Renee would always know he'd slept with her mother. But he couldn't do anything about that except not make the same stupid mistake again . . . .

While stepping through the door of Penelope's All Night Doughnuts he saw Lou Cotton perched in a booth sitting across from two Mexicans dressed like members of a street gang. He waved hello but the guy responded with a scowl, letting him know he'd mistaken him for someone else. Motioning for the two dudes to follow, the look-alike whisked past him like he had leprosy or something, and led them outside.

Excuse me for breathing, thought Ronnie angrily. The ill-mannered butthead not only looked like the redneck he'd met at Brad Barron's, but wore the same type of cowboy boots as well. He watched the whiskered asshole guide the Mexicans past the glass storefront. When they disappeared from view he took a seat at the counter and ordered coffee, resisting a strong temptation to splurge on an apple fritter. His nose was being titillated by a heavenly aroma wafting from a plastic bin filled with the scrumptious ameba-shaped pastries, testifying they'd been freshly removed from the fryer.

¶

Something bad was happening in Baltimore, Arnon could feel it in his spirit. Some form of evil had been growing for years like a fungus hidden in the darkness of a kitchen cabinet, nourished by a leaky water pipe. The Lord had called for its exposure and termination. Woe to those involved. His intuition couldn't decipher any more detail than that, but The Almighty wouldn't have alerted him to it only to leave him in ignorance. He dreaded the revelation that would surely be forthcoming in some form or fashion, and figured it was bound to tie with Charley's blip and the vision he'd had that same night.

TWELVE

"Why didn't Ronnie follow us out here like you said he would?" Ursula complained as Veronica and Renee walked in from the kitchen, each carrying two glasses.

Taking one from Renee, Nanatobi crossed one red-clad leg over the other, and beckoned Ursula to have a seat beside her on the couch. "I'm totally surprised he didn't. Guess he got overwhelmed at the notion."

The statuesque blonde wore a low cut dress meant to be alluring to Ronnie. Her expression as she adjusted it to sit down revealed great disappointment that she'd worn it in vain.

Nanatobi sympathized, having so looked forward to fucking him herself. Renee had told her what she'd feared Veronica had fantasized as soon as they left Ronnie's apartment. Her protests had been merely for show, to keep Ronnie from getting suspicious. It hadn't occurred to her that Renee would have been concerned over that. She'd figured Veronica had fantasized about getting dicked by Ronnie, and she'd wanted to hear the juicy details, having clearly seen the lust that came over her when she and Renee had walked in with him. Apparently Renee hadn't spotted the hungry look in Veronica's eyes because she'd flipped out at first upon hearing her mom had screwed him at a motel.

Veronica had demanded to know if Renee had broken the code and told him about their most closely guarded secret.

"Of course not, Mom," Renee had assured.

"Then where the fuck did he get the idea of an orgy with the three of us?"

"I have no idea," Renee had lied through her teeth.

Veronica had then given her the evil eye. "How do you figure he did, Nanatobi?"

Knowing there was no way she would believe the truth that Ronnie had learned about one of their orgies by reading

Renee's mind, she'd lied too. "Good grief, Veronica, he's a man isn't he? What dude wouldn't love the idea of having three hot chicks like us at the same time?"

She tossed those thoughts aside and smiled at Ursula. "Um, I didn't exactly tell you everything earlier when we were having lunch because I was afraid if I did you might not come with us. We need you to pretend to be a witch for Ronnie's sake. You see, Veronica told him this cock-and-bull story about us being witches when in reality we're nothing more than free spirits who occasionally like to do the same guy at the same time."

Ursula accepted the glass from Veronica. "Why'd you do that?"

Veronica raised hers and gazed at the potion invented by her mother many years ago. "Because I thought my darling daughter had divulged—well let's just call it a little family secret for now. I had the hots for Ronnie so I seduced him, got him into a motel room, and we had a ball. Afterwards he said a particular thing to me that made it seem like he knew about the little family secret. I tested him to see if he really did by pretending I thought Renee had told him we were witches. I made up a lie about there being twelve of us but we needed thirteen. And if he'd followed us tonight like he was supposed to, we were going to make out like we were trying to induct you into our coven as the thirteenth witch.

"Nanatobi and I planned to explain everything to you in another room while Renee entertained Ronnie in here. It wouldn't have mattered if you'd agreed or not so long as he thought we really were witches. But since he didn't follow us, we need to pretend for his sake that we went ahead and tried to induct you."

"Why? He's not here so what's the point?"

"So Renee can tell him we made the attempt. It'll buttress the illusion that we're really witches and keep the little family secret safe."

Ursula had taken two gulps of the potion while Veronica began weaving her verbal web. Nanatobi could tell it had started to take hold by the calmness in her voice and lack of concern. What she'd just been told would have made anyone apprehensive without having their faculties altered. The potion worked very subtly, yet swiftly.

"Well what do you want me to do?"

Veronica took a sip of her drink and sensuously traced her full lips with the long polished nail of her left pinky finger. "Pretend we succeeded in inducting you by getting naked with us."

"Excuse me?" Ursula expostulated, gawking at Veronica. "The only person I'd planned to be naked with was Ronnie. Nanatobi didn't say anything about hanging around in the buff with you guys. She told me he was a super stud but it looks to me like he's a dud."

"Oh he's a super stud all right, dear, and we'll catch him some other time. For now, let's just say we need to do a little rehearsal for when we do."

"Well can't we do this rehearsal with our clothes on?"

A brazen smile leisurely traversed Veronica's sexy face as her dark eyes fastened themselves to Ursula's confused blue orbs. "We can't go down on each other with our clothes on, dear."

Nanatobi had to bite her lip to keep from laughing over the horrific shock radiating from Ursula, rendered speechless by the explanation. All she'd been told over lunch was that she'd have Ronnie all to herself during her turn at riding his rod, and that she'd be wearing a sheer gown during the interim.

"Oh my god, you're all bi." Ursula spoke the words barely above a whisper, a trace of fear mingled with the repugnance tainting her pretty features.

Veronica lowered her gaze to the hot blonde's cleavage. "Have you ever had your mouth on a pussy before?"

"Heavens no!"

"Ever had one on yours?"

"Not a woman's. Look, I can see I made a big mistake in coming here. Please take me home."

Nanatobi glanced at Renee and frowned. She appeared distracted and bored. She'd been acting strange ever since they left the store where Ronnie worked. If she didn't know better she'd think her best friend actually seemed relieved he'd punked out. That couldn't possibly be the case because when Veronica told them what a fantastic lover he was, the three of them had gotten so excited anticipating an orgy with him they'd eaten each other. Afterwards they'd drawn straws to see who'd get first crack at him, and Renee had won.

Veronica set her glass down, nonchalantly took off her blouse, and slowly shed her bra as if she were a topless dancer entertaining a bunch of horny men.

Mortified by the action, Ursula cupped her hands over her gaping mouth.

"Ever felt of a boob other than your own?" Veronica began fondling her large breasts.

"God no!" Ursula shouted into her palms. "Put your clothes back on!"

"I will after you feel my tits. Go ahead, they won't bite you."

"Not on your fucking life." She dropped her hands and glared at the topless whore, eyes saturated with repulsiveness. "Come on, Veronica, at least put your damn bra back on, it's not gonna happen. I came out here because Nanatobi got me intrigued about an orgy with Ronnie. She didn't say fucking word one about doing it with any of you. If she had, I wouldn't have come out here."

"Just one quick feel, dear. Then I'll put my bra back on . . . if you want me to."

Ursula's carefully made-up face turned livid. She launched from the couch and almost lost her balance. Once her feet got settled she shouted, "You're disgusting! If you don't take me home right now I'm calling a cab."

"Nonsense." Veronica waltzed up to her. "Here, give them a good squeeze. I'd hate to have my husband fire you."

"I thought Jesse didn't know what you guys did here?"

"He doesn't."

Ursula shot her a defiant smirk. "Go ahead, tell him to fire me. Then I'll tell him what I know about your secret life, you bitch."

Veronica reached up and caressed the blonde's cheek while gazing into her eyes. "Never threaten me, dear. I have such high hopes for you, it would be so disappointing to find out you're not worthy of my admiration. We *will* get Ronnie out here at some point and trust me, you don't want to be left out when we do. And once he's had a taste of being pleasured by us, he'll be begging to come out here as often as possible. Now all I'm asking of you is to feel my tits, then I'll take you home if you still want to go."

The change in Ursula's demeanor didn't surprise Nanatobi in the least. Veronica could talk a corpse into taking a breath with her incredible powers of persuasion. Red-faced with embarrassment, the tall blonde awkwardly put a lovely hand on one of Veronica's outstanding mammary glands and immediately pulled it away. "There. Satisfied?"

"No, you barely touched it. Give them both a good feel, then I'll be satisfied. But enjoy some more of your drink first."

Veronica resumed feeling herself up as Ursula took several pulls from her glass, eyes focused on the erotic action. Giving her nipples one last tweak, Veronica lowered her arms and smiled. "Okay, dear, put your drink on the table and give my boobies a nice long feel."

Nanatobi's pulse quickened as Ursula nervously gave it a

second try, this time with both hands, and lightly cupped Veronica's jugs. "Your nipples are hard as stone."

"Oh are they? Hmm, well I guess that means they must like the way your hands feel on them. Now squeeze them—squeeze my tits as if you were kneading a ball of pie dough."

Ursula's long pretty fingers pressed into Veronica's gorgeous mounds, groping them in a manner that left no doubt she'd begun to derive pleasure from feeling their silky yet firm texture. Seeing the voluptuous bitch had gotten aroused at last, Nanatobi stood up, took off her shirt, and freed her boobs from a red-laced bra. "Want to squeeze mine?"

"Oh god—!" Ursula spun away from Veronica. "I can't do this, I'm not into lesbianism."

A sultry laugh ascended from Veronica's graceful throat. "Neither are we, dear, but we *are* into orgasms. Aren't you?"

"What else is there?" The perturbed blonde fingered the space between her eyebrows as if trying to relieve a headache.

"Well haven't you ever made yourself have one?"

"Of course I have. Everybody masturbates on occasion."

"Don't you achieve orgasm when you masturbate? Isn't that the whole point?"

Ursula grabbed her glass and took a deep swig as if to gather strength, little knowing it would only further weaken her resolve. Turning to face the seductress, she discharged a quick breath with an annoyed sigh. "I wanna go home."

Veronica merely smiled. "Come here, Nanatobi. I'll feel your tits and you feel mine."

She clutched Veronica's firm exquisite breasts, exulting in the sensation of the beautiful whore's lithe fingers groping her own.

"Mmm, that feels good, Nanatobi."

"You're making me feel good too." She looked at Ursula while speaking. Intrigue had replaced shock. Her big blue eyes were affixed to their mutual breast massage. The look on her face depicted blatant confusion over how something she found so disgusting could stimulate her.

"Now feel your own boobs and I'll feel mine." Veronica eyed Ursula while once again fondling herself. "Even though this feels pleasant, it doesn't feel nearly as good as it did when Nanatobi was doing it to me. What do you think, Nanatobi? Which do you prefer, my hands on you or your own."

"Oh yours feel so much better than mine."

"Now then, Ursula, that being the case with my boobs, I wonder whose hand will feel better on my snatch—Nanatobi's or mine. Which do you think?"

"I wouldn't know," she brusquely rejoined.

"No, because you've never tried it. But even if I did prefer my hand over hers, I can't lick myself can I? And a tongue feels oh so much better than a hand, don't you think?" Veronica took off her pants, slipped out of her panties, and planted her right foot on the couch. "Do me the kindness, Nanatobi."

She dropped to her knees and went to work on Veronica's snatch.

"Ah, that feels marvelous, dear. Want to taste it, Ursula?"

"Hell no, it's repulsive!"

"Your lips say no, but I notice you've hardly blinked your eyes since I pulled off my panties. Why is that? Why are you staring at us if it's so repulsive? Why aren't you looking away?"

"I-I don't know."

Nanatobi thrust her tongue in and out of Veronica's dripping slit with increasing frequency until it started spasmodically contracting and the pleasured vixen collapsed on the couch with a loud moan, whereupon she started mauling her swollen clitoris. Veronica grabbed the back of her head as the nympho's body began shaking worse than an epileptic's during a grand mal seizure, and panted a chorus of obscene declarations before squeals of pleasure filled the air.

She waited until the throes of Veronica's multiple orgasms ceased before withdrawing her mouth. Then she stood up and took off the rest of her clothes. "I'd love to eat you too, Ursula. Are you sure you don't want me to?"

Beautiful face now a bright shade of crimson, Ursula stood with mouth ajar, slowly shaking her head.

"Are you ab-so-lute-ly one hundred percent certain you don't want me to?"

"I-I don't know."

Nanatobi grinned. "You saw how good that felt to Veronica. See how she just lays there on the couch, so sated and relaxed. Please let me, I'm dying to taste your sweet pussy."

Ursula swilled more of the potion and wiped her mouth. "I can't, it'll make me a lesbian . . . I don't want that."

"Nonsense, lesbians don't like men," proclaimed Veronica, lazily rising from the couch. "We *love* men. I'd give anything if Ronnie was here right now, but he's not. It's just us girls tonight. But I can see it's no use, your mind's made up. Guess we might as well get dressed and take her home, Nanatobi."

Playing along, she picked up her panties. "Yeah, I suppose so. What a shame."

"Wait!"

Nanatobi's crotch twitched. "Wait for what, Ursula?"

Nervously grasping the bewitching brew with both hands she meekly uttered, "You know."

"You want me to do down on you now, is that what your saying?"

She closed her eyes and nodded.

"Well I can't do it with your clothes on."

"Let us help you, dear . . . ."

Veronica assisted her in stripping the gorgeous blonde and they guided Ursula down the hall.

"Where are we g-going?" she stammered.

Nanatobi could tell the potion was peaking, rendering

Ursula's will completely malleable. Dazed perplexity gripped her face as she surveyed the large dodecagon-shaped room. In the center sat a bed with no headboard. It was twelve feet square and covered with a black sheet embroidered with red arrows. There were no other bedclothes as it hadn't been designed for sleeping. On one side of the room a long counter with shelves beneath held every sex gadget known to man, and some that didn't exist anywhere else. A clothing rack with numerous see-through gowns hanging on it loomed beyond the other side of the bed. Beside them hung a heavy black robe with a hood.

The ceiling displayed an enormous painting of a centaur circled by the rest of the zodiac illustrated much smaller. Besides his bow and arrow, he sported a huge erect penis. Veronica's mother, the inventor of their religion, had been a Sagittarius and believed the supreme being was a centaur, and that he'd revealed that truth to her in a dream. A large portrait of the matriarch rested on an easel near one of the room's twelve corners, depicting her superb nude body, immortalized during the prime of her life.

Ursula slowly turned all the way around, taking everything in. Then she looked up at the ceiling and gasped. "O my god, you *are* witches!"

Veronica smiled at her. "No, dear. That was just the lie I told Ronnie. We call ourselves The Order of Centaurians. It's our religion."

"What do Centaurians do, worship the devil?"

"No, dear."

"You said it was a religion, you must worship something."

"Yes, we do."

"Well what do you worship?"

"Sex."

Turning away from Veronica and the flabbergasted Ursula, Nanatobi again frowned at Renee, the only one still wearing clothes. "What's with you tonight? Why haven't you uncovered your glory?"

Unenthusiastically Renee unbuttoned her blouse with Ursula watching her every move. Nanatobi sighed when her best friend's perfect tits came into view because the reluctant blonde was ogling them. By the time her pretty auburn pussy made its presence known she noticed the pubic hairs surrounding Ursula's crack were moist. Renee took a deep breath and walked over to the tall blonde. Grabbing the back of her neck, she gave her a quick but firm kiss, and stepped away, pointing at the bed. "Lie down in the center."

Ursula obeyed.

Renee stood with hands on naked hips. "Good. Now act like you're making a snow angel but leave your limbs spread out."

Veronica crawled up the bed, buried her face in Ursula's cunt, and soon had the busty blonde gasping with pleasure. Renee maneuvered to one side of her chest while Nanatobi slithered to the other. With their lips manipulating her nipples, hands squeezing her breasts, Veronica administering oral delights, Ursula was soon arching her back and thrashing about as she telecasted an intense climax.

The three of them rolled away from her but remained on the bed. Ursula let out a bitter groan. "I can't believe that just happened. I never dreamed I'd ever let a woman even touch me erotically much less have one make me come while two others were sucking my tits. God, I've become a lesbian."

"You're not a lesbian, dear," Veronica soothingly reassured. "We'd all rather have a stud than some butch with a strap-on dildo. But I've yet to meet the man who isn't turned on when he sees beautiful women make love to each other. We're merely preparing you so that you'll enjoy the experience when we all share the same man, because he won't like it if you don't. Ronnie will think he's died and gone to heaven, believe me."

Nanatobi turned her head towards the remorseful blonde. "Did you like what we did to you?"

"Yes, but I feel ashamed that I did."

"That's only because it was your first time, it'll pass. We want you to join us."

Veronica took over. "I told Ronnie our membership consisted of thirteen witches and one warlock which was simply an exaggeration of the truth. In reality Centaurianism is limited to four women and a man only on rare occasions. As you can see there's only three of us. We need a new fourth. The requirements for membership are stringent. No one who doesn't posses superior beauty, intellect, and the capability of what outsiders would consider to be extreme egregious behavior behind closed doors can even be considered for membership. You're a gorgeous woman and I've been around you enough to know you fit intellectually. When you had lunch with Nanatobi earlier today she determined you have the erotic capabilities required by your eagerness to have an orgy with Ronnie. Now we're here to see if you can pass the final test.

"The drink you enjoyed is a potion my mother created when I was a child—very powerful but quite harmless. You've been under its influence until now, but its effects will soon wear off. When it does, we'll see whether or not we have a new member. Of course if you don't want to join, there's no point in going through with the final phase."

Ursula raised up on an elbow. "What happens if I join?"

"Then you'll become part of us."

"No, I mean what exactly would I be doing? Do you have rituals, secret handshakes, that type of thing?"

Veronica sat up and crossed her legs. "The only ritual is the initiation. After that what you'll be doing when we're all together is experiencing one orgasm after another through various means. We like to get together at least once a week, but since we want this kept secret at all costs that isn't always possible. Nanatobi happens to be spending a few days at my house, so she, Renee, and I have had several opportunities to drive each other mad. But when the three of us aren't together, you'd never know Renee and I were anything but your typical mother and daughter. And when I'm not with them, they simply carry on like the two best friends they are."

While absorbing that, Ursula glanced at her, then Renee, then the sex gadgets before refocusing on Veronica. "You and Nanatobi never touch each other in that way when Renee isn't present? Is that what you're saying?"

"Right. And the same holds true for the two of them when I'm not there, just as it does for Renee and I when Nanatobi's not there. No one gets left out. If you join us, the only time the three of us will be doing anything like this is when you're with us. This is the spiritual aspect of the order and why we call it a religion.

"To use Ronnie Garr as an example. I met him when he picked up Renee for a date. Neither he nor Renee did a thing for my libido even though I saw he was a good looking guy. But one night Nanatobi and Renee brought him to the house. The three of us being present in the same place made me so amorous for Ronnie I almost raped him right in front of my husband. I knew I had to have him, and succeeded in doing so."

"Were Renee and Nanatobi there when you had sex with him?"

"Mm mm. It was just the two of us."

Ursula assumed the same position as Veronica and glanced down at her breasts. "I can't believe I'm sitting here naked with three nude women."

Nanatobi chuckled inside. The potion had rendered Ursula completely uninhibited.

"So the three of you don't have to be together when you

want to do it with some guy?"

"No," said Veronica. "That's the power of our order. We only get amorous for one another when the three of us are together. If you join us it will have no affect whatsoever on your particular taste for men. If you and these two girls were to get together without me there and one of them tried anything it would repulse you, just as it would either of them if you put a move on. But let the four of us get together at the same time and horny ain't the word for it, dear. At least that will be the case if you join."

"How can that be? I don't understand."

Veronica laid down on her side—legs stretched, ankles crossed, head resting in her hand. "That's why we call it a religion, it's some sort of unexplainable spiritual thing."

Ursula coughed out a harsh laugh. "Spiritual thing, my ass, it's the potion isn't it. The reason you all get the hots for each other when you get together is because you all drink the potion when you do. Am I right?"

"No. The potion does contain an aphrodisiac and we enjoy its effects, but it has nothing to do with what I just explained to you. Speaking of that, it's bound to have worn off by now, so the time has come for you to make a decision."

The busty blonde pouted with thought for a few moments before aiming a quizzical squint at Veronica. "Why did you say all that stuff earlier, about needing Ronnie to think you were witches and all?"

"Because Centaurianism has to remain a secret between us women. Though a man is required on special occasions, he can't know the truth about the order, so we make out like we're witches in his presence. We want Ronnie to be that man for the time being."

"Why can't the man know? This is so confusing."

"Not now, dear." Veronica crawled to the edge of the bed and stood up. "I can tell you the rest only after you become a

Centaurian."

Thinking about what Ursula was going to learn upon joining, Nanatobi grew wet between the legs. During the next three days she'd experience more orgasms than most women have in a year. She'd be violated by every gadget in the room, and by the time they were through with her the hot bitch would realize she'd never been truly fulfilled sexually before becoming a member of The Order of Centaurians. Of course she'd have to give herself to the centaur first—the so called final test—but that was meaningless. That stupid horse-man didn't exist and she'd barely been able to keep a straight face while reciting the prayer of dedication seven years ago. Only Veronica and her mother ever believed it did. The centaur was a joke to her and Renee but the vows and codes were not. Neither she, Renee, Veronica, or their founder had ever broken one.

Neither had Veronica's two aunts, who were her mother's first recruits. One of them had died shortly before Renee reached puberty. The death of the other had led to her being brought in to again raise the membership to four, as she was Renee's best friend and possessed the qualities required. Veronica had so mourned her mother's loss she'd been reluctant to seek a new fourth member but had recently changed her mind for reasons she wouldn't explain.

Nanatobi would never forget her three day initiation. Though only fourteen at the time, she'd learned how to make herself come over a year prior, but she'd never experienced anything like the erotic heights attained while being on the potion. It not only greatly enhanced sexual climax, the intoxicant eliminated the normal post-orgasmic reaction of a deflated libido. A woman or man under its influence could have sex unlimited times without having to wait for their systems to reset for another bout. And the desire to do so didn't decrease one iota until the potion dissipated.

Since Renee's grandmother's death only Veronica knew how to make it. The secret recipe would be passed on to Renee when she turned thirty-two. Veronica had chosen that age for sentimental reasons. That's how old she'd been when her mother taught her.

The basement of the country house contained a small laboratory designed strictly to produce a product resembling talcum powder. Like her mother before her, Veronica rendered half of each batch into pills. One tablet, half the size of an aspirin, achieved maximum affect, but the potion was preferred because it lasted almost twice as long. It consisted of a pinch of powder mixed with fruit juices and a half ounce of tequila. Nontoxic in low levels but dangerous beyond two tablets or the equivalent amount in potion form, only one dose was allowed within an eight hour span.

Veronica had lied to Ursula when she'd said it had worn off by now, for the pill itself lasted two hours. But she hadn't prevaricated about the order needing a man, and only Veronica could choose him. For some reason the males who'd been brought here through the years had never returned, and it mystified all of them as to why they'd refused Veronica's invitation for an encore since each had been thrilled by the experience. The man wasn't allowed to know they worshiped the centaur, though only Veronica actually did.

It had always irritated her that Veronica refused to say how or where she met each man. Not only were she and Renee never told that, they weren't allowed to know anything about him—address, occupation, marital status, not even his name. And she never understood why Renee's grandmother, who'd started the order, had become subservient to Veronica where the men were concerned.

According to Renee Veronica had completely taken over that aspect by the time she'd spent that eventful weekend with her and returned to Taylor's mansion a Centaurian. Renee said that when her grandmother used to orchestrate the male orgies, they took place every winter and summer solstice with the same guy—a handsome well-endowed catholic priest. Veronica's mother had selected him to seduce because he dared not say a word to anyone for fear of being defrocked.

Veronica had changed all that. There was no longer any set time—it happened whenever she desired—and she'd instituted a strict rule that the basement was off limits to anyone but her when they had a real dick at their disposal. Renee didn't know what became of the priest but hadn't seen him since the first male orgy arranged by Veronica.

There'd been only five men brought here since Nanatobi joined—three before Renee's grandmother died, two after. To keep them in the dark about each member's identity they used stage names as if they were pornographic actresses. She went by the moniker of Scarlet O'Cunt.

Veronica always drove the man to the country house where they waited in their gossamer gowns. Once inside, she'd remove his blindfold, offer him the special drink, and leave him in their care while she changed into her gown. By the time she returned he'd already be feeling the effects of the potion. They'd take off his clothes and put the black robe on him. Reciting a fake witch's chant, they'd slowly circle around the salivating male, giving the potion time to render him incapable of losing his erection. When Veronica gave the word they'd shed their gowns, strip the black robe off the man, and seat him in a chair specifically designed for female-on-top intercourse. While one member gratified herself with his ultra-stiff penis, the remaining tended to each other. After they all fucked him, he'd be led to the giant bed for the duration of the orgy, which continued until the potion wore off.

Then every member except Veronica, who always stayed behind to take the man home, went to a quaint all night diner in Roland Park. She'd always suspected Veronica insisted on that job in order to have him all to herself for awhile. When Veronica finally joined them they'd split a coconut cream pie, their founder's favorite. The pie had been divided into thirds the last two trips to the restaurant and Renee couldn't handle such a large portion. She and Veronica could gorge endlessly on sweets, so they'd divvied up Renee's leftovers. Ursula's membership would reduce the portion to a quarter again.

Ronnie had been the first male chosen whom she and Renee knew anything about, and had he not backed out, would have been the only one allowed to drive himself to the country house. All the others had been blindfolded and brought there by Veronica in order to keep them from knowing its location. They also wouldn't have performed the bogus ritual or insisted Ronnie wear the black robe. Veronica had explained the exception after instructing her to approach Ursula: "We'll never get him beneath the centaur otherwise."

Nanatobi knew they'd eventually have him lying on the giant bed with a perpetual hard on, and the thought of riding it made her exceedingly horny. Ronnie may have thwarted Veronica this time but sooner or later he'd give in and follow them out here. The beautiful slut always got what she wanted.

Always.

THIRTEEN

Brad frowned at the phone he'd just cradled. Ursula had called in sick, saying she'd come down with some sort of flu and figured to be out of commission for at least three days. Tapping his calendar blotter with a Cross Classic Century Ballpoint, he couldn't get past how contrived her voice sounded. He'd worked with her for the last six years and she'd always been a dedicated professional, but he couldn't shake the feeling she was faking it. Each time he replayed the conversation in his mind it bothered him a little bit more.

He'd asked if she'd seen a doctor and she hadn't, so how did Ursula know she'd be ill for a minimum of three days? The call came from her cell according to the ID and she'd claimed to be in bed. He dialed her home number and let it ring fifteen times but she never answered. Though she may have turned off the ringer, he suspected she wasn't there.

Hilda Weiss walked in with an application. "Ursula's sure running late this morning."

"She called in sick," he said with a neutral tone, keeping his doubts to himself. Hilda left and he perused the information a twenty-three year old male had jotted down in the hopes of obtaining a programming position at Mirror Tech. Picking up the phone to verify his degree and employment history, Brad's thoughts again shifted to Ursula. Ordinarily he'd have passed the chore on to her.

After confirming the young man's résumé, Brad took the document into Jesse's office to get his approval. His boss was on the phone.

"For three days? Won't Renee get bored? . . . Oh, Nanatobi's going too . . . Okay, hon, enjoy yourself . . . Love you too."

Jesse hung up the phone and Brad handed him the document. He gave it a once over and signed it. "That was my wife on the phone. Looks like I'll be having dinner at the club the next few days. She's taking Renee and Nanatobi on a road trip, even though it will cause the two of them to miss some classes. Who could know the logic of a woman, eh?"

Back at his desk Brad's mind whirled around two words: *Three Days.* It was an extremely anomalous coincidence, considering the fact Nanatobi happened to stop by yesterday and had lunch with Ursula. Mirror Tech offered five personal days a year and Ursula had her full compliment. Why pretend to be sick if she wanted to go along on Veronica Van Cedar's road trip? Jesse certainly would have allowed it since it was his wife asking her to go.

¶

Ronnie had woke up in a jubilant mood. He'd altered fate last night by refusing to follow Veronica, and in doing so felt like one of the good guys again. A long and arduous road lay ahead. It wouldn't be easy freeing Renee from witchcraft since she obviously didn't want to be liberated. Having no idea how to perform the task, he opened the yellow pages, searching for churches.

An hour later he realized that wasn't the answer.

Except for two, the pastors that actually talked to him were aloof and disinterested upon learning he didn't belong to their congregations. One told him to seek God's guidance, offering nothing beyond that. The other had seemed to want to help but admitted dealing with witchcraft loomed beyond his training. He'd been certain of one thing though, which stuck in Ronnie's brain: *"A witch is in bondage to Satan, whether or not she believes he exists."*

"Thou shalt not suffer a witch to live," he said aloud while rising from his desk where he'd been stewing over the matter since last hanging up the phone. He wished he had a Bible so he could read those lines again. Reciting it a second time, he put on his coat, grabbed his microbiology and biochemistry textbooks, and headed for the door.

¶

Arnon set a bucket beneath his milk cow's udder, latched on to two teats, and proceeded with Tuesday evening's milking, the last chore of the day. He dreaded the first one he'd have to perform tomorrow. Mary Jo usually gathered the eggs while he slopped the hogs but her being away had altered his morning routine. One of the roosters just knew he was out to romance the hens and always tried to chase him out of the pen. A swift kick to the backside was the only way to make the big Rhode Island Red stop attacking and the bird couldn't remember from one day to the next that was all he'd get for his trouble. More than once he'd been tempted to wring his neck, pluck his feathers, throw him in the stew pot along with an onion, simmer him for a couple of hours to tender him up, and have him for supper.

He stopped squeezing and yanking as an image started forming on the milk's surface. The face of a man gazed up at him with sorrowful eyes, the rest of his features vague and undefined. Arnon waited for the picture to become clear, certain that it would, but his hunch proved incorrect. As it faded away so did any intuition of the guy's identity. Somewhere some fella needed help but all he could for him was pray, which he proceeded to do while his hands went back to work.

¶

"Ever since the eighteen hundreds when John Dalton, after

proving the atoms of any particular piece of matter are linked together in a quantitative arrangement to form a molecule, it has been theoretically possible to alter any element consisting of diatomic molecules, which of course you all learned—or at least should have learned in basic physics—means any molecule comprised of two atoms, unlike the monatomic elements that are comprised of molecules containing only one atom . . . ."

Part of Ronnie's mind strove to absorb the physics of the low-browed professor's lecture, but another section of his brain kept storming around the fact that science didn't know everything. Other realities existed which no branch of it could explain. He needed an expert to talk to about Renee's problem with witchcraft, and also hoped someone could explain what was happening to him. Of the billions of people populating the planet, surely he couldn't be the only one experiencing these supernatural events. But where could he find such a person?

"For what would happen if we were able to split a diatomic molecule?" the professor continued. "Each of the two atoms is identical to the other, and bound together they form their particular elementary molecule. But what are they when isolated? Take oxygen for instance. An oxygen molecule consists of two atoms. But what exactly are these atoms? Hydrogen is one atom with an atomic weight of one, simple enough. But the diatomic molecule that makes up oxygen— with an atomic weight of sixteen, which is a round number used for the element that has an actual weight of fifteen-point-nine-nine-nine-four, the weight of course calculated at one twelfth the weight of carbon twelve—is two atoms bound together . . . ."

Ronnie stopped taking notes and waited for the professor to quit speculating and start relaying facts again. From the corner of his eye he noticed a girl looking at him who seemed familiar. It took him a moment to place her as the dingbat who'd screwed up his first approach towards Renee by bragging about going out with Danny Hill. Back then he'd thought her to be an olive-skinned Caucasian, but the hood of a winter coat had concealed the coarse curly hair spiraling past her shoulders, signifying she was part black. He met her gaze. A shy smile sprang up and she quickly looked away.

When class ended he beat her to the hall and waited. As she stepped out he blocked her path. "Hi there. My name's Ronnie Garr and we have a mutual acquaintance."

"Oh really?" she replied with a smile. "Who might that be?"

"Renee Van Cedar."

"Is that right. Well pleased to meet you, Ronnie. I'm Louise Hudson."

Accepting the hand she held out in greeting he said, "Same here. Well I suppose I should let you get to your next class."

"Actually I have an hour to kill before it starts. I usually go for coffee after Physics."

He'd figured on having to say hi and bye a few times before asking if they could go somewhere to talk, but she'd just presented an opportunity for him to do so without appearing too forward. "I have the same schedule—an hour between morning classes. I could use a cup. Mind if I tag along . . .?"

¶

Thin yet shapely, Louise Hudson had delicate features that alternated between being merely cute to quite pretty, depending on her expression. They were having coffee at a place near his apartment called Betty's Café. Eating out to him meant hamburger joints as restaurants were a luxury he could seldom afford, so he'd never been there. She frequented the place because her grandmother owned it. Her Aunt Chloris ran it now.

"So I messed you up with Renee, huh?"

He grinned. "Yeah. I'd finally worked up the nerve to introduce myself but before I could circle for a landing you came running up ranting about some guy named Danny Hill asking you out."

"Danny Hill . . .?" she made a sour face. "That lasted two whole days."

"Chemistry wasn't right I take it."

"Chemistry was the problem. He had too much of a certain kind if you know what I mean."

"Oh." He took a sip of coffee. "How long have you known Renee?"

"Since fourth grade."

"Are you close?"

She gave him a knowing smile. "You're using me to get to Renee, aren't you."

"No, we've dated since I finally managed to meet her."

"She didn't tell me she was seeing anyone. But then I haven't talked to her since December. We're in the same art history class this semester but she hasn't attended once. Of course we're only talking two absences thus far so I guess it's not that big a deal. Renee only goes to college to appease her dad anyway."

He'd wanted to talk to her because of the possibility she might be one of the twelve witches. Renee wouldn't tell him anything about the coven, but if he could find one of the other members he might learn more about it and glean some clues on how to fight it. Though Louise Hudson didn't look like a person who secretly practiced witchcraft, neither did Renee.

"When's the last time you saw her?" she asked over the rim of her cup.

"Night before last. She dropped by the grocery store where I work part time." He shook off a mental image of what happened afterwards at that house in the country. "She was with Nanatobi Cain. You know her?"

"Oh yeah, what a character."

"How long have you two known each other?"

"Same as Renee, since fourth grade."

The coincidence stirred him. Maybe she'd gotten inducted into the coven too, being friends with the two witches from such a young age. "Are you guys close?"

"Yeah, the three of us are pretty tight. But Renee and Nanatobi are much closer with each other then either are to me or anyone else. They've been best friends since first grade. Well it's been real, Ronnie, but we need to get back. Thanks again for chauffeuring me."

He didn't learn anything important during the drive to the university. While getting out of his car, he asked if they could have coffee again after Friday's physics class.

"Sure."

Instead of walking off after saying goodbye, she ran up to him and pulled his head down for a kiss. An instant later he realized it never happened. Watching her walk away, he wondered why Louise had felt passionate enough about such an innocent fantasy to draw him into it. If only she'd fantasized about an orgy like Renee had, he'd know for certain she was part of the coven. Then maybe he could trick her into leaking some information about it without breaking his promise to Renee.

¶

Charley sat down at his usual booth and opened a newspaper. The waitress brought him a cup of coffee he hadn't ordered. Everyone who worked there knew that would be the first thing he'd ask for every time. "I'll have a Reuben and fries."

His cousin Chloris, who now ran the place since Aunt Betty Louise was getting on up there in years, walked over from the counter. "We're fresh out of sauerkraut, Charley. What else can I get you for lunch besides a Reuben."

"Out of sauerkraut? Hell that's un-American!"

She snickered. "Unless you're willing to settle for a plain old corned beef on rye I can't help you none. Now if you want to trot down to a supermarket and pick me up some, I'll be glad to fix you one. Otherwise you'll have to wait an hour until this week's food order gets here."

"That's all right, I'll live. But if you're going to be in a bind before your delivery gets here, I'll be happy to go get you some."

"No, we'll be fine."

"Okay, then bring me a corned beef on rye and fries." Before he could return to his paper another relative walked in. "Hey there, Louise! Come have a seat."

"How are you, Charley?" she said with a smile.

"Feeling pretty good at the moment because I'm on vacation. But don't ask me after I get back to the salt mine in a few days or some of my language might offend you."

"That bad, huh . . .?" she scooted across from him.

He nodded.

"So you're not too happy with your job right now I take it."

"Bingo. Think it's time to start looking for something else, that's why I'm pouring through these want ads."

The waitress came over with a menu and coffee.

"Nothing for me," said Louise.

She topped off his cup and headed for another customer.

"So what you up to these days, girl?"

"Just college and work same as always."

"Still working at that clothing store part time?"

"Yeah, Cathy's Boutique. I'm on my way there now as a

matter of fact. I saw your car in the parking lot and thought I'd drop in on you."

He grinned, reached across the counter and gave her a love pat on the shoulder. "Well I'm glad you did."

"What's up with you these days besides hating your job?"

"Went to see Arnon the other day."

"How is the old prophet?"

Louise said it in jest, but that description fit Arnon if it fit anybody living in these godless times. "He's doing fine other than having to batch it for awhile. Mary Jo's away at her sister's. He ragged me real good when I asked if she'd taken Beatrice and Bessie with her. I'd forgotten they'd grown up."

"You're kidding!" she giggled. "Gosh, Bess and Bea have been in Annapolis for several years now. Well gotta run. It was great seeing you, Charley."

Watching her head out the door, he heaved a sad sigh. Louise was the only member of the Hudson-Green clan that had white blood. She'd never been told the bitter truth about how that came to be. Even Arnon played along, and lying set about as well with the seer as a mouse sitting on a cat's back. She'd been conceived as a result of his cousin Mabel's rape, and poor Mabel hadn't survived Louise's birth. Betty Louise's husband John shot and killed the white son-of-a-bitch who committed the crime. When he got arrested for it, John hung himself in jail, fearing the outcome of a trial of a black man killing a white man, no matter how justifiable, would be life without parole at best. Uncle John had chosen death rather than a life behind bars.

While Louise knew that Mabel died giving birth to her, and she'd been born illegitimate, she thought her granddaddy passed away of natural causes. She'd been told her father was a white English tourist who'd fallen in love with her mother while vacationing in the States. His death had been conjured as a plane crash fatality when he'd flown back to England after his vacation ended, never knowing he'd left a child in Mabel's womb. Aunt Betty Louise concocted the fabrication and had threatened every member of the family that knew the truth with their very lives if they ever told Louise anything but that version of events. So far Aunt Betty Louise hadn't murdered anybody.

¶

Ronnie decided to splurge on a hamburger at Betty's Café, hoping Louise might be having lunch there. As soon as he walked in a large black man with a newspaper waved at him. "Did you get your T-Bird fixed?"

Recognizing him as the guy that helped him when his fuel pump gave out, he broke into a grin. "Well hello there! How are you doing?"

"Fine. Care to join me?"

"Sure." He slid into the booth and shook hands with him. "Thanks again for helping me the other night. I'm sorry, but I've forgotten your name."

"Charley Hudson, and don't feel bad about it. I remember yours though—Ronnie Garr."

He tilted his head quizzically. "I met a Louise Hudson this morning at the university and she introduced me to this place a few hours ago."

"Pretty, good build on a light frame, looks half white?"

"Sounds like you know her. Are you guys related?"

"If she mentioned being kin to the owner of this café then we're talking about the same girl. The Louise I know is my first cousin once removed."

"Unreal, she sure did."

Charley laughed. "Small world ain't it? First Brad Barron, now Louise."

Hearing Brad's name made him recall Charley saying he was an air traffic controller. A waitress came over and started to hand him a menu. "I won't need that, ma'am. I'd like coffee and a hamburger with mustard." He leaned forward the moment she left. "You're the one who saw a UFO on radar the night of the blackout, aren't you."

The big dude's eyes flared. "How did you know that?"

"Brad Barron told me. I should have connected the dots at the time because I knew you were his neighbor, but I just now remembered what you do for a living."

"He did, huh." Charley started scratching his chin. "Did Brad mention anything else to you?"

"Like what?"

"Never mind."

His tense expression betrayed he knew some secret of Brad's. Since he'd asked if Brad mentioned anything else in connection with the UFO, Ronnie figured he knew which one. "He told you about his out of body experiences, didn't he."

Charley lowered his hand and relaxed. "You know about it then."

"Yeah. Do you believe him?"

"Mm hmm . . . and I think it's damn strange it started the night of the blackout."

"Likewise." There was something special about Charley Hudson that made him feel very comfortable talking to him. The waitress brought his coffee and he waited till she left before saying, "So you guys never did figure out what that UFO was?"

"No, and I don't think anybody ever will. I just hope whatever that thing is, it never comes back. My cousin Arnon has what some folks call *The Sight,* meaning God reveals things to him on a pretty regular basis. I talked to him about what's been happening to Brad because Arnon had an out of body experience when we were kids. He's a very spiritual man, knows his Bible inside out, and sometimes has visions. He had one the night of the blackout and fears it's an evil omen." Charley blew out a heavy sigh. "Arnon has never had a vision that didn't come to pass."

Shivers assaulted the back of Ronnie's neck as a skin-prickling sense of foreboding enveloped him. He didn't doubt this Arnon's authenticity because of the overt reliability of the man who'd communicated the disturbing revelation. But consternation got trumped by elation as it dawned on him he'd unwittingly located the perfect person to help him free Renee from Veronica's cult. "I'd like to meet your cousin."

"You would? Why so?"

"Because of what you told me about him. I need spiritual guidance on something. The reason I don't have a problem believing Brad really goes astral is because I've been dealing with some weird phenomena since the night of the blackout myself."

"Oh?" Charley hoisted his cup. "Mind if I ask what?"

"I seriously doubt you'd believe me."

"Try me." He took a sip.

"All right, but it's really crazy. Did Brad tell you the details about his out of body experiences and a girl named Nanatobi Cain?"

The big guy nodded. "It happens to her every time it happens to him, and he always goes to her bedroom when it does."

"Well, Charley, the day after the blackout I took her best friend out to dinner, then to my place, then drove her home. Shortly after I got back to my apartment the entire date repeated itself but I was the only one who knew it. I'll spare you the gory details but another series of events almost happened twice after that but I interceded and prevented the second outcome from going down like the first. I've come to the conclusion that only the second outcome really happens and the first is a vision that's so realistic I think I'm actually living through it." He cleared his throat and moistened it with coffee. "Well if that's not freaky enough for you, if somebody near me is imagining something strongly enough, I see it play out as if it's really occurring. Brad can verify that for you because I saw a fantasy of his spring to life."

Brows almost reaching his hairline, Charley roughly massaged his jaw as if the action could somehow help him absorb the irrational tale he'd been told. Exhaling a breath through his nose, he relaxed his face and stabbed a finger through the handle of his cup. "Man, that *is* tough to swallow. And all this started the night of the blackout?"

"Nanatobi's and Brad's did. My deal started the next day when that date repeated itself, but I believe it's all a result of whatever caused the blackout."

Charley gulped some more coffee and wiped his mouth. "Speaking of that, it's a pretty odd coincidence we hooked up twice and both times learned you'd recently met somebody connected to me—first Brad, then Louise."

"Yeah, pretty strange indeed."

The waitress brought his hamburger. It came with complimentary potato chips and the hefty beef patty was slightly larger in circumference than the over-sized bun. He picked it up carefully so as not to lose any of the veggies and took a bite. "Mmm, I won't be buying burgers anywhere else from now on—talk about getting a bang for your buck. Anyway, do you think your cousin Arnon can help me?"

"Yeah, most likely. There's nothing to lose if we find out he can't. He lives on a farm an hour's drive from here. I'm on vacation until next Monday so I'm flexible. How about you?"

"I've got classes during the day and work nights through the week, but we could go Saturday evening after I get off work."

"Fine. I'll call him right now . . ." Charley frisked himself.

"On second thought, no I won't. Left my cell at home. Let me get your number and I'll call you after I talk to him. I'm sure he won't mind us coming up Saturday. We'll take my car."

Ronnie grinned. "I was hoping you'd say that."

FOURTEEN

Brad sat at his desk fuming over Ursula's irresponsible actions in playing hooky from work. It was four o'clock Thursday afternoon. He'd called her house and cell several times on Tuesday, Wednesday, and today but she never answered. Her answering machine and voicemail had been conveniently turned off. He had no choice but to reprimand her. Though it would be her first write up, Mirror Tech allowed only two. A third infraction necessitated immediate termination.

¶

Ronnie hadn't called Renee because he knew she'd be irate about him not following her mother's car to that house in the country. At first he'd been relieved that neither she nor Nanatobi had made contact. But three days had passed since that fateful Monday night and now he was concerned about not hearing from her. Having to leave for Riley's in five minutes provided a handy excuse to bail from an argument so he phoned her, intending to hang up if Veronica picked up the phone.

Jesse answered and said she wasn't there.

"Um, could you give me her cell phone number please?"

"You don't know it?" he replied with a surprised tone.

"I'm not up with the times, Mister Van Ce—"

"Call me Jesse. What do you mean you're not up with the times?"

"I don't have a cell phone so I depend on Ma Bell. It never occurs to me to ask people for their cell numbers . . . ."

When she didn't answer he let it keep ringing so he could leave a message on her voicemail, but the damn thing never directed him there.

The phone rang while he was putting on his coat.

Charley Hudson called to say his cousin Arnon had agreed to talk to him and expected a visit from them on Saturday.

¶

Nanatobi walked into the parlor with two minutes to spare.

Taylor looked up from his easy chair. "You made it by ten o'clock Thursday just as you promised."

"Yes, sir."

"And you're sure you'll be able to make up for the classes you missed."

"Yes, sir."

"Did you have a good time?"

"Oh yeah, it was great getting to meet the actors and see what all goes on behind the scenes of a television series being filmed on the streets of New York."

"I'm sure it was most memorable for you."

"Yeah, it's so cool that Renee was allowed to bring two friends with her."

He frowned. "I thought you said her mother won the contest?"

"Oh, I'm sorry, did I say that? No, it was Renee . . . ."

¶

Friday morning Ursula strolled into the break room with a nonchalant "Good Morning", helped herself to coffee, and started for her office.

Brad detained her. "Come with me, Ursula, you've got some explaining to do."

She followed him into his office and he closed the door. "So, why haven't you been to work these last three days?"

Her immaculate nose bobbed with a frown. "I told you, I

had the flu."

"Why didn't you answer your phones? I've called your house and cell at least a dozen times each over the last seventy-two hours."

"I was bed ridden and didn't want to be disturbed so I turned them off." The frown had turned to a worried glower. "What, you don't believe me?"

"No," he stated emphatically. "Why'd you turned off your voicemail? It couldn't have *disturbed* you."

"I-I had no idea it was turned off . . ." Ursula went on and on about how sick she'd been, and started crying. "Why won't you believe me?"

Brad didn't buy a word of it and her audacity in insulting his intelligence in such a manner really pissed him off. "I'll have to write you up. If this happens again I'll do it a second time, and you know what that means."

Still weeping, she meekly nodded.

He wanted to tell her he knew she'd gone on Veronica's road trip, but didn't because he couldn't prove it. If Veronica covered for her Jesse might write him up for making false accusations against a fellow employee. So he let the matter stop there, reporting only what he thought—that she'd lied about being sick in order to miss three days work without using any of her personal days. "Okay, we're done. You can go now."

¶

They left Friday's physics class together and went to Betty's Café for coffee, but this time took Louise's car—a red Nissan as old as his Thunderbird which came off the assembly line twelve years ago. Her wheels might have been humble but not the chic dress she had on. It really showed off her petite figure.

"Don't you want some cake to go with that coffee?" asked the black proprietor while setting their cups on the table.

Louise grinned. "Don't tempt me, Chloris. You know I only allow myself to eat your special chocolate cake on weekends. Otherwise I wouldn't be able to get through the door."

Chloris shifted her gaze to him. "How about you, young fella? We make it from scratch and it's the most popular item on the menu."

"Maybe some other time." As she walked off he smiled at Louise. "After you introduced me to this café two days ago I came back for lunch and ran into your cousin Charley Hudson."

She brightened with surprise. "You know Charley?"

"Yeah. We met one night when my fuel pump died. I was heading for a payphone and he pulled over to see if he could help me out. He hollered at me when I came in here and asked me to join him. I couldn't remember his name and after he refreshed my memory I mentioned meeting you and asked if you guys were related."

"I saw him here last Wednesday too. We must have just missed each other."

"Apparently so . . . ."

They traded life stories as well as phone numbers. Louise's was a cell. Her white father died in a plan crash without knowing the black woman he'd fallen in love with and planned to marry was carrying his baby. Another tragedy followed several months later when her mother died bringing her into the world. He now hoped she wasn't a witch. Though desperately needing information about the coven, he didn't want to learn that the sweet sincere girl she appeared to be secretly belonged to a sex cult. Her fantasy had only involved kissing him which made him wonder if she'd ever gone beyond that stage with anyone. If that was the case, she couldn't be a member of the coven.

"Well, Ronnie, I guess we'd better get back to the university so I can get to art history on time. What's your next class?"

"Psychology. Want to meet back here for lunch afterwards? I love their burgers and they're reasonably priced."

"Can't. I'll be munching on a tuna sandwich on my way to work."

Just as well, he thought, *I'd be putting a strain on my weekly budget.*

An odd expression came over her. He started to ask if she felt okay but didn't get the chance. She got up, walked around the table, and fastened her lips to his in a passionate kiss.

"Is something wrong?" Louise asked from the chair she'd never vacated.

"Huh? Oh, no I'm fine . . . ."

¶

His psychology professor had given a reading assignment of three chapters which he'd been studying since coming home after his last class of the day. Confident he now had a solid handle on the subject matter, Ronnie put away his notes and called Louise's cell.

"Hello?"

"Ronnie here. Wanted to verify I had your number written down correctly."

"Um . . . hi."

"You sound funny. Did I catch you at a bad time?"

"Yeah, I'm still at work and we're quite busy at the moment."

"Sorry my timing was bad. I'll let you go."

"Oh, guess who made it to art history this morning."

"Renee?"

"Yeah, and boy is she jealous of me now. I told her about meeting you and she went berserk. I said, 'Renee, all we did was have coffee together!' She told me to stay away from you. Can you believe that?"

He hoped she'd told the truth about being busy and wasn't trying to ditch him because of Renee. "I'll talk to her and explain we're just friends, don't worry about it . . . ."

After hanging up with Louise, he tried Renee's cell again and this time finally heard a hello. As he anticipated, she didn't sound too pleased with him.

"Why didn't you follow us like you were supposed to?"

"Because of what happened the first time," he answered without hesitation.

"First time? What are you talking about?"

"It happened again. I relived the same thing twice, and the first time I did follow you."

An awkward silence passed before she spoke again. *"I don't believe you. You're just making all that up to keep from looking like the chicken shit you are. Guess you're just not man enough to handle more than one woman at a time, huh?"*

Letting the insult pass he told her the route to the house, what the exterior looked like, described the furniture in the living room and paused, giving her a chance to respond. When she didn't, he continued. "You, your mom, Nanatobi, and a fourth woman were wearing see-through silk robes. We were all drinking a blue concoction. And in case you doubt me still, let me tell you that the fourth woman was Ursula Winston."

A loud gasp pierced his ear. *"My god, it really* did *happen! What made you not want to follow us the second time?"*

"I'm not going to tell you. Time to change the subject."

She tried to force it out of him but he wouldn't budge. He wanted her first memory of them making love to be romantic and just the two of them, not a replay of the orgiastic lust-filled scene forever locked within his on. "I met your friend Louise Hudson in physics class and we had coffee together."

"I know, the fucking half-breed told me."

He dropped his jaw and damn near did the same with the phone. "Don't call her that! I can't believe you, Renee."

"Well that's what she is, her mom was a nigger. That bitch had better stay away from you if she knows what's good for her."

"Chill out! I asked her to have coffee with me and all we did was talk."

"Yeah, that's what she said. Why'd you ask her to have coffee with you?"

Renee obviously thought more had gone down than mere conversation over a cup of joe. "When I first tried to talk to you at school she came up and told you this guy named Danny Hill had asked her out. When I recognized her in class I wanted to meet her out of sheer curiosity, that's all. I was hoping she'd give me some insight into your twisted psyche."

"So you honestly just wanted to talk to her about me? You weren't trying to get into her pants?"

"Not at all."

"Oh my . . . guess I owe her an apology for chewing her out then."

He heaved a big sigh of relief. "You sure do."

¶

Ursula walked into his office at four-thirty. He could see the write up weighed on her heavily—she looked as if she'd just lost her best friend. "Brad, we need to talk. Could we go somewhere after work, maybe have dinner . . .?"

¶

Brad stopped by a delicatessen on his way home from the office. Retrieving an imported beer from the fridge, he twisted off the cap and took a swig before unpacking his bounty: shaved smoked turkey, thinly sliced brisket, pepper jack cheese, hot mustard, kosher pickle, an eight inch sub roll, and a plastic container of diced onions, tomatoes, and Anaheim pepper. He ran a knife through one side of the freshly baked bread, leaving the other intact for a hinge, and opened it on a plate. Then he slathered mustard on the bottom, covered the smear with generous portions of the rest of the deli items except the pickle—which he took a big bite of—closed the loaf as far as the top would go, and sat down to eat his perfectly constructed submarine sandwich.

Ursula would be coming over later. She'd wanted to treat him to dinner, any restaurant he wanted. He'd declined the bribe but told her she could come to his place after dinner if she wanted to talk. As the day wore on he'd developed mixed emotions over the reprimand and considered shredding her write up. By the end of business he had neither destroyed nor filed it which would have made it impossible to rescind. It lay harmlessly in his desk drawer.

The doorbell rang five minutes after he finished eating.

When Ursula took off her overcoat, the casual attire she wore shocked him. Then he laughed at himself. There'd been no need for her to dress up. She had immaculate taste in clothes for work or an evening out, and they'd never been together in a setting that wasn't one or the other before now. Disappointment filled a naughty cranny of his brain in which had lurked a hope that she'd try to bribe him through his penis since her attempt at his stomach had failed. However, the greater part of him felt relieved that her loose sweater and unflattering winter boots indicated otherwise. "I was about to make myself a drink. Want one?"

"Please," she said with a grateful smile as he hung up her

coat.

She sat down on the couch while he whipped out two dry martinis. He handed her one and went back to the bar. "Okay, Ursula. You wanted to talk? Start talking."

A squint twisted her exquisite nose a tad. "Won't you sit down? You make me nervous just standing there."

Eyeing the nasal masterpiece, he exaggerated a sarcastic smile to assure his underling she wouldn't find it easy to fool him. "I'm comfortable here, thank you very much. You said you wanted to talk to me, so do it."

Tears sprang to her eyes. She choked back a sob and broke down. "Oh, Brad, something awful has happened . . . I've made a huge mistake . . . You're right . . . I lied about being sick, but oh how I wish I had been instead of being with—"

"Veronica and Renee Van Cedar and Nanatobi Cain?"

Her face ignited with an astonished gape. "How did you know that?"

"I happened to be in Jesse's office when his wife called and told him she was taking Renee and Nanatobi on a three day road trip. This happened not long after you told me you'd probably miss at least three days from work. Your three day statement juxtaposed too your having lunch with Nanatobi the day before, made me suspicious. Plus you sounded like you were pretending."

The sobs halted but she remained tearful. "I've never been a good liar, and I'm even worse at pretending."

"What I don't understand is why you didn't just use your personal days. Why lie about wanting to go on a three day trip? You know Jesse would have okayed it."

"That's what I need to explain. Veronica made me lie."

He dropped his jaw. "Veronica Van Cedar made you lie about being sick instead of just having you ask her husband if you could go with her on a three day vacation?"

Responding with a nod, she vigorously rubbed her eyes

with her forefingers, which caused her sexy nose to twitch tantalizingly.

"Why?"

The action stopped and she began wiping away mascara trails with her fingertips. "Veronica has a secret life Jesse knows nothing about, and she wants to keep it that way. She knew he'd wonder why I'd been invited along since we barely know each other, and he'd ask about how the trip went, etcetera, and I might inadvertently contradict some lie Veronica told him about the excursion. And he might have become suspicious if I asked for three days off at the same time she told him she was taking Renee and Nanatobi on a road trip that would last the same length of time. It's a long sordid story, and it wasn't any road trip. I've spent the last three days in a weird house just outside Baltimore undergoing an initiation into a group called The Order of Centaurians."

"What?" His chin fell again.

She pulled a hanky from her purse and blew her nose. "You're not going to believe what I'm about to tell you—*god* this is so embarrassing. Nanatobi came to Mirror Tech last Monday for the sole purpose of getting me to have lunch with her so she could entice me into having an orgy with Ronnie Garr. I've been attracted to him since you introduced us, and when she went on and on about what a great lover he was I became intrigued by the idea and agreed to join in. Later on I found out Nanatobi had never made it with Ronnie, it was Veronica that screwed him and raved about his performance."

"Wow . . .!" he slapped his forehead. "Does Renee know about that?"

"Oh yes."

"So Veronica runs around on Jesse, who'd have thunk it? Poor guy."

Nostrils flaring with a blast of air, she crossed her arms and said, "Brad, this is very hard for me. If you don't let me tell it all now I may never be able to. This is all so fucking twisted it kills me to put it into words."

"Sorry. By all means continue."

"After work I got all gussied up for Ronnie and joined Nanatobi, Veronica, and Renee for dinner. Afterwards we took Veronica's car and drove to a grocery store where he works. I waited in the car while they went inside to coax him into following us to that house I told you about. Well, he followed us out of the parking lot all right but turned the opposite direction from the way we went. Veronica said she wanted to show me the house in the country anyway. After we got there she made drinks for all of us, and only after I was totally intoxicated did she tell me it was a potion created by her mother. But before confessing that, she and Nanatobi . . . ."

"She and Nanatobi what?"

The angst on Ursula's face deepened. "Listen, Brad, I don't like women—let me make that clear—but Veronica managed to seduce me because I was under the influence of that potion. Nanatobi had a lot to do with it too, and later Renee joined in. Anyway, there was an orgy after all, only Ronnie didn't star in it, I did. That potion enhances sexual pleasure while at the same time making you unimaginably horny. It's impossible to adequately describe its effects—it's unbelievable. Anyway, I'd never had sex with a woman before that night. But for the next three days that followed I can't tell you how many times I did with Veronica, Nanatobi, and Renee—sometimes one at a time, sometimes two at a time, sometimes all of them."

"Wow." The exclamation carried little volume because he'd almost swallowed his tongue.

She downed the rest of her martini and heaved a pungent sigh. "Now that I've managed to confess that, I'll tell you how I became a member of The Order of Centaurians . . . ."

Ursula's shocking sex-laden occult tale held him absolutely spellbound. The fact that it involved Nanatobi made it all the more astounding. She finished with a plea for him to take her word at face value, apparently thinking there was no way he would. "I believe you and not to worry. Your write up is still in my desk, I'll shred it tomorrow. I didn't tell anyone I thought you were playing hooky."

"Oh thank you, Brad!" She vaulted from the couch and almost suffocated him with a grateful hug. "I'm surprised you believe what I just told you. I wouldn't believe it if anyone had told me."

Pulling away, he took a deep breath. "I've got something to tell you that *you're* going to find very hard to believe. It not only also involves Ronnie Garr and Nanatobi Cain, but yours truly as well."

He told her everything, including how Ronnie had read his mind and saw the fantasy he'd had about Renee and Nanatobi—an extremely censured version of it that didn't incorporate his actions. She'd appeared skeptical early on and the expression only intensified by the time he concluded.

"Brad, that's a little—"

"Far fetched, out there, over the top, looney tunie? Whatever cliché you want to use, it's true nonetheless. Just ask Ronnie and Nanatobi . . . ."

¶

Ronnie tossed his coat on the recliner and started for the kitchen to grab a beer but the phone rang before he could manage it. He angrily reached for the receiver. *Whatever happened to not calling after ten?*

He'd expected it to be Nanatobi since telephone courtesy seemed to be an alien concept with her, but to his surprise it was Brad Barron asking him to come over because he needed his help. "Why do you need my help? Man, I just got home from work."

"I'll explain everything after you get here."

¶

"Can I get you anything?" said Brad while hanging up his coat.

"Yeah, I'll take a beer if you've got one."

"Aren't you going to say hello, Ronnie?"

He cut his eyes towards Ursula Winston, sitting on the couch holding a martini. Recalling her breathtaking nakedness marred by a tattoo—the way her large breasts bounced while her pouting lips slid up and down his cock, and so erotically waggled in rhythm to her climactic screams when Nanatobi and Veronica assaulted her groin—it felt odd to see her fully clothed and breathing normally. "Hello."

Brad handed him a sixteen ounce bottle with the name engraved in fancy silver lettering. He'd never heard of the brand, had no idea how to pronounce it, but after taking a swig he wouldn't shell out any of his hard earned cash for a six pack of it. "Okay, what do you need my help for?"

Briskly rubbing his hands together, Brad nodded towards the dishwater blonde. "Ursula and I have been discussing what's been happening with you, Nanatobi, and me since the night of the blackout. She doesn't believe me."

Stupefied with shock and anger, Ronnie leered at him—so enraged his free hand knotted into a fist as the other threatened to crush the bottle. "What kind of idiot are you? Why the fuck did you tell *her*, dumbass?"

"B-Because of what she's gone through the last few days, Nanatobi was involved!" Brad yelped it from behind crossed forearms while fearfully stepping back.

A cold blast of regret instantly cooled his temper, and he

barely managed to keep a straight face. This was awkward enough without adding insult to injury by laughing at the poor guy. "Relax, man, I'm not gonna deck you."

"I thought for sure you were, you looked so pissed." Brad's tan began seeping back into his relieved mug, no longer protected by arms that now gestured to convey gratitude. "I've only been in one fight in my life and that was only because I couldn't run fast enough to get away."

"Sorry I blew, but you really freaked me out." He felt horrible about it, knowing how embarrassed Brad must be to have Ursula witness his lack of moxy. "How much have you told her?"

"Everything. And what she has the hardest time believing is that you actually relived the same thing twice."

"Oh boy . . ." he sucked down some beer.

"You need to hear her story, Ronnie. But first please help me convince her I'm telling the truth."

He turned to Ursula. "It all really happened just like Brad said."

"So tell me about it." Her tone was flat and patronizing.

"Look, I don't care if you believe me or not, and I'm tired. So if there's nothing else you guys need me for, I'll be heading back home."

"At least hear what happened to her before you leave," pled Brad.

Ronnie took another pull from the bottle and wiped his mouth. "Since it involves Nanatobi I can pretty much give you a partial synopsis. Tell me, Ursula, did Veronica Van Cedar drive you, Renee, and Nanatobi Cain to a house in the country last Monday night?"

"Yes."

"I was supposed to follow Veronica out there but I didn't. I don't know if you were expecting me to, but the other three sure were."

A hint of arousal attached itself to the blonde's demeanor. "I was, and must confess I was quite disappointed when you didn't."

"Oh but I did follow you guys out there the first time, but the second time—and that's the only one you'll recall—I didn't. You see, I relived that time sequence twice. And while I was there you were all wearing sheer white robes which you soon took off." He gave her a devious grin. "You have a red heart tattooed just above a certain part of your anatomy. Rather tasteless if you ask me."

Ursula wheezed and had a coughing fit. She'd been taking a drink when he mentioned the tattoo. Brad ran over and repeatedly slapped her on the back to help dislodge the blockage. When the coughs finally subsided she harshly cleared her throat and choked out: "How in fucking hell were you able to do that, Ronnie?"

"All I can say with any certainty is nothing like that ever happened to me until after that long blackout on January sixth." He told her everything except for her coworker's fantasy, filling in the blanks that Brad didn't know. Each narrated episode seemed to leave Ursula more unsettled, as if his words sucked energy from her like a vampire draining its victim of blood.

When he finished she asked Brad for another drink, voice weak and tremulous, then unsteadily rose from the couch. "Can I tell you what happened to me now, or have you already read my mind?"

This time he offered a friendly smile. "No, I haven't read your mind, nor can I. Whatever this thing is, it only works when someone's really passionate about whatever they're thinking. So go ahead and tell me."

She waited until receiving her martini, turned it up twice, and covered her mouth to catch a burp. The alcohol appeared to help, her eyes were no longer gaping as if she stood on a hanging platform watching her executioner climb the steps.

"I'm no lesbian, Ronnie, but Veronica and Nanatobi seduced me while I was under the influence of an extremely powerful aphrodisiac invented by Veronica's mother. After an orgy that included Renee, I became a member of their secret club known as The Order of Centaurians. Veronica calls it a religion, and it was founded by her mother because of a vivid dream she had when Veronica was a child.

"She dreamed a centaur told her that because she'd been born a Sagittarius, was extremely beautiful, had a superior intellect and many talents, that she'd been chosen as a portal for him to work through. He gave her a sign to prove he was the supreme being and had chosen her to be his prophetess. The day that sign came to pass she dreamed about the centaur again and he gave her detailed instructions to have a special room constructed—a holy of holies for The Order of Centaurians if you will—and revealed to her how to make that aphrodisiac I spoke of. Veronica calls it a potion, and I have to admit it's effects *are* otherworldly, it so greatly intensifies sexual pleasure. Anyway, obeying a strict command of the centaur Veronica's mother enticed her two older sisters to drink it and once they were under its influence, told them they'd been chosen to help her. They became the first members but The Order of Centaurians didn't become official until Veronica was inducted when she had her first period.

"In order to become a member I had to give myself to the centaur by saying a prayer of dedication Veronica recited to me line by line. Afterwards I had to take a sacred vow that I would keep the Centaurian code—that I would never tell anyone about the order, never attempt to have sex or even flirt with any member without all members being present, never miss an official meeting, and make sure I never contracted any form of venereal disease. And then . . . well, the next three days are pretty much an orgiastic blur in my memory.

"Veronica's mother was obviously a nutcase because the order is about nothing but sex. I don't believe in the centaur, of course, and didn't want to say that prayer, but Veronica had me so fucking curious about Centaurianism I went along. She wouldn't tell me the details about it until I became a member. The membership is limited to four because of the four elements associated with the signs of the zodiac—earth, air, water, and fire. Renee and Nanatobi replaced Veronica's two deceased aunts. I became her mother's replacement.

"Veronica told me that Centaurianism on rare occasions requires a man for all the members to gratify themselves with. Such men can't know what the order is really about and are led to believe they're merely participating in a witch's ritualistic orgy. She plans on you being the next one at bat. According to Veronica, her mother received a stern warning from the centaur that every member would incur his wrath if any man were to learn the truth about Centaurianism. And there you have it."

At last he knew the facts. Though she called herself a Centaurian, Veronica was still a damn witch. The group worshiped a mythical being and used a potion, so to him their order definitely qualified as a form of witchcraft. Veronica had lied to him at the motel about being led to the group by her best friend. She'd grown up in the cult founded by her mother. They weren't composed of twelve women in need of a thirteenth, but three requiring a fourth, and Ursula had been duped into filling that vacancy.

A promise meant something to him and he was reluctant to break one made to anyone, much less the woman of his dreams. He'd planned on talking to Charley's cousin about witchcraft in general without mentioning Renee and the strange faction she belonged to, hoping he'd be able to tell him how to pull someone out of it. Now he had a way to give the specifics about it without breaking his word. Ursula could tell Arnon everything. That way he could look Renee straight in the eye and swear he'd kept her confidence. He took a gulp of lame-tasting beer and gazed sympathetically at the newest victim of Veronica's cunning. "Do you have any plans for tomorrow night?"

¶

"Dammit, Ronnie, pick up the fucking phone!" Nanatobi shouted in her mind after the eleventh ring. It was midnight so he couldn't be at work, and she knew he hadn't gone somewhere with Renee because they'd talked earlier and she'd said Veronica wanted her to spend the evening at home for some quality family time.

She called him again at twelve-fifteen, twelve-thirty, twelve forty-five, and one o'clock but he still didn't answer. She'd wanted to have phone sex with him but he either wasn't there or had been so sound asleep that even a telephone ringing off the hook couldn't wake him.

Frustrated, she finally gave up and crawled beneath the covers. Too aroused to sleep, she tumultuously besieged herself with both hands until loudly sighing his name. Now relaxed, she felt the first hints of approaching slumber dissipate when a tingling sensation traversed her skin.

She was hovering beneath the ceiling of Renee's parents' bedroom. Jesse lay on his back with Renee and Veronica taking turns sucking his dick. She couldn't believe the transaction taking place below. They weren't allowed to so much as give each other a sexy look without every member being present, and Jesse wasn't supposed to even know anything about such activity, much less be a participant.

Oh this is beyond atrocious—they're breaking the code!

While angrily observing their debauchery she realized Jesse seemed unaware of what was happening. He lay like a corpse with his hands limply resting on his chest. Not once did he so much as twitch a finger.

Nanatobi abruptly opened her eyes. She'd returned to her body.

Grabbing her diary she hastily wrote out the scene she'd just witnessed, concluding with: *There's no way a man could just lie there like that without somehow reacting to it. They must have drugged him so he wouldn't know they were using him for sex. But why were they using him???????*

¶

Ronnie helped Brad up from the floor. Ursula had panicked, but having been rudely educated about it when Nanatobi passed out at his apartment, he'd told her to calm down, that Brad had left his body and would wake up any second. The astral traveler had been standing at the bar and his left arm took the brunt of the fall when his lifeless form landed sideways on the carpet.

Rubbing his dinged elbow, Brad inhaled a deep breath and blew out an anxious sigh. "Nanatobi's upset."

"You saw her this time?"

"No, Ronnie, I didn't see her—just somehow felt it while I was in her room. I was also aware she'd gone astral from her bed, but the canopy prevented me from seeing her body. This trip was different. I've never sensed her emotions before."

FIFTEEN

Since it would be his first meeting with Arnon Green, Ronnie decided not to bring Ursula after all. He needed to test the waters first, see what the guy was all about. His own saga would be hard enough to believe, so he thought it best to do it in stages. If all went well he'd bring her next time, assuming there would be one.

Charley picked him up at his apartment and stopped at Betty's Café for some takeout coffee. They ran into Louise.

"So what are you two up to?" she asked while forking off a bite of chocolate cake.

"Stopped by to fetch some coffee for the road," said Charley. "We're on our way to see Arnon."

Her brows rose. "Ronnie knows Arnon?"

"Um, no, I'm taking him out to the farm to introduce the two of them."

"Oh yeah? Mind if I join you?"

"Sorry, Louise," Ronnie answered for Charley, who'd uneasily cut his eyes to him. He didn't want Louise to know anything about the weird events he, Nanatobi, and Brad had been experiencing. "Charley told me Arnon's a very spiritual man and I asked to talk with him about a private matter I'm pretty sensitive about. Otherwise I'd love for you to."

¶

A big man like Charley, Arnon had to be at least six-seven. He wore faded overalls, a plaid flannel shirt with sleeves rolled up to the elbows, and lace-up work boots. As he shook the snowy-haired black man's hand, Ronnie intuitively knew he'd done the right thing in coming. The guy possessed the same intangible comforting quality as Charley, making him feel totally at ease. His bearded face and bright eyes, twinkling behind a pair of gold wire-frames, reeked of experience and wisdom, while the calluses on the gnarly hand that shook his testified he was no stranger to hard labor.

Arnon led them to his kitchen. "So how is it you hooked up with this negro?"

Charley laughed while taking a seat at the table. Stifling one, Ronnie joined him and relayed how they'd met.

"Well I'll be. If even an uppity Baltimore nigger can be a Good Samaritan, there may yet be hope for mankind."

Unable to hold back this time, he chuckled along with Charley who said, "You gonna insult me all night or bring me some damn coffee?"

"Hmm, let me think on that," sniggered Arnon. "How do you take yours, Ronnie?"

"Black."

He served them and sat down with his cup. "Charley tells me you've had some oddities come over you of late. Why don't you tell me all about it. Take your time, and make sure you neither exaggerate nor play down anything. If I can be of any help, I can only help you to the extent of your honesty."

¶

Nanatobi had called Brad earlier in the day to verify he'd left his body as she had hers.

"Yeah, it happened again," he'd said, *"and while I was in your bedroom I had the strangest feeling you were upset about something."*

"That's the understatement of the century."

"What got you so upset?"

"I don't want to discuss it," she'd firmly replied.

He'd then informed her that Ursula had spilled her guts about Centaurianism. Brad in turn had told the blonde tattletale of their astral trips and Ronnie's strange abilities. Ursula hadn't believed him, so he'd asked Ronnie over to verify it, and they'd both been at his apartment when he'd gone astral.

Instead of going ballistic over the code of silence being broken like she'd have done if not being aware of Veronica's and Renee's treachery, she had formulated a plan and suggested he invite Ronnie and Ursula to his place so the four of them could brainstorm. Brad had said Ronnie wouldn't be able to come because he'd taken a trip with the man who saw the UFO on radar the night of the blackout. Though very disappointed to hear that, she'd told him to have Ursula over anyway and the three of them would try to find a logical explanation for their out of body experiences and Ronnie's peculiar abilities. When he'd then asked if she wanted Renee to come as well, she'd forced herself to remain calm and replied, "You don't want that, Brad. Renee can never know Ursula broke her Centaurian vow of silence because she might tell Veronica and all hell would break loose."

The tall blonde had been very nervous at first, obviously expecting a severe tongue lashing for telling Brad about The Order of Centaurians.

"No hard feelings on my part," she'd assured Ursula, "but I strongly advise you not to say anything to Renee or Veronica about breaking the vow. You don't want to be the object of Veronica Van Cedar's wrath, believe me."

They'd been conversing less than ten minutes, sipping alcohol, not yet discussing possible theories that might account for all that had been going on.

Brad made the first attempt at analyzation. "I have the feeling that if I could have remained in your room just a little while longer, I would have known what upset you."

She gouged him with a sharp stare. "I'd have been devastated if you'd learned what displeased me."

The troubled look on his face amused her, for little did he know how much he would enjoy this evening as a direct result of what had caused her such distress. Hidden within her purse were some tiny pills. When the opportunity presented itself she'd medicate his and Ursula's drinks, then the games would begin. What a shame Ronnie wasn't present.

¶

"Nanatobi is out for the evening," he informed Renee, who'd phoned.

"Where did she go, did she say?"

His employer being within earshot, Jim markedly cleared his throat.

"Oh I get it. She's supposed to be with me, and Taylor can hear you, right?"

"Very good, ma'am. Thank you for asking."

"Okay, I'll find her. Bye."

He deleted the number from the Caller ID.

"Who was that?" asked Taylor from his easy chair.

"Betty Solomon, Sir, calling for Nanatobi."

"What was very good?"

"Sir?"

An impatient frown pounced upon Taylor's face. "You said *Very good, ma'am, thank you for asking.*"

"Oh that. Miss Solomon kindly asked how I was doing."

¶

A phone call interrupted their discussion and Brad went to answer it. When Nanatobi heard him say "Oh hi, Renee" she hurried across the room and yanked the receiver away from him. Renee must have been looking for her and that meant her cell was on the blink again or she'd have called it. She hoped the bitch hadn't gotten her in trouble with Taylor. When she didn't want the meddlesome grouch to know her whereabouts she always used Renee as an alibi, something she shouldn't have done this time since the slut hadn't been informed of it because she'd intended not to speak to her until exposing her duplicity face to face. Fighting back fury, she took a deep breath, sighed it out slowly, and brought the phone to her ear. "Hello, Renee."

"Nan, why didn't you tell me you were going to Brad's tonight? He better not be having a party and invited you without inviting me!"

Her cheeks burned as the vexation of betrayal shot flames of wrath throughout her insides. She wanted to scream at the unfaithful whore but reeled in her emotions enough to sound calm. "Um, he asked me over for a drink. Sort of like a date, you know."

"Oh. Well I called your house and asked for you when I couldn't get you on your cell, but Jim covered your butt."

"Good . . ." she clinched her eyes shut and gritted her teeth.

"I guess I shouldn't come over then if it's a date and all, huh?"

"Um, well we decided we should get to know each other a little better—the metaphysical connection and all that— dissect the out of body thing, you know."

Renee heaved a sigh. *"Damn it will be a boring Saturday. Ronnie told me he was going to a farm with a new friend, so he's not home. Oh well, guess I'll just hang out with Mom and Dad for the evening."*

YOU FUCKING WHORE! she screamed in her mind before vocalizing, "Okay well, I'll let you go then . . . ."

Brad grinned as she hung up. "So we're having a date, huh?"

She glared at him. "Don't press your luck, stud."

¶

Ronnie told the big farmer about what had been happening to him, Nanatobi, and Brad, but didn't mention witchcraft. He also kept mum about following Veronica's BMW to that house in the country. "None of us have ever experienced anything abnormal before so I think what's happening is connected to whatever caused a power failure that affected the whole city of Baltimore."

"It happened the same night I saw that weird blip on the radar I told you about," said Charley.

Arnon refilled their cups and sat back down. "Okay, Ronnie, before I say my piece I need to make sure I'm tuned in right. You were raised by a single parent—your mama—and never saw your father because he died before you were born on a cold morning somewhere in the rocky mountains. You wound up in Baltimore because of a stint in the military and your innards have been orbiting around a certain pretty girl since the day you first laid eyes on her. Am I wrong?"

"No, sir, you're dead right." Neither the astral projections of Nanatobi and Brad nor the paranormal events he'd lived through amazed him like what he'd just heard. Charley hadn't exaggerated. This man had *The Sight* all right.

"I believe your story to be true and factual," Arnon continued, "but I sense there's something you're wanting to tell me but are afraid to—the existence of a great evil you became aware of because of a sexual sin you committed that you're real ashamed of. That evil involves a group of women and you want to fight it because the pretty girl I mentioned earlier is tangled up in it. You hope to make her your wife. Am I wrong?"

"No, sir, you hit the nail square on the head again."

"Don't be afraid, son . . ." Arnon leaned back and folded his massive hands across his stomach. "Go ahead and tell me all about it."

Dazed by the man's special gift, he proceeded cautiously so as not to inadvertently break the promise he'd made to Renee. "There's a woman I'd like you to meet who can give more specific details about the evil you spoke of, but the sin I committed was adultery." He cleared his throat, deeply ashamed of what he had to say next. "And the woman I hope to marry is the daughter of the woman I slept with."

He noticed Charley's brows shoot up at his confession, but the calm expression on his cousin's face never wavered. "The mother of the woman you hoped to marry seduced you. Am I wrong?"

"No, sir, but I'm just as guilty. I could have backed off but didn't. I um, wanted it to happen. My only defense is I thought at the time that the woman I hope to marry didn't want me."

Arnon pursed his lips and quickly parted them, making a popping sound. "It's impossible but that offenses must come, but woe to them through whom they come. A fountain of offenses springs forth from this woman, but she too can be saved if she repents and takes the Lord into her heart. The devil holds her in the palm of his hand but she's too wise in her own conceit to be aware of it. The woman you spoke of who leaves her body—Nanobie I believe you said her name was—is she the one you hope to marry?"

"No, sir. And her name is Nanatobi. She's Renee's best friend."

"Nanatobi, okay. So Renee's the one you want?"

"Yes, sir." He'd tried to keep from mentioning Renee by name but it had slipped out.

"Nanatobi's part of the evil too. Am I wrong?"

"No, sir."

"What about the man who always leaves his body when she leaves hers? Brad I believe you said his name was. Is he part of the evil?"

"No, sir."

"Hmm . . ."Arnon formed a steeple with his long index fingers and tapped them against his mouth for several moments. "Tell me all you know about Nanatobi and Brad besides their out of body dreams."

A snicker left Charley when Arnon said *out of body dreams.*

Ronnie barely held one in, due more to the infectious nature of Charley's laugh rather than the odd phrasing. "Nanatobi's a beautiful freckled redhead. She's a college senior and lives with her uncle Taylor Cain. *The* Taylor Cain. She's intelligent and aggressively goes after what she wants—pretty much your typical spoiled rich brat—but seems to be sincere otherwise. I'll let Charley tell you about Brad since he knows him better than I do."

"Brad's a sissified yuppie," Charley snorted, "but he's a great guy—real honest and thoughtful, mannerly to a fault. He's a swinging bachelor, I guess, because I've never known him to have a steady girlfriend and he likes to throw parties at his place. He's got a high-paying job at a software company and dresses and drives to show it—trades his car in for a new one every year. I met him two years ago after I moved out of the house when Loretta and I split. His apartment's next to mine. He's lived there since the place was built and has a ten year lease with a fixed rate. The lucky dog pays about half the rent I do. If memory serves he's got about three years before his lease expires, and he plans to buy a house when it does. That's about all I can tell you."

Arnon raised his cup and held it at his chin. "Doesn't sound like Brad has any insight that could be helpful on this matter, but I need to meet Nanatobi. Can you bring her out here, Ronnie? I guess I could drive to Baltimore, but man I'd hate to do that."

Charley winked at him. "He gets claustrophobia in city traffic, least that's what he started claiming a good while back. Myself, I think the negro just don't like to drive."

"Guilty as charged," chuckled Arnon. "How soon can you bring her out here, Ronnie? Assuming she's willing to come that is."

"Probably next weekend. We could leave after I get off work Saturday. I'd also like to bring the woman I told you about. She can tell you more about the evil in case Nanatobi refuses to open up about it."

"Fine. Just give me a call and let me know when to expect you."

¶

Brad opened his eyes to see Ursula standing over him clutching her hair, asking if he was okay.

"Yeah, I'm okay." He tried to wipe the smirk off his face but couldn't. "How long were we gone?"

"Less than two minutes, I'd guess. My god, Brad, what if this happens when one of you is behind the wheel? Nanatobi fell over on my lap while we were sitting on the couch but you're lucky you didn't hit the floor face first . . . ."

As Ursula continued voicing her concerns he eyed Nanatobi. A deep frown revealed that she too was trying to reason it all out. Their astral selves had intertwined. The two of them had merged into one entity for a brief moment. He had no idea where they'd floated off to when the oneness occurred because unlike the other times, he hadn't been able to see.

Ursula finally gave her mouth a rest and he got up from the floor. "I couldn't see anything this time, could you?"

Still pensive, Nanatobi slowly shook her head.

"I wonder if that happened because we were in the same room when we left our bodies?"

"What are you talking about, Brad?" asked Ursula.

"This time was totally different." He continued eyeing the dazzling redhead who appeared quite taken aback by what they'd shared. "I don't know where I went but Nanatobi was there and we somehow meshed into each other. We became one essence, that's about the only way I can explain it."

The trembling smile Nanatobi acquired when he said it, made his heart leap and his penis stretch.

¶

They drove through the cold Maryland night, heading back to Baltimore. Ronnie stared blankly through the windshield, not paying attention to anything visual because his thoughts were intensely focused on Arnon. He'd never had a brush with anything supernatural until the day after all the lights went out in Baltimore, but that farmer had dealt with it his whole life. At the conclusion of their visit Arnon had told him not to fear "the oddities" he'd been experiencing because God in His infinite wisdom had either bestowed those abilities or was allowing them to happen for a reason.

"So what did you think of the brother?"

"He's amazing, Charley . . . ."

¶

The pills were still in her purse and would remain there. After leaving her body a short while ago Nanatobi no longer had the desire to violate the Centaurian code by enticing Ursula into a threesome with Brad. And it wasn't from having second thoughts about being disloyal to those two bitches over at Wine's Gate, who were probably in the very act of once more desecrating the rule they claimed to hold so precious and dear. She simply wasn't about to share Brad Barron with Ursula Winston or anyone else.

SIXTEEN

They left Monday's physics class in his Thunderbird and found Betty's Café packed, so he asked Louise if she wanted to have coffee at his place instead.

She gave him a sly grin from the passenger's seat. "Come into my parlor, said the spider to the fly. Are you trying to bait me to your lair with coffee? It'll take something a little more worthwhile."

Surprised by her reluctance, Ronnie slowed down and started to turn into Betty's parking lot, explaining he'd only made the suggestion because he lived nearby.

"I was only teasing, silly. By all means let's go to your place."

¶

Resting her head in one hand while doodling in a spiral notebook with the other, Nanatobi pretended to take notes as her civics professor droned. At some point she'd started drawing little hearts and had formed Brad's name with them. What they'd shared two days ago when their astral states merged was indescribable. Their thoughts, memories, hopes, fears, dreams, and fantasies had intertwined. They'd caught each other in flagrante delicto as all their decadent passions and secret desires melded into absolute singularity.

She'd been too embarrassed to look at him at first. He had explored her very soul, and though neither could recall the contents of each other's invaded psyches, the memory of that remarkable intrusion remained. Mere words couldn't explain the unequivocal intimacy that had transpired between the two of them. There could be no other man for her just as no other woman would suffice for him. Some cosmic force, whether benevolent or malevolent—she didn't give a damn which—

had bestowed upon them the gift of absolute homogeneity, if only for a few brief seconds.

Nanatobi had never kidded herself about her sexuality. Since she'd first explored her vagina as a child and found she could produce pleasurable sensations by touching, rubbing, and poking, she'd been blatantly wanton. She suffered none of the inhibitions or moral misgivings that afflicted most of her peers, and after first attaining orgasm her erotic appetites had grown to nymphomaniacal proportions. But what happened with Brad Saturday night went beyond sex.

When Taylor came home from church yesterday she'd joined him for lunch and made a request that had thoroughly shocked the old boy, which hadn't surprise her in the least. He'd given his permission but she hadn't extended the invitation yet. Giggling within, she drew a big heart and wrote *Nanatobi loves Brad* inside it.

¶

"So how did it go with Arnon Saturday?" Louise asked over a cup of coffee, sitting across from him at his kitchen table.

"Awesome. He's the most remarkable man I've ever met."

"Listen," she said cautiously, "he's a nice guy who means well but he's very eccentric, Ronnie. Don't take him seriously. My cousins and I make fun of the old fool."

He reared his head back with shock. "Why? Don't you know how special he is, what supernatural insight he has? The man's a modern day prophet."

She laughed. "That's what I call him—The Prophet."

"Then why do you make fun of him?"

"Because he's not one, that's why. He has this round building he built way back when and sometimes locks himself up in it for days on end to fast and pray. Occasionally, due to a chemical imbalance brought on by lack of food I'm sure, he hallucinates and mistakenly thinks he's receiving a vision from God."

Her unbelief baffled him. "I can't believe I'm hearing this. Arnon may be eccentric as you say, but he's definitely got a gift. Charley called it *The Sight.*"

"What makes you think so?"

"He told me about some things going on in my life that he couldn't have known otherwise, that's why."

"Such as?"

"Never mind, it's way too personal."

"How convenient." Her pretty brown eyes gleamed with skepticism.

"I can tell you he knew my dad died before I was born and my mom raised me as a single parent."

A knowing smile quickly manifested. "I never said Arnon wasn't intuitive, he has a very discerning spirit, but so do a lot of dedicated Christians. That doesn't make them prophets. You look like a guy that's had to fend for himself without a father's guidance, that's what Arnon picked up on. He happened to guess right, your dad died. But your father could have abandoned your mom as well, and if he had, you wouldn't be so impressed with Arnon."

"Then how did he know where I was born?" he challenged.

"Did he state the specific town and state or merely a region of the country?"

It bugged him that he couldn't answer yes to the first part of her question but that didn't dilute his opinion of the man. "He said I was born in the rocky mountains."

The smile widened. "Ronnie, if I didn't already know where you were raised, I'd have guessed Colorado or Wyoming because of your accent. The rocky mountains run through both."

Her assumption irritated him—it seemed unlikely she'd

have narrowed it down to only those two states. His accent wouldn't have been noticeably different if he'd hailed from Utah, Arizona, Nebraska, or Kansas. Nonetheless he didn't want their disagreement to escalate into a full-scale argument so he didn't voice it. "Think what you want, but I know what I know. Arnon Green is a very special man. He has *The Sight* just like Charley says."

She brushed a crop of curls off her shoulder. "Okay, here's how the legend goes. Or did Charley tell you already?"

"Legend about Arnon?"

"Yeah. He was born at seven minutes after seven o'clock on July seventh. Get it? The seventh day of the seventh month. And he's supposed to be the seventh son of a seventh son of a seventh son."

"Really?" He laughed with amazement. "How cool is that?"

"Don't be too impressed. While it's true he was born on July seventh and has six older brothers, he isn't the seventh son of a seventh son. Arnon's father, who made up the story, was an only child which makes it rather difficult for him to have been the seventh male to come along, wouldn't you say?"

The cute expression she wore when posing the question made him chuckle. "Why did he make that up?"

She shrugged. "To look superior, I guess. The elder members of the Hudson and Green families are a very superstitious bunch. When Arnon came into the world at seven after seven on the seventh day of the seventh month and happened to be the seventh male child born, he was anointed by my relatives as someone special from that moment on because they believed the man who sired him was also a seventh son born to a seventh son.

"Now I don't blame Arnon. He's never made a big deal of it and always pooh-poohs it anytime it gets brought up in his presence. I'm the only one besides one other member of my family that knows it's a lie. My grandmother found out the truth after Arnon's father passed away. Up until then she believed it too. Most of the family treasures Arnon's ties with the number seven and they really believe the old fool has *The Sight.* She threatened me with my life if I ever told any of them the truth. She's content to let them believe the legend."

None of what she said affected his faith in Arnon. The remarkable farmer could have been sired by the first born son of a nanny goat for all he cared. "Why did she tell you if she wanted to keep it a secret?"

Louise took a sip of coffee and sighed. "I don't know. I've always wondered about that myself . . . ."

¶

Brad shredded Ursula's write up first thing after he got to work and gave her a big grin when she walked in a few minutes early. The tall blonde returned his smile, causing the nostrils to flare on her majestic nose.

They were so busy the morning flew by. When lunchtime arrived he considered his restaurant choices while reaching for the ringing phone. It figured to be Ursula. Though he'd turned down her dinner invitation on Friday, he'd let her spring for Monday's lunch.

"Hello?"

"Brad? It's Nanatobi."

His heart lurched as he involuntarily rose to his feet. "Hey, what a pleasant surprise!"

"Listen, if you don't have any plans for the evening I'd like to invite you to my house for dinner."

Currents of elation surged through him. She *had* felt it too, the dinner invitation confirmed it. They'd bonded in a manner that couldn't be defined by rational explanation. He'd watched her closely that evening after they returned to their bodies, looking for the slightest hint she wanted him as badly as he did her. The only signal he'd picked up was that quavering smile she'd worn, and he'd lacked the courage to find out if it meant she felt the same.

Something rudely sprang to mind—the only thing besides his height that kept him from being a spectacular male specimen. Anxiety ransacked the raw excitement of knowing she had her sights set on him. There was no way to keep her from eventually finding out about it. She had to know he wasn't really five-ten because of his footwear—but how would she react upon discovering his other flaw?

"Brad? Are you there?"

Hooking a finger in his collar which seemed to have instantly shrunk a size, he nervously slid it back and forth behind the knot of his tie. "Yeah, sorry. Your invitation surprised me and I was a little taken aback."

"Well?"

"Um, yes of course, I'd love to."

"We dress for dinner, so be sure to wear your very best suit. I want my uncle to like you."

¶

Charley's shift started at three. An hour had yet to pass on his first day back from vacation and his nerves were already on edge. A cargo plane experiencing altimeter problems had just made it safely to the runway, but damn near gave him a heart attack.

An oncoming from Boston needed to get into the circular arc in the air space above BWI to await its turn at descending in intervals each time another plane landed. "Delta fifty-one, adjust altitude to forty-one thousand feet." His voice sounded calm but he felt anything but.

"Roger, Baltimore . . . ."

¶

Arnon slowly rocked back and forth in his chair, thinking about Ronnie Garr and the saga he'd been told last Saturday night. Besides the *knowing* that had come over him about the sin involving some women and Ronnie, he'd simultaneously received a vision. He hadn't shared it—not from fear the young man wouldn't believe him—he hadn't had the heart. The revelation had been short, clear, and simple. Ronnie stood by an open casket within which lay the corpse of a beautiful young lady. Grief stricken, tears streaming down his face, he kept crying out, "Why, Renee?" This had occurred between the first part of Ronnie's tale and the second. The poor boy hadn't said the name Renee in real life until after the vision. Unfortunately that verified it came from on high and Arnon felt in his spirit its fulfillment didn't lie far ahead.

¶

Brad had never been so nervous in his life. A servant had been waiting for him at the gates, the very ones he'd never dreamed would open to grant him entrance onto the Cain estate. Now a British butler dressed in tails was leading him into an opulent dining room with a vaulted ceiling of stained glass held in place by arching redwood beams from which hung crystal chandeliers. Objets d'art lined the walls, and antique credenzas supported lavish display cabinets filled with artifacts ranging from ancient Egypt to nineteenth century weaponry. At the end of an exquisite Louis XIV dining table, sat the legendary Taylor Cain. The butler pulled out the first chair to the billionaire's left and beckoned him to be seated, across from Nanatobi, wearing a gorgeous red evening gown.

She looked at the stern-faced lord of the manor and smiled sweetly. "Uncle Taylor, this is Brad Barron, the young man I told you about."

"It's an honor to meet you, sir." He started to extend his hand but froze when her uncle merely gave a silent nod of acknowledgment.

"Brad works at Mirror Tech."

The maid tucked a napkin in Taylor's collar and filled their soup bowls. Brad unfolded his and placed it on his lap, following Nanatobi's lead. He wanted to dampen his dry throat with water or wine, both of which sat before him in crystal glasses, but wasn't sure of proper formal dining etiquette other than knowing the host was supposed to begin supping first. So he waited.

Taylor picked up the spoon lying at the outside end of his silverware row and started in on the soup. Brad mimicked the tycoon, sipping the delectable consommé from the edge of the engraved sterling silver implement.

"Did I tell you Renee's dad is Brad's boss, Uncle Taylor?"

He glowered at her. "What's with the uncle all of a sudden? You haven't called me that since you were twelve."

Her smile grew all the more engaging. "Can't a niece be in an affectionate mood for her uncle once in a while? By the way, I love your beard now that you've shortened it a smidgen." She reached out and touched the neatly groomed whiskers on the mogul's cheek.

The elder Cain's scowl softened into an expression that seemed hopeful yet cautious.

"I'm not blowing sunshine, Uncle Taylor, I mean it."

Like a layer of invisible ice, the air of inapproachability surrounding the most powerful man in Baltimore melted instantly away as an appreciative grin appeared. "Why thank you, young lady. Exactly what does your young man do at

Mirror Tech?"

Nanatobi giggled. "Um, you wanna take this one, Bradley?"

Brad cleared his throat and gave account of himself. By the time the delicious dinner of standing rib roast with yorkshire pudding was over, he found himself talking business with Taylor Cain, an unimaginable event he couldn't wait to brag to Lou and everyone at the office about. Their conversation obviously didn't interest Nanatobi in the least, but she kept cheerfully adoring her uncle all the way through.

"I'm an excellent judge of character," said Taylor, "and am always looking for good people to work for me. Whatever they're paying you at Mirror Tech, I'll double it. I want you to come to work for me, Brad."

A thrill shot through him. It was the first time he'd spoken his name all evening. Taylor nodded at the butler, who immediately tended to his chair, sliding it from the table as the renowned tycoon rose. When Brad started to scoot his chair back the maid hurried over and assisted him while the butler helped Nanatobi from hers.

Giddy with headiness, he seemed to be walking on air as the three of them exited the room. "I'll give my notice in the morning, sir."

"Excellent." Taylor turned to Nanatobi. "What are the two of you planning on doing this evening?"

She gave her uncle a glittery smile. "If it's all right, I plan to change into something more comfortable, then we'd like to spend the evening at Brad's apartment listening to music."

Taylor eyed him for a long moment as if summing up his moral fiber, then turned to Nanatobi. "You young people enjoy your evening, but I expect you home by eleven. You have school tomorrow. Come sit in the parlor with me, Brad, while Nanatobi changes."

¶

Ronnie was stocking shelves at Riley's when a vision of beauty appeared in his peripheral vision. He turned to see Renee walking down the aisle. The last time he'd seen her she'd sat naked at his feet, stroking his thigh, whispering she loved him. Those magical words had catapulted him back to reality. Fearing Veronica and Nanatobi were about to show up and try to lure him to that house in the woods, he glanced warily back and forth.

She folded her arms and smiled. "Don't worry, Curly Sampson, I came alone."

"Man it's wonderful to see you, Renee! I've missed you so bad."

"Me too."

He'd been holding two cans of green beans in each hand since spotting her. He placed them on the shelf and reached into a box for four more.

"I called Louise Hudson and apologized."

"Good, I'm glad."

"How was your trip to that farm?"

"Oh it was great—" he grabbed another round of cans "—I spent the evening with a prophet."

That induced a giggle. "A prophet? Well tell me about it."

"I talked to him about what's been happening with me, Nanatobi, and Brad. I'll give you all the details some other time. Let me finish emptying these boxes and I'll see if I can get out of here early. We can go back to my place and have a beer if you'd like. I've got a piece of a twelve pack left."

Her emerald orbs twinkled with a flirtatious smirk. "Why don't I go get us something a little stronger and meet you there . . . ?"

Ronnie managed to get home by nine and found Renee

waiting in a parking space near his apartment. She got out of the Camaro holding a brown paper sack. Taking possession of it, he walked her inside and to the kitchen.

"Well look what have we here." He transferred a pint of tequila, a quart of grenadine, and a carton of orange juice from the bag to the table.

"In memory of our first date. You made tequila sunrises for me at Brad Barron's that night. Remember?"

"Oh yeah, I'll never forget." Her perfume took him back to the enchanting dance that would stay locked in his memory forever. He'd intended to tell her what Ursula had relayed at that very apartment but that would have to wait. Tonight belonged only to them and he wasn't going to let anything spoil it. "Life hasn't been the same since."

Renee held her nose. "Well one thing hasn't changed. You still use that same disgusting cologne."

"Aftershave," he elucidated with a grin. "Do you really hate Old Spice?"

"Mm hmm. But it's tolerable because of the way I feel about the man who wears it. But what I won't tolerate is you ever shaving your head again, Curly Sampson, so beware."

"No fears." He fixed them a round in juice glasses and guided her to the living room. Motioning for her to take his office chair, he lowered himself into the recliner.

Still on her feet, she took a sip and set the glass on his desk. "Don't you think it's a little warm in here?"

"Sorry, I'll turn the heat down."

"No need . . ." she started unbuttoning her blouse. "I'll just make myself a little cooler if you don't mind."

His heart threatened to burst from his chest as she came out of her clothes. The immaculate splendor of her body took his breath away, even more so than when he'd first seen it at the country house. He knew why. That setting had been tainted with evil and he'd been used as a lustful pawn in an orgy. Now it was just the two of them, each motivated by love. She stabbed her pretty fingers inside his waistband and pulled him towards the bedroom. "We have some unfinished business that's long overdue, Curly Sampson . . . ."

Renee's astounding beauty, coupled with his deep love and burning desire, produced an erection every bit as stiff as that induced by the potion. Her hot, tight, wetness felt as thrilling as before, but this time they were in his bed rather than a witch's chair, and he was on top of her. Since to Renee this was their first intimate union, he'd entered her very gently and moved slowly until she'd begun undulating her hips with frenzy. When urgent, impassioned cries started spewing from her panting lips as she writhed in orgasm, he ecstatically pumped his semen inside her.

In the same manner as she'd done in the vision, kissing his chest rather than his thigh she whispered, "I love you."

This time he had the chance to respond. "Mere words can't express how I feel about you, Renee. An army of poets, a thousand Shakespeare's couldn't come close to describing what you mean to me. I fell hard when I first saw you at Maryland and my love for you has only grown stronger since."

Her tender lips quickly found their way to his mouth. She gave him a deep kiss and sighed. "Oh, Ronnie, I've never felt this way about anybody. When I asked why you wanted to marry me, you said you weren't sure you wanted to any more. Are you still undecided?"

"Oh no, that was nothing but my injured pride talking." He caressed her left breast, reveling in the feel of her perky nipple hardening against his hand. "I've wanted to marry you since the moment I first saw you. Are you still going to refuse me?"

Joyful tears glistened in her eyes. "There's only two things I want from this crazy world, Curly Sampson—you and to bear your children. Hell no I'm not going to refuse you. I can't wait to become Mrs. Ronnie Garr."

The exhilaration of winning her heart exceeded his wildest expectations. Happiness like he'd never known seemed to hurl his inner being to the farthest reaches of the universe, making him feel as though *he* was having an out of body experience and his astral essence had actually entered heaven itself. "Man I wish we didn't have to wait until I get my doctorate to get married."

She squinted at him. "Who says we do?"

"Necessity, that's who. I'm barely able to feed myself—there's no way I could take care of you before then. Of course if I toss my goal of being a professor and try for some type of research gig after I get my bachelors in May, we could get married as soon as I land a job."

"Screw that," she spouted irately. "I don't want you to give up your goal. I graduate in May too. I'll ask Nan's uncle to give me a good job at T-Cain Corporation and I'll put your sweet ass the rest of the way through college. Taylor's always been fond of me. I'll have my degree, so I know he won't turn me down."

The thought of changing her name to Garr this coming May produced an instant hard on, it so excited him. "Are you sure you'd be willing to do that? We're talking several years before you'd be able to quit."

"Mm hmm . . ." she grasped his rigid shaft. "I want to get married the day after we graduate."

¶

Nanatobi sat on the couch sipping a glass of white wine. Brad had made himself a martini and stood nervously at the bar. "Come sit beside me, Brad, but first take off that stupid coat and tie."

It took two martinis before he finally started relaxing. Seeing she'd have to make the first move or the evening would be wasted, she took his drink from him, placed it on the coffee table beside her wine, and kissed him. When he returned her kiss she took his hand and put it on her breast. He moaned and immediately started squeezing. Relishing his massaging fingers, she slipped her hand inside his pants. Brad wasn't very big despite being hard as a rock. The moment she started fondling him he ejaculated.

¶

Charley belted back two Johnny Blacks at the bar and headed for home. When he got there Brad Barron was sitting cross legged in front of the door holding a bottle of scotch— drunk and looking real troubled. "Brad, what are you doing out so late on a Monday?"

"G-Got a minute, Charley?"

He summoned a supportive grin. "Sure."

"This is ex-extremely embarrassing, b-but I need some advice. I've never learned how to d-do it right. Fact is you could c-count on one hand how many times I've d-done it my entire life."

"Done what, Brad?"

"You know, f-fuck a girl."

"Oh . . ." he tried to hold in a lightning bolt of shock. Brad came off like the archetypal playboy who got laid on a regular basis. "Let's go inside."

He started a pot of coffee for Brad, grabbed a beer for himself, and went back to the living room where he'd left his troubled neighbor lying on the couch. Brad had his head propped up on the arm and left hand dangling to the floor, clasping his hooch. Occasionally he'd lean over for a swig.

Charley felt embarrassed for him, knowing that when morning came Brad would deeply regret confessing he was a premature ejaculator.

"You ever h-have that problem, Charley?"

Nervously clearing his throat, he planted his butt on the recliner and gulped a mouthful of beer. "It happens to the best of us sometimes."

"W-Well it happens to me every damn time. You g-got any ideas on what I can d-do about it?"

Exasperated, he leaned back and eyeballed the ceiling. Of all the damn things to have to deal with after his first day back at work, why did it have to be Brad Barron's sex life? He took another pull from his beer and offered the only help he could. "When I was young I used to beat off before a date so I wouldn't get too overly excited. You might try that. And while you're doing it with your lady, try to think of something boring. That's about all the advice I can give you."

Brad slowly sat up on the couch, his unfocused eyes brimming with frustration. "Think of s-something boring, huh?"

¶

A most unfortunate turn of events took place after we got to Brad's apartment, Nanatobi wrote in her diary. *Brad suffers from an extreme case of premature ejaculation. We tried to do it twice after he blew in his trousers but he can't last more than two seconds. What to do? The man I love can't fuck worth a fuck.*

SEVENTEEN

Classes on Tuesdays and Thursdays lasted ninety minutes instead of an hour like courses on the other three week days. Ronnie left the microbiology laboratory with two-and-half hours to kill before biochemistry at one o'clock. He spent the time studying in the library. When he arrived for Tuesday's class he found a note taped to the door announcing it had been canceled because of a death in the professor's family. On the way to his car he spotted Louise in the parking lot and detoured her direction.

"Where you headed?"

She favored him with a cute smile. "Advanced calculus."

"Ouch! I took basic calculus to satisfy the math requirements for my major and barely got through it by the skin of my teeth. Come on, I'll walk you to class."

They strolled across campus—passing giggling coeds, suspicious nerds, arrogant jocks, and bashful wallflowers along the way.

"So you barely passed basic calculus, huh?"

"Yeah . . ." he opened the door for her and they entered the hall.

"What did you make, a C minus?"

"You know, I actually managed to get it up to a B by acing my finals."

Louise giggled. "You call a B getting through by the skin of your teeth? What's your GPA?"

"Three-point-three. What's yours?"

"Four-point-o."

"Wow, kudos!"

A sad smile came to her. "Don't be so impressed. It would probably be a two-point-something if I had a life. Well, here we are."

He left Louise at the door of her class and headed back to

the parking lot where he heard a sexy voice exclaim, "Hey, Curly Sampson, wait up . . .!"

¶

They spent the afternoon at his apartment making love, holding one another, whispering sweet nothings in each others' ears until hunger forced them out of bed. Renee wanted to treat him to dinner and he gratefully accepted her generous offer. Being strapped for cash, he'd have had to settle for leftover tuna casserole otherwise.

She ran her fingers through his hair, now long enough to need combing. "So what are you in the mood for, Curly Sampson?"

"Your dollar, your choice."

"How does pizza sound?"

"Like a million bucks."

They went to a pizza parlor and he let the glutton in him come all the way out. Renee, who'd eaten only two slices of the house special, grinned at him when he grabbed the last piece, brought it to his lips and said, "Are you sure you don't want this?"

"Would it matter if I did?" she laughed.

He chuckled out a "No" and took a huge bite.

They parted at seven thirty. He had to be at Riley's in an hour.

¶

Having his second dinner at the Cain mansion in as many days had him pinching himself. They'd dined on vichyssoise for the first course and delectable veal cutlets served as the main entree. Nanatobi had consumed two helpings of strawberry shortcake for dessert and Brad, who'd limited himself to only one, marveled the girl wasn't fat.

Taylor signaled the maid to remove the napkin from his collar and cut his eyes towards him as she performed the task. "Did you give your notice?"

"Yes, sir."

Jesse had said he hated to lose him but understood that such a huge opportunity couldn't be passed up. Then he'd congratulated him with a warning. "It's a well known fact Taylor Cain's a real bastard to work for. That's why he pays his people so well—so they'll stay with him."

Brad didn't know that, but figured since Taylor was one of the richest men in the country, maybe it took being a bastard to get to the top. He planned to excel at his new position no matter how difficult the circumstances, and prove himself worthy of further advancement.

Ursula had been very disappointed at the news until later in the day when Jesse said he was considering her as his replacement.

Taylor rose from his chair. "So what have you young folks got planned for tonight . . .?"

¶

Brad hung up his overcoat and went to the bedroom to change. Once his dinner jacket and forty-dollar luxury silk necktie were properly put away, he took off his cufflinks and stripped. Dreading the inevitable, he returned to the living room wearing a polo shirt, jeans, and loafers. Now aware of his true height, Nanatobi had insisted he not enhance it when they were alone. She sat on the couch with legs crossed, looking delectably luscious in a clingy red sweater and tight black slacks. Flipping a martini glass over at the bar, he quickly filled it and took a big gulp to calm his nerves. "Um, what's your pleasure?"

"Nothing for me, I'm all set at the moment."

Her tone made him take another long pull before joining her at the couch. She turned sideways and began toying with a lock of his hair. "Brad, we need to talk."

"I know . . . I have a problem but I'll solve it, I promise. Please don't give up on us because of last night."

Now curling the strands with her slender fingers, she donned a reassuring smile. "Oh I'll never give up on us. And yes that is a problem we definitely need to address, but that's not what I'm talking about. As you know I'm a Centaurian, and now that you and I have happened I must leave it. When I went astral the time before last—you know, the time you sensed I was upset—I witnessed Renee and Veronica breaking our second most sacred code, the first being the code of silence. I've been a member since I was fourteen, and it isn't going to be easy for me to leave. It must be sort of like what one goes through when giving up drugs. You know, withdrawal.

"I must ask you never to speak with Renee again ever. You are not to invite her to a party, you are not to ever, ever call her for any reason, and if she comes to the office before you leave Mirror Tech you must give her the cold shoulder. The same goes for her mother. Do you understand?"

Inundated with relief she hadn't told him they were through, he nodded.

"Good." She slid her hand to the back of his neck and pulled him to her for a kiss. After probing his mouth with a hungry tongue, she withdrew it, stood up, and started taking off her clothes. "I hope you're into oral as much as I am, Brad."

¶

Renee clowned around with him as he swabbed the deck—poking him in the back, tickling his side, pinching his butt. Ronnie battled back when he could, careful to allow only a moment for each retaliation so he could finish mopping the floor in time. After work they went to his apartment and made love. With each passionate union, his love for her deepened, just as he'd known it would.

The hour grew late. She got dressed and he put his clothes on too so he could walk his beautiful fiancé to her car. When he reached for the doorknob she grabbed his hand and gave him a bad-news look.

"Mom won't give up on the idea of an orgy, Ronnie. I'm in love with you and don't want to do it, but she's insistent."

He released the knob. "There's not going to be any orgy."

A sigh of desperation wafted from her pretty throat. "Try telling Mom that. She always gets what she wants. We're just going to have to give in, and hope once is enough for her."

"We're not going to give in." He wanted to tell her of his plans to free her, but now wasn't the time. He needed Arnon's guidance and counsel before instigating the attack on Centaurianism. "It's late, you need to get home."

¶

Brad has the most marvelous tongue, but for some reason I can't make him pop orally. He can't last in my snatch and yet can't cum in my mouth. What a dichotomy!

Nanatobi put away her diary and fell asleep thinking about Brad's face between her legs.

¶

Nanatobi was supposed to be in her Wednesday morning

civics class but had cornered Renee in the parking lot. "Come with me, we need to talk."

"I don't have time, Nan, I've gotta get to art history."

"Cut it."

"I can't. I've already missed three classes. I skipped two and couldn't make the other because of Ursula's initiation, and I barely convinced the professor to let me make up a pop quiz instead of giving me a zero. I suspect he's going to give another one today and I'm afraid I won't be able to sway him a second time."

Hissing an angry sigh, she pointed at her red Porsche. "Get in the car, Renee, *NOW...*!"

She drove to a video store that had gone out of business. They wouldn't be disturbed there. Killing the engine, she turned towards the one person she'd never thought would betray her. "I left my body again the other night, Renee, and the funniest thing happened. I was floating in your parents' bedroom. Three guesses as to what I saw."

Renee looked puzzled.

"Let me give you a hint. All three of the Van Cedar bears were on the same bed."

"Oh god . . .!" she opened the door and spewed her breakfast on the parking lot.

Nanatobi knew right then she'd been forced to participate.

Renee dug some tissues from her purse and cleaned the vomit off her lips, crying all the while. "Nan, I'm so sorry you had to witness that horrible filthy scenario. It's that damn thing with Mom over Ronnie. It's gotten to her mind. She made me do it. We were pretending Dad was Ronnie. Mom drugged his drink, and when he started feeling sleepy she made him go to bed before he passed out cold. That's the only time we've ever broken the code, I swear. I was *so* grossed out at the whole idea—my own father! But Mom made me take two pills, and you know you have no control over your will under that strong a dosage."

Nanatobi had the very same pills stashed in her purse. During Ursula's initiation she'd pocketed some, knowing Veronica couldn't possibly miss a dozen from a jar containing hundreds. Even if she had noticed them missing, there was nothing in the code forbidding a member using them on their own. Taking something from the country house without asking would have been the only reprimand incurred if she'd gotten caught, and the penalty wouldn't have amounted to anything more than a tongue lashing from Veronica. She'd stolen them initially in order to drug Ronnie the next time she went to his apartment—and after witnessing Renee's and Veronica's misconduct, had planned to use them that night at Brad's. But neither Ronnie nor Ursula would ever have the special mickey slipped into their drinks now that she'd fallen in love. She reached over and caressed the tear-soaked cheek of her dearest friend. "I believe you, sweetie, please stop crying."

Bent forward with heaving shoulders as deeper sobs commenced, Renee grabbed her hand and squeezed. "I'm so sorry, I would never intentionally betray you, Nan."

Freeing her fingers from Renee's, she tenderly stroked the beauty's auburn curls until they finally quit bouncing in rhythm to flooding emotions. When her teary-eyed passenger had regained enough composure to sit erect, Nanatobi turned the ignition and headed back for the university. "There's something I need to tell you. Ursula told Brad about her induction."

"Ursula broke the code of silence?!" Renee screeched with astonishment.

"Oh most assuredly. Brad got an earful, and now Ronnie knows everything as well. I like Ursula, and I don't want Veronica to ever know she broke the code. Do we understand each other?"

A meek nod shook her cinnamon coils. "I won't tell Mom, but you know how she can get anyone to give up their secrets. If Ursula acts funny, which she's bound to do the next time we have a meeting, Mom will sniff it out like a bloodhound and you know it."

She drew a deep breath and sighed. "There isn't going to be another meeting for me, sweetie. I'm finished with that shit."

A blood-rush of excitement colored Renee's face. "Do you really mean it?"

"I sure do."

"Oh, Nan, I've fallen deeply in love with Ronnie and I don't want to cheapen myself like that ever again. I want out too . . ." she slumped in the seat. "But Mom will never let that happen."

¶

Seeing Veronica Van Cedar step out of the elevator, Brad ducked back in his office before she could spot him. He'd always kissed up to her when she paid a rare visit to Mirror Tech, but now she had no power over him. Ursula had officially been chosen to take his place when he left, and his remaining time at Mirror Tech would be spent training her. He picked up the phone and called next door to warn her Veronica was there.

"Oh my god, thanks for the heads up, Brad! I won't step out of here until she's—well hello, Veronica . . . ."

Fifteen minutes later Ursula walked into his office looking pale and shaken.

"What's the matter?"

"Nanatobi called Veronica a little while ago and told her she was no longer a Centaurian."

He didn't know why that would be such a shock to her. "She told me last night she was quitting. You are too, aren't you?"

"Brad, think!"

Grasping her predicament, he laughed in spite of the fact it obviously wasn't funny to Ursula. "Ah, Jesse's the problem. What are you going to do, just play along with it like you want to be a member?"

She raised a sexy hand to her forehead. "I don't have any other choice if I want to keep working here. Veronica has Jesse under her thumb and I know she'd convince him to fire me if I quit. And I can't tell Jesse what's going on because Veronica would shoot me down and make me look like a lying fool, and Renee would back her up all the way."

¶

"That looks scrumptious. What kind of bird is it?"

"Pheasant under glass," answered the butler, who Brad now called Jim.

"It's Uncle Taylor's favorite," said Nanatobi with a wide smile, sitting across from him, decked out in a black dress with red trimmings. She'd pulled her hair back in a pony tail, held in place with a black ribbon laced with the same trim as her dress. Her cute ears were as freckled as the rest of her skin. He now knew only her lips, palms, and the soles of her dainty feet were free of them.

Taylor gave her a brief smile from the end of the table before looking at him. "Do you play the market, Brad?"

He'd quickly learned to wait until Taylor spoke first before addressing the magnate. "No, sir. I view the stock market much as I do Las Vegas. A total gamble."

"And if you owned a successful company, would you go public with it?"

"No, sir."

"Even if it meant increasing its worth tenfold?"

"No, sir."

"Why not, pray tell?"

"The possibility of a hostile takeover. Unforeseen financial difficulties might force me out of being the majority stockholder. The only way I would go public with a company is if I were financially secure enough to guarantee I'd never have to liquidate any of my stock in said company."

"Smart lad." His benefactor spoke it through a jovial grin which not only amazed him but seemed to astonish Nanatobi. The look of surprise on her pretty face intensified when Taylor continued. "I don't play the market either, I *work* it. I only deal with the stock exchange when I want to take over a company, and I'm in the process of buying the majority of stock in one that produces computer software. Perhaps you've heard of it. It's called Mirror Tech."

Brad was flabbergasted. "Um, am I still leaving that company, sir?"

The smile broadened. "Nanatobi has never invited a date here for dinner before. Since reaching puberty she hasn't treated me with a modicum of respect or called me Uncle Taylor until you showed up. She thinks I'm a grouchy old miser who's forgotten how to have any fun." He shifted his gaze to Nanatobi. "Well how's this for a lark? I'm buying your boyfriend's company and promoting him to administration. I'll appoint one of my aces to train your young man on the job and watch over him until he acquires the savvy and experience to operate on his on—capabilities he can't possibly have now since he's been in personnel his whole working life. We wouldn't want this new toy to lose its luster by having it go under, now would we."

Nanatobi affectionately ran the back of her hand over his bearded jaw. "You're the greatest, Uncle Taylor."

Brad was dying to know what his new position would be,

but feared the billionaire would think him presumptuous if he asked.

After dinner Nanatobi left to change clothes and he walked towards the parlor with Taylor. They turned down a hallway the width of his living room and impatience got the better of him. "Um, sir, might I ask what administrative slot I'll be filling?"

Taylor stopped and turned towards him. "If I tell you, I expect the information to remain solely between the two of us until I inform otherwise, and Nanatobi is no exception."

"I understand, sir."

"So I have your assurance that it will?"

"Definitely, sir."

"I'm making you the new vice president."

The jubilation he'd felt since hearing Taylor's plans flittered away. He'd be replacing Jesse who'd always treated him well. "Um, what about the current vice president, sir?"

"He's out."

¶

Sitting in his parlor, Taylor lit a pipe, savored a mouthful of heavily flavored tobacco for a second or two, and languidly released it with a smile. The glow that had emanated from Nanatobi when he'd agreed to let her invite a suitor to dine with them revealed she thought she'd found Mister Right. After spending only a few minutes observing him, he'd clearly seen Brad was smitten with her as well.

Little did the two lovebirds know he'd already learned the pertinent facts about Bradley Boston Barron before meeting him.

"What's your suitor's name?" he'd inquired after getting over the initial shock of her asking permission to have a young man join them for dinner.

"Brad Barron."

"Is he enrolled at Maryland?"

"No, sir, he's already finished college and has a very good job."

The conversation had taken place over Sunday's lunch, and the moment Nanatobi had left the dining room he'd called his right-hand man and issued a directive to have Brad checked out immediately. Every report came back positive. The lad had never been arrested or married and wasn't paying child support as a result of sewing wild oats. He'd graduated from Maryland eight years ago with an excellent academic record, secured a job at Mirror Tech, and worked his way to the top of the personnel department.

For several months Taylor had been keeping an eye on two software companies, planning to purchase one or the other as neither had a dominant shareholder. Their market values were so similar he'd almost decided to flip a coin for a decision. Already aware from the investigation that Brad had an exemplary work ethic, once he'd become satisfied the young man had nothing but the most honorable intentions towards his niece and would have been just as infatuated with her if she lived in a ghetto, the choice had been easy. He'd ordered his broker to start buying shares of Mirror Tech.

Barring certain criteria failing to be met, before year's end Nanatobi's beau would have an overseer from T-Cain Corporation hanging around him to learn the strengths and weaknesses of his administrative acumen. Once any detected flaws were corrected, he'd become the president of Mirror Tech. The current one held his position because of nepotism, being the chairman-of-the-board's son, and relied on Jesse Van Cedar to keep the ship afloat. When he gained control of Mirror Tech the entire chain of command would be replaced, starting with the chairman.

He brought the pipe to his lips and let his mind float down the river of his memory that encircled his precocious niece. His brother and sister-in-law had perished in a freak boating accident two weeks after Nanatobi's eleventh birthday. The sole child of his only sibling, she had always been a powerful force to be reckoned with. From day one she'd captured his heart and he loved her as if she were his own daughter. She'd barely turned twelve when he first had to reprimand her for using makeup despite being forbidden to do so until reaching thirteen. He'd grounded her for three days.

The punishment had been pointless, however, for she could sneak in and out of the house with stealth a mouse would envy. That prompted him to have a lock installed on the door of her bedroom suite which could only be unlocked from the outside. He'd then reinstated the three day sentence. By noon the first day another problem had manifested. His gardener almost had a heart attack upon witnessing Nanatobi try to climb out of her room using sheets as a rope. So he had bars installed outside her bedroom windows.

From that day forward until two nights ago, she had neither called him uncle nor displayed any real feelings of affection towards him except those feigned when she wanted something. Soon she would inherit his brother's estate. He'd known without doubt that once she did, Nanatobi would move out, quit college, and go absolutely wild. But that tragic course got altered when she'd invited a very well mannered, nicely groomed, intelligent young man over for dinner, and started calling him Uncle Taylor again. Brad was an answer to prayer. It now looked like there might be hope for his beloved niece after all.

¶

They'd spent an hour looking through her yearbooks and

family photo albums as she told Brad all about her childhood, her wonderful father, her beautiful mother, and the tragedy that had befallen them when she was only eleven. Because they'd made such a late night of it two nights in a row, they were both tired and Brad had gone home at eight-thirty.

After he left she'd kissed Taylor on the cheek, something she hadn't done in ages, and told him goodnight. He'd given her a peck on the forehead and said, "Goodnight, Freckle." Elation had inflated her when he'd called her that. It'd been so long since he had, she'd all but forgotten his pet name for her.

¶

They'd once again merged into one essence but this time she could see, hear, and smell. Aware Brad could as well, due to their thoughts being one, they hovered above Veronica and Renee standing at the top of the stairs arguing. Renee had apparently told her she wanted out because whatever discussion had been taking place, they'd arrived in time to hear Veronica scream, "You cannot leave the order! He's trying to corrupt your mind with lies!"

"No!" Renee screamed, hands covering her ears. "I love Ronnie and I'm going to marry him! Grandmother was crazy and so are you!"

"Like hell . . .!" Veronica slapped her hard on the face.

Renee started crying.

Nanatobi woke up in bed, shook her head to summon alertness, and called Brad. It was no dream, he'd been there too.

¶

Brad lay on his back, thinking about what he'd experienced along with Nanatobi as they'd somehow observed an argument between Renee and her mother. Why had they been endowed with such a strange uncontrollable ability? If bestowed by a higher power then it surely served some sort of purpose, but what would that be?

Tired of pondering that, he thought about the earlier part of the evening when Nanatobi had shown him her childhood memorabilia. She heavily favored her mother, a beautiful woman of obvious breeding. Her father and Taylor looked a lot alike in the many aged snapshots chronicling the lives of the two brothers. Brad figured they still would had her father lived. She'd shown him a very touching photograph of her and Taylor that had been taken not long after her parents' demise. The obvious affection they had for one another in the image made them appear much more like father and daughter than uncle and niece. Sadly, they were the last living members of the Cain family and Nanatobi had never gotten close with any of her mother's relatives as they all lived in Sweden.

Good fortune had smiled upon him. Not only was the woman he loved beautiful, rich, and shorter than him, albeit only by a quarter inch—he'd asked her height and learned she stood five-five and three quarters—her uncle was about to elevate him several rungs up the corporate ladder. Ironically, the opposite seemed to be true for the Van Cedar household and that saddened him. He turned over on his side and tried to go back to sleep.

¶

Arnon rubbed his eyes and reached for his glasses on the night stand. It was two in the morning. He'd been awakened by a vivid dream of a white tornado traversing the streets of Baltimore without causing any structural damage. The dream ended with Charley watching the cyclone on a radar screen, saying to Ronnie Garr, "That's what it is, and that's what it was."

¶

His eyes had popped open for no apparent reason. For three hours he'd been tossing and turning, unable to go back to sleep. Ronnie groaned and rolled over on his stomach. If he didn't get some more sack time this was going to be a very long Thursday.

¶

The damn sandman just wouldn't pay him another visit. Charley got out of bed and brushed his teeth. It was ten after five so he'd finally given up hope of returning to dreamland after being yanked from it at straight up two o'clock. Betty's Café opened for business at five-thirty on weekdays and he decided to go there for an early breakfast. Arnon called while he was putting his shoes on.

¶

Despite a growling stomach, Ronnie only ordered coffee. He'd kill for some pancakes but had to watch his pennies. Tomorrow was payday at Riley's, and Saturday he'd get paid by Ben Palloy. He only had twelve dollars in his pocket and ten of that was allocated for gas. Though it would have been more frugal to brew a pot at home, he'd decided to splurge because the walls were closing in on him after laying around there since two.

"What are you doing here so early on a Thursday morning, Ronnie?"

He turned to see Charley Hudson heading for a booth.

"Well hey there! I'm surprised to see you at this hour. I woke up in the middle of the night with a bad case of insomnia and bailed from my apartment to keep from going stir crazy."

"Well how peculiar, that's my story too—been up half the night. I finally gave up on trying to go back to sleep and decided to grab some breakfast. Come sit with me."

Charley looked troubled. Ronnie had a feeling it didn't have anything to do with lack of sleep. "I need to head home and fix something to eat before my stomach cannibalizes itself. My money's too tight at the moment to afford breakfast out."

A huge black hand motioned for him to come over. "I'll treat you to some chow. Let's visit a spell."

"Aw, thank you so much, man." Mouth watering, belly flip-flopping, he grabbed his cup and moved to the booth. "Next time we both suffer insomnia the same night, breakfast is on me."

Charley responded with a short laugh that didn't alter the worry on his face. "Arnon called me awhile ago. Seems he's been up since two, same as me."

That floored him. "Would you believe I've been up since two as well?"

"No shit?" The anxiety blanketing Charley's features grew deeper, borderlining fear.

"Yeah. I don't know what woke me up but I never could get back to sleep."

"Likewise," stated Charley, wearily massaging his brow. "But a dream woke Arnon up. You and I were in it. Now me finding you here, well it's just too damn weird."

Hunger pangs gave way to a spiraling current of shock that twisted his stomach into a knot of eerie astonishment. "What a weird coincidence."

"Too much of a coincidence if you ask me."

A chubby black waitress set a cup of coffee in front of

Charley and asked what he wanted. The distressed air traffic controller gave his forehead a rest and used the hand to elevate the vessel to his mouth. He took a light nip and said, "Three eggs over easy, sausage, home fries, and toast. My friend here will have breakfast too. Put it on my tab."

"And what can I bring you?" she smilingly inquired.

Innards churning with another hunger rumble, he ordered a four-stack of pancakes.

"That comes with a choice of three strips of bacon, two sausage links, or a slice of ham to go with them."

"Just the pancakes please."

Charley cocked his head. "A man that doesn't eat pork with hotcakes must be Jewish. Hope I didn't offend you by ordering sausage with my eggs."

"No, I'm not Jewish. I love pork but I watch what I eat. Renee spoiled me with a trip to a pizza joint and I far exceeded my weekly allowance for fatty meats. They smothered that pie with pepperoni, Italian sausage, hamburger, Canadian bacon—"

"Shut up!" barked the plump girl through a grin. "I'm on a diet and you're making me starve for pizza, which is off limits."

"Sorry." Despite the feeling of dread that had gripped him over the oddity of he and Charley being in Arnon's dream on top of the three of them having their sleep disturbed at the same hour, he had to laugh.

So did Charley. The moment she left, he relayed Arnon's dream.

"Does he think it means something?"

"When that negro dreams anything, it always means something."

"What does he think it means?"

"He thinks the tornado is symbolic of the blip I saw on radar the night of the blackout."

A shudder ran through him. "Which means what, Charley?"
"Don't know, Arnon didn't say."

¶

Biochemistry lasted an eternity. When Ronnie wasn't yawning he had to stifle one. He couldn't wait to get home and crash for a few hours before going to work. Wilhelm Bach, a tall black-haired German with a pronounced widow's peak, instructed the class. He spoke articulate English with a heavy Deutschland accent. While lecturing on gene splicing, he wrote letters on the blackboard to represent the particulars, turning to face the class with an explanation after each one. Ronnie failed to stop a wide yawn as the professor turned around after chalking a series of three D's on the board.

Bach looked at him sternly, hands behind his back. "Am I boring you, Mister Garr?"

"No, Doctor Bach, I didn't mean to yawn. I didn't get much sleep last night."

"I see."

Ronnie pictured him clicking his heels like a Nazi as he turned back to the board without conveying one way or the other whether the explanation satisfied him. Some of the students snickered, but he could only yawn.

¶

Nanatobi was having a drink with Renee at a club called The Point, a popular hangout for college students. Though not yet twenty-one, she'd never been carded there. She relayed in detail the argument she and Brad had witnessed last night from their astral perspectives.

Renee frowned. "Nan, that never happened."

"What?"

"Mom *was* upset but not with me. She was angry over you quitting, but she was bitching about it in the kitchen, not the top of the stairs, and I never sassed her at all, just listened."

Dumbstruck, Nanatobi looked down at her wine cooler. "The last two times have been different. I wonder if it's evolving or something."

"Different how?"

"The night Ursula told Brad about the order, he and I left our bodies and our astral selves merged together . . . ."

¶

"Good evening," said Jim with a pleasant smile as he let him inside the Cain mansion.

"Hello, Jim. What's tonight's delicacy?"

"Tonight's dinner was prepared by McDonald's."

Brad entered the dining room to see three trays on the lavish table. The one in front of Nanatobi's chair contained a Big Mac, an order of fries, and a strawberry shake. Taylor's held two Big Mac's, fries, and a chocolate shake. The tray awaiting him was chock full of food items and three different shakes. He stood beside Jim as Taylor escorted Nanatobi to the table and gave her a courteous bow after seating her.

The mogul then fired a smile his way. "Welcome, Brad. We didn't know your preference so we ordered a bit of everything."

Before long Brad felt like a fifth wheel as niece and uncle relived different things the family had done together during Nanatobi's childhood. They were jocular and animated and so enamored with each other's company, an uninformed guest would have sworn this was the first time they'd seen each other in years. Jim seemed to be thoroughly enjoying the rapture between his employer and Nanatobi, smiling all the way through the meal, but Suzanne the maid appeared puzzled by it.

¶

Once again Renee showed up at Riley's Grocery. Spotting her before she saw him, Ronnie snuck up from behind and pinched her beautiful ass. She spun around with a raised fist, prepared to knock the shit out of the offender. He grabbed the hand, gave her a quick smooch, and grinned. "We've got to stop meeting like this."

¶

Alfred had been given the night off since his services weren't required, and had retired to his quarters for the evening. Jim sat with Suzanne in the kitchen where they were sipping tea.

"The old coot was certainly in a good mood tonight, wasn't he?" said Suzanne. "I didn't know the man even had a sense of humor."

Jim smiled at her. "Oh if I could take you back in time you wouldn't know Taylor Cain, believe me. You came aboard after he and Nanatobi had already gone to war with each other. They used to be very, very close."

Brows forming steep rainbows, she gawked at him for a speechless moment before reaching for a chocolate chip cookie. "I thought he was going to ground her for sure when she had the nerve to ask if they could have McDonald's for dinner. And when he said that was a splendid idea, why—I nearly fainted, I did."

He laughed. "They used to have McDonald's fare for dinner

once a week when she was growing up. And believe it or not Taylor actually dined at the place rather than have me pick up their food as he did this evening. He'd fetch her at her parents' house and take her there every Thursday, and even after their deaths he continued the tradition until she became a self indulgent adolescent twit."

"Why, this is a Thursday."

"Indeed it is . . ." he raised the teacup to his lips.

"Did you hear what he called her when she left for the evening? I couldn't quite make it out but I know I've never heard him use the term before."

"It's the nickname he used to call her when she was a child. It's a very fitting soubriquet as well."

She heaved an impatient sigh. "Well, what is it?"

"Freckle."

¶

"SW eighty-four, make your altitude thirty thousand feet," said Charley. As he listened to the pilot's reply he imagined a white tornado swirling across the radar screen which took him to the mysterious blip, then Brad's out of body experiences, and lastly the poor guy drunkenly asking for his advice. They hadn't seen each other since, and he hoped his neighbor wasn't too humiliated to face him again.

¶

They were in his bed and Brad wanted to kill himself. "I'm so sorry, Nanatobi. I failed you again."

"No, my darling, you didn't fail me. You lasted a little longer, and it will only get better. We'll get through this, you'll see. I confronted Renee yesterday and I'm lifting the ban, you can talk to her again. She was a victim. We had a drink after classes today and I told her about what we saw going on between her and Veronica last night."

"Was she embarrassed we caught them squabbling?"

"No, and you wanna know why?"

"Why?"

"Because it didn't happen."

He sat up and peered down at her. "You're kidding."

"Nope . . ." she pulled him back to her side.

"She's lying."

"No, Renee's not lying. It never happened."

Seeing she was certain, he tried to make sense of their last astral flight. Why had they so clearly witnessed a fictitious event? Before long an incredible possibility occurred to him that he immediately voiced. "What if it's *going* to happen? What if we saw something that will happen in the future?"

Nanatobi sprang to a sitting position, freckled face glowing with sudden vibrancy. "Oh, Brad, that must be it! I've been wondering if whatever's happening to us isn't evolving and becoming more complex."

EIGHTTEEN

Renee snuggled next to him, purring through her afterglow. His squeaking mattress springs had been given a severe workout. He'd been putting off telling her he knew the truth about the cult and figured now was as good a time as any. "Brad called me the other night and asked me over because Ursula—"

She sealed his lips with her fingers. "I know. Nan informed me Ursula told you and Brad about The Order of Centaurians. So now you know the sordid details. Did she tell you that I was inducted into it right after I had my first period? Mom took me to my grandmother's house and I became a Centaurian for life."

Though Ursula had told him, hearing it again turned his stomach, making him want to strangle Veronica. "What kind of mother would do that to her own daughter?"

"That's what her mother did to her." She sounded on the verge of tears.

"That's sick beyond words."

"I know—" her voice broke as she started crying. "When my grandmother's oldest sister died I was chosen to take her place. Nan was my other great aunt's replacement."

He held her tightly and let her bawl. Renee had suffered the strangest form of child abuse he'd ever heard of, yet she apparently viewed Veronica as a victim like her. That didn't wash with him. The evil bitch might have been coaxed into The Order of Centaurians but that was no excuse for dragging her daughter into the cult.

When her weeping finally subsided, she sniffled and said, "Nan told me she and Brad have had some more out of body experiences."

"Yeah, I was there for one of them. He was standing by that fancy bar of his and just keeled over."

"The last time she left her body she saw something that didn't really happen—Mom and me arguing."

That mystified him. "Nanatobi always goes to where you are during her astral projections, so why would she see you doing something that you really weren't?"

Renee shrugged. "I don't know, but she didn't go to where I really was this time. Nan said Mom and I were at the top of the stairs arguing. We didn't have any type of conversation there."

"What were the two of you arguing about?"

"My leaving the order—but like I said, nothing of the sort really happened. Mom and I haven't fought in ages, and I would never dare tell her I was quitting, even though I want to. After you earn your doctorate we'll bail from Baltimore and I'll finally be through with that shit. But until then, I'm stuck."

Not for long, he thought. *Arnon Green will show me how to solve this wicked mess.* "I wonder why she saw something that didn't really go down?"

"I have no idea. Brad was there too. Nan said the last two times it happened their minds melded together like they were the same person."

"Brad also saw you arguing with your mom?"

"Yes. And the time they left their bodies before that, they were like inside each other, but couldn't see or hear anything. Neither of them had any idea where they were. Nan thinks it's evolving. And guess what else. She's fallen for Brad."

He raised his brows. "No kidding? I never would have put those two together."

"Well they are. She called Mom and quit the order because of it."

His pulse elevated upon hearing that. With Arnon's guidance and Nanatobi's help, Renee would soon be free of Centaurianism forever.

"I'd give anything if I could quit too, but like I said, Mom will never allow me to."

Her defeatist attitude nauseated him. "She can't stop you. You're twenty-one years old—of course you can quit."

"No . . . I can't." She spoke as if it was a tragic, unalterable fact.

"Yes you can."

"No, you don't understand."

"Nanatobi quit, and you can too."

Renee sadly shook her head. "I've got news for you, Nan won't be able to follow through with it. Mom won't let her."

"Veronica can't keep her from quitting."

She got out of bed and started putting her clothes on. He did likewise because she had to leave soon.

"What Ursula told you about Centaurianism is only part of the story, Ronnie. Mom has this power that neither Nan nor I can resist when we're in her presence. Perhaps no one can, I don't know. Ursula certainly can't. When you didn't follow us that night, she didn't want anything to do with us, she just wanted Mom to take her home, yet now she's a Centaurian. As soon as Mom and Nan are face to face, she'll renounce any desire to leave the order, even if it means giving up Brad."

¶

"You little bitch! You'll do exactly as I say!"

"No! It's over and I'm out. You can't control me anymore. I don't know how you ever did, but now I'm free of your spell."

She and Brad, viewing through their combined essence, watched the scene unfold after the part where Veronica had slapped Renee when they were last there. When she'd first found herself intertwined with him above the stairs, they'd seen a repeat of their last astral trip. Now they were observing the subsequent events. The argument below suddenly became inaudible until just before they returned to their bodies, whereupon Veronica shouted, "I'll see you dead first!"

They didn't have to phone one another to verify the reality of the incident. Nanatobi was lying beside her lover in his bed.

¶

He walked Louise out of Friday's physics class and they went to Betty's Café for coffee, which had pretty much become a ritual.

Ronnie ordered a glass of water.

Louise frowned. "What, no coffee?"

Embarrassed, he confessed he couldn't afford it. He'd shelled out the last of his cash for gas that morning and didn't have a red cent.

"Chloris, Ronnie will have coffee too!" she yelled to her aunt, who'd walked away after taking their order. Then she turned to him with a cute smile. "On me."

Feeling humbled yet grateful, he thanked her. "I'll square up with you Monday. Today's payday at the store, and tomorrow I'll get paid from the trucking company."

"Don't worry about it. This will be the first time I've ever paid for a cup of coffee here. So how are things with you and Renee?"

"Great." He tried to sound cheerful. Glumness over her adamancy of not being able to leave the cult had clung to him all morning.

"Glad to hear it . . ." she flipped a shock of curls off her shoulder.

Her deportment didn't match the enthusiasm of her words. Louise appeared to be jealous, but that seemed unlikely since she no longer fantasized about him, at least not passionately enough to produce a vision, according to Nanatobi's theory. "So how about yourself? How's your love life these days?"

"Ha! Love life? What is that?"

He held back a laugh and tried to look sympathetic. "No new Danny Hills in the picture then I take it."

"Nope."

"I'm glad you and Renee patched things up."

"Me too."

The same thing happened again. Her expression didn't mesh with what left her lips. If it wasn't jealousy, something else about Renee was bugging her.

"We ran into each other in the parking lot this morning and got to visit for a few minutes. She told me Nanatobi has a new boyfriend."

"Yeah, I heard about it last night. He lives next door to your cousin Charley as a matter of fact."

Chloris brought their coffee.

"So you know him then?"

He took a quick sip. "A little. His name's Brad Barron."

"How well do you know Nanatobi?"

"Not much better than I know her boyfriend."

"But you do know she's Taylor Cain's niece, right?"

"Yeah, I know that much about her."

Louise grasped the handle of her cup but didn't raise it. A moment later she abandoned the coffee and brought her hands together beneath her chin, appearing to have gotten lost in thought. "I felt so bad for her when her parents were killed. It was just awful."

"What happened?"

"They were out sailing with some friends. A man got thrown from his speedboat and it crashed into their vessel and exploded. Nobody survived. We were just fifth graders, but I'll never forget how shallow I was when I heard about it. I thought, 'Well at least you got to be with your parents for eleven years, I never even got to see mine.' Of course I never told her that."

A spark of guilt fluttered through him. He'd been angry throughout his childhood over having only one parent. "That's sad."

"Yeah . . . she was a totally different person for months afterwards. Looking back, she handled it a thousand times better than I would have, I'm sure. So tell me what you know about her boyfriend Brad."

I could tell you a tale that would straiten the curls right out of your pretty hair, he imagined saying. "He's about my age, appears to be your basic successful pen-pusher type, and he's a nice guy."

"What does he look like?"

"Blonde, tan, smiles a lot."

She aimed an impatient squint at him. "So is he handsome, ugly, in between, or what?"

"Hmm . . . I guess you'd call him handsome."

"But?"

"No buts."

"You hesitated before you said he was handsome."

"Did I? Didn't mean to."

A skeptical grin popped up. "Come on, what are you not wanting to say?"

"Well he seems a little pretentious in my opinion. But I barely know the dude, so don't judge him on what I say."

"Be more specific."

"I guess it's the way he carries himself, I don't know, and he dresses sort of pompous. He has a perfectly even tan that obviously comes from a heat-lamp rather than the sun, and his teeth are so white and straight they look false."

She laughed. "Maybe his teeth *are* false."

"Maybe so. Why are you asking me all these questions about Brad Barron?"

"Just curious as to what Nanatobi finds so appealing about him, that's all."

"I'm sure they probably just have a lot in common." *One thing in particular*, he snickered to himself.

"Nanatobi could get just about any guy she wanted. That's why I'm so curious as to why she settled for this one."

"Well the thing to do," he said firmly, tired of being interrogated, "is ask her instead of me."

¶

Brad had started training Ursula and she caught on quickly as he'd expected. He wanted to tell her about Taylor's plans to take over the company but didn't dare. Jesse was in the process of deciding who would replace her when she stepped up. Everyone assumed it would either be Ava Blanc or Hilda Weiss. If it were up to him he'd pick Hilda because she worked harder. Jesse would make the choice before his two weeks notice passed, and he hoped Ava didn't get chosen. She'd have to relinquish her new position when he assumed the vice presidency, and he hated the thought of having to tell her that.

He felt like a traitor. A few minutes after he'd gotten to work that morning Jesse had called him into his office and said, "It looks like Taylor Cain is interested in Mirror Tech. You know anything about that?"

"What?" he'd exclaimed, faking surprise.

"Yeah, it appears he's planning to become the majority stockholder, and that probably means a lot of us are going to be looking for work. Maybe even me. So which one of the many companies under the Cain umbrella are you going to work for?"

It had been extremely difficult to disguise his nervousness.

He'd cleared his throat and replied, "Um, he just told me he wanted me to come to work for him and that he'd double my salary."

"Did he say anything to you about Mirror Tech?"

"No. He asked me where I worked and I told him. That's the only time it was brought up." He'd hated lying to Jesse, but felt he had no choice.

"I see. Well if you get any info on what he has planned for this company you *will* pass it on to me of course."

"Of course," he'd lied again, feeling like a contemptible snake.

It was now half past three and he couldn't bear the guilt any longer. He returned to the scene of the crime, closed the door behind him, and inhaled an anxious breath. "I owe you an apology, Boss—a big one. I lied to you this morning."

Jesse sat stoically with arms folded as he bared his soul, including the fact that he'd be replacing him when the takeover was complete. When he finished, Jesse rose from his desk and turned towards a large window facing the Inner Harbor. "Thanks for telling me, Brad. I'd have probably lied too if I'd been in your shoes. If you'll excuse me, I'd like to be alone now and let it all sink in."

Shortly after he got back to his office the phone rang. "Hello?"

"Congratulations, Brad. You passed the test."

He knew the voice, but couldn't believe it was him calling. "Um, sorry, but I don't know what you're referring to, sir."

"Jesse Van Cedar will explain it to you. See you tonight at dinner."

¶

After classes she'd insisted Renee come with her to The

Point. Nanatobi had chosen a table located in an area sequestered from the main part of the club where the bar and pool tables were located. She babied a wine cooler. A beer sat before Renee, untouched. "Okay, here's what's up. Last night Brad and I returned to the same scene at your house. We saw it replayed exactly like before, but this time we saw and heard more afterwards. We're both convinced that what we are seeing is something that's going to happen and possibly very soon."

Renee imparted a reproachful frown. "You made me come here to tell me that? Why didn't you just tell me in the parking lot or phone it in? I wanted to hang out with Ronnie before he went to work, not sit here and listen to you speculate about what's happening to you and Brad. Even if you're right, big deal. A mother and daughter are going to have an argument. Gee, go figure that one."

She slapped the table. "You're not getting the importance of what I'm trying to tell you, Renee!"

"So what are you trying to tell me?"

"That if you don't move out of your parents' house you might get killed."

"Killed?" Renee laughed out incredulously. "Who'd want to kill me?"

"Your mother, that's who."

¶

Dinner consisted of crown rib of pork for the main course and cherry pie for dessert. Nanatobi was spending the evening with a friend she'd forgotten making a commitment to several weeks ago. She had promised to attend a surprise anniversary party for the girl's parents. At least that's what Taylor maintained she'd asked him to pass on. It deeply concerned

Brad that she hadn't called and told him herself.

¶

"Oh lick it! . . . Lick it! . . . Oh shit, Renee, eat it!" Nanatobi screamed, grinding her hips against Renee's delightful hungry mouth while Veronica and Ursula muff-dived each other. When the multiple orgasms besieged her—powerfully enhanced due to the potion—she cursed herself for being so foolish as to think she'd ever wanted to give this up. Oh what a stupid foolish bitch she'd been . . . .

¶

Ronnie kept expecting Renee to grab him from behind and yell "Surprise!" or catch him coming around an aisle, or walk in while he was bagging groceries as she'd done the last few nights. But she didn't. Even when he walked out of the store after closing, he still half expected to see her pull into the parking lot. But she didn't. He called her cell from his apartment expecting her to answer.

But she didn't.

¶

Brad lay in his bed, hands behind his head, worrying about Nanatobi. She was in trouble, he felt it in his gut. He'd called Renee after leaving the Cain mansion and Jesse had answered the phone.

"Renee's out and about," his lame duck boss had informed. *"I don't know if she's with Nanatobi or not."*

He'd wanted to ask if Veronica was there but hadn't dared

because it would have raised suspicion. He feared she'd gone out for the evening as well, which very likely meant Nanatobi had been seduced back into the cult.

When Taylor passed on Nanatobi's message at dinner Brad had been so shocked over her last minute change of plans that he'd lacked the presence of mind to ask the girlfriend's name. Afterwards he hadn't been able to muster the nerve to change the subject, as his host had spent the remainder of the meal explaining the test he'd arranged.

Taylor had called Jesse, told him his plans for Mirror Tech, and instigated a covert evaluation to determine if "Nanatobi's suitor" was an overly ambitious back-stabbing stone-stepper who cared about no one but himself. The truth would be learned through how he answered the questions Taylor had instructed Jesse to ask. He'd unknowingly been given to the end of business to pass or fail. The magnate had allocated that amount of time to take into consideration that he might initially lie due to a sense of loyalty to his girlfriend's uncle.

"I knew if my instincts about you were correct," Taylor had said at dinner, "you wouldn't have been able to go very long without coming clean. Jesse called me right after you told him the truth. I've been researching the company and its employees for quite awhile, and am aware Jesse Van Cedar excels at his job. I have no intention of hurting the man. My saying he was out marked the beginning of your testing. After you assume the vice presidency, Jesse will undergo special training in one of my other companies to replace the retiring chief executive officer. If you'd failed the test, you would still have been made vice president because I'm a man of my word. But I'd have had you sign a sixth month contract, and half a year from now you'd have been looking for a job."

¶

Nanatobi was crying as she wrote in her diary.

Veronica somehow knew Renee and I were at The Point and found us right after I told Renee I feared for her life. I don't know how she managed to do it, but neither of us could resist her when she insisted we go with her to the country house, and neither of us had the willpower to refuse the potion. I wanted to call Brad and tell him I couldn't keep our date but Veronica forbade it and made up a lie for me to pass on to him through Taylor. I called Brad after I got home and he was pissed, but he understands everything now. Oh how I hate that evil bitch!

¶

Brad pounded his pillow and buried the left side of his face in it. Nanatobi had called and confirmed his worst fears. Veronica had somehow gotten her and Renee to go with her. They and Ursula had been at the country house all evening. He'd gotten angry with her and she'd started crying. Upon being reminded that she had told him it wouldn't be easy for her to quit for good, he'd forgiven her for standing him up. While trying to fall asleep, he wondered what would happen if he were to tell Jesse about his wife's evil secret life.

NINETEEN

Saturday dawned with a horrible snow storm. Ronnie called Charley from Palloy's Transportation to see if they'd be able to make the trip. The big man had already spoken with Arnon, who'd told him not to come because of the weather conditions. The snow plows always got to the country road leading to his farm last so it wouldn't be passable for several days.

He left work with his regular pay in his wallet plus a fifty dollar bill, courtesy of the generous Ben. On the way home he treated himself to a case of beer along with the necessities and jumped in the shower when he got everything put away.

Eyeing his wet hair in the mirror, a part of him wished Renee didn't like it so much so she'd let him shave it off. He ran a comb through it and headed to the kitchen for a beer. She called right after he cracked it open.

¶

With Taylor's kind permission and insistence upon having their meal placed on his account, Brad took Nanatobi to a pricey restaurant on Charles Street for dinner in his recently purchased Shelby Mustang GT500 Super Snake. She wore a mini dress of shimmering scarlet with a plunging neckline that revealed an abundance of freckled cleavage. Uncertain which of them appeared taller due to her pumps, he felt self conscious when they walked in, until a mirrored wall confirmed his reflection stood a smidgen above hers.

Sumptuous aromas of diverse cuisines being prepared by expert chefs titillating his nostrils alongside Nanatobi's delectable perfume, Brad smoothed the lapels of a blue dinner jacket he'd shelled out six hundred dollars for, placed a hand on the small of the breathtaking beauty's back, and made his way to the maître d'. "We're the Barron party . . . ."

As they were being seated he requested caviar and the bottle of the restaurant's exclusive pinot noir Taylor—who'd recommended the wine and made their reservation—had called ahead to have opened before they arrived so as to let it breathe. The dancing flame of a sculpted candle six inches in diameter reflected in Nanatobi's glorious green eyes. Knowing their appraisal found him desirable filled him with immense pride as well as wonderment that she still wanted him despite his glaring inadequacy at sexual intercourse. He'd always felt cheated that the length of his penis, like his height, had failed to reach that of the average male's, and suspected an inferiority complex over both had a lot to do with the problem.

The waiter returned with the readied wine and poured a small amount in his glass. Brad tasted it, verified the quality with a nod, and the server filled their glasses. Meanwhile a waitress placed an hors d'oeuvres platter on the table and took their order. They snacked on sturgeon roe, toast points, and deviled egg until the main course arrived. At least he did. Nanatobi had accused him of being gauche when he'd dipped his caviar spoon into the bowl a fifth time. She'd done so only once.

Having eaten his fill of grilled salmon and red roasted garlic herb potatoes, he sipped coffee while admiring the freckled goddess sitting across from him, working on the second of two desserts she'd requested. He'd learned Nanatobi ate only tiny portions of a meal so the ample amounts of calorific confections she consumed afterwards wouldn't expand her narrow waistline. They'd avoided the subject throughout the evening and he hated to bring it up, but had no choice. "We've got to do something about Veronica."

Nanatobi looked up from a rapidly disappearing wedge of cherry cheesecake. "I know."

"Do you think Jesse suspects anything?"

"No. Veronica's very surreptitious."

He lowered the delicate cup onto a saucer. "I'm wondering if I shouldn't tell him about it."

Raising only one eyebrow to show how ludicrous she found the idea, Nanatobi reinforced it with a brief sardonic smile. "You do that and Veronica will own your ass. She'd sue you for slander, and Jesse would never believe a word of it anyway, she'd see to that."

"But I have you as a witness."

That pulled a sarcastic laugh from her. "She'd tear up my testimony like confetti, Brad. You don't win an argument with Veronica Van Cedar. Whatever she wants someone to think, they think it. At least while they're in her presence."

Her utter certainty over the matter amazed him. "How is she able to do that?"

"Through her incredibly strong powers of persuasion."

He pictured Veronica mesmerizing Nanatobi and Renee with her sultry dark eyes widened like those of Charles Manson in that horrific picture taken of him after the Tate and LaBianca slayings. "Sounds like hypnosis."

"It almost is."

¶

Charley normally hated snowstorms because it made the already tense work environment all the more strained. This one annoyed him because it prevented the drive to Arnon's. He hoped the weather cleared over the weekend so he wouldn't have to deal with it when his shift started Monday evening. The television flickered between his feet as he relaxed in his recliner, but his mind kept wandering back to his cousin's dream and the peculiarity of Ronnie and him not only being in it, but waking at the same time as Arnon.

The telephone rang.

A slew of cuss words flew out of his mouth when he checked the ID. He never got a call from BWI when he was off duty unless they needed him to fill in for another controller.

¶

Ronnie set a freshly opened beer on his desk and went to answer the door, grinning because Renee had apparently changed her mind. She'd called earlier to say she was staying home tonight due to fatigue over an all-day shopping spree with Nanatobi. The smile faded and his gut twisted when he opened it to find Veronica and Ursula standing there.

Ursula looked dazed—glassy-eyed stoned—but her sleazy companion appeared sharp as a tack, smiling seductively, dark eyes brimming with assertiveness. "Hello, Ronnie."

Veronica's assuming tone turned his stomach another nauseous degree. The arrogant bitch thought she could entice him into having the orgy, the only possible reason for this surprise visit. He wanted to slap her. "Where's Renee?"

"At home with a headache."

It puzzled him that she hadn't forced Renee to come, being she was the only other member of her cult besides Ursula now that Nanatobi had quit.

"Aren't you going to invite us in?"

"No, I'm sure not. You should have taken the hint when I didn't follow you the other night. Don't embarrass yourself by ever trying this again."

He slammed the door.

Several moments went by without him hearing another knock. He didn't think she'd give up so easily. Cautiously, he opened the door a crack to be certain they'd gone. A shocking scene awaited him. They were holding their coats open and both were topless. When Veronica saw he'd taken full note, she turned towards Ursula, pulled the blonde to her mouth, and they started kissing, passionately.

Speaking into Ursula's lips Veronica said, "Bend your knees until your nipples touch mine, dear." A moment later their breasts were melded as tightly as their mouths.

"Stop it," he yelled, "someone's liable to see you!"

Veronica pulled away long enough to say "Well you'd better invite us in then, hadn't you" and resumed sucking face with Ursula.

"All right! Knock it off!" Though practically dilapidated, the apartment rented cheap and he couldn't afford to get kicked out.

The black-eyed witch tried to pat his cheek as she stepped inside but he dodged her hand. She lowered it and took in the bleak surroundings. "My, Ronnie, you live in absolute squalor, don't you. Why don't we go some place a little less poverty stricken?"

"No way. Look, just leave me the hell alone."

"May I . . .?" she strolled to his desk and took a sip of his beer before he could answer.

He jerked the can away from her to show the twisted slut she wasn't welcome to it, and angrily downed a mouthful. "The only reason I let you in here is because this dump is all I can afford and I don't want to get evicted, which is what's liable to happen if one of my neighbors were to see you two sucking face and rubbing chests!"

Veronica started toying with the phone cord, gazing upon it as if the black coils fascinated her. "But we love to rub chests, don't we, dear."

"Oh yes." Ursula's voice came out husky and inebriated.

"If you still want us to leave by the time you finish that beer—" she released the cord "—we will. Let us stay at least that long so we can warm up a little. It's cold out there."

He took another gulp and glared at her with contempt. "You wouldn't be so cold if you had shirts on."

¶

They were in Brad's bed and he was castigating himself over his lack of staying power. He'd ejaculated after making love to her less than ten seconds. Nanatobi consoled him, but badly wanted him to use his tongue. She wasn't about to mention it however, figuring the thought of putting his mouth on her slit with his semen oozing from it would totally gross him out. "Brad, lets get dressed and brainstorm—try to figure out a way to defeat Veronica instead of worrying about it. You'll learn to hold it in time, darling, you'll see."

¶

Violently thrusting her hips back and forth, a deep groan blasted from Ursula's throat and she cried, "Gawd this feels good, Ronnie—I-I'm so close!" He lay on his back with the tall blonde riding his cock while Veronica gyrated against his mouth. Despite not wanting to go with them, he was now lying naked on the living room carpet of that house in the country.

"It's to the b-bed for you next, Ronnie," moaned Veronica. "The b-biggest fucking bed you've ever seen in your l-life. Oh fuck!" Grabbing the back of his head, the wanton witch jerked him tighter against her inflamed clit. A high-pitched refrain of blasphemies streamed from her mouth as she climaxed.

Ursula broadcasted her orgasm a mere second before his load rocketed into her spastic cunt. "Oh yes! Squirt it in me, baby, squirt it all in me—"

Ronnie snapped to in his apartment. It hadn't happened yet.

A quick glance at the clock warned him he had exactly five minutes to get out of there before Veronica and Ursula would be arriving. Grabbing his coat, he made a mad dash for his Thunderbird and drove to Betty's Cafe.

He settled at a table and ordered coffee from a waitress he hadn't seen before. The place was almost empty. A white man taking his meal at the counter and two black old timers engaged in jovial conversation at a booth were the only patrons besides himself. Tuning out their discourse, he tried to figure out why he hadn't been able to resist Veronica in the end. Somehow in the short time it had taken him to finish his beer, at which point she'd agreed to leave, he'd become putty in her hands. Recalling her taking a drink of it first, a light bulb flashed in his head. *"That bitch put something in my beer and drugged me!"*

¶

Brad stood at the bar making his martini swirl, idly staring at it. "I don't buy that Veronica's powers of persuasion alone made you go with her since you so adamantly want to leave the order. She obviously somehow drugged the two of you. Either that or you aren't as hostile to the cult as you maintain."

An aggravated grunt entered his ears. "Both of us want out, Brad. But when you're on the potion all you want to do is have sex, and the more aberrant the better."

The erotic avowal forced his eyes to Nanatobi. "So you agree with me that you had to have been drugged."

"No, dammit, we weren't given the potion until we got to the country house. I don't know how Veronica even knew we were at The Point. It was my idea, and we went there straight from campus so Renee couldn't have told her even if she'd wanted to. Veronica said she usually stopped in for a drink every time she was in the vicinity and was totally surprised to find us there, which is a bald faced lie."

Having hung out at The Point himself during his days at Maryland, he figured that was indeed a lie. The Veronica Van Cedar's of the world didn't usually patronize establishments that catered to college students.

"She ordered a beer and made small talk," Nanatobi continued. "I was nervous the whole time, waiting for her to ask me back into the order, trying to gather the strength of will to refuse when she did. Then she casually said, 'I've decided to have an official meeting tonight and have informed Ursula to go to the country house when she gets off work. I'll let you girls finish your drinks, then you're coming with me.' I wanted to tell her I wouldn't go with her, but the next thing I knew Renee and I were in her car, looking forward to drinking the potion."

He carefully examined the scenario she'd presented. "So she must have slipped something in your drink before mentioning the meeting, or you'd have resisted her."

"She couldn't have, Brad. I never left the table, and her hands never went near my wine cooler or Renee's beer."

"Hmm . . ." he put himself in Nanatobi's shoes. Being rudely surprised by Veronica's intrusion would have made her cautious and acutely aware of the woman's actions. "Maybe she didn't put anything in your drinks."

"I believe I just told you she couldn't have." A sarcastic sneer accompanied the retort. "She just has some sort of weird hold over Renee and I that I can't explain. It doesn't have anything to do with drugs."

"I'm not agreeing you weren't drugged, merely that it might not have come through the drinks."

Nanatobi grunted again and snapped, "How else could she have done it? We weren't eating anything."

"Did she hug you or touch the two of you in any way?"

"She gave us both a love pat on the cheek before she sat down. That was the only physical contact she made with either of us."

"Did you feel a sting or pricking sensation or anything like that?"

"No."

"Then it had to have come through the drinks. She must have diverted your attention while she medicated your wine cooler."

A hot breath whooshed through her pretty nose as she angrily firmed her lips. "You're barking up the wrong fucking tree, Brad! I know she didn't put anything in my drink. She couldn't have or I'd have seen it."

"Then she must have done it by touching your faces, using some type of drug that only requires skin contact to be effective. Just don't let her touch you, or drink or eat anything she might offer you, and she'll be powerless to seduce you again."

Her posture destabilized from rigid defiance to slumping futility as an aura of sadness encased her. "Oh, Brad, I wish that were true, then Renee and I could resist her. I'm sorry, but her power over us just doesn't come from a laboratory."

¶

Ronnie was working on a second cup of coffee when he heard "Hello, Curly Sampson" as another feminine voice greeted him by his given name.

Renee and Louise had entered the café.

Offensively surprised, he stood up, thinking she'd better have been looking for him or she had a pissed off fiancé on her hands. "I thought you were staying home tonight."

"I was but Louise talked me into going out for some chocolate cake." She pecked him on the lips and sat down.

He threw her a derisive smirk while reseating himself. "You were too tired to go out with me, yet Louise was able to talk you into coming here for cake? That must be some tasty cake."

"It's the best," said Louise, smiling cutely while taking a chair. "So what are you doing here? I thought you were going to Arnon's tonight?"

"The weather put a kibosh to that." He noticed Renee trying to communicate something to him with her eyes as he said it.

"Oh the snow storm this morning, of course. That road Arnon lives on will be impassable for awhile."

Renee frowned. "Who's Arnon?"

"Louise's cousin. He's the farmer I went to see last Saturday."

"Why were you going to see him today?" Whatever signal she'd endeavored to send had dissipated.

"I was going to fill you in last night—figured you'd drop by the store again. When you didn't I called your cell phone after work but couldn't even get your voicemail to answer. Anyway, Arnon had a vision the night of the blackout. I told him about—" he stopped mid sentence, clearly understanding the message Renee was eye-casting this time. Her dazzling orbs warned him to proceed no further.

"You and I meeting that night?" she quickly offered with a nervous grin.

Feeling like a fool, he stifled a laugh. He'd almost blurted out information that would have made Louise think them crazy.

The waitress arrived. Louise did the ordering and turned to Renee. "A lot of the members of my family think Arnon is some sort of prophet, and apparently Ronnie does as well."

"I know he does," affirmed Renee light heartedly. "That's what he called him instead of telling me his name when I asked about his trip to the farm."

It looked like her ploy had worked. He breathed an inward sigh of relief.

"So what was it you told him about?" asked Louise.

Renee raised her brows as a warning to be careful.

He acknowledged her caution with a subtle nod before answering Louise. "You remember that blackout that lasted so long several weeks ago?"

"Yeah."

"Charley saw a UFO just before it happened. He told Arnon about it, and Arnon told him he had a vision that same night and—"

"Charley saw a UFO?" Louise laughingly interrupted.

"Uh, no, not a flying saucer or anything like that, just a blip on his radar that shouldn't have been there. Anyway that was the night I finally managed to introduce myself to Renee, and I think it was fate—kismet, cupid, whatever—and wanted to see what Arnon thought about it. Of course that's not why I went to see him. That matter has to remain between him, Charley, and me for the time being."

"How romantic." Louise sounded sincere but once again her demeanor betrayed some sort of problem with Renee, who would have picked up on it too had she been looking at her instead of him.

"And I nicknamed him Curly Sampson that very night," Renee reminisced with a sentimental smile.

Louise grinned. "Yeah, she told me about you shaving your head, Curly Sampson."

"Hey, nobody calls him that but me!"

"Okay!" sniggered Louise, hands raised in surrender. "I promise I won't do it again, so chill."

As the two of them giggled he realized it might be concern

rather than jealousy he'd detected, because Louise now had a protective air. "So Renee told you about my nickname."

"Mm hmm, after she started speaking to me again."

The waitress delivered the girls' coffee and cake.

Renee immediately took a bite of hers and dangled a forkful in front of his mouth. "Try this, you'll love it."

A burst of rich chocolaty flavor delighted his taste buds. "Man, that *is* good."

"And extremely addictive," warned Louise while shoving a large portion between her lips.

"Yeah, I can see I'd better leave it alone."

As they consumed their creamy dark desserts, he wondered why Renee had turned him down with a lie in order to spend a night on the town with Louise. Though exceptionally delicious, he didn't buy the special chocolate cake as the reason, having no doubt she wanted to be with him as often as possible.

He thought of the communicative look she'd given him earlier, and the mystery unraveled. Veronica had wanted to have the orgy but Renee had refused to go along with it, so the evil bitch had forbidden her to see him tonight because she'd planned to proceed anyway. He needed to inform her that as far as Veronica and Ursula knew, the threesome never took place. "I saw your mother earlier."

"Oh really?" The statement clearly cut her like a knife but she'd managed not to let it show in her voice.

"Yeah. She was with Ursula Winston."

Her eyes screamed for him to shut up about it. Pain glistened in the twin emerald ponds as if she were being physically tortured. He quickly got to the point. "They were eating cake too—offered me some—but I managed to resist the temptation and turned them down. Got to watch the ol' Garr figure, you know."

A joyful tear found its way down Renee's cheek as her

wondrous visage blossomed into a beautiful flower of relief.

Louise noticed it and laughed. "Boy, Ronnie, she must really be concerned with that figure of yours."

"Oh believe me I am," said Renee with a glowing smile.

¶

"Oh never mind that bitch for now, we're getting nowhere discussing Veronica. Stand up, baby." Hot to work on another challenge since they couldn't solve hers with the cult, Nanatobi unfastened Brad's pants and pulled them down along with his underwear. Teasing him like a stripper, she slowly took off her clothes—tossing each item on the couch—and knelt in front of him.

¶

Louise excused herself and went to the ladies room. They took the opportunity to fill each other in. He'd been right in his assumption. Veronica *had* told Renee to stay away from him when she'd refused to participate in the orgy.

"At first I was amazed at being able to resist Mom when she demanded I go with her because I'd never been able to do that before. She finally gave up and said, 'All right then, but you stay away from him tonight. Tonight he's mine.' I realized then she'd only been going through the motions and didn't really want me to come along for some reason.

"I couldn't tell you the truth when I called because she was hovering over me listening to every word I said, making sure I passed on the lie she told me to tell you about being exhausted from shopping. After she left I tried to call you back and explain what was going on but Dad got an important call. The battery on my cell phone died earlier and it hadn't charged up enough to work. By the time he got off the phone I was afraid Mom had already made it to your place, so I was too scared to call. I was just sick, my imagination was running so wild.

"I needed some sort of diversion to keep from losing my mind. Nan had plans with Brad so I called Louise and lied to her about why you and I weren't together tonight. I said I wasn't feeling well earlier in the evening and by the time I felt better you weren't home. She wanted to have cake and coffee, then see if we could find you. Of course I didn't think we would, figuring you were with Mom and Ursula at the country house, drugged with the potion."

Afraid Louise might return before he could get it all out he rapidly said, "It happened again, Renee. Your mom and Ursula came to my place. Veronica somehow drugged my beer and took me to that house in the country, but suddenly I was back in my apartment. I'd noticed the time when Veronica knocked on my door and knew they'd be arriving soon, so I hightailed it out of there and came here."

Her face paled. "Why is this happening to you? And why are Nan and Brad having astral projections?"

"I wish I knew."

"Well thank God it did happen again and you were able to escape. Let's ditch Louise and go to your place."

"Too risky, Veronica might try again. Let's just go somewhere, the three of us, and hang out. Your mom's too slick. I just can't take the chance of seeing her because I know she'll wind up getting me doped up somehow."

An exasperated sigh passed through her pretty lips. "She is a tenacious shit, isn't she. I thought you were going to spill the beans earlier. Can you imagine what Louise would have thought?"

He grinned. "Oh by the way, Louise, I read minds don't you know."

Renee snickered but quickly sobered.

"What's so funny?" queried Louise, walking up from behind him.

¶

Nanatobi had worked on him until her jaws ached but still couldn't make him shoot. She'd never gotten a complaint about the way she gave head. Every guy fortunate enough to have received oral pleasure from her hadn't been able to last more than a couple of minutes without popping. So why didn't Brad like it? Totally perplexed, angry at herself for failing, she gave up and rose to her feet. "I'm not doing you any good, baby, and I'm so sorry. What am I doing wrong?"

Features sagging with a defeated mope, he pulled his briefs up and grabbed the waistband of his pants. "I've never been able to do that. It's not you, Nanatobi. Once again the problem is with me, I'm afraid."

"Then it's not me? You really like the way I do it, promise you do?"

"I promise. Not many girls have gone down on me but none of them were even remotely in your conference. You're absolutely amazing. I've just got some sort of mental block that keeps me from being able to . . . you know. Ironic isn't it, since I can't hold back during intercourse. I think it's because I'm so self conscious of my size, the way I am of my height."

His confession infused her with relief as much as the compliment warmed her insides. "It's just another thing we've got to work through then." As she reached for her panties a tempting thought crossed her mind, making her naked nipples harden. She grabbed her purse instead.

Brad took note of her T-H-O. The puzzled look on his face made her giggle. Retrieving one of the pills, she held it up between her thumb and forefinger for his perusal. "Quit ogling my boobs and check out this tiny tablet I'm holding. I promise it won't hurt you, baby. It's not an illegal narcotic and it's not habit forming. I want you to take it for me, okay?"

¶

Louise directed Renee to a bar near the airport. They climbed out of her Camaro and entered the establishment.

"Why this place?" asked Renee as they sat down at a table for four.

"I figured Ronnie might want to visit with Charley, and he always comes here after work."

"The guy that saw the UFO?"

"Yeah," he answered for Louise. "I'd like for you to meet him but unfortunately it won't be tonight because he's off."

"He was supposed to be off tonight," said Louise, "but I saw him earlier at Betty's. One of the controllers came down with the flu and Charley had to take his shift. He wasn't real pleased about it to say the least. He'd dropped in for some takeout to eat on his meal break."

A middle-aged woman with a leathery face depicting she'd weathered many storms in life but had refused to be defeated by any of them, arrived to take their order.

Renee smiled at her. "I'll have a margarita, please. I'm only going to allow myself two though, so ignore me if I ask for more after the second one."

"Designated driver, huh?"

"I'm afraid so." She turned towards him and placed a hand on his thigh. "Your first two drinks are on me. After that you're on your own, Curly Sampson."

He reached down and snaked his fingers through hers. "I appreciate you trying to help out the poor but since my boss surprised me with an extra fifty bucks when I got paid today, I'll be able to manage."

Still eyeing him she told the waitress, "Don't let him pay until I give the okay."

"Whatever you say, honey. What'll you have, handsome?"

Ronnie chuckled and gave her a wink. "How about a Manhattan, gorgeous."

Her wrinkled lips parted with a dry laugh. "Oh that's me all right." She cut her eyes to Louise. "How about you, hon?"

Louise grinned at Renee. "Are you paying for mine too?"

"If you need me to."

"Just teasing, I just got paid too. Did I tell you I got a nice raise?"

"No!" Renee gushed through a big smile. "Congratulations!"

"Oh it was such a surprise, let me tell you about it . . . ."

He thought of how silly the two of them had acted that day Louise had bragged about being asked out by Danny Hill. They giggled back and forth about the salary hike until the weary waitress impatiently cleared her throat.

"Sorry," said Louise, "guess I'll have a margarita too . . . ."

Before they'd finished their first round Charley walked in. Ronnie waved him over. The waitress strolled up shortly after he introduced him to Renee.

"What'll it be, Charley, the usual?"

"Yeah, and bring me a draft too."

Ronnie noticed a bartender looking their way, wagging a raised hand. "I think you're being paged."

Charley turned and gestured back. "That's Harry, a real nice guy."

When the waitress returned, Charley quickly downed a whiskey, asked for another, and took a long pull from his beer. The big man's hand was shaking as he sat the mug down.

It apparently caught Louise's eye too. The smile on her face disappeared as she said, "Rough shift?"

Charley nodded. "We had a flight from Cleveland that almost wound up on the scrap heap. One engine shut down and the other was acting up, but we managed to get it to the ground in one piece."

¶

Although he still couldn't last beyond a few seconds, his erection refused to wane. Gritting his teeth after each climax, Brad forced himself to keep moving through the extreme discomfort of post ejaculation and stepped up the tempo once pleasure returned. After several more eruptions he wanted to climb the Empire State Building and pound his chest like King Kong when Nanatobi's vaginal canal suddenly started convulsing and she went berserk. Frantically thrashing her hips, clawing at his back, blissful obscenities along with his name spewed from her arching throat . . . .

¶

At Louise's insistence he relayed what happened the night of the blackout. Glad to get past the eerie recount, Charley popped some cashews in his mouth and brooded over Ronnie's girlfriend as he chewed. Renee Van Cedar was a real beauty— eye candy of the finest quality—but something in those sexy jade orbs troubled his spirit. He sensed she'd been deeply wounded and had carried those emotional scars for a long time. Despite her friendly smiling demeanor, an aura of sadness hung about her. The Almighty hadn't given him *The Sight* or Arnon's incredible grasp of scripture, but occasionally he'd come across a person whose insides were as apparent to him as the clothes they wore. This poor girl happened to be one of them. Arnon could pinpoint the trouble and help her get right with the Lord. He washed down the nuts with beer and turned to Ronnie. "What do you think about taking your sweet thing along when you're able to go see Arnon again? I'd like for him to meet her."

On his way to getting drunk Ronnie stammered, "F-Funny you should say that, Charley. I was just thinking that very thing."

Louise, a bit soused herself, started giggling. "Well I want to go see the old prophet too. Did you know Ronnie's convinced Arnon has *The Sight*, Charley?"

Oh the foolishness of youth. Most of the young folks in his family had lost respect for Arnon's gifts, though they all still loved him. Their change in attitude mystified Charley. Every one of them had once held him in esteem as the man of sevens, but now they made fun of him behind his back. The shift had happened around the time Aunt Betty Louise got miffed at Arnon for not coming to one of the reunions. Arnon had explained why he couldn't come, that he'd developed claustrophobia in heavy traffic, whether driving or just riding, but she'd gotten mad at him just the same.

¶

Beneath the covers of her bed, pen in hand, Nanatobi wrote: *I didn't take one, but Brad made me have multiple orgasms through intercourse tonight after I gave him the pill! As he continued making love to me after each premature ejaculation, I realized his johnson fits inside me perfectly and that's what drove me insane with pleasure—another sign that we were made for each other! I can see now that if he doesn't learn to last without them, I must go to one more meeting at the country house to garner a big supply of pills for my dearest Brad. I have never experienced anything like what happened tonight—being in love while cuming so hard through missionary sex—and cannot, will not, shall not live without it!!!!!*

TWENTY

Something tickled his nose. Ronnie awoke to find his face pressed against the back of Renee's head. Trying to recall how they'd wound up in his bed but unable to, he attempted to ease away from the thick mass of auburn curls without disturbing her.

It didn't work. She turned over and slowly opened her eyes. Recognition swam into them and she smiled. "What time is it?"

He looked at the clock. "Ten-forty."

She sat up and swung her legs over the side of the bed.

"Not so fast." He wrapped his right arm across her naked breasts, forced Renee onto her back, and feasted on her glorious nipples while massaging her labia.

"You're gonna get peed on if you don't turn me loose, Ronnie."

"Oh, sorry. Hurry, I've gotta go too." The hard on he'd woken up with had quit suppressing his bladder's signal the moment Renee made her complaint.

When he came back to bed she had her legs spread, waiting for him.

"Oh, Ronnie, I love you so much," she moaned in his ear as he slid inside her.

"I'd die if I ever lost you, Renee. I love you more than you'll ever know—more than life itself." He gave her a deep wet kiss and started moving his hips. "Baby, this is heaven . . . ."

¶

Nanatobi sat on the divan in the parlor visiting with Taylor as he relaxed in his easy chair smoking a pipe. The exotic smell of his special blend of tobacco took her back to the days when she used to sit on his lap with a toy pipe, blowing bubbles instead of smoke. Her mother had guffawed when she'd first caught them doing it, and jokingly accused him of teaching his niece bad habits.

They'd moved to the parlor after finishing lunch. She'd had it waiting for him when he came home from church. It was the only thing she knew how to cook but he'd always claimed she made the best grilled cheese sandwiches in the world. She'd prepared four and had eaten one. Taylor either still liked them or so wanted her to think he did that he'd forced down the rest. The happy look on his face had spoken volumes when she'd hurried from the elevator as he was leaving for the service and hollered, "Please don't have lunch in town, Uncle Taylor! I'll have a surprise for you when you get home."

She hadn't cooked for him since he'd first grounded her, and had quit going to church after turning thirteen. He'd promised she could make her own decision about attending upon reaching that age. Though very upset about it, he'd kept his word and she hadn't set foot in the large Presbyterian church since. Now wanting to please her beloved uncle, she'd even considered accompanying him that morning but had woken up too late to get properly attired for the occasion. He didn't attend the evening services so she'd have to wait until next Sunday to surprise him, providing she could tear herself away from her dearest Brad in time to get a decent night's sleep first.

He exhaled a smoke ring and grinned at her. "Has Brad broached the subject of marriage yet?"

Smiling inside and out at the thought, she gave him a wink while crossing her fingers. "Not yet."

"It seems unavoidable that he will, don't you think?"

"Yes, Uncle Taylor, I most certainly do."

¶

Renee drove him to Betty's Café so he could get his car, then she headed home. When he got back to his apartment Ronnie did his daily exercises—one-hundred pushups, fifty sit-ups, and twenty-five deep knee bends—before scrambling some egg whites. He sat down to a late breakfast, thinking about last night. He'd gotten pretty sloshed and Louise hadn't fared much better. She'd been a happy drunk, laughing at everything he said whether it was meant to be humorous or not. Charley and Renee had shown a lot of tolerance for their immoderation, considering they'd put up with it sober. Renee had stopped after her two allotted drinks and Charley hadn't drank much after a few initial belts. They'd closed the bar, and he now vaguely recalled Renee driving him home and saying, "Okay, Curly Sampson, let's pour you into bed." By all rights he should be battling a terrible hangover, but he felt pretty decent considering the amount of booze he'd consumed.

After breakfast he settled at his desk and began studying an assignment issued last Friday. He found it difficult to concentrate. Even the technical jargon of physics made him think of Renee.

¶

Charley got out of his car and stretched his weary back, trying not to let the doldrums over having to fill in for the flu-bitten relief controller again get him down. Never bothering with Sunday school, he usually made it to church in time for the sermon but not today. It would have been too hectic having to rush home, change clothes, grab a bite, and make it to the airport by three. At least he wouldn't be missing any late games or Sunday Night Football since the season had recently ended. He ambled into Betty's Café for a hot meal an hour before his shift started, and was surprised to see Louise there.

He took a seat at her table instead of his traditional booth. "Girl, I figured you'd be in bed all day with an icepack on your head the way you kept slamming back those margaritas last night."

She grinned. "I was pretty anemic when I woke up, but feel much better now."

Chloris brought his coffee. "You're in luck, Charley. I made one of my special meatloaves today."

"Well in that case bring me a cheeseburger and onion rings."

Louise shook her head at his dry joke as Chloris walked away chuckling. "Having to fill in again, huh?"

"Yeah. I hate having to work on my days off. So what are you up to?"

"Guilty pleasures." She pointed her fork at a three-layer triangle of chocolate cake.

"Yeah, I know what you mean. Excuse me a minute. Hey, Chloris, bring me a piece of that cake Louise is having!" A few minutes later his taste buds were in chocolate heaven.

"Ronnie's an intelligent guy," said Louise, who'd become contemplative as he stuffed his face, "yet he thinks Arnon really has *The Sight*. Why does he think that, Charley?"

He drug a napkin across his lips. "Because he does, that's why."

"You really believe that?"

"I know it to be a natural fact. You kids . . . I don't know why you can't see it."

A refuting gleam bloomed in her eyes. She leaned over and whispered, "I happen to know Joshua Green was an only child, therefore Arnon cannot be the seventh son of a seventh son."

"Say what?"

"It's true, Charley."

"No that's not true! Who told you that?"

She shushed him. "Keep your voice down."

He glanced around guiltily, realizing he'd bellowed it out. "Who told you that?"

"I can't tell you."

"Well whoever told you that is crazy out their ass because that's a lie."

"The source is ultra reliable."

"The hell it is—" he shot her a reprimanding frown. "I met all six of my Uncle Joshua's brothers, so how could he have been an only child?"

Louise's face lost a shade of color as she gawked at him with utter shock. "You met his brothers?"

"Sure did. While it's true they were much older and had all passed away by the time you were old enough to hear about them, there were six of them and Joshua was the youngest which makes him the seventh born. Now who told you he was an only child?"

"Grandma," she said weakly, a stunned expression leaving no doubt she believed him.

"Aunt Betty Louise told you that?"

She leaned over and shushed him again. "Keep your voice down."

"Who else did she tell that to?"

"Only me, and she'll have me boiled in oil if she knows I told you."

"Who else have you told?"

"No one else in the family, but I did tell Ronnie when he was going on about Arnon the other day."

He bit his lip and angrily shook his head. "Why did she tell you that? Did she say?"

"No."

His gut tightened with bitterness as the motivation hit him. At last it all made sense. "Louise, I bet she told all the younger kids the same thing and swore them to secrecy too."

"She said I was the only one she over told. Why did she lie to me, Charley?"

A harsh sigh forced its way out. "I've always wondered why you younger kids didn't believe in Arnon, and now I think I know. He ticked Betty Louise off a good ways back without meaning to. He couldn't make it to one of the family gatherings and she thought he was just making excuses because he didn't want to come. Truth is he wanted to but just flat out couldn't. That's the only reason I can think of for her telling you that bull about Joshua. I bet she either told the other kids the same lie, or made up something else for each one to discredit him."

Louise cast a nervous glance at Chloris, handing a customer change at the cash register. Satisfied they weren't being overheard, she refocused on him. "She didn't discredit Arnon, only his father. I've never heard Arnon brag about all his sevens, and I've always thought he was a great guy. I just never thought he had *The Sight*. Now, with Ronnie going so gaga over him, and you telling me Joshua really was a seventh son, I'd like to talk to him."

It was plain to see that for some reason she now wanted Arnon to be a prophet. "Louise, what's the matter? What are you needing Arnon's help with?"

A blush flooded her cheeks. "Why would you ask me that?"

"Because it's obvious. Now what's bugging you?"

She looked down at her plate, a few crumbs of dried chocolate the only clue of what had been served on it.

"Come on, Louise, you can tell me."

Several moments of silence rolled awkwardly by before she raised her eyes. "I've had some weird dreams."

"Oh? Well tell me about them."

"How long before you have to leave for work?"

"Gotta run here pretty quick."

"I'll tell you about them some other time then."

"It's Arnon you're wanting to tell them to, isn't it? Just give him a call."

"Can't. Used up most of the free minutes on my cell this month and can't afford the phone bill this would run up."

He thought about loaning her his, then got a better idea. Rising from the table, he pulled a ring of keys from his pocket, slipped one off, and handed it to her. "I keep a spare apartment key in my car. My telephone package includes toll free calls anywhere in the country. Use my phone and lock up when you leave. Remember how to get to my place?"

"Sure. Thanks, Charley."

¶

Arnon eased himself out of his rocking chair and answered the phone, figuring the caller to be Mary Jo checking in.

"Hello?"

"Hi, Arnon, it's Louise."

He grinned with surprise. "Well hey there, girl! How are things in Big B?"

"Cold," she giggled.

"Yeah, I'm snowbound up here on the farm."

"I figured as much after that snowstorm yesterday."

"Yeah, It was a doozy all right."

"So are you okay? Got food and all?"

"Oh yeah, I never let supplies run too low during wintertime on account of occasions such as this. So what's up? I don't recall you ever calling me before, child."

"Um . . . remember that white boy that came to see you the other day, Ronnie Garr?"

"Yeah." Hearing the name caused an uneasy feeling to stir in his spirit. She obviously hadn't called just to chat, and he dreaded learning the reason she had.

"That's what's up."

They spoke for an hour. Arnon hung up the phone and blew out a worried sigh. He'd known from a vision had long ago that somebody in his family was going to receive *The Sight* but never figured it would be the one member of the clan that was half white. Now he fully understood the white tornado he'd dreamed about. It represented Louise as well as Charley's radar blip. That's why Charley had said to Ronnie Garr in the dream, "That's what it is and that's what it was." *What it was* meant the blip, and *what it is* represented Louise. A spiritual rope tied her, Ronnie, and the couple who'd had the out of body dreams together. God had seen to it Charley saw the blip the same time he'd received the flash in the vision so the events that followed could be verified as being brought on by His hand. The omen was both good and bad. Only time would reveal The Almighty's true purpose in the event, but he now felt it was good for Ronnie and the out of body dreamers, but dreadful for the woman the young man hoped to marry.

Louise knew none of this, including the fact she'd been given *The Sight.* She'd be contacting him again once the revelations started coming upon her in broad daylight instead of merely in dreams. It was a heavy burden to bear, but at least she wouldn't have to deal with it alone as he had all his life. Some troubling dreams involving Ronnie Garr had prompted her to call this time, and she'd wanted his advice. The counsel he'd given her had been simple: "Tell your dreams to Ronnie, and God will take it from there."

¶

Louise arrived five minutes after he finished dinner. She'd

phoned earlier and asked if she could come over to discuss something with him. They were lounging around his kitchen table, drinking coffee, laughing about how silly they'd been at the bar last night. Her mood turned serious when he asked what she wanted to talk to him about.

"I called you right after I had a long conversation with Arnon over the phone. He advised me to talk to you about some dreams I had."

Ronnie didn't know which surprised him more—Arnon's peculiar advice or Louise actually taking it. "Why?"

"He didn't say, just told me to tell them to you. Before I do, I need to tell you something else. I told Charley about Arnon's dad being an only child and found out I was lied to. Charley verified that Arnon's dad was indeed the seventh son of a seventh son. So I apologize for trying to convince you he didn't have *The Sight*."

"No need to. You were the one concerned with his pedigree, not me. And your skepticism didn't sway me at all. So you believe he's a prophet now?"

"Mm hmm, but it's more you being so impressed with him than learning I was lied to that changed my mind." She imbibed some coffee from his best cup, a Baltimore Raven's mug, and eyed it for a moment before resting it on the scratched up tabletop. "Anyway, on to my dreams. In the first one I saw you and Nanatobi talking to some blonde guy I've never seen before. I wasn't in the dream, just you guys, and I was viewing everything like I was watching a movie. The three of you were very animated about something. I couldn't hear what any of you were saying, but I somehow knew the blonde guy was concerned about his height. He and Nanatobi floated up in the air like two helium balloons, grabbed each other's hands, and started kissing. I thought it was all really happening until I woke up and realized I'd been dreaming.

"When you told me Brad was blonde, I thought that was

pretty weird. That's why I kept pumping you for more information because if you'd said he was short without me asking his height, it would have confirmed to me that he was the man in my dream. I didn't have time to quiz Renee after she told me Nanatobi had a new boyfriend because I was on my way to class. I tried to get her to talk about him last night before we ran into you at Betty's but she seemed preoccupied with something and wouldn't elaborate on him. So I didn't get a validation from her either."

Louise's dream impressed him. Nanatobi and Brad floating made him think of their astral flights. "When I met Brad I couldn't help but notice the fancy boots he was wearing because they had real tall heels. He's worn something similar every time I've seen him since. So yeah, I'd say he was concerned about his height."

Her nostrils flared with a frustrated breath. "If you'd said that before I told you what I was trying to get you to say, I'd bet he was the man in my dream. Guess I'll never know for sure now. Anyway, I thought it was just an odd dream until I had the second one and you, Nanatobi, and the blonde guy were in it too. The three of you were discussing something going on between Renee and her mom, and you were very upset. I somehow knew without hearing you say it that something was really troubling you about Renee's mom. I didn't know exactly what, but I was aware it had something to do with group sex."

An icy rush swam over him. Those two dreams weren't merely abstracts flashing in Louise's brain during REM sleep, they were epiphanies. "How did you know that?"

"I don't know, I just did, the same way I knew the blonde guy's concern. Anyway in the third dream—"

"Third dream? How many did you have?"

"Seven . . . I dreamed them all the same night." She lowered her gaze to the Raven's cup. "And they've really been nagging at me."

"Well let's hear the others."

Louise took a slow sip of coffee and resumed eye contact. "The blonde guy wasn't in the third dream, just you and Nanatobi. The dream started with her telling you about some woman being a Sagittarius. I have no idea who she was referring to but I somehow knew she was a relative of Renee's. You were furious and said you'd give anything to be able to go back in time and stop her even if you had to resort to murder. I don't know what you wanted to stop her from doing.

"Nanatobi had a Bible and started looking for a certain scripture that you'd read a long time ago. I guess she found it because she shouted 'Here it is!' and suddenly I saw a woman tied to a tree and a crowd of people were throwing rocks at her. I screamed for them to stop but they wouldn't listen to me, just kept trying to kill her. Another woman came running up and they all fled like they were scared to death of her. She freed the woman and at that instant I knew they were both evil and I'd been wrong to try to prevent the first woman's death. Neither of them were anyone I know in real life but in the dream I knew they were also related to Renee."

So that's what's been troubling you about her! he almost blurted aloud. Glad to know it wasn't jealousy he said, "Go on."

"The fourth and fifth dreams were real short. In the fourth one you told Nanatobi she'd made the right choice, and the blonde guy was congratulating her over it. I didn't know what you meant by that and was very confused. You were with a blonde in the fifth dream too, but this one was a woman. You were discussing something with her that I couldn't quite make out, but at the end of the dream I clearly heard her say she wanted to quit but couldn't. The sixth dream was—"

"Whoa, wait a minute! Can you describe this blonde woman?"

"No, she was just a generic white girl."

Despite her inability to verify his assumption by saying she was tall, he felt it had to have been Ursula wanting to bail from the cult. "What was it she wanted to quit?"

"Smoking or drinking or some other bad habit, I guess. I have no idea."

"Okay, continue."

"The sixth dream was different from the others, but you were in it too, and in the seventh dream you were crying and kept saying 'Why, Renee?' over and over. That's it."

Surely Renee wasn't going to break up with him. Just the thought made his bowels cramp. "What was Renee doing?"

"She wasn't there—you were the only person in that dream. I don't know what prompted you to keep repeating the question but you were extremely upset. Those dreams weren't like any I've ever had, Ronnie. I can remember all seven as vividly now as when I had them."

As he stewed over her final dream, it dawned on him she'd completely glossed over the one preceding it. "Tell me about the sixth dream, maybe it'll clue me in on why I was so bummed about Renee."

"I did already."

"No, you only said it was different and I was in it."

She nervously shifted in her chair. Something about that one troubled her and she didn't want to tell him about it. He pressed anyway. "Come on, tell me the sixth dream."

"I'd rather not, okay? It's embarrassing."

He didn't want to make her uncomfortable but needed to hear it because the others were undoubtedly connected to what had been going on since he'd made the awful mistake of going to that motel with Veronica. Something dreadful must have happened or he wouldn't have been crying in the seventh dream. And the fact he was apparently bawling over Renee made it all the more unnerving. "Listen, I understand now why Arnon told you to relay them to me—those dreams are prophetic. Please tell me what happened in the sixth one."

Louise started fidgeting with her cup handle. "The prospect scares me. Do you really think they are?"

"Without a doubt. If Nanatobi and Brad were here right now they'd totally freak. So please, tell me the sixth dream."

A quick intake from the Ravens mug served as her only response. She swallowed nervously.

"Did you tell Arnon the sixth dream?"

"A very condensed version of it."

"Well now you've really got me intrigued."

"Please don't make me do it. I'd much rather hear why you think the dreams are prophetic."

He got up and headed for the phone. "I don't think it, I know they are, and I'll prove it to you. What's Nanatobi's cell number?"

Louise recited it and he dialed.

"Hello?"

"Nanatobi, it's Ronnie Garr."

"Hey, Ronnie." She sounded cheerful but confused as to why he was calling.

"Can you meet me at Brad's?"

"That's where I am. What's up?"

"A friend of yours, Louise Hudson, just told me some dreams she had. They involve you, Brad, me, Renee, and a blonde woman."

"Louise doesn't know Brad."

"She didn't call him by name but he fits the description of the guy in her dreams. You both need to hear them, they're prophetic."

"Seriously?"

"Yeah. Mind if we come over?"

"God no, get your asses over here . . . ."

He hung up the phone and turned towards the kitchen. "Nanatobi's at Brad's place. Let's go over there so you can tell them your dreams, and we can tell you what's been going on and how the two are connected. Um, I'd leave out the part about the blonde guy's concern with his height. Brad's pretty sensitive."

¶

When he pushed the doorbell a male voice hollered for them to come in. Ronnie followed Louise inside and took in the snuggling couple sitting cozily on the couch. Brad looked confident and laidback rather than high-strung and overly attentive. His pretentious air was gone as well. The freckles on Nanatobi's face appeared to be dancing with happiness.

Louise turned to face him and whispered, "He looks just like the blonde guy in my dreams. This is scary, Ronnie."

Nanatobi rose from the couch, pulled Brad to his feet, and introduced him to Louise. Then she aimed a beaming smile his direction. "Did Renee tell you Brad and I have fallen in love?"

"Yeah, congratulations, you two." He said it with a smile that didn't linger, wanting to get on with the business at hand. "Before you hear Louise's dreams let's fill her in on what's been happening to the three of us, and you need to tell her about the cult."

If he'd just called her a whore Nanatobi couldn't have looked more incensed. "Have you lost your fucking mind?"

"That's debatable, but she needs to hear everything."

That didn't appease the annoyed redhead at all. "I figured her dreams had to be connected to our paranormal activity since you said they were prophetic, but why does she have to hear about the order?"

"You'll understand once she tells you her dreams."

"I'd better." She gripped her waist and eyeballed Louise, whose mouth had fallen open the moment *paranormal activity* left Nanatobi's. "Sit down, you don't need to hear this shit standing up. What I'm about to tell you is liable to make you faint . . . ."

Though Louise never lost consciousness, her face exhibited more expressions than a mime pretending to watch a horror movie as she listened to Nanatobi's shocking narrative. He chipped in to clarify the parts of it involving him, and Brad did likewise. Hands glued to the sides of her face, Louise glanced at the liquor bottles neatly arranged on the bar. "May I please have a drink to settle my nerves?"

Brad turned a martini glass upright. "What would you like?"

"Could you make me a margarita?"

"Sure." He flipped it back over, rotated a tumbler, and working efficiently as a professional bartender, soon fulfilled her request.

Louise gulped a mouthful, drew a deep breath, and downed another. "Land o' Goshen, I am *totally* blown away by all this. It feels so freaky to know my dreams are prophetic."

"Well tell them to us," said Nanatobi, now keyed up and bright-spirited. She'd been quite moody, almost surly, while conveying the perverse activities of the cult.

Either forgetting or ignoring his advice to omit the blonde guy's concern about his height, Louise laid out dream one. The faces of Nanatobi and Brad grew increasingly awestruck as she relayed the rest.

"Fucking amazing," lauded Nanatobi, standing beside Brad at the bar. "Why'd you skim over the sixth one?"

"Because it's too embarrassing to tell in detail." Louise's lips quickly sought refuge on the rim of a highball glass.

"What if you just told me? We can go in the bedroom for privacy. I won't tell anyone, I swear."

"Girl, don't do this to me." Louise's panicked eyes spoke much louder than her voice.

"C'mon, I swear on my mother's grave I won't tell a soul."

Apparently that vow carried a great deal of weight with Louise because she reluctantly gave in. When they returned to the living room several minutes later Nanatobi tossed him a knowing smile embellished by a wink, neither of which could be seen by Louise, trailing behind her. She then gave him all the details about hers and Brad's latest astral trips. "So what do you think, Ronnie? Are we seeing what will happen in the future or what?"

He pondered the meaning of her wink but knew better than to ask about it in front of Louise. "Yeah, I believe you are. Do you remember me saying I thought you were having a vision instead of really leaving your body?"

"Yes."

"Well even though I was wrong about your first few experiences, maybe that's what's happening to the two of you now."

Nanatobi cut her eyes to Brad, then aimed them back at him. "Well whatever's happening, we both fear Renee's in danger and needs to get away from Veronica."

"Don't expect any argument from me." He knew all too well that whatever Veronica used on him could make anybody her puppet if she managed to get it into their system. And that drug had another insidious quality that totally baffled him— he'd been completely unaware of any alteration in his metabolism. It seemed at the time that he'd simply decided to go along after all for no logical reason, the same way he had at Riley's. Demanding she get the hell out of his apartment one minute, he'd found himself in Veronica's BMW the next, wedged between the wanton slut and Ursula.

But he hadn't been drinking anything at the store when he'd followed her to that house in the country, so how had she manipulated him then? An eerie chill coiled in his gut as he recalled her caressing his face.

That's how she did it! She couldn't sway me the second time because she never touched me. That's why she tried to pat my cheek when she came over with Ursula. When I avoided her hand, she decided to drug me through my beer.

But what kind of drug could alter somebody's will by a mere touch without affecting the one administering it? A macabre thought came to mind that made him feel creepy all over: maybe it wasn't a drug at all, but some form of black magic. He couldn't deny the feasibility of that gruesome prospect, having had the reality of supernatural abilities forced down his throat.

He glanced at Louise standing at the bar, margarita in hand, a faraway look in her eyes. She'd been through enough for one evening, so he kept the speculation to himself.

Brad guided Nanatobi to the couch and they sat down.

Louise took a long drink and daubed her lips with a cocktail napkin Brad had provided. Her frail countenance looked as if it might shatter like humpty dumpty if any further shocking revelations entered her ears. "I can't believe Renee's mom is a witch. She seems like such a sweet normal lady."

"Centaurian, Louise, not witch," Nanatobi clarified.

"And you're not exaggerating about what you guys have done to each other?"

Nanatobi's mouth slackened as she aimed a stunned glare at Louise. "Hardly. I watered it down for your sake. Veronica's mother was quite the inventor, at least concerning means of enhancing sexual pleasure. I've had my orifices invaded by more devices than you've ever heard of and have participated in more sapphic sex orgies than I can count."

"Since you were fourteen?" Of all the startling revelations thrown at Louise, the sexual activities of Centaurianism seemed to have shocked her the most.

Nanatobi nodded. "Renee's been in it since she started

menstruating. And the blonde woman in your dream? I think that's a woman that works with Brad named Ursula Winston, the latest recruit."

"I think so too," said Brad.

He echoed Brad's statement and added, "The cult is bound to be what she wanted to quit and I'm sure she eventually will. I want to get Arnon's counsel on how to fight this thing and liberate Renee from it once and for all."

"Who's Arnon?" asked Nanatobi.

"The farmer I went to see. He's related to Louise and Charley, the man who saw the UFO the night of the blackout. He has a gift of being able to intuitively know things without being told about them. I discussed what's been happening since the blackout with him, and he wants to meet you."

She appeared impressed yet skeptical. "Sorry, Ronnie, but this Arnon won't be able to help you with Renee. The only hope of freeing her from Centaurianism is to keep her away from her wicked mother."

Brad put his arm around her and said, "Charley told me Arnon had an out of body experience when they were kids, babe."

"Well that's interesting but it won't help Renee. Like I said the only—"

The sentence was left unfinished because Nanatobi passed out.

So did Brad.

¶

Their combined essence once again viewed the scenes they'd witnessed on their previous two excursions from their bodies. After Veronica said "I'll see you dead first!" she picked up a vase of flowers and shattered it on Renee's head, causing her to tumble backwards against the banister which broke on impact.

Rendered unconscious from the blow, she plummeted to the living room floor. Her blank face looked towards the ceiling but her breasts were pressed against the carpet. She'd broken her neck.

"*GODDAMMITT!* Oh what have I done, what have I done? Renee . . .!" Veronica rushed down the stairs. Kneeling beside the lifeless form of her daughter, the black-eyed bitch from hell wailed, "Why, my precious baby, why? Oh why? Why, Renee, why . . . *WHY, RENEE?!*"

¶

Ronnie told Louise not to be afraid, that Nanatobi and Brad had temporarily left their bodies and would come to any second. The statement sounded ridiculously stupid to his ears despite being true.

As soon as she opened her eyes Nanatobi lunged to the edge of the couch, grabbed the telephone sitting on an end table, and punched the numbers so fast her fingers were a blur. "Oh, Renee, thank God you're alive!"

His knees turned weak. "What happened, Brad?"

"Listen and you'll find out." The words came out fearful.

Panic gripped him in a frigid vice as Nanatobi told Renee what she'd seen from her astral body. It hadn't happened yet but he knew in his gut it most certainly would if she didn't get the fuck out of that house.

"Let me talk to her," he demanded when it became clear Nanatobi couldn't convince her to leave.

The redhead heaved a frustrated sigh and said "Lots of luck" while handing him the phone.

"Renee, you've got to get away from there! I believe Nanatobi and Brad are witnessing a future event that some form of providence is giving you a chance to avoid."

"That's silly, Ronnie. Mom would never harm me."

"Listen, Louise is here. She had seven dreams the same night and they're prophetic. They point to you, me, Nanatobi, Brad, and Ursula. In the last dream I'm crying and keep saying 'Why, Renee?' even though you're not there. That can't be good, baby—it can't be! Please, you've got to move out and—"

"Tell me the other dreams," she interrupted, sounding very curious but not the least bit concerned for her safety.

Begrudgingly he fulfilled her request, explaining after he finished that Louise wouldn't tell him the sixth dream.

"Why won't she tell you that one?"

"Louise said it's too embarrassing. Anyway, what's it gonna take to make you see you've got to move out of your parents' house and stay away from your mother?"

Her response floored him. Blowing out a haggard breath, he motioned to Louise. "She wants you to tell her the sixth dream."

As she accepted the phone Nanatobi urgently shook her head, silently mouthing *Don't do it.*

Louise slapped her hand over the mouthpiece. "You think I have a death wish, girl? No way I'd tell Renee that dream."

¶

Stewing over Renee, he didn't say anything while driving back to his apartment. Apparently lost in thought, Louise's lips remained motionless as well. He parked and escorted her into the living room where he finally broke the silence by asking if she was okay.

"Yeah, I guess. But it seems like the whole world just got turned upside down."

"I know the feeling, believe me."

"This is all too freaky, Ronnie. How have you guys kept your sanity?"

He forced a grin and tried to lighten the heavy mood. "Who says we have?"

"Ha, ha, very funny." She unzipped her coat and took it off. "I just don't know what to make of all this."

"Neither do we." He hung his on a plastic hook screwed into the wall and turned the office chair around for her to sit on. "Nanatobi winked at me when she came back into the living room after hearing your dream. Wonder why she did that?"

Louise draped her jacket on the back of the chair and sat down without responding. "Got anything to drink besides coffee?"

"Cola, but it's generic."

"I was referring to alcohol."

He fetched two beers, handed her one, and took the recliner. "Louise, I really need to hear that sixth dream. There may be some clue you're oblivious to that might enlighten me about the meaning of the last one."

"There's not, trust me."

"How can you be so sure? Please tell it to me."

"No."

"Pleeease," he begged with a childish pout, trying to shame her into doing it.

"No, and stop asking me!"

"Well at least tell me the condensed version you told Arnon."

Honing in on him with an angry glower, she took two stiff pulls from the can in rapid succession, exhaled a harsh breath, roughly wiped her lips dry with her free hand, and slammed it on her thigh, not blinking once during the process. "You wanna hear the damn thing? Okay, but just keep in mind I can't help what I dream."

Gone was any hint of embarrassment—he'd clearly pissed her off. "Of course you can't. Now please tell me."

"You and I were standing next to each other beside this huge bed—I mean gargantuan—and Renee was lying on her back in the center, hands crossed at the base of her throat. She looked over at me and said, 'Take care of Ronnie for me. I give him to you with my blessing.' Right after she said that, you and I were alone at my house and . . . ."

"And?"

"We were in my bed." She downed a big gulp of beer. "I think you can fill in the rest without my saying it."

"We had sex?" It flew out of his mouth on the wings of a surprised laugh.

Louise took another quick swig and made a sour face while swallowing. "Give the boy a gold star."

"Man, no wonder you wouldn't tell Renee." While trying to figure out what that dream could possibly represent, he suddenly found himself on top of Louise in an unfamiliar bed. She moaned into his mouth as their loins united, whereupon they both immediately climaxed. He snapped to, horrified to learn his pants were bulging with a hard on. Hoping she hadn't noticed it, he maneuvered off the recliner with a twist to get his back turned towards her quickly as possible, and made for the bathroom where he stayed until his penis deflated.

Self-consciousness overwhelming him, he returned to the living room and faked a yawn. "Boy I'm beat. We need to call it a night or we're liable to keep each other up until the wee hours of the morning worrying about Renee." Though true enough, the real reason she had to leave was so they wouldn't wind up doing something they'd deeply regret.

At least he would . . . .

He couldn't sleep. Concern over Renee's safety had his

nerves on edge, and Louise's erotic fantasy stubbornly refused to vacate his mind. Apparently, finally telling him the sixth dream had caused her to fantasize about it really happening. They way they'd both reached orgasm immediately made him feel pretty certain Louise had never slept with a man. Sex in real life didn't work that way.

Surely she didn't really want that dream to happen. They were friends, nothing more, and that would never change, at least on his end. His heart belonged to Renee and no woman could alter that fact. Unfortunately his libido seemed to have a mind of its own at present. Despite his concern over Renee's welfare, his cock was on the juice again and he couldn't think it back down. Afraid it might keep him awake all night, he finally gave in and masturbated, careful to focus on a mental picture of Renee—and *only* Renee.

TWENTY ONE

"Avogadro's law states that equal volumes of gases under the same pressure and temperature will have identical molecular quantities...."

Trying to get past Louise's fantasy she'd had when class first started, Ronnie scribbled notes as the low-browed professor lectured. She'd envisioned the two of them alone in the classroom, making love on the instructor's desk, once again instantly achieving simultaneous orgasm. Evidently concentrating on physics afterwards, no further imaginings ensued from her.

Louise had to run an errand so he drove to Betty's Café alone. When she finally arrived he felt compelled to explain that he was living out her fantasies, hoping she'd resist the urge to daydream in his presence. Though neither had really happened, they made him feel unfaithful to Renee and he couldn't bear that.

She denied ever having any sort of fantasy involving him.

"So you don't believe me, huh?"

"Nope," she stated resolutely.

"I really hate to do this." He cleared his throat. "Just before class started you and I were doing it on the professor's desk."

"Oh shit . . .!" she jerked her head sideways, the olive tone of her face turning crimson.

He felt horrible but it had to be done. "I'm really sorry. I know how embarrassed you must feel, but I think you can understand why I had to tell you. It happened with Nanatobi too. In fact living out other people's fantasies started with her. I should have been more specific at Brad's last night when the three of us were explaining everything. Since the night of the blackout, not only do I sometimes relive the same string of events twice, if someone near me feels strongly enough about what they're thinking, I see it played out like it's really happening. Nanatobi came up with that theory, and it looks like she's right."

Still looking away she said, "I wonder if Charley's blip is responsible for my dreams as well?"

¶

Arnon stretched out on the couch for a short afternoon nap but soon fell into a trance instead, whereupon he saw a man tied spread-eagle to a massive bed, naked from the waist down. A long golden arrow, centered between his feet, pointed towards his groin. Thirteen women chanted unintelligibly as they slowly marched around the poor soul. Twelve of them wore sheer garments somewhat resembling negligees, but one had on a black robe with a hood hanging down the back. After they circled the bed several times, the female in black pulled the hood over her head, picked up the dart, and all the women stopped moving. Raising it high with both hands, she looked to the ceiling. Strange words issued from her lips as she appeared to be praying. She stopped speaking, lowered her gaze to the helpless man, and with a mighty thrust, impaled the arrow into his chest.

The vision had been a strong one and flustered Arnon so badly he barely made it to the bathroom before vomiting.

¶

"Hello, Curly Sampson." Renee was peeking around the end of the soup aisle, smiling broadly.

Clutching two cans of chicken noodle in each hand Ronnie turned towards her and grinned. "Something I can do for you, miss?"

Less then an hour later they were in his bed.

The mattress springs had quit complaining and they were both sated. Renee lay beside him, lightly stroking his chest. "I wonder why Louise won't elaborate on her sixth dream. All the others seem to tie with the order so I'm really puzzled what she finds so embarrassing about that one."

"Beats me." He didn't want to lie but wasn't about to tell her that dream—she'd go ballistic and demand he keep away from Louise. As far as she knew the contents of that one hadn't been shared with any of them.

"What really baffles me is why Nan and Brad keep seeing Mom and me fighting when we haven't been. I know you guys think they're seeing into the future but they're not. Mom would never hurt me . . . at least not in that way."

He knew what she meant. Though she'd never suffered physical injury at the hands of her mother, Renee had been psychologically devastated by the sex maniac. Musing on that caused him to have a little fantasy of his own about chopping Veronica to pieces with an ax. "They have to be seeing into the future because no other explanation makes sense. Look at Louise's final dream. I'm crying and keep saying your name which implies something awful has happened to you."

She continued the chest massage. "True, but she didn't see me in the dream. I really hope I'm wrong, but my hunch is you're crying because I couldn't break free of Centaurianism and you had to give up on me."

Her statement rattled him—she might have just vocalized the dream's actual meaning. But he soon relaxed. That interpretation couldn't be right because he'd never give up on her. "You don't believe that and you know it. Where there's a will, there's a way, and you want to quit—you know you do."

She kissed his chest and sighed. "That's true, I do want to quit, *badly* . . . but I know I won't be able to."

"Oh yes you will."

"You're grossly underestimating my mother, Ronnie.

There's no way she could have known Nan and I were at The Point, yet she somehow uncannily did, even though she claimed to be stopping by for a drink and was surprised to see us there. I thought I'd be able to break free of her if we moved away from Baltimore, but I don't think so anymore."

That spooked him until he thought on it a moment. "Assuming she's lying as you say, she merely saw your cars in the parking lot while passing by, that's all. That's how she knew you guys were there."

"No, our cars were parked at the university. We walked to The Point from campus. Mom's not very computer literate but even if she was, she couldn't have found us through our cell phones because Nan and I keep our GPS Locators turned off to save battery power."

¶

After dinner she and Brad spent the rest of the evening with Taylor, vegetating in the parlor watching TV. Nanatobi felt ever so content, letting all worries escape for the moment, relaxing with the men she loved.

Taylor rose from his chair. "Come tell me goodnight, Freckle, it's time for this old man to count sheep."

She crossed the room and kissed his cheek. As Taylor pecked her forehead Brad cleared his throat.

"Um, sir, I uh—I beg your permission to ask Nanatobi to marry me."

Electrified by sparks of jubilation, she slapped both hands over her gaping mouth. She had no idea he'd planned to propose tonight. Not only had that come as a delightful surprise, it never occurred to her Brad thought he'd have to clear it with Taylor first.

She knew the stern look of indignance draping her uncle's face was contrived but poor Brad hadn't a clue. "Just what makes you think you're worthy of her, young man?"

The tan seem to flee from his features as the unwitting dupe struggled to answer.

"Well?" Taylor impatiently barked.

"B-Because I love your niece more than any man could ever possibly hope to, sir."

"Oh . . .?" he turned towards her. Brad couldn't see him wink. "Nanatobi, do you believe that to be the case?"

"Yes, Uncle Taylor."

"And how do you feel about him?"

"Not sure yet, depends on whether or not he brought a ring with him."

"Well did you?" Taylor inquired, turning to face him.

"Um no, sir. I want Nanatobi to pick out her engagement ring because I don't trust my judgment on such an important matter and fear I'd choose one she might not like."

She heaved a sigh of fake disappointment. "Looks like you're out of luck then."

"It does indeed," affirmed Taylor, stone-faced.

The pained expression that came over Brad amazed her. How gullible could he be?

Taylor broke down which caused her resolve to crumble. When their laughing fit finally petered out, Brad glowed with exultation as her loving uncle said, "Welcome to the family, son."

¶

The phone woke him. Ronnie grimaced when he saw the clock.

It was two a.m.

"Hello?"

"Ronnie, it's Louise!" She sounded terrified.

"What's wrong?"

*"I had an awful nightmare, and I'm afraid it's prophetic!
Can I please come over . . .?"*

He dressed and made coffee. When Louise arrived she
wasted no time telling the dream.

"I saw a man who sort of looked like Professor Bach bound
and gagged in an open car trunk. Then Professor Bach walked
up and closed it—got in the car and drove off. Next thing I
knew the man was lying on an enormous bed like the one
Renee was on in my sixth dream. His ankles and wrists were
tied with ropes running to each corner of the bed and beneath,
where I assume they'd been fastened to the frame. Renee's
mom walked into the room followed by Professor Bach. They
took off their clothes and Veronica started going down on the
professor. She suddenly pulled away and he ejaculated on the
man. Veronica had this horrible wicked smile on her face as
she raised her arms, looked up at the ceiling and said, 'Oh
Mighty Centaur, we prepare for you this sacrifice.'

"Then everything went dark and a spotlight came on,
shining on a centaur putting an arrow on his bow string. He
drew it back so far I thought the bow would break, but it
didn't. He shot the arrow and the lights came back on. I was
very confused and kept looking around, trying to figure out
where the arrow went. Then I saw it sticking out of the man
tied to the bed, and woke up screaming. Oh, Ronnie, I'm afraid
the dream is a warning that Renee's mother and Professor
Bach really did kill somebody. I'm so scared. Why have I been
given this revelation? I mean, what can I do about it?"

He wanted to give the nerve-racked girl a reassuring hug
but didn't, fearful he'd find himself living out a fantasy
triggered by the action. "I think that one was just a nightmare,
Louise. You had a lot dumped on you last night and the cult
really flipped you out. Since you knew about it before having
the dream, the centaur can't be a validation that it's prophetic.
You've known Renee since grade school. Learning the truth

about her mother—especially Veronica's sexual deviancies— must have shocked you as deeply as if you'd been told she'd killed somebody. Wilhelm Bach is my biochemistry professor, another fact you already knew. With that creepy widow's peek of his, I can see why your subconscious would throw him into the mix. The man looks like a warlock."

A flicker of hope danced across her troubled face. "You think so?"

"Yeah. It was just a nightmare, that's all. It's doubtful Veronica even knows Doctor Bach exists since Renee's never taken biochemistry."

Holding her cup with two unsteady hands, she took a tiny nip of coffee. "I forgot to mention that the car was painted weird."

"How so?"

"The doors and fenders were brown, the hood and trunk were white, and the top was blue."

"Now I'm positive it was a nightmare," he snickered. "What an outlandish color scheme."

It evoked a nervous laugh but her bearing remained grim. "I don't suppose you've ever seen Professor Bach's car have you?"

"No."

"Neither have I."

"Bach dresses too snazzy to drive a bomb like that. More evidence it was just a nightmare."

¶

Louise's dream lay at the forefront of his thoughts when he got to biochemistry. Ronnie glanced at Wilhelm Bach and inwardly chuckled. He'd have made an excellent poster boy for the Nazi Gestapo.

"Pop quiz," announced the professor. "Assume I know nothing and write an essay explaining to me everything we've covered so far concerning recombinant DNA. When you finish, hand it in and you may leave, but you must complete it by the end of class."

Suffering another bad case of the yawns from lack of sleep, he was grateful for the pop quiz. He'd been dreading another reprimand for appearing bored during the lecture, now he didn't have to worry about it.

It took him the better part of an hour to complete the assignment. Bach looked up from a book when he laid the essay on his desk. "Another restless night, Mister Garr?"

His esophagus constricted. How did Bach know he'd had a restless night? He thought of Renee's statement about Veronica's ability to know where she was without any apparent means of being able to, and his imagination went wild. Veronica knew about Louise coming to see him in the wee hours of the morning, why she'd done so, and had informed her accomplice. Until that moment he hadn't even considered the possibility Louise's dream might be prophetic. Now he couldn't help viewing the professor in a different light. "Uh . . . what makes you say that, Doctor Bach?"

"I saw you yawning . . . ."

Ronnie had a good laugh at himself over his exhausted brain making him temporarily paranoid over Bach. But while heading for his Thunderbird his mirth vanished when he saw a brown and white two-tone sedan whose top hadn't received its finish coat which would have covered the blue primer. It could be mere coincidence but he didn't think so. Louise might have seen the car some time ago, forgotten she had, and subconsciously used it as a prop in her nightmare, but he didn't buy that either. He had only one smidgen of hope the car didn't belong to Bach: it wasn't parked in the area reserved for faculty. Ben Palloy's best friend was a retired police sergeant who had two sons in the Baltimore Police Department. Fearful of what he would learn, Ronnie jotted down the tags, got in his T-Bird, and headed for Palloy Transportation.

Ben was lining out one of his drivers when he entered the shop but stopped and turned to him with a grin. "What brings you here on a Tuesday afternoon, Ronnie?"

"Wanted to talk to you about something but it can wait."

The burly guy resumed his instructions. When the driver left to make his delivery Ronnie handed Ben the slip of paper he'd torn from his notebook. "Do you think your policeman friend would mind getting someone to check out this license plate for me?"

A frown jumped on Ben's face. "What, you think your girl's two timing you with whoever owns this vehicle?"

"No, nothing like that. I saw the car parked on campus and want to find out who did the beautiful two tone paint job on it. I know it's a customized job because the top's only got primer on it. It's not that big a deal, but if your friend won't mind, I'd really appreciate it."

"Nah, he won't mind, be back in a minute."

While waiting, Ronnie admired a new set of mags hanging on a rack. As the minutes passed, the sense of dread he'd felt upon seeing the car mounted, reaching a crescendo when his boss returned with the information. Beneath the tag number Ben had scribbled down the name *Wilhelm Bach.*

TWENTY TWO

"Have you been crying?" Nanatobi asked Louise as they strolled across the campus parking lot with Renee.

"No, why'd you ask me that?"

"Your eyes are puffy."

Louise blew out a deep breath through puckered lips. "It's from lack of sleep. I had the most horrible nightmare last night—I saw a man bound and gagged . . . ."

Nanatobi had cringed while hearing the details, but laughed over Louise's fear that it might have been a revelation. "Professor Bach looks like the type of character that would do something like that, but Veronica's many vices don't include murder."

"Oh really?" chided Renee, making a tart face. "Then why do you think she's going to kill me?"

"She's not going to intentionally kill you, sweetie, she's going to accidentally kill you."

Renee giggled and so did Louise.

"You know what I mean. There's no way your nightmare can be prophetic, Louise. There aren't any sacrificial rites in Centaurianism. The order is purely about sex and that's it."

"Nan's right. Disgusting though it is, the order doesn't espouse any form of violence. Are you going to tell Ronnie about it like you did the others?"

"Um, I already have," Louise nervously responded. "We talked earlier."

Seemingly unconcerned about the twitchy way her question got answered, Renee said, "So what does he think?"

"That it was just a nightmare."

Nanatobi studied her best friend's face. If Renee knew, she hid it well. The way Louise had avoided eye contact while relaying the sixth dream in Brad's bedroom had roused her suspicion. It had grown stronger after they'd returned to the living room and she'd caught her gazing at the hunk while he wasn't looking her direction. Her turning into a bundle of nerves over Renee asking if she was going tell him the nightmare confirmed it.

Louise had developed a thing for Ronnie.

¶

Ronnie went to Academic Affairs hoping to find out whose death had caused Bach to cancel last Tuesday's class, and the sex of the deceased if the name crossed genders. No one in that department knew him so they wouldn't be able to tell the professor who'd made the inquiry. Hopefully Bach would never hear anything about this visit.

A thin woman with frosted hair smiled at him from behind a desk adorned with frilly bric-a-brac. "Can I help you?"

"Could you tell me who passed away in Doctor Wilhelm Bach's family last week? I want to offer my condolences."

"How thoughtful of you. It was his cousin, Jon Bach."

So it *was* a man. "Uh, do you happen to know what he died of?"

"He was killed by a mugger . . . ."

Ronnie hurried to the library, impatiently waited until one of the computers became available, called up *The Baltimore Sun,* and searched for Jon Bach.

His body had been found in Druid Hill Park where he'd been stabbed to death in an apparent mugging. The article read like he'd been killed there but Ronnie knew better—his cousin had chosen that location to dump the corpse after Veronica slew him. If he had to drag Renee out by the hair she was no longer going to reside in that house at Wine's Gate. Her mother wasn't merely a perverted nymphomaniac, but a cold blooded killer as well.

He drove home, scribbled the number for the police department on an index card, and walked to the front of his apartment complex to use a payphone so his identity wouldn't show up on Caller ID. But the moment someone answered he hung up as something dawned on him. If they didn't find any evidence in Bach's trunk, having the cops question him would only serve to alert the bastard that someone knew what he'd done. Being such a brilliant man, the odds were heavily stacked against the professor leaving anything incriminating in his car. Veronica was dangerous enough without being forewarned.

The sticky situation left him helpless to do anything about it. Feeling panicky over Renee's safety, he went back to his apartment and called Louise. He could tell by the background noise she was at some bar. "Where are you?"

"At The Point with Renee and Nanatobi."

"I saw the car you dreamed about. It is Professor Bach's."

"Oh no! So it wasn't just a nightmare?"

"No. Fill Renee and Nanatobi in, and tell Renee to plan on staying at my place tonight."

¶

Ronnie got off work an hour before Riley's closed but didn't drive home. Instead he went to Brad's as instructed to by Nanatobi, who'd called him back after he'd gotten off the phone with Louise earlier. She'd logically pointed out that his apartment would be the first place Veronica would look for her daughter. Renee had made arrangements to spend a week with Nanatobi instead. It hadn't aroused any suspicion because they often spent stretches of several days at each other's houses. What Veronica didn't know was that Nanatobi had told her uncle Renee would be staying with her the rest of the

306   ARLEY OWENS, JR.

semester. The need to be away from the distractions of regular life so she could better concentrate on college during this crucial last phase had been given as the reason.

Renee answered the door and greeted him with a kiss. He waved at Louise, perched at the bar—said hello to Brad and Nanatobi, sitting on the couch—and briefed everyone on all he'd learned and done since leaving biochemistry that afternoon.

Nanatobi was livid. "Oh what an evil shitty bitch! All these years Veronica's been deceiving Renee and me about what her true religion really is. God I feel so filthy knowing I've had sex with a fucking murderess."

Not feeling very clean over the matter either, Ronnie glanced at Louise. "You need to call Arnon and tell him about your dream. Or have you already?"

"No, I haven't had the chance since learning it was prophetic after all. Shouldn't somebody call the police?"

"I did already, but hung up without saying anything when something occurred to me." He explained why they should leave law enforcement out of it for the time being.

"Good point," said Brad. "Lou might be the solution. He's made friends with a lot of cops through the years because he offers them a discount to repair their personal vehicles. Maybe he can convince one of them to sneak a peek inside the professor's trunk while he's in class. If the guy finds something, one of us can call the police anonymously and say they need to check it out in connection with the death of Jon Bach."

Ronnie thought that over a minute and nixed the idea. "We'd have to tell him everything. He'd never believe us."

"Oh I think he will," Brad confidently asserted. "He already knows a great deal about what's been going on."

"That's true, Ronnie," said Renee. "He was here when Nanatobi told Brad about her astral projections, and he heard about your visions the same time I did. I know he believes their out of body experiences really happened."

That put the matter in a different light. He dug Bach's tag info out of his pocket and handed it to Brad. "All right then, give him a call."

Brad phoned Lou, laid everything out, passed along the tag number, and hung up the phone smiling. "Well, folks, we have another believer. Lou's positive one of his cop friends will do it and keep mum if nothing turns up in Bach's trunk. Let's just hope there's enough forensic evidence for the police to make a case."

"Dammit!" Ronnie raked a hand through his hair. "I should have thought of it right away. The man was alive when Louise saw him in her dream. Bach obviously transported him to the country house in his trunk but that doesn't mean he took the corpse to Druid Hill Park in it. Better tell Lou to hold off for now. His friend won't find anything other than maybe a few strands of Jon Bach's hair. Doctor Bach can easily account for that by saying his cousin accompanied him on a trip somewhere and must have shed some hair while storing his luggage in the trunk or taking it out. Bach's too intelligent to have used his own car to carry the body away from that country house."

Nanatobi shot him a frown. "You can't know that, Ronnie."

"Sure I can. I wouldn't take such a chance and the professor's a hell of a lot smarter than me. What happened to Jon Bach wasn't a crime of passion, it was a ritualistic slaying, obviously carefully planned out. So you can bet Veronica and Bach made sure nothing would lead the police back to them when they disposed of the body."

"So we're screwed. Is that what you're saying?"

"At least as far as the police being able to help us right now we are."

"I'm afraid Ronnie's right," said Brad resignedly. "I don't

know Wilhelm Bach, but a man with enough brains to earn a doctorate in biochemistry is certainly witty enough not to risk leaving incriminating evidence in the trunk of his car. I'll call Lou back."

As Brad relayed the message to Lou, Ronnie pulled Louise aside. "You need to call Arnon and tell him your dream so we can get his counsel on what to do."

"It's pretty late."

"I don't care, you need to call him."

"Okay, but I'm going to tell him you insisted. I'll do it at Charley's next door. It won't be a toll call from there."

"I thought he didn't get off work until eleven."

"He doesn't, but he gave me a key to his apartment."

Renee sank into an armchair crying the moment Louise left. He stepped behind her and massaged her shoulders. "Hang in there, baby, we'll get through this."

"I knew my mother was an extreme oddball," she sniffled, "but I never dreamed she was capable of murder."

"Oh, sweetie . . ." Nanatobi hurried over and grabbed her hands. "Please stop crying. You're safe. Veronica wouldn't dare try to make you leave my house against your will. Taylor would never take her word over yours and mine, and she knows what a powerful man he is."

"I'm not worried about me!" Renee bitterly ejaculated. "It's you I'm crying over. I love you so much, Nan, but I wish we'd never met, then I wouldn't have drug you into this fucking nightmare."

"Enough of that shit!" Nanatobi leaned forward and embraced Renee, cheek to cheek. "You didn't force me to join—I chose to of my own free will. Ronnie's right, we'll get through this and finally be free of Veronica's hold over us."

Brad hung up the phone and joined forces with them. They spent the next half hour trying to cheer up Renee, and had almost succeeded when Louise walked in with a pallid expression on her face, several small squares of blue paper in her hand.

"What's that?" queried Brad, pointing at them.

"Arnon's vision. I made him repeat it so I could write it down on Charley's notepad. Let me read it to you." She wiped a tear from the corner of her eye and began. "He saw a man tied to a bed with an arrow lying between his feet, and thirteen women chanting as they circled the bed . . . ."

The frightening similarities between Louise's dream and Arnon's vision made Ronnie shudder with awe. He could tell by the look on Nanatobi's face, the way Brad's mouth hung open, and the utter shock in Renee's weepy eyes, they felt the same.

Louise lowered her notes and sighed. "He said his vision and my dream were one, and that the centaur with the arrow in my dream was the woman with the arrow in his vision. The man in his vision and my dream wasn't a prophetic warning of what was to come but a picture of what had already happened."

Renee broke down again. Nanatobi kissed her forehead, hooked an arm in Brad's, and led him to the couch. Ronnie tried once more to assuage her grief but stopped when Nanatobi started speaking.

"Those garments in his vision are hanging on a rack in the country house. The black one was only to be worn by the male chosen for the orgies, that's what Renee and I had always been told. There were never thirteen women, only four. Until Ursula joined there was just the three of us after Veronica's mother died. There were only five meetings I was a part of where we actually had a man wearing that black robe. Five different men—men neither Renee nor I knew.

"Veronica chose each one. She'd seduce him, bring him to the house in the country, drug him with the potion, and then we'd all have sex with him. I've always wondered why there

310 ARLEY OWENS, JR.

was never a repeat performance. Every one of them wanted to come back for more, yet we never saw them again. I should have realized there was more than met the eye all along because of the numerous white gowns hanging in that room when the membership was limited to four. Veronica's mother said the centaur had magically put the others there and they were never to be touched. Renee and I knew that was a crock of shit but we put it off to just another one of the woman's deluded superstitions. Whatever The Order of Centaurians really is, it involves twelve women Renee and I have never seen. Since Arnon saw thirteen women when the man was sacrificed, there's one murderess, Veronica, and twelve accomplices." She cut her eyes to Brad. "I'm starting to feel tingly which always happens before—"

Nanatobi slumped over on the couch.

So did Brad.

"Unbelievable," uttered Louise, staring at their limp forms.

Renee grabbed his hands and squeezed.

Twenty minutes passed before the astral travelers woke up. Brad's sunlamp-toned face turned white as he came to.

Nanatobi's blazed with terror. "Renee, you're not going home again *EVER!*"

TWENTY THREE

After Wednesday's physics class, Ronnie chauffeured Louise to his apartment for coffee so they could discuss what Nanatobi and Brad had seen the night before. They couldn't risk being overheard at Betty's Café.

¶

Still deeply unnerved by the ordeal, Brad sat in his office recalling the bizarre scene they'd witnessed from their combined astral essence. Nanatobi theorized it happened because Renee had been present when she left her body. With the exception of the first time they'd become one and neither of them knew where they'd been taken, she'd always gone to where Renee was. But last night they'd found themselves floating beneath the ceiling of the living room of what Nanatobi referred to as the country house.

The horrid scene played out in his mind:

They saw twelve women speaking with Veronica Van Cedar and Wilhelm Bach. The ladies may as well have been nude because the sheer robes they wore hid nothing, but Veronica and Bach were fully clothed. Nanatobi didn't recognized any of them. They looked very much alike with features resembling the painted faces of porcelain dolls, but their appearances soon transformed. Like Nanatobi, he unerringly sensed that Veronica and Bach not only didn't perceive the change, they were completely unaware of the true likenesses of the dozen unworldly beings.

Their splendid hair disappeared as the lovely pale faces contorted into gargoyle-like countenances with eyes shrunk down to blazing red dots centered in hollow sockets. Horrible fangs protruded from ghastly black lips. Talons erupted through fingertips elongating from hands no longer creamy but ash-gray and scaly. Exquisite, thrusting breasts withdrew into bony rib-cages covered by skin resembling weathered leather. Curvy hips and shapely legs gave way to bare sinew and stringy muscle. Delicate bare feet contorted into cloven hooves, parted in thirds. Then, as if whatever power bestowing their astral abilities knew their minds would snap if they beheld the hideous visages any longer, the beings abruptly reacquired the illusion of feminine beauty as observed by Veronica and Bach.

The macabre women had been discussing what to do about the problem with Renee. One of the ghouls, whose human disguise was a shade fairer to behold than the rest, spoke. "This young man has a powerful gift that's been given to him from the side of the light. If Renee cannot be persuaded to separate from him, we must remove her from this plane of existence. The omen is clear. We cannot harm the gifted one or another from the side of the light will be sent with even greater power. Therefore, since your efforts to corrupt him and bring him to our side have been thwarted, he must now be avoided at all cost."

"I don't sense any such power in him," Veronica skeptically replied.

The professor buttressed her statement.

"Fools!" shouted the woman.

The way Veronica and Bach recoiled from the reprimand made it obvious this entity disguised as a human female was really the one in charge of the cult.

"No such power you say? How about this for power? The night you first tried to lure him here, he *was* here and you almost succeeded, but the power from the side of the light granted him a reprieve. He went back in time to the beginning, and refused to follow you a second time. His visions are so strong, he perceives them as if he actually lives them. We have never witnessed such occurrences before."

Veronica squinted at her with a bewildered frown. "With all due respect, Holy One, are you certain of this? If it happened, why can't I remember?"

A burst of derisive laughter streamed from the woman's painted lips. "You need only ask Renee, she'll tell you it happened. Or ask Ursula. She too will verify that it did."

"How is it they can remember it when I can't?"

"They do not recall it, foolish one, because it never really happened except in the young man's perception. He proved it to them by describing certain things he couldn't have known otherwise. The powers of light also warned him about you and Ursula by giving him a vision of the two of you bringing him here. He fled before you arrived at his apartment to enchant him. Any further attempts will prove just as futile.

"You know that we feed off the energy created on the bed, and for that purpose we need Renee to stay on this plane. But it would be far better to suffer the hunger of one less than to have you all exposed and face total starvation. You have one week to convince her to renounce the gifted one or you must destroy her. That is all for now." The twelve hideous creatures disguised as beautiful human women dematerialized and a dozen piles of silk littered the floor.

At that moment he, like Nanatobi, inexplicably ascertained that those beings weren't aware that Ursula had broken the code by telling him, and later Ronnie, about the cult. They only knew that Ronnie had told her and Renee about his mysterious first visit to the country house.

Veronica gathered the garments while Bach took off his clothes. The naked academician, whose identity he knew only because of being metaphysically bound with his fiancé, followed her into a large twelve-sided room in the center of which sat the biggest bed he'd ever seen. Veronica stripped, exposing a body so dazzling it aroused him even in his astral state, and lay down on the giant bed.

When the German climbed on top of her, he and Nanatobi had opened their eyes in his apartment to behold the concerned faces of Ronnie, Renee, and Louise.

¶

"I'm glad you made me call Arnon again afterwards," said Louise, referring to the demand he'd made after Nanatobi and Brad had recounted their out of body ordeal.

Ronnie swallowed a slurp of coffee and gazed at his cup. "I can't believe he thinks there's hope for Veronica."

"Me either. But if he's right about those twelve women being demons whose power over Veronica can be neutralized once her eyes are opened to the truth, she might prove to be as normal as you or I."

"Speak for yourself," he said dryly. "I'm no longer what most people consider normal."

¶

Arnon rocked back and forth, teacup in hand, musing on what Louise had laid on him about the out of body dreamers' latest astral excursion when she'd called a second time last night. He'd advised her what he knew in his spirit to be true. Veronica Van Cedar thought she only came in contact with the twelve women at that house, believing them to be spiritual advisors sent from the centaur she worshipped. They were really imps of Satan—fallen angels who never ventured away from the misguided soul, invisibly manipulating her like a dozen puppeteers. Jesus Christ was the only hope for that woman.

The Lord had given him a vision of her as a child, weeping over her father who'd been laid to rest the day before. While

Veronica mourned in her bedroom, her mother—an amazingly handsome woman—was busy decorating her house with obscene paintings of a centaur. A *knowing* had come to him that The Order of Centaurians was really birthed from the woman's desire to be worshipped, not from a dream she'd falsely claimed to have had. Taking advantage of her self-idolatry and lascivious mind, the devil had given her a means to achieve that end by supplying her with a recipe for a concoction only the strongest wizards and witches of ancient times were familiar with. Having no idea those thoughts were implanted, she assumed it to be her own invention, though she claimed to have received the formula from the centaur.

Through the power of that potion she convinced her sisters to worship the centaur and to do so by paying homage to a nude portrait of her, insisting he'd called for that method of obeisance because she was his only prophetess. As the years passed after she brought Veronica into the fold, the deluded woman got far more than she'd bargained for, though she never knew it. Veronica became such a strong believer in the centaur that she'd unwittingly completely opened herself up to Satan.

Eight years ago her mother had a real dream—a nightmare in which she learned to her horror that the centaur really did exist, totally ignorant of the fact it was merely a demon in disguise. The evil spirit told her she'd find twelve additional gowns hanging in the ritual room upon waking, which she did. Those garments were symbolic of the twelve signs of the zodiac and were never to be moved, she'd been told. He warned her to teach Veronica how to make the potion or she'd surely die, and commanded that she let Veronica chose the male for the rituals she'd feigned to be a revelation from the creator of the universe. Upon receiving that authority Veronica was sent a dozen emissaries to help her—the twelve demons beheld by the out of body dreamers. Under their direction she began secretly offering the highest gift possible to the centaur—a human sacrifice.

¶

"What are you going to do about biochemistry?" asked Louise as he refilled their cups.

"Somehow I'm going to have to act normal and not arouse his suspicion." Ronnie put the pot back on the burner of his cheap coffee maker and returned to the table. "I can't afford to drop the class even though there's nothing I want to do more. It's going to be creepy as hell being in the same room with Bach after what I've learned about him, but I don't have any choice."

Louise grimaced. "I couldn't do it. I'd drop biochemistry like a hot potato if I couldn't switch classes, and make it up in the summer."

"My schedule won't allow it. As things stand now I'll be graduating at the end of this semester, and I want to work for Ben Palloy full time all summer to build up a stash and start working towards my masters next fall." He didn't tell her that *stash* would be used to buy Renee a beautiful wedding ring to replace the cheap one he'd be forced to put on her finger the day after they graduated. No one knew of their wedding plans and they intended to keep it that way until the last moment because Renee felt that was the only surefire way to keep Veronica from finding out. He'd ask Ben Palloy to be his best man and Renee would have Nanatobi as her maid of honor in a quick civil ceremony.

¶

Brad had never seen Renee in formal attire. The sequins on

her mauve cocktail dress glistened like diamonds as she strolled into the dining room appearing as much at home in the opulent chamber as Nanatobi, decked in black with scarlet accessories.

His future employer smiled as Jim and Suzanne seated them. "I understand you'll be spending an extended period of time with us, Renee."

"Yes, hope it won't be an inconvenience."

Taylor's smile brightened. "Not in the least, glad to have you."

"Thank you."

"Not that I mind, since I'm not expecting company any time soon, but why have you decided to use the guestroom this visit?"

"So Nan and I won't get on each others' nerves during my prolonged stay."

Nanatobi giggled. "We love each other dearly but we don't do well sleeping in the same bed. Renee snores something awful."

"Nan!"

"Well you do."

"Oh yeah? And just who hogs the covers, huh?"

A sheepish grin was Nanatobi's only reply.

Taylor laughed and glanced his way. "Tell me, Brad, have you ever seen two lovelier young ladies?"

"No, sir," he cheerfully agreed, "I certainly haven't."

Nanatobi pecked her uncle on the cheek as Renee said, "How sweet of you to say, Mister Cain."

The tycoon exaggeratedly cleared his throat. "Renee, we've known each other since Nanatobi came to live with me. I think it's about time you started calling me Taylor, don't you?"

"Renee and I are closer than sisters," Nanatobi broke in before Renee could reply. "Would it seem inappropriate if she were to call you Uncle Taylor too?"

"Well I'd be delighted. Unless of course she doesn't want to."

A blush tainted Renee's beautiful cheeks, framed by lavish swirls of ginger. "Thank you, *Uncle Taylor*."

The industrialist beamed.

Brad couldn't recall witnessing such a radical change in anyone. When he'd first sat down at this table Taylor Cain had been extremely aloof, very intimidating, and came off like an old cantankerous eccentric ready to bite the head off anyone who displeased him. Those traits had started to ebb the moment he'd quit feeling patronized by Nanatobi's affection and had steadily regressed since. Now cordial and happy, the man looked ten years younger. Jim and Suzanne had changed as well, smiling a lot and obviously enjoying their jobs—a far cry from the way they'd acted at first, always stiffly at attention with expressionless faces.

Delicious crab cakes, French fries, coleslaw, and chocolate sundaes were greatly enhanced by the merriment of an uncle conversing and joking with his niece and her best friend. Brad didn't participate much but thoroughly enjoyed their witty bantering. After dinner Nanatobi gave Taylor a goodnight kiss, bade Renee to do likewise, the two girls changed clothes, and the three of them went to his apartment.

Brad eavesdropped on their conversation while making a round of drinks.

"What's gotten into Taylor, Nan? I hardly knew the man sitting at the head of that table tonight."

Nanatobi donned a big smile. "When I fell in love with Brad I somehow fell back in love with Taylor as well. He's really loosened up, and when you get to know the new him, you'll really be getting to know the old him before I started acting like such a bitch towards him."

A patronizing laugh vacated Renee's pretty mouth. "Oh you can be a real bitch all right. I, on the other hand, well I'm just sweeter than sugar at all times."

"Sure you are," Nanatobi teased. "You're the only person I know that can top me in the bitch department, especially when you're PMS-ing."

"When *I'm* PMS-ing—give me a break! Only Mom tops you in that department, honey." Renee's face dropped immediately after the statement left her lips. "Sorry I brought her up. Anyway, back to Taylor. I wonder why he never got married?"

Brad perked his ears, very curious to hear.

"Oh, sweetie, it's such a tragic, heartrending story. He fell in love with a girl he met in kindergarten and they were sweethearts all the way through school. They both got accepted by Harvard and planned a June wedding once they'd graduated college. But the summer of their junior year they went on a safari with her father and the poor girl got bitten by a tsetse fly. She died of trypanosomiasis."

"What's that?"

"Sleeping sickness," he spouted involuntarily, moved by the tragedy.

"How horrible!"

"Yeah," sighed Nanatobi. "Anyway, that was the only girl for him. He never even dated another woman."

"Wow, no wonder he's such a grouch."

"No, Renee, that was because of me. Like I said, wait till you get to know the real him. He's the greatest guy in the world. We were super close until the first time he grounded me. I was bound and determined to prove he couldn't enforce it, and when he put the lock on my bedroom door and bars on the windows I just hated him for it. I know now he had my best interest at heart and was just trying his best to raise me properly. Secretly I knew it all the while but was just too spiteful and prideful to admit it. The more I disrespected him, the more respect he demanded, and the stricter he got."

Brad chuckled. "He put bars on your windows?"

"Oh yeah . . . ."

¶

Taylor was having a brandy and cigar. Still astounded by the offer, so was Jim. The billionaire owner of T-Cain Corporation had actually asked—and rather persistently—that he join him in the study. He'd been the head of Taylor's household staff five years shy of two decades and never had such an invitation been extended. At his employer's insistence he sat on a brown leather Chesterfield sofa facing the lone exterior wall where four immense floor-to-ceiling windows offered a graphic view of the magnificent grounds from the second floor. It felt strange being in this luxurious room without serving something or helping one of the housekeepers tidy up. How often he'd wanted to pilfer a snort of the expensive liquor when refilling the crystal decanter. Now he held an eighteenth-century snifter full of it while smoking a forty dollar cigar.

Sitting behind his massive Napoleonic desk, Taylor exhaled a perfect smoke ring and watched it float towards the ceiling like a wavering doughnut. "I don't know if you're aware of it or not but I wasn't always a man of means, Jim. My father sold life insurance and left a sizable policy when he died of a heart attack, I believe brought on by the sorrow and stress of losing my mother to leukemia only three months before. My brother and I split that policy. He was twenty, I was twenty-three. I started T-Cain Corporation with my half while he sank his into real estate.

"He made his first million before I did but I was a billionaire by the time I turned thirty. I surpassed him because I kept my nose to the grindstone while he enjoyed the life of an international playboy until meeting a beautiful Swedish model at thirty-seven. She was only eighteen. They soon wed and she gave birth to Nanatobi a year later. This mansion was under construction at the time. Before it was completed I'd made a trip to England to find the best people for my household staff.

"Six years later my butler inherited a rare stamp collection which he sold for several million dollars. No longer having to work for a living, he left my employ. When I went to London to find a replacement for him at the British Butler Institute, I held little hope of locating his equal. I recall such mixed emotions—happiness for him as he set off to enjoy a life of ease, bitterness on my end that his good fortune had taken him from me. Ah but then I took a chance on you and have never regretted it. I'm raising your salary twenty percent. You've served me exceedingly well and have put up with me for a pittance of what you should have received, working for such an ogre. My apologies for almost a decade of ill temperament and my assurances that those days are over. Isn't it wonderful to have our old Nanatobi back? It's given me a new lease on life."

His jaw slackened at hearing the wonderful surprise but he soon firmed it with a grateful smile. "It is indeed, Sir, and thank you for the elevation of my salary. You've been most generous since I've been in your employ these fifteen years, but the increase is very greatly appreciated."

Taylor laughed as if hearing something absurd. "Humph! You're not going to admit you've worked for a boorish tyrant for the last nine of those fifteen, are you?"

¶

Charley's fingers trembled at his temple. "Orb five-nine-nine, do you read me?" He kept repeating the message and getting no reply. Right after the passenger jet entered BWI airspace, the pilot had requested emergency clearance to land because he'd just learned the electrical system had been sabotaged by a suicidal flight attendant.

¶

Brad answered the doorbell to let Louise in. She looked very upset.

"What's wrong?" asked Renee.

"I just heard on the radio there was a plane crash near BWI. A hundred and thirty people were killed."

Nanatobi switched on the TV and flipped to a local channel where a news commentator was concluding an announcement of the calamity . . . .

¶

Having to work till close, Ronnie couldn't meet with everyone at Brad's. He hoped their brainstorming session would yield a means to nail Veronica and Bach because he sure hadn't been able to think of a way to do it. What a crazy world. People with good intentions seemed to be dunces when it came to thwarting the slick maneuverings of evil minds. The animal kingdom reflected that sad fact. Prey knew only to flee from danger, while the predators alone had the wherewithal to entrap and kill.

Pushing a shopping cart stuffed with a dozen bags of groceries, he followed an elderly Portuguese lady to her car. A Riley's regular, the poor dear seldom purchased anything with cash, using food stamps instead.

"Such a shame about all those people," she said as he filled her trunk.

"What people are you referring to, ma'am?"

"Those poor souls on that plane that blew up while trying to land at BWI."

Ronnie hoped the casualty hadn't been under Charley's supervision.

¶

He found a parking space, shut off the engine, and lowered his forehead to the steering wheel. When the tears finally stopped, he got out of his car and went inside. His favorite bartender had obviously heard the news.

"I'm sorry, Charley." Harry set a four-ounce glass on the bar and filled it with Johnny Walker Black. "On the house . . . ."

At first he thought the mental image of a coffin stemmed from obsessing over the death of all those people aboard that sabotaged jet. But when Ronnie Garr walked up to it bawling, asking the same question over and over, it finally dawned on him that for the first time in his life he was having a vision. The thing vanished from his mind's eye as abruptly as it started and he felt compelled to call Ronnie despite the fact his watch read twelve-fifteen. He left a tip for Harry and pulled out his cell while making for the door . . . .

TWENTY FOUR

The big black man greeted him with a cup of coffee. Ronnie could only imagine how bad he felt—the plane that went down *had* been under his guidance. They'd talked about the crash over the phone, but weren't discussing it at the moment. A queasy feeling cramped his gut over what had prompted this visit. "Okay, why are you so fearful trouble lies ahead for Renee and me."

Charley ran a hand over his face and fueled his lungs with a deep breath. "Man, nothing like this has ever happened to me before. I was feeling sorry for all those people aboard that plane, furious at the sicko that caused their deaths, and kept picturing a coffin. Then I saw you walk up to it and realized I was having a vision. You were bawling your eyes out and kept saying 'Why, Renee?' while looking down at it. The casket was closed but by the way you were acting she must have been in it. I hated to call so late, knowing you were bound to be in bed, but something told me I had to and that you needed to hear it in person."

A tremor of dread radiated from the pit of his stomach. "Louise dreamed practically the same thing, except she didn't see a coffin."

Charley nervously rubbed his jaw. "So she told you her dreams?"

"You know about them then?"

"She didn't get a chance to elaborate, just told me she'd had some odd dreams. I told her to call Arnon and tell them to him."

Ronnie felt putrid all over, but the sensation failed to quench a spark of hope that whatever power was acting upon him, Nanatobi, Brad, Louise, and now Charley, had done so in order to forewarn them so Renee's fate wouldn't be decided at the hands of Veronica. "Those dreams were prophetic, and she had another one about a human sacrifice."

Charley grimaced while hearing the details of Louise's night vision starring Veronica and Bach. His hands were shaking.

¶

Ronnie was glad to be so sleepy this time as he walked out of biochemistry. The fatigue affected him like a sedative, allowing him to calmly sit through the lecture. He'd even managed to laugh along with his fellow students when Bach stopped mid sentence and said, "Can anyone spare a sleeping pill for the yawning Mister Garr?"

He drove to his apartment, stripped to his skivvies, and crashed.

¶

After work Brad met Lou for a beer at a sports bar in Fell's Point where they sometimes took on some of their high school buddies in a game of foosball. Due to Lou's talented wrists, they usually won. He reiterated in greater detail everything he'd told him over the phone. "Ronnie thought you wouldn't believe me until Renee convinced him otherwise."

Lou swallowed a mouthful of beer and grinned. "We've been buds too many moons for me to doubt you, partner."

"I appreciate that."

"Besides, I never would have believed you if Nanatobi hadn't dropped that bomb the night she came to your party."

"Up yours, Lou," he jokingly retaliated while turning up his bottle.

The Okie did likewise and started scratching his stubbly Adam's apple. "Are you sure you don't want me to talk to my cop buddy?"

"Mm hmm. Ronnie and I both fear nothing incriminating

would be found and we can't afford for Veronica to sniff out any possibility we know what she did. I think Veronica and Bach may be responsible for five other deaths as well."

Lou narrowed his eyes. "Why's that?"

"Nanatobi said Veronica has brought five different men to that house in the country for an orgy since she became a member. Each one had been enthralled with the experience and yet, according to Veronica, none of them ever accepted an invitation back." His cell started playing *Love Is All Around* by The Troggs. He'd chosen the ring-tone for Nanatobi's calls. "Hey, babe, what's up?"

"Renee, Louise, and I have decided to have a girls only night, baby, so I won't be seeing you until tomorrow evening."

That devastated him. He'd been thinking of nothing all day but making love to her after having devised a means for them to be alone. "I'd hoped to have you all to myself tonight while Ronnie took Renee out on the town, compliments of yours truly. I have a very romantic evening planned."

"Sorry, Romeo, but I shalt not suffer thy presence until the morrow . . . ."

¶

She and Renee were at Louise's house. The rambling two-storey edifice standing on an acre of land in the heart of Carrollton Ridge cut quite a contrast to the rowhouses in the area. A liberated slave had built it after the civil war. He'd taken on his master's surname Hudson upon being given the land along with his freedom. It now belonged to the widow of his great-great grandson, who'd raised Louise.

Nanatobi loved the old style atmosphere of the place and savored an aroma that permanently lingered in the kitchen—an amalgamation of scents lying somewhere between those of a bakery and a fried chicken joint. Betty Louise—she refused to be called just Betty—was at the stove stirring a big steaming pot of peaches in preparation for a cobbler. Her fat-gorged waist strained at a thin apron string tied in back of a blue frock which ended at the middle of two shapeless cellulose-quilted calves, supported by wide feet inserted into orthopedic shoes. They were chatting with the old woman while waiting for Louise, who'd gone upstairs to pack a bag for an overnighter at her house.

"How's your uncle getting on these days, Nanna-toe?"

"Nanatobi," she giggly corrected. Though often protesting it, she secretly enjoyed hearing Betty Louise call her that.

"You'll always be Nanna-toe to me, child . . ." she turned from the stove just long enough to make a face at her.

This time Renee laughed too.

"Taylor's doing great."

"Glad to hear it."

¶

When Betty Louise used the term Nanna-toe again, Renee thought back to when she'd first started calling Nanatobi Nan. It had slipped out naturally not long after they met, and she'd rarely used her full name since, unless referring to her when speaking to someone else. Some of their friends, including Louise, liked the shorten version as well and had tried to use it, only to receive a stern reprimand. Through the years any new acquaintance that tried got the same rebuke—"Only Renee can call me Nan!" Not only did she alone have that privilege, Nan had never invited any friend but her to Taylor's mansion. This would be Louise's first time to see the magnificent edifice from the inside.

How she wished she'd never asked her dearest friend to spend the weekend that fateful day seven years ago when her mother came into her room and said, "Renee, I think it's time for Nanatobi to visit your grandmother's country house." Having dealt with the horrid shame of Centaurianism for two years at the time, she hadn't wanted Nan to suffer the same fate, but had been powerless to resist her mother. So at the tender age of fourteen her best friend was mesmerized by the potion, then molested by her mother, her grandmother, and her.

Nan had relished it from the start, which somewhat lessened her sense of guilt as time went on, but never completely. Oceans of it washed over her now as she quietly observed *Nanna-toe* kidding around with the jolly fat lady stirring syrupy peaches. An aura of happiness shrouded her, stemming from being in love with Brad and her rekindled affection for Taylor.

They'd had so much fun as innocent kids before she'd woke up one morning with blood on her panties and went crying to her mother. "Nothing to worry about, Renee," she'd been told. "You've just had your first period that's all. Welcome to womanhood."

She'd gotten inducted into the order three days later. After that, only Nan remained innocent . . . until . . . .

As she thought of her culpability in corrupting the sweet girl clowning around with Louise's grandmother, remorse overwhelmed her and a reckoning occurred deep within. There was only one way to rectify what she'd done to that precious freckled redhead she so deeply loved.

¶

Mopping the floors at Riley's Grocery, Ronnie hoped Renee's girls only night with Nanatobi and Louise wouldn't be spent at a nightclub full of handsome men. He'd be off work in ten minutes and his batteries were fully charged because of a long afternoon nap. Caught up on his studies and not having his sweetheart to spend the remaining hours of wakefulness with, a boring night lay ahead.

¶

It was a sad ol' sorrowful night. Arnon had awoke at dawn with the notion he should drive to Baltimore and have Charley find out Veronica Van Cedar's address from Ronnie so he could go see her. He'd hoped to enlighten her to the fact she'd been enslaved by those twelve demons and would never be liberated from them without asking Jesus into her heart. But despite his concern that the task would never be accomplished otherwise—due to people like her requiring someone with a vast amount of patience, an unshakable faith in God's word, and the spiritual gifts to break through the formidable Satanic barriers blinding her to the truth—he couldn't do it. Not because of the road, it had finally gotten plowed yesterday, and not due to claustrophobia.

The Lord forbade it.

He knew this because his morning meditation had been interrupted by a thump as his Bible hit the floor, dropping off the coffee table for no apparent reason. It had fallen open, and when he picked it up these words jumped out at him from the page: *Thou shalt not go with them.* It was from the book of Numbers, chapter twenty-two, verse twelve. He'd closed the leather-bound King James Version and attempted to put it back on the coffee table but the book had slipped from his fingers as if being knocked away by an invisible hand, falling open at the exact same spot. That time the last two words of the declaration had appeared too blurry to read, as had all the other text except *Thou shalt not go.*

Since he hadn't told anyone about his plans, no one could accuse him, as Aunt Betty Louise had years ago, of faking claustrophobia because he didn't want to drive in the city. Unable to track Veronica down, he'd tried to devise a plan to get her out to the farm, but after hours of deliberation he'd finally thrown in the towel. Short of breaking the law and having Charley kidnap her, he couldn't think of any way to lure that woman to him.

Why was The Almighty preventing him from helping that poor misguided soul?

¶

Nanatobi sat in Taylor's easy chair. He'd just gone to bed after entertaining the three of them with his amazing repertoire of card tricks which she'd begged him to demonstrate for her two guests. Renee and Louise had chimed in with her, and they'd finally coaxed him into giving in. Jim, Alfred, Suzanne, and the housekeepers had retired to their quarters so they had the whole first floor to themselves. She glanced at Louise, sitting on the davenport next to Renee. "So what happened to you and Danny Hill?"

"He tried to move too far, too fast."

Renee leaned forward and took a lemon drop from a crystal basin on the coffee table. "I was so jealous of you over that."

Louise laughed. "You think I don't know you were only pretending for my sake? He doesn't have the guts to approach you or Nanatobi. He saw me as an easy conquest. It's a shame such a handsome guy has to be such a jerk. He just *could not believe* I wouldn't sleep with him on the first date. He said, 'Look, baby, we both know it's gonna go down anyway, so why waste time?' I can still picture that look of absolute astonishment on his face when I told him no thanks and made him take me home. I was obviously the first girl that had ever refused him, and his ego just couldn't allow his brain to process such information."

"I've never slept with a guy on the first date," said Renee, reaching for another candy. "Not even Ronnie."

"Prude," razzed Nanatobi. "I'm not sure I've ever not slept with a guy on the first date. Of course I always made them use a rubber. Brad's the only exception, but I was already in love with him before we did it."

Cheeks turning pink, Louise timorously cleared her throat. "Girls, I have a confession to make. I've never slept with a guy on any date."

"You're a virgin?" she blurted along with Renee, who looked as stunned as she felt.

"Yeah."

She winked at Renee and gave Louise a flirty smile. "Ever done it with a woman?"

"Don't start, Nan."

Louise shook her head, now fully blushing. "I've never done it with anybody."

¶

Betty's Café was packed so they went to his apartment for their tri-weekly coffee date. Ronnie brought their cups to the table and sat down across from Louise. "Did you guys enjoy your girls only night?"

"Mm hmm."

"Did you go clubbing?" He was apprehensive of the answer but had to ask.

"No, we just hung out at Nanatobi's. Her uncle amazed us with some card tricks. He's quite a magician."

The thought of billionaire Taylor Cain spending some of his valuable time entertaining his niece's friends both amused and relieved him. "Sounds like an innocuous enough evening to suit me. I was picturing the three of you at a nightclub with Renee dancing the night away with the proverbial handsome stranger."

Louise grinned. "Hardly. Nanatobi wanted Renee and I to get to know Taylor better. What a charming guy. After he went to bed we just sat around and visited. I'd never been inside the mansion before. That thing is four stories tall and you can reach each level by either climbing beautiful curving stairways or riding an elevator. Nanatobi's and Taylor's bedrooms are on the third floor, the servants quarters are on the fourth. Renee and I slept in the guestroom on the second floor. It's set up like a fancy hotel suite built to accommodate an entire family. You would not *believe* how swank everything is. Except for Taylor's parlor, which is rather modest compared to all the other rooms Nanatobi showed me when I begged for a tour, you'd swear you were in a palace."

"Some people have it rough, don't they?" he chuckled out. "I saw the outside of that sucker so I'm not surprised to hear the interior's so impressive. Did you girls come up with any ideas on how to solve the problem of ensnaring Veronica and Bach?"

She shook her head despondently. "I'm afraid the problem remains as enigmatic as always."

¶

"Great," said Taylor when his broker called him with the news. He pressed an intercom and told his secretary to get Brad on the phone. A few minutes later she had the two of them connected. "Brad, you're talking to the new majority owner of Mirror Tech . . . ."

¶

Brad hung up the phone and waltzed into what from henceforth would be his office. Sniffing a deep breath through his nostrils, he raised his right hand and said, "Give me five, Boss! The deed is done."

Jesse launched from his desk and high-fived him before they hugged each other in mutual congratulations over their career advancements. "How sweet it is, Brad boy, how sweet it is!"

¶

"Hello, Arnon."

"Well now how did you know it was me calling, Charley?"

A laugh filled his ear. "I've got Caller ID, you old fool."

"Oh. Mary Jo wanted to get one of those things but I told her no, on account it would up the phone bill a few dollars a month. Anyway, the road's passable and Ronnie needs to get out here lickety-split if not sooner."

"I'll let him know."

"Remind him to bring Nanatobi, and I'd like to meet his girlfriend as well. I want to hear all the ins and outs of that cult they belong to. I'll be expecting them tonight."

"This is a Friday, Arnon, he works at a grocery store on week nights."

"Not this one he won't . . . ."

¶

Ronnie picked up the phone. "Hello?"

"Charley here. Gotta make this quick because I'm at work. Arnon called me this morning and he wants you to come see him tonight. I told him you wouldn't be able to but he won't take no for an answer. Think you can get the night off?"

He turned shivery. "Just a few minutes ago my boss called and told me not to come in because he had to close the store due to no electricity. A transformer went out in a substation that powers the area around Riley's Grocery and it'll take the electric company several hours to replace it."

"Well, can't say I'm too surprised to hear that. Arnon said you wouldn't be working tonight. He wants you to bring Nanatobi and Renee along so they can educate him on whatever that bad thing is they're involved in."

"Okay. I'll round them up an be on my way, but first I need directions. I hardly ever remember a new route when I'm just a passenger."

¶

With Renee by his side, Ronnie steered his Thunderbird towards Arnon's farm. He glanced at Louise through the rearview mirror, sitting in back with Nanatobi. "If I'd known you were coming along, I wouldn't have had to ask Charley for directions."

"No, it's a good thing he gave them to you. I haven't been out there in so long I'm not sure I remember the way myself."

He no longer needed Ursula to inform the farmer about Centaurianism because Renee and Nanatobi were going to, though neither thought doing so would help matters. If they had a change of heart he'd do it, since Renee had released him from his promise not to mention the cult to anyone.

"The scenery is so pretty out here," said Nanatobi. *"Over the river and through the wood, to grandfather's house we go.* Sing with me, Renee!"

"The horse knows the way to carry the sleigh through the white and drifted snow-oh," Renee giggled as much as sang.

He grinned as the two best friends, in heartfelt unison, crooned, *"Over the river and through the wood, to grandfather's house away. We would not stop for doll or top for this is Thanksgiving Day-hey. Over the river and through the wood—"*

"That's Arnon's place up ahead on the right," interrupted Louise. "I see the tower."

Ronnie recognized the house and a structure composed of various-sized rocks cemented together, illuminated by a safety light perched on a telephone pole in between them.

Renee leaned towards the windshield. "I don't see a tower."

"It's what my family calls that round building."

"Why do you call it a tower?"

"Don't know how it got the nickname, but it wasn't Arnon who dubbed it that. He locks himself in there, sometimes for days at a time, when he feels the need to pray and meditate."

He turned onto a dirt drive and parked near the gate of a four-foot tall chain link fence surrounding the dead lawn of white clapboard house. Arnon opened the door before they got to the porch. His massive frame blocked most of the light emanating from the living room.

"Welcome to the farm," he bellowed.

"Hi, Arnon . . .!" Louise ran up the porch and gave him a hug.

"Remember me?" said Ronnie, grinning.

"Sure do, come on inside."

Arnon seated them at his kitchen table and stood like a waiter. "What can I get you young folks, coffee or tea?"

Everyone agreed on coffee.

"Figured as much, so I used my big pot."

Watching coffee flow from the tap of a thirty cup dispenser, Ronnie thought of the huge ones in the mess halls during his marine days. His buddies had always bitched about the flavor but he'd never minded his java being a little too strong. It was a weak mix he couldn't tolerate.

Arnon distributed the steaming cups and pointed to a big jar of powdered creamer sitting next to a sugar bowl at the center of the table. "Your doctoring's are over there. The wife has to have her cream and sugar but I take mine black. Who needs doctoring? I'll get you a spoon."

Renee and Nanatobi raised their hands. Arnon took care of them and sat down. "First thing I need is to remember who's who between you two pretty girls. You are Renee?"

She gave him a polite smile and nodded.

"Then you must be Nanatobi."

"Yes, sir." Nanatobi echoed Renee's expression.

"Good. Second thing I need is to know who knows what, Ronnie."

"Everyone knows everything."

The big man leaned forward, hands clasped in front of his face, index fingers extended. "Okay then. Third thing I need is for you to tell me everything."

"You're up to date," said Louise. "Nothing new has happened since I called you the other night."

"No, I mean about the cult."

Louise gazed at him cautiously. "Arnon, it's . . . it's—"

"I know it's offensive, child. Go head, young ladies, I need to hear it all. Don't worry about offending me and don't exaggerate or play anything down."

"Don't say I didn't warn you." Louise rolled her eyes and took a sip of coffee.

Arnon listen intently as Nanatobi and Renee relayed all they knew about The Order of Centaurians. Nanatobi did most of the talking after Renee broke into tears while explaining how the cult originated. Bouncing his fingers off his lips the whole time, he never commented or changed expression.

When they finished, he lowered his hands and looked at Renee. "So you were only twelve years old when you first learned about the order?"

She wiped her eyes and nodded.

"My sweet Lord . . ." his face contracted into a mournful grimace. He turned to Nanatobi. "And you were fourteen?"

"Yes, sir."

"And you want out, but Veronica won't allow it."

"Yes, sir," they both answered.

He leaned forward, slipped a handkerchief from his back pocket, removed his glasses, and started wiping them. The delicate lenses looked tiny in his immense hands. "First thing we need to do is get one thing crystal clear from the get-go. Satan didn't create sex, God did. Is that much understood by both of you?"

Nanatobi shrugged. "I've never really thought about it one way or the other."

"Me either," said Renee.

"Well it's the truth. Sex is not evil in and of itself, but outside the boundaries God intended for it to be used, it becomes sin and therefore, like any sin, becomes a tool for the devil." He simultaneously stuffed the cloth back into his overalls and positioned the glistening frames on his wide nose. "The myriad demons in league with Satan use them to set up strongholds in the minds of their victims. The longer a body continues in the sin, the more powerful the stronghold becomes, eventually making the victim the puppet of the wicked one. This is what has happened to Veronica. She can be freed from the chains of hell, but she must want to be free— be willing to change. God won't force it upon her."

"She doesn't want that, believe me," spake Nanatobi sadly.

Arnon turned his hoary head towards her. "She doesn't think she wants it, true enough, child. But in reality she wants nothing more desperately than to be free. Her mother is the chief offender. She started the cult and beguiled her daughter into it. Then had her daughter pull her granddaughter into it. Veronica's mother is the bad egg here—unredeemable as Cain—but not Veronica. She's a puppet on a string—she just doesn't know it yet. Now for the big question. You two girls want to be free from the order, but do you want to be free from sin altogether?"

Nanatobi brightened with curiosity. "What do you mean?"

"We're all sinners, child, born in sin, ever blessed one of us without exception. That's why Jesus came, that's why He died on the cross—to pay for our sins. You can be free from sin only one way, accept Jesus Christ into your heart . . . ."

Two hours later everyone was crying and hugging each other, and as they were leaving, Arnon reminded them, "If any man be in Christ, he is a new creation. Old things have passed away, and behold, new things have come."

¶

"Bad news, Charlie Brown. You just sold a kilo of blow to a cop." Lou flashed his badge.

The punk took off running down the alley but a single shot fired skyward made him stop in his tracks. Hands held high in the cold night air, he slowly turned around. "I trusted you, man!"

"Yeah well, it breaks my heart to disappoint a lowlife like you." Lou relished the pained expression on the thug's weasel face. He pulled out his cell and dialed with his thumb, careful to keep the snubnose forty-four he kept hidden in a holster sewn inside his right boot aimed at the drug-dealing piece of shit who called himself Pablo.

"Got a live one for me?" said his contact, one of only three people that knew he'd been working undercover for the

Baltimore Police Department for the last five years. They were all badges. No one else had a clue—not even his parents or his best friend Brad.

"Yeah. We're in the alley behind Penelope's All Night Doughnuts."

¶

Nanatobi told Renee goodnight in the guestroom and took the elevator to the third floor.

The most unbelievable thing happened to me tonight! she wrote in her diary. *I became a born again Christian and so did Renee and Ronnie!!!!! Louise accepted Christ as a child but said she'd drifted from her faith through the years. She rededicated her life to Jesus and is as excited about the future as Renee and I! I can't wait to tell Brad and get him saved!*

¶

Cloaked in comforting darkness, Renee lay in one of the luxurious beds of Taylor's immense guestroom. She'd pretended to go along with Nan in accepting Jesus after that big nigger told them they were sinners and needed to do so. She had even cried like everyone else. The tears weren't fake but they had nothing to do with religion. They'd sprang forth because of pent up emotion being released over what she'd done to her best friend. As the resolution that had come to her at Betty Louise's house solidified, she'd bawled like a baby. Although undecided about *when* to do it, she knew exactly *what* to do.

TWENTY FIVE

It was Saturday, March eighteenth. Nanatobi had stopped counting the days until her twenty-first birthday because she wouldn't be leaving Taylor's house until her wedding. Twenty-four of them had passed since they'd learned the truth about Veronica. Renee had gone back home the Monday after their conversion despite knowing twelve demons had commanded her evil mother to destroy her if she wouldn't leave Ronnie.

"I'll just pretend I broke up with him and everything will be fine," she'd said. Nanatobi had been baffled and devastated. They both knew all too well it wouldn't be possible to hide it from Veronica for very long. She'd solicited Ronnie's help but even he hadn't been able to convince Renee, despite begging with tears in his eyes after throwing a fit over her stupid decision.

Something else troubled her as well. Renee didn't like discussing Jesus and had no interest in the Bible, while she'd been reading hers voraciously starting the day after they'd gotten saved. That book had been in her possession since birth yet she'd never bothered reading a word of it except for her mother's dedication on the first page. Now she considered it her most priceless treasure. She couldn't understand why Renee didn't have the same burning desire to learn the truth.

Brad resented her new faith and refused to ask Jesus into his heart, believing the resurrection of Christ to be a mere contrivance of His disciples. But it didn't worry her too much because she knew now that it was the Lord rather than some mystical cosmic force that had drawn them together. Feeling God wouldn't have done such a miraculous thing only to have Brad forever remain at odds with her over the issue, she firmly believed he'd someday be converted. For now, she at least had the comfort of knowing he believed in a higher power.

He wouldn't have been so unhappy about her beliefs if she hadn't refused to have sex with him again until they got married. After Jesus filled her heart she hadn't permitted Brad to so much as touch her breasts. Though her sex drive remained strong as ever, more often than not her reborn spirit brought it under subjection, managing to subdue the carnal urges. She occasionally slipped in moments of weakness and masturbated, but unlike Renee she'd avoided Veronica like a plague, knowing she couldn't resist her manipulation. The strongest saint wouldn't be able to refrain from sex while under the influence of the potion.

Taylor would walk her down the aisle on the eighth of April and she'd become Mrs. Bradley Boston Barron. They'd exchange vows in Taylor's church even though she'd fallen in love with Charley Hudson's and became an official member. She and Louise had accompanied him the Sunday following that fateful trip to Arnon's farm. The congregation was predominantly black but they'd accepted her with open arms. That morning Louise had called and invited them still burned in her mind. She'd gone to the guestroom and told Renee, "Louise has invited us to the Baptist church Charley Hudson attends. He'll be picking us up at Betty Louise's in an hour so you need to get dressed, sweetie."

"Charley's black," she'd responded with a deep scowl, "so that church he goes to is bound to cater to his own kind."

"I suppose. So what's the big deal?"

"Nan, I wouldn't set foot in a church full of niggers."

"Good grief, Renee," she'd scolded, "we grew up with Louise. She's half black and lives in her black grandmother's house. You've been in that house countless times, you hypocrite."

Renee had shrugged that off. "That's different. We know them."

So even though Taylor was willing to give her away at

Charley's Baptist church, she'd be marrying Brad in her uncle's predominantly white Presbyterian house of worship. For despite Renee's stupid prejudice, no one else could be her maid of honor.

¶

Ronnie couldn't go on like this any longer. He didn't understand why Renee hadn't changed the way he and Nanatobi had since accepting Christ as Lord and Savior. She constantly tried to lure him into bed and he always refused, puzzled why she couldn't comprehend the reason they had to wait until their wedding night before having sex again. As the days passed after their visit to Arnon's he'd grown increasingly suspicious that she hadn't really been born again. Not due to her persistently trying to seduce him, but because of flagrant disinterest in anything spiritual.

They were in his living room arguing over the sex issue again and he finally voiced his doubt. "You know what I think? I don't think you accepted Christ that night at Arnon's. I think you only pretended to, and I want to know why."

¶

Renee seemed to float home on a cloud she felt so wonderful. The Lord Jesus Christ had liberated her from bondage to Satan and freed her from the penalty of sin. Now she understood why Nan had no concerns about fraternizing with a black congregation. Ronnie made her see that Christ paid the price for everyone. Black or white, Jew or Gentile, rich or poor, bond or free—all had sinned and fallen short of the glory of God. But none need perish in hell because of what happened when Jesus sacrificed Himself on that cross and rose from the grave three days later. Now she too was a child of God, a *New Creation* as Arnon had said.

She had planned to kill her mother, seeing that as the only way to truly liberate Nan from the order and undo the wrong she'd done to her best friend. Strychnine smuggled from a chemistry lab at the university had been the chosen method. She'd intended to poison the woman who'd given her life that very next day, March nineteenth. Nan's mother would have turned forty on that date, the age her anticipated victim happened to be. That's why she'd chosen it. Serendipitously, her father had flown to New York that morning for two weeks of preliminary training before being groomed to take over one of Taylor's companies, leaving only the two of them in the house, perfectly setting the stage. After poisoning her mother she'd planned to write a full confession in a suicide note before slashing her wrists.

But her eyes had been opened to the wonderful light of the truth. Arnon had been right. Her mother needed Jesus—He could save her. Entering the living room, she spotted her arranging flowers in a vase on the second floor. She hurried to the stairs shouting, "Oh Mommy, I love you!"

¶

Charley relaxed in his recliner drinking beer on a Saturday night, relishing the absence of a radar screen. Brad had come over to have a cold one with him, and kept bitching about Nanatobi. He chuckled even though he could understand his neighbor's frustration. Brad had found a solution to his sexual problem only to have Nanatobi refuse to spread her legs now that she'd become a Christian.

"The last time we did it was the greatest performance of my life, Charley. It was great—I was great—and she loved it. Now she won't even let me touch her tits."

¶

Arnon stood at the lone window of his sanctuary. Those young folks had truly been a blessing. Nothing brought joy to his heart like witnessing a sinner accept Christ, and he'd had the privilege of delivering salvation's message to three of them that Friday night Ronnie came out. Though he'd been keenly aware Renee hadn't left his farm a true convert, a *knowing* had risen in his spirit that her name was indeed written in The Lamb's Book of Life which meant she'd become one before leaving her earthly tabernacle.

A body's brief sojourn on earth was filled with highs and lows—some mountaintops so delightful life couldn't possibly get any sweeter, some valleys so abominable death appeared to be the only relief. He'd had his share of both like everyone else, but most people didn't have to experience the troubles of others in their insides like he did.

On a lazy summer afternoon long ago he'd been playing in the back yard when a daydream popped into his mind that really frightened him. Only three years old at the time, he thought it was a great big alligator up in the night sky trying to knock all the stars down with its tail and succeeding in making a bunch of them fall. He told his mama about it while the family was gathered round the supper table. Her eyes had grown wide and she'd turned them towards his dad.

"Did you hear what that boy just said, Joshua?"

"Yeah," his dad had replied, looking real stunned. "He saw a reenactment of Revelation twelve four. Arnon, what you saw was a dragon, not an alligator. The Lord done gave you a vision of the devil stealing away a third of the holy angels for his army. Your grand-pappy predicted this when you was born. Son, you've been blessed with *The Sight.*"

Blessed was hardly a word he'd use for the endowment at

the moment. He wept within his spirit for the time had come. The omen was now to be fulfilled . . . .

¶

Ronnie couldn't wipe the smile off his face. Renee had balked at first when he'd challenged her veracity about accepting Jesus at Arnon's, but finally confessed she'd only pretended to get saved.

He'd pressed her for the reason.

"Because I belong in the hottest regions of hell along with my mother and grandmother. I know Christ can't save me and Mom, but I wasn't going to spoil it for you and Nan. It was a very special night. Even I could feel the holiness in that house, and of that man, even if he is a nigger. I knew you'd all try to convert me and it would have ruined the evening if I'd said what I really thought so I pretended it happened to me too."

Upon hearing that he'd relayed something a preacher had taught him via television last Sunday. "Renee, if your sins had not been paid for by the sacrificial death of Jesus then Christ couldn't have risen from the dead. But He did rise which means He bore the punishment for everyone's sins. If you can't be saved as you claim, then your transgressions are bigger than the Son of God and He wasn't really resurrected from the dead."

That had gotten her to thinking, and after letting that sink in he'd asked why she was prejudiced against blacks.

"I'm not prejudiced," she'd protested. "I just don't like being around niggers I don't know. They scare me."

At that moment it had dawned on him she honestly couldn't perceive her bigotry, so he'd silently prayed for Jesus to open her eyes to the truth. A few moments later her physical orbs had ignited with recognition. "Oh my god, I *am* prejudiced, aren't I?"

Again he'd stressed that Christ bore the punishment due her because of her sins so that His righteousness could be imputed to her. "But you have to accept it, Renee. He won't force it on you."

Renee had again asked Jesus into her heart, this time sincerely petitioning Him through what Arnon called The Sinner's Prayer. His spirit had borne witness to her conversion and they'd rejoiced together for awhile before she'd excitedly said, "Oh, Ronnie, I have to go! I must go tell Mom the good news and get her to say The Sinner's Prayer with me . . . ."

¶

"Well I love you too, dear." Her mom walked along the banister, towards the landing.

"Oh Mother, there's hope for us! Jesus saved me, and he can save you too!"

"What . . .?" her eyes flew wide. "Have you lost your mind, Renee?"

"No, no, it's true, Mother!" She bounded up the stairs two at a time. "I know it sounds crazy, but I just got saved. Ronnie led me to the Lord Jesus Christ."

Her dark irises became daggers. "You told me you were through with him! I told you to stay away from him, Renee!"

They met at the top of the stairs.

Raising her hands in a pleading motion she cried, "No, Mother, you don't understand, please listen to me! Ronnie and I were meant to be together, I can't leave him. And now we both have Christ in our hearts, and we're free from sin, and you can be too. Please listen to me!"

Venomous anger distorted her mother's face into a blazing portrait of outrage as she shouted, "You cannot leave the order! He's trying to corrupt your mind with lies!"

"No!" she screamed, covering her ears, refusing to listen to the sin-blinded woman's accusations and demands. "I love Ronnie and I'm going to marry him! Grandmother was crazy, and so are you!"

"Like hell . . .!" her mom slapped her.

She started crying and the poor Satan-bound fool hit her twice more with vicious fury. "You little bitch, you'll do exactly as I say!"

"No, it's over!" she sobbed. "I'm out . . . you can't control me anymore. I don't know how you ever did, but now I'm free of your spell."

They argued back and forth, screaming at each other for several minutes before a peacefulness swept over her. The tears stopped and she calmly said, "I'm going to pack my things, Mom. I'm sorry you can't accept the truth about Jesus, but I have, and now I'm leaving."

Her mother's face turned flaming red. "I'll see you dead first!"

Everything seemed to move in slow motion as she watched the woman who had both nurtured and corrupted her, pick up a clay vase and hit her with it.

TWENTY SIX

Brad stood at his bar sipping a martini. It was far too early in the day, but being a Sunday he'd made an exception. Frustration over Nanatobi had him tied in knots. She'd become a self righteous prude since her so called conversion.

Lou, who'd dropped by unannounced a short while ago, sat on the couch drinking coffee. The Okie leaned forward and set his cup on the coffee table. "There's something I need to tell you, partner."

"Oh, what's that?"

"I'm an undercover cop."

He swallowed a gulp of booze and grinned. "Oh yeah? Well I'm a double agent for the CIA."

"I'm serious, Brad. I got recruited five years ago after I helped the police catch a big time drug dealer who had a stash of cocaine hidden inside a dummy firewall. While I was tuning up the guy's engine I noticed the passenger side of the firewall stuck out several inches further than the driver's side. I knew that set of wheels hadn't left Detroit like that so I suspected it had been constructed to carry some form of contraband. When the guy drove off I called one of my cop buddies and told him about it. Sure enough my hunch was right and they busted the guy.

"A few days later my cop friend said his captain wanted to meet with me and I agreed. The dude said I had the perfect cover, being the owner of a successful auto repair business who likes to hang around town most of the time and let my shop managers keep the mechanics in line. You know I've always worn my hair long but I needed a shave when I went to see the dude, and he asked if I'd mind keeping the stubbly look because it made me look even less like a cop."

Astounded to hear Lou wasn't joking he said, "Who all knows about this?"

"You're the only civilian I've told, and you damn well better keep it to yourself. My parents would worry themselves sick if they ever found out. Anyway, despite you telling me to hold off, I talked to my cop friend. We went to the university the next day and located Bach's car. My friend jimmied the trunk open but failed to find any evidence of foul play, at least none that could be detected by the naked eye. Remember telling me about Nanatobi saying there'd been five men involved in the orgies and none of them ever came back?"

He nodded, still dazed by Lou's shocking confession.

"That was the break my buddy needed. He checked the files and here's what turned up. Over the last seven years, besides Jon Bach, five white affluent males have been found in various locations at Druid Hill Park. Each was stabbed in the heart with a narrow weapon, and their bodies were moved after they'd been slain. The police reported each case as the victim of an apparent mugging to avoid panicking the public, but they knew they were dealing with a serial killer.

"The detectives hadn't been able to find a common tie between the victims until Jon Bach's murder. He was in charge of the blood bank at Williams-Hathaway Medical Center. They discovered that the five previous victims had given blood there shortly before their demise. Donated blood is tested for everything, including AIDS and every other sexually transmitted disease. My buddy and I think Wilhelm Bach got the tests results through his cousin for Veronica Van Cedar's sake, and Jon Bach put the pieces together and either tried to blackmail his cousin or threatened to tell the police what he knew. Whatever he was up to, it scared Wilhelm Bach enough to take him out. But we can't prove it. I need directions to that house in the country where the cult holds their meetings . . . ."

¶

Ronnie didn't know which church to attend and hadn't bothered looking for one because he'd happened across Dree Gillis, a preacher from Texas with a television ministry. He dressed like a cowboy, delivered his Bible-centered messages clearly, and never asked for money. Gillis had played backup tight end for the Miami Dolphins for two years but left the NFL because of a neck injury. Ronnie's spirit soured while listening to this Sunday morning's message, but he didn't get to catch the end of it because Brad called.

"We have a radical new development, Ronnie." The astral traveler sounded slightly inebriated. *"You think you know somebody—especially your best friend—but Lou just told me he's an undercover cop. He's convinced Wilhelm Bach killed Jon Bach but he needs proof. He wants you to take him to that country house, as Nanatobi calls it. She's at church and planning to have lunch with her uncle in town afterwards, so she couldn't do it anyway, but Lou wants this kept between you, me, and him for now."*

He frowned and shoved a lock of hair back from his forehead that had fallen when he'd leaned forward to answer the phone. "What good will that do?"

"Don't ask me. I'm just the vice president of a software company, not an undercover cop."

"When does he want to do it?"

"As soon as possible."

"Well I'm free all day so name the time."

"I'll tell him, hold on . . . Ronnie's game and it's up to you when."

"Tell him I'm on my way," he heard Lou say in the background.

Brad relayed the message and they hung up.

¶

Sitting in the passenger seat of a Corvette ZR1, Ronnie guided Lou to the house in the country, a place he'd really never been before but had visited twice in his memory. Along the way Lou filled him in on the evidence that had him convinced but was of no use without being able to tie Wilhelm Bach to it. He also apologized for snubbing him at the doughnut shop. It *had* been him with the two gang members. "Couldn't take a chance on blowing my cover."

Lou pulled over on the far side of the road and peered cautiously through the driver's window. "I don't see any cars but there could be one in the garage. Do you think anyone's in there?"

"I doubt it. From what I know about the cult, they always meet at night."

He got out of the car. Ronnie did likewise and followed him across the street.

"The trunk won't nail the bastard but maybe the tread of his tires will. My buddy told me there were some well defined prints near Bach's body." Lou snapped several photographs of tire-rutted soil between the road and driveway. "Okay, we're done. I'll drop you off and get these snapshots to my friend so he came compare them to the pictures the police took . . . ."

Lou's contention that Wilhelm Bach used his cousin to check potential victims for sexually transmitted diseases made Ronnie wonder if Centaurianism forbade the use of condoms. He hadn't worn one at the motel or the two envisioned episodes at the country house. If so, it made perfect sense that Veronica would want to be certain she wouldn't contract a disease from her victim. It wouldn't be hard for her to talk most men into having their blood tested for the chance to get her in bed. But why had she risked having unprotected sex with him? He'd been so overcome with lust that night she'd led him to the motel, he hadn't given a second's thought about buying a rubber first. But she'd planned the escapade in advance, so why had she been willing to take him on bareback?

He thought of a ghoulish possibility. Maybe the twelve demons became aware of him because of the mysterious abilities he'd been given, supernaturally ascertained he didn't have any form of venereal disease, and had informed Veronica as much.

¶

At four o'clock Brad called to say none of the tire tracks matched the ones found at Druid Hill Park. Ronnie cradled the phone and it rang before he took his hand off the receiver. He picked it back up and Nanatobi said hello.

"Is Renee there?"

"No, sorry."

"I tried her cell a gazillion times but she's not answering. We always call each other on Sundays if we don't get together."

"Try her home phone, maybe her cell's acting up."

"No way! Veronica might answer. I can't take a chance on even hearing her voice. I'm worried, Ronnie. I've got this awful feeling in my spirit."

Unnerved to hear that, he told her about Renee finally seeing the light yesterday and leaving his apartment with high hopes of getting Veronica saved. "I'll get Louise to call the house phone. I can't since Renee's pretending she dumped me."

"Good idea. Tell her to have Renee call me if she gets hold of her...."

Louise agreed to make the call and phoned back a few minutes later.

"Veronica said Renee went to town after lunch and she doesn't know when to expect her back, but would tell her I *called . . . ."*

After filling Nanatobi in he drove to Wine's Gate to verify Renee's car wasn't there. The garage being reserved for her parents' vehicles, she parked her Camaro in the drive which lay empty. It looked like Veronica had told Louise the truth but he couldn't shake the notion that something was terribly wrong. He turned around at the cul-de-sac and immediately braked to a stop.

Veronica's BMW was backing onto the road.

She drove towards Baltimore and he pulled into her drive. He hoped to find Jesse home and ask where Renee went because there'd be no reason for him to lie about her whereabouts. Though he'd likely tell Veronica about it, she couldn't blame Renee for her jilted boyfriend stopping by uninvited.

No one answered the door. Heaving a disappointed sigh, he started for his car but a rapping noise from above made him turn back. Renee was gagged and apparently bound because she'd poked her head between the curtains of an upstairs window to tap it with her forehead, a look of sheer terror in her eyes.

He ran to the door but found it locked. His first instinct was to kick it open but that would be breaking-and-entering and play right into Veronica's hands. If Renee was doped up with the potion she'd probably say whatever Veronica wanted her to, even lie to the police and claim he'd tied her up.

Backing away from the porch so she could see him he yelled, "Can you hear me?"

She nodded.

"The door's locked! I'm going to have one of your neighbors call the police!"

First she violently shook her head no, then kept jerking it to the left, obviously trying to tell him something.

"Are you telling me there's a hidden key?"

Again she nodded, excitedly.

Rushing to the porch, he examined four clay pots stuffed with artificial flowers but couldn't find anything within or underneath any of them. A rectangular wall-mount mailbox caught his eye. He stuck his hand inside it and felt around. A piece of tape covered something thin on the bottom. It proved difficult to loosen with his fingernails but he finally succeeded and came away with a key which he promptly stabbed into the lock on the front door.

Less than five minutes later he peeled out of the driveway with Renee at his side. She was either drugged, had a concussion, or both. A purple knot protruded from her right temple. Though practically incoherent, he managed to make out from her slurs that Veronica had hit her with a vase but the blow hadn't left her in this condition—she'd been drugged. Renee then laboriously communicated that she didn't need medical attention and warned him not to take her to his place.

He drove to Brad Barron's.

¶

Since Veronica knew of his relationship with Nanatobi, Brad feared she might come to his apartment looking for Renee after failing to find her anywhere else. The wicked bitch also being familiar with the black Thunderbird her daughter had escaped in, Lou had driven it to Ronnie's place and waited for him while he took Renee and her rescuer to the Okie's house. He pulled into the parking lot of a rundown apartment complex. Lou got in and they headed for Wine's Gate in his Shelby.

They assumed Veronica had left her house in order to establish an alibi while Wilhelm Bach murdered Renee. He planned to either kill her there and make it look like she'd been the victim of a surprised burglar, or kidnap her and do it elsewhere. Renee's account of what happened created the assumption. With Jesse in New York, Veronica's plan would have gone down without a hitch if Ronnie hadn't happened by.

Brad spotted Nanatobi's Porsche parked at the appointed place, stopped to pick her up, and they continued their journey.

Feeling horrible for Jesse, who had a nightmare of a surprise awaiting him, he bade his passengers good luck as they got out of his car. He watched them enter the house using Renee's key, then drove away. There couldn't be any vehicles in the driveway when Wilhelm Bach showed up.

¶

Lou bound and gagged her, then gently maneuvered her on Renee's bed so she lay with her back to the door. Armed with a pistol, he hid in the closet to await the arrival of Wilhelm Bach. Nanatobi marveled that Renee was still alive. Veronica had hit her with the vase exactly as she and Brad had seen it, but the railing wasn't broken on the upstairs hall. According to what they'd witnessed, Renee should have fallen back against the banister and wound up on the first floor with a broken neck. Another puzzlement was Louise's dream of Ronnie crying and saying 'Why Renee?' over and over, while she and Brad had heard Veronica say those words after witnessing Renee's accidental murder from their combined astral essence. Further complicating things, Charley Hudson had spiritually visualized a coffin with Ronnie repeating the phrase. Nanatobi felt the Lord must have intervened and altered her best friend's fate.

When Ronnie phoned to say Louise had been told Renee wasn't home, she'd set out for Wine's Gate to see if her

Camaro was gone. Halfway there Brad had called her cell.

"Where are you?" he'd asked.

"On my way to Renee's. I'm really worried about her, Brad."

"She's with Ronnie at Lou's house. Pull into the nearest place where it's safe to leave your car and we'll pick you up. Lou has a scheme to end this shit with Veronica once and for all."

The plan called for Bach to think she was Renee. When he made his move Lou would spring from the closet and place him under arrest. Veronica would be arrested as well for assault, but for the time being they needed the evil witch to think her plan had succeeded. Hopefully Bach would break and tell all because she knew Veronica wouldn't.

She'd checked the garage and Renee's car was in the spot where her father usually parked. Brad had told her Jesse flew to New York yesterday so he'd evidently driven himself to the airport. She didn't know who'd parked the Camaro there, but Ronnie not seeing it in the drive had almost cost Renee her life. If he hadn't seen Veronica leave he wouldn't have stopped. The thought of what would have happened to Renee if he hadn't, made her shudder.

Brad had relayed all the details of Renee's rescue after picking her up. "Can't you see the hand of Jesus on all this, baby?" she'd gushed excitedly. He'd silently answered with a sour face as if she were insulting his intelligence.

His reaction had broken her heart.

¶

Sitting on Lou's sofa with Renee snuggled against him, Ronnie thanked the Lord for the umpteenth time for all He'd done in warning them beforehand and delivering Renee from Veronica in the end. If Nanatobi and Brad hadn't envisioned

Renee's death—if Louise hadn't told him her seventh dream—
if Charley hadn't had that vision of a coffin—fear for her
safety wouldn't have driven him to Wine's Gate, and he'd have
never seen Renee alive again.

After he'd forced some black coffee down her at Brad's,
she'd tried to explain all that happened. Now completely
coherent, she recounted everything in greater detail.

"When I came home last night after leaving your place I
tried to convert Mom and she went ballistic. While we were
arguing it dawned on me we were at the top of the stairs just
like Nan and Brad had seen us from their astral states. I
realized we'd been saying things very similar to what they'd
heard. So instead of just standing there like an idiot and
letting their vision of my death come to pass, I tried to go to
my room. I thought I'd altered the outcome until Mom hit me
with the vase. I blacked out and later woke up in my bed to
find she'd tied my wrists together, my ankles together, gagged
me, and drugged me. She kept checking on me all night long,
dosing me each time she found me almost alert. I had no idea
she knew how to give shots and don't know what got pumped
into my arm each time she sedated me.

"About an hour after I finally woke up today, she came into
my room with a tray of food and a glass of water. She helped
me use the bathroom, forced me back on the bed, pulled the
bandana off my mouth, and fed me—begging me all the
while to renounce Jesus and stay away from you. I told her I
couldn't do that and pleaded with her to accept Christ. She
angrily gagged me and stabbed the needle in my arm. I didn't
see her again until shortly before you rang the doorbell. She
had a horrible expression on her face—one I've never seen
before—and said, 'I'm leaving now, but you're going to have a
visitor soon, and he'll be the last person you'll ever see. I'm so
sorry it has to be this way but you've left me no choice.'

"When I heard her drive off I managed to get on my feet

but I was too woozy to try hopping down the stairs. I knew I'd fall and feared I'd break my neck because of what Nan and Brad saw. So I just kept praying for Jesus to help me, and when I heard the doorbell I somehow knew He'd sent you to save me. I was *so* afraid you wouldn't find that key in time."

¶

It seemed like she'd been laying on Renee's bed forever. With each passing minute Nanatobi grew more concerned they'd arrived too late, that Bach had already come and gone and was even now telling Veronica of Renee's escape. That worry got instantly replaced by stark fear when she heard the bedroom door open. Terrified, she clinched her eyes shut, praying Lou would catch him in time.

"What a pity you wouldn't listen to mama, Fraulein."

A fresh wave of fright rippled through her at hearing Bach's accented voice. Then the sound of another door opening entered her trembling ears.

"Hold it right there, motherfucker, you're under arrest! Drop that gun and get your fucking hands in the air or I'll blow you away!"

Nanatobi hadn't realized she'd been holding a deep breath until it blasted through her nostrils upon hearing the gun hit the floor. Lou removed the gag and untied her with one hand while aiming his pistol at Wilhelm Bach with the other.

Astonishment radiated from the professor's Dracula-like face as he glared at her with rude surprise. "Who are you?"

"The woman that's gonna put you away," said Lou, pulling a cell phone from his shirt pocket.

Tears of relief pouring from her eyes, she silently praised the Lord for delivering her from harm and saving Renee's life by guiding Ronnie with His mighty hand.

TWENTY SEVEN

Nanatobi sat on the passenger side as Brad drove. They'd just left Renee's house, following a police car that had arrived shortly after Lou called. He was riding in it along with Wilhelm Bach, sitting in the secured back seat wearing handcuffs. A warrant could now be issued for Veronica's arrest for attempted murder. Feelings of extreme relief that she'd escaped without so much as a scratch from the wicked professor were overrode by dreadful sadness over what would happen next.

Her relationship with Taylor was about to be severed.

"What's wrong?" said Brad.

Morosely anticipating Taylor's shock and subsequent rejection of her when he learned the truth, she'd started crying. "When the facts about Veronica come out, so will all the sordid details of Renee's and my involvement in that perverse cult, and I'm going to lose Taylor. He'll disown me and never speak to me again."

¶

Taylor took a deep sniff, savoring the aroma of roasted pheasant fresh off the rotisserie, magnificently prepared as only Alfred could do it. He'd be dining without the pleasant company of his lovely niece because she was off somewhere with her fiancé. He winked at Jim, who'd made the evening's desert. "If that cobbler doesn't taste as good as it smells, you're fired."

Suzanne giggled. "Trust me, Sir, he won't be unemployed. He made me give it a taste test to verify it was par, and it's marvelous."

"Are you willing to back that claim by putting your own job on the line?"

"I am indeed, Sir," she affirmed with a grin.

"Very well. We'll soon see if I'll be looking for a new butler and maid or not." He said it tongue in cheek as Suzanne unfolded a napkin. While raising his chin to receive it, a numbing sensation traveled up his left arm, followed by a sharp pain in his chest.

TWENTY EIGHT

Ronnie was now working full time for Ben Palloy. He'd made arrangements to return to Riley's Grocery on weeknights come fall, though he wasn't under the same financial stress as before. His wife also had a job and was the main breadwinner. They'd gotten married the day after graduating from the University of Maryland in May. He'd received a bachelor of science degree while a bachelor of liberal arts had been bestowed upon her. He no longer lived out other people's fantasies nor relived the same events twice.

Two days after Wilhelm Bach's arrest a second lengthy blackout occurred. Charley had seen another mysterious blip on radar while Arnon beheld a flash while deep in prayer. Arnon said it meant things had gone back to normal. Nanatobi and Brad hadn't left their bodies since seeing the twelve demons. So far Charley hadn't had another vision but Louise's gift would remain with her for life as she'd been given *The Sight.*

The Order of Centaurians was now nothing but a bad memory. Wilhelm Bach had confessed but swore he'd never killed anybody. Although he'd been charged with first degree murder, Veronica had slain the six men whose bodies Bach left at Druid Hill Park to make it look like each had been the unfortunate victim of a mugging. The district attorney had offered him a deal—life without parole rather than the death penalty—if he'd plead guilty and save the state of Maryland the cost of a trial. Discovering a camouflaged portable metal building deep in the woods behind the country house, detectives had found a van parked inside whose tire treads matched those at Druid Hill Park. They'd also located some discernable foot prints the size of Bach's shoes leading to and from the residence, indicating the bodies had been carried to the van by Veronica's accomplice. Confronted with the evidence, Bach had agreed to the deal but denied knowing anything about the body of a catholic priest buried in a shallow grave twenty yards beyond the building, sniffed out by a police dog.

Ronnie had been in the courtroom the day Bach, as a condition of the plea bargain, had to state what happened and tell it truthfully. The cult was never mentioned by name, and the twisted professor never said a word about Renee or Nanatobi.

Veronica and Bach had been lovers for the last seven years, a fact that Jesse Van Cedar, also in the courtroom, had never suspected. Bach had told the court that because of overwhelming infatuation with Veronica, he had assisted her "when the woman's strange religious fixation called for a human sacrifice." He'd lied and said her beliefs didn't have a formal title. Ronnie suspected fear of retaliation by the twelve demons had prompted it.

When Veronica felt compelled to offer a sacrifice to her unnamed deity, she'd seek out a particular type man— handsome, white, and affluent—beguile him with her charms, and insist on proof that he had no communicable diseases before she would sleep with him. Each was instructed to donate blood at Williams-Hathaway Medical Center, and do so discreetly as a thoughtful citizen. Least any of them lack such discretion Veronica never revealed her true identity and made up a different name for each one. Bach then obtained the test results from his cousin Jon who worked there.

"Veronica had a morbid distaste for condoms," Bach had said in his heavy German accent, "and that's what made the blood tests necessary. If all the tests had been negative, there'd have been several more victims, but some of the men tested positive with some form of venereal disease."

According to the German, Veronica drugged the victim's drink with a medication that caused him to attain and maintain an erection no matter how many times he ejaculated or how frightened he became. After a round of foreplay on the sacrificial bed—underneath which lay Bach, hiding with a golden arrow and a plastic mask—she'd entice the hapless fool into putting his shirt back on, claiming the sight of a man naked only from the waist down really turned her on. The real reason was to make it appear the poor devil had been stabbed as the result of a robbery. A dead man couldn't put an unmarred shirt over a chest with a bloody hole in it. Under the guise of wanting to have kinky sex, she'd then tie him to the bed.

Once she had him bound, Bach would make his presence known—hand her the mask, place the arrow between the man's spread out legs, take off his clothes, and fetch a black robe with a hood for Veronica to put on. As calculated the sight terrified the offering, who'd start struggling against his bonds to no avail. The more fear that could be induced, the more pleasing the deity found the sacrifice. Veronica would then perform oral sex on Bach. When he neared the verge of ejaculating he'd pull away, whereupon she'd cover the man's frightened face with the mask for Bach to deposit his semen on. She'd then remove the soiled plastic shroud, lick the sperm off it, and recite a prayer. Ignoring the frantic pleas of the terrified victim, Veronica would pick up the arrow, mount the man's erect penis, and thrust the golden shaft into his heart the moment she climaxed.

Jon Bach thought he was delivering the tests results to his cousin as part of the latter's private research in biochemistry, having no idea what they were really for. Wilhelm Bach had claimed to be researching the genetic parallels of similar white males, maintaining he required only a few drops of blood for his research but also needed the hospital's test results because it would be unethical to conduct private research at the university's expense and he lacked the facilities for such examinations in his small home laboratory.

Bach's cousin had believed the lie until seeing a picture of the last victim on TV while the newscaster reported his death as an apparent mugging at Druid Hill Park. He'd drawn the man's blood himself, something Jon Bach rarely did. Realizing the test results had been requested only a few days before the man died, he became suspicious. Unbeknownst to the professor his cousin had kept a record of all the blood tests he'd copied and passed on. After discovering four others had been murdered in the same fashion, Jon wanted to know what was going on. Bach had told him it was mere coincidence and felt he'd convinced his cousin as such, but when Veronica heard about it she told her paramour they'd have to silence him permanently.

Veronica murdered Jon Bach but offered him as a sacrifice without having sex with him as she had the others. He'd also been the only victim brought to her ceremonial abode against his will, bound and gagged instead of merely blindfolded. Bach had drugged his cousin and transported him to his waiting executioner. He'd then used the hidden van to deliver the body to Druid Hill Park as he had the other five victims. That vehicle served no other purpose. Until the police found it, no one but he and Veronica knew of its existence.

Only two of the murders besides Jon Bach's had taken place since Veronica's mother died, which meant she'd been alive when three of them were committed. Bach never mentioned the cult's founder.

Nanatobi pieced together what went down when there was on orgy with a male participant, and had shared it with him as they'd all exited the courthouse in a surreal daze. "Since Professor Bach didn't recognize me when Lou arrested him, he couldn't have been hiding in the country house secretly watching us, waiting for everyone but Veronica to leave. There're three ways to get in and out of the basement—a door in the kitchen, one outside, and a trapdoor under the giant bed. Now I know why we were forbidden to go down there for any reason when we had an orgy with a man. Bach was down there waiting for a signal from Veronica to alert him we'd left and the coast was clear. That's how he got under the bed without the man seeing him. Veronica's mother had the trapdoor installed as an emergency exit in case of a fire. Her husband died while trying to save a baby from a burning apartment building so I don't doubt that was its original purpose."

He'd later learned from Arnon that Veronica hadn't insisted on the blood tests to merely screen potential victims for venereal disease. If there were any impurities at all the man wasn't fit for an offering. The prophet's testimony wouldn't have stood up in court because the Lord had revealed that truth to him in a vision.

Ronnie stood in front of the bathroom mirror and combed his hair, still wishing he hadn't been forbidden to shave it off. It was their bedtime. He walked into the bedroom and smiled while looking down at his lovely wife, kneeling on the floor beside the bed. Luscious curls hid the sides of her face as she leaned her head towards hands folded in prayer. His life had sure taken some mysterious turns since that night he'd finally managed to meet Renee. He studied his bride for a moment, admiring her as she silently petitioned the Lord. Then he knelt beside her and also began to pray.

¶

Nanatobi sat in her uncle's chair at the dining table. It wasn't dinnertime, lunchtime, or breakfast time, and there were no servants standing about. She was alone. Over three months had passed since her twenty-first birthday and what was supposed to have been her wedding day eight days following. Though still in love with him, she'd changed her mind about marrying Brad on that date because of his hostility towards her faith. It wouldn't be wise to become unequally yoked with an unbeliever. Still, she believed that one day he'd see the light, and when that happened they'd be united in holy matrimony. He'd become somewhat of a workaholic since replacing Jesse and she suspected it had more to due with frustration over her refusal to sleep with him than dedication to duty.

Jesse had been promoted to chief executive officer of a nation-wide investment company as promised by Taylor. Purchased by T-Cain Corporation thirteen years ago, the enterprise had three main branches and he'd chosen the one in San Francisco as the site of his administration because it was the furthest away from Baltimore, the place where his world had been so rudely turned upside down.

Lou Cotton had been converted as the end result of defending Brad one evening while Ronnie was helping her try to enlighten the spiritually blind exec.

"Leave the boy alone," he'd growled. "Brad has just as much right to his opinion about Jesus as you two have."

"Do you believe in Jesus, Lou?" Ronnie had asked.

"That He exists? Yeah, but I can't call myself a believer. Organized religion repulses me. I'd rather be horsewhipped than sit in a pew listening to some guy recite a sermon that's supposed to be inspired by God but only bores me to tears if it doesn't put me to sleep. I've tried to read the Bible but the words go right over my head. I can't believe in something I don't understand."

Smiling, Ronnie had responded with, "I challenge you to come over to my place next Sunday morning and watch a non-denominational Christian broadcast with me. You won't be bored and the preacher is about as far from organized religion as you can get. He makes the Bible come to life for me, and I think you'll find he will for you too. I've begged Brad to watch him but the stubborn mule won't even consider it."

Lou accepted the challenge and had been so moved by the preacher's message that he'd felt God was speaking directly to him. He'd left Ronnie's apartment a staunch believer.

The lovable redneck had gone out on a date with Ursula the night before his conversion. She'd cornered him at a party Brad had thrown a week prior and demanded to know why he'd never asked her out. "Because you're the type of woman that could really get under my skin," he'd said, "and I'm afraid I'd wind up with a broken heart."

After picking her jaw up off the floor Ursula had slapped her hands on her hips and said, "You're afraid of me? I'm the one risking a broken heart, you stud nut."

Nanatobi didn't know how the rest of the conversation went because she'd left at that point when Brad tried to get frisky. Ursula's success in convincing Lou to take her out had resulted in them falling in love soon thereafter. The tall blonde now went by Ursula Cotton and she'd recently gotten saved. Having Brad's old job kept her near him during business hours, so besides his fiancé and his best friend, the vice president had another believer he couldn't avoid, striving to get him to see the truth of the gospel.

Louise had quit attending church. A televangelist based in Texas—the same one Ronnie had challenged Lou to watch—had captivated her and she wouldn't leave home until his Sunday morning broadcasts were over. Nanatobi had to admit there *was* something very special about the guy. She'd love to meet the incredibly handsome cowboy turned preacher, Dree Gillis. She taped all his messages and watched them first thing after coming home from church, where she always sat beside Charley during the sermon. The big guy didn't attend Sunday school like her.

At least once a week she'd drive out to see Arnon, and begged him to come visit her on occasion. He'd told her he got claustrophobic in traffic so it seemed unlikely he ever would. The adorable farmer simply amazed her and she loved having Bible studies with him and his wife. Not once had she left his farm without some deeper truth or a surprising enlightenment on an old one burning in her spirit.

The day she turned twenty-one she'd received twelve-point-six million dollars, the entirety of her father's estate, but that was a mere pittance compared to the huge financial empire of T-Cain Corporation she'd inherited when Taylor died from a heart attack while sitting in the very chair she presently occupied. She'd sat there like a zombie for the last fifteen minutes, crying for the better part of it, but the tears had finally subsided—at least outwardly.

Rising to her feet, she scooted it back to the table that had adorned this regal dining room since its construction, and went to the parlor. She stood for several minutes touching the top of Taylor's easy chair, looking down at the sad, vacant seat. He'd died before she came home the day Lou arrested Wilhelm Bach. Not having the heart to tell her the tragic news by telephone, Jim had broke down the moment she'd walked in the door. Weeping bitterly he'd said, "Nanatobi, I don't know how to tell you this, but your uncle suffered a fatal heart attack shortly after sitting down for dinner."

The memory of that fateful Sunday would forever torture her. She referred to it in her diary as *The Day The World Ended.*

Two hours after Professor Bach's arrest Veronica had been taken into custody, but Renee inexplicably refused to press charges. Then, in another incomprehensible move, Renee had gone home with her after she'd been released. Afterwards the police came to make an arrest again, but this time they took

Renee to jail. She'd called them herself to confess stabbing her mother in the heart with a boning knife.

Nanatobi would never forget the way Ronnie had kept crying and saying "Why, Renee?" when Lou convinced the officer in charge to let the two of them see her. No, she would never forget that, but what haunted her even more was Renee's answer. Smiling sweetly, she'd stuck her arms through the cell bars and caressed Ronnie's cheek with one hand while gently stroking her hair with the other. "Oh how I love you, Curly Sampson," she'd tenderly cooed, "and how I hate to see you hurting. Why did I do it? Why did I kill my mother? Before I answer that, I want you to know that I've known for some time that Louise has fallen in love with you. I can't be there for you, badly as I want to, my darling. I give you to her, please go to her . . . she'll love you forever just as I will."

"No, Renee, no!" Ronnie had cried, bawling again.

Renee's beautiful green eyes had sparkled with tears of their own, but the smile remained on her face. "Please don't cry, my darling. It's okay."

He'd clutched her hand and pressed it against his face while sobbing out, "Why are you talking like that? You'll probably only get probation if not outright released when the truth comes out. Even if you do get jail time I'll wait for you, baby. Even if they give you life without parole, I'll still wait for you!"

Freeing her thumb from Ronnie's fingers, Renee had gently rubbed it back and forth beneath his eye, wiping away half his tears. She'd sobbed uncontrollably as Renee kept stroking her hair in an effort to console her. "My darling, Ronnie . . . my dearest, Nan . . . I ate a brownie a short while ago. I hid it in my bra when the police came for me. It's starting to take affect and soon I'll be with Jesus, and I'll see you both when you get to heaven. I was going to give it to Mom before I got saved. It's laced with strychnine. And now to answer your question, my darling. Why did I kill my mother? I did it for Nanatobi, to forever free her from Mom's clutches because I knew she wouldn't have remained behind bars for long. I did it for my dearest best friend Nan."

"Get help!" Ronnie had yelled to the guard. "She's poisoned herself and needs her stomach pumped! Get help . . .!'"

But help arrived too late. Renee had gone into convulsions by the time they put her in an ambulance. She died on the way to the hospital.

Two days after losing her and Taylor, she'd invited Ronnie and Louise to the mansion for dinner, hoping she might be of some comfort to them, knowing their spiritual presence would definitely console her. Jim and Suzanne had barely cleared the table when a second lengthy blackout occurred. Face illuminated by candlelight, Louise had told Ronnie, "This probably isn't the time or the place, being her funeral's tomorrow and Nanatobi was her best friend, but I've got to get something off my chest. I felt deceptive towards Renee while she was alive and feel like I'm betraying her now that she's with the Lord. I think the blackout is a sign for me to bare my soul. I-I'm in love with you . . . I realize you only see me as a friend but I had to tell you."

He'd been speechless so she'd intervened. "It's okay, Louise. Renee knew you were in love with him."

Louise had shaken her head, a pained expression on her face. "She couldn't have, Nanatobi. I never told her."

"I don't care, she knew. She told Ronnie and I just before she died."

"Yeah, she knew," Ronnie had sadly muttered. "Not only that, she wanted us to be together. Correction, she *wants* us to be together but I can't do it, Louise. I'm truly sorry. It's not that I can't see us becoming more than friends. It would be unfair to you because my love for Renee will never die and no one could ever possibly replace her in my heart."

Tearfully, Louise had replied, "As long as you don't expect me to compete with a ghost I can accept that, Ronnie. Dree Gillis said something the Sunday before Renee died that's been haunting me since we lost her. He was explaining how marriage symbolizes Christ and his bride. There's only one head but many members. Jesus is the groom but His bride is composed of a multitude of believers and He loves each one as if there were no others, yet each has a unique function within the body. Dree said, 'If your spouse departs for heaven, don't feel guilty about loving a new one. God didn't send you a replacement, but an addition.' I believe the Lord sent me to you, Ronnie—not to replace Renee but to be your additional mate. Hearing she knew how I felt and wanted us to be together, well that's divine validation if you ask me—a signal from above that I was meant for you. I believe that in time you'll see it too."

It hadn't taken long for Louise's prediction to come to pass. Taylor was interred the following morning and that afternoon she'd stood beside Louise and Ronnie, viewing Renee before the funeral began. She had been looking down at her best friend's beautiful face when Ronnie weepingly said, "Renee, if you can hear me from up above, then you know what I'm about to do is because I believe it's God's will, and I believe that because you told me it's what you wanted, baby."

She'd kept her eyes on Renee as Ronnie said "Will you marry me, Louise?" and could have sworn the corners of her best friend's cold lips had turned up ever so slightly when Louise wept out a yes.

Ronnie's boss Ben Palloy was best man and she'd been honored to serve as Louise's maid of honor at their wedding. Louise had begged him to pick another date after learning he'd planned to marry Renee the day after graduation, but Ronnie wouldn't budge.

"Since that's the time she chose for me to become a

married man," he'd said, "I'm going to carry out her will. And this way she'll always be a special part of our anniversary."

She was very happy for the two of them. As happy as she could be these days.

Now sitting in Taylor's easy chair, she was looking at a picture of Renee and her he'd taken not long after her parents died. It was summertime and they were wearing swimsuits, standing on the shores of Chesapeake Bay. They were both eleven . . . just two silly little innocent girls posing with their arms around each other, making pretty for the camera. She looked at the ceiling and started crying again.

She'd lost her adoring uncle, whom she had grown to love as much as her father. Her faithful best friend, with whom she shared a bond and love stronger than that between any two sisters, had been taken from her. Both had left her on the very same day. They were with Jesus and she'd see them in heaven, but here on earth, oh how she missed the two of them.

She knew, as the old saying went, that life must go on, and she had to live out the rest of hers. And how fortunate a life it must seem, she thought, being Nanatobi Cain—dangerously pretty and worth eight-point-four billion dollars. But the truth was she'd give every cent of it away in a heartbeat and flip burgers at McDonald's for the rest of her life if she could only have the two of them back.

About the Author

Arley Owens, Jr. is a musician, composer, author, and rancher who resides in his native Texas with his lovely wife Cristi. He's a member of the musical group TORN PAGE.

Website:
http://www.tornpageband.com

Other books by Arley Owens, Jr.
A Tale of the Mojave
The Cyrus Syndrome
A Texas Ghost Story

Read Arley Owens, Jr. on your Kindle
http://www.amazon.com/author/arleyowens

SHORTY MAE PRODUCTIONS
P.O. BOX 81102
MIDLAND, TEXAS 79708

www.ingramcontent.com/pod-product-compliance
Lightning Source LLC
Chambersburg PA
CBHW070259030726
47505CB00004B/862